Darkest Hour
By
Matt Hilton

Sempre Vigile Press

Darkest Hour

By Matt Hilton

Published by Sempre Vigile Press

Copyright © 2012 Matt Hilton

ISBN-13: 978-1477647318
ISBN-10: 1477647317

Cover image design © 2012 Matt Hilton and Nicola Birrell

DARKEST HOUR

This one is dedicated to Lee Hughes

"…if we fail, then the whole world…including all that we have known and cared for, will sink into the abyss of a new Dark Age made more sinister, and perhaps more protracted, by the lights of perverted science."
Winston Churchill June 18, 1940

September 1912
Hofburg Museum, Vienna

'Snap out of it my friend.'

The young man, whose paint-flecked jacket was at odds with the palatial surroundings, continued to stare, his gaze transfixed. Around him was displayed the Hapsburg treasures, beautiful, priceless, but only one display case held his attention, and had done so on all subsequent visits to the museum. His friend, Walter, glanced to the object that fascinated him. He nudged the young man gently.

'Are you entranced by its exquisite beauty, or has that confounded Eckhart been filling your head with his ridiculous stories again?'

The young man finally blinked, allowing a pent up breath to slip between his lips. Unconsciously he ran a hand over his dark hair, his gaze never straying. Walter shoved his hands into his trouser pockets, searching for his watch. He pulled out a handkerchief, a couple of loose coins, before shoving them awkwardly away. He dug in his jacket pocket and finally found his silver timepiece. He flicked it open and held it in front of the young man's nose. 'You see. We must leave now. It is almost time for the museum to close.'

'A minute longer.'

Walter snorted. 'I swear this has become an unhealthy fascination: you should put all thoughts of this...this *talisman* aside. I blame Eckhart for this madness and shall be having words with him next time we meet.'

'Unhealthy.'

'Pardon me?'

'You said "*unhealthy*".'

'Pah!' Walter again glanced at his watch before putting it away. 'How would you describe your state of mind?'

Finally the young man's gaze left the object of his fascination. He blinked languidly as he brought his older colleague's features into focus. 'I do not follow you, Walter.'

'Then I'll explain in a way that shall hopefully make sense: you have stood here for the best part of an hour.'

The young man's brow creased. 'That can't be so? A couple minutes at most.'

Walter grabbed for his watch again, as though it would offer proof. '*Fifty-six minutes* to be precise. You have been in so deep a condition of trance you haven't noticed my comings or goings, regardless of my exhortations.'

'I've been entranced?'

'I'd say. So much so that I'd swear you were suffering complete sense-denudation and a total lack of self-consciousness.'

The young man looked past Walter to where visitors were filing from the Hapsburg Treasury, an aged curator directing the flow of foot passage with exaggerated hand gestures. The curator, for all his hand-slashes were less genteel than his prim demeanour would suggest, held the attention of those passing by. They demanded total obedience. The young man pursed his lips in consideration, before firmly clasping his hands in the small of his back. He turned his attention to the display cabinet, but this time his eyes were focused, burning with determination.

'One day I shall make it mine again,' he said.

Walter glanced round furtively, as though checking that his friend's words had gone unheard by the curator. 'Even in jest you should not say such a thing.'

'I do not jest. The talisman spoke to me, Walter. Some hidden meaning which still evades me, something I inwardly know yet can't bring to consciousness.' He unclasped his hands, reaching towards the glass case, his fingers trembling, the object of his desire just out of reach. 'I felt as though I myself had held it before in some earlier century of history. That I myself had once claimed it as my talisman of power and held the destiny of the world in my hands...as I shall once again.'

Walter laughed, but his humour held a note of disapproval. 'My young friend, those are grand imaginings indeed...for a struggling artist. You'd best put these silly notions out of your head, concentrate on your water colours for it is through them that your name will be remembered.'

The young man dropped his fingers so that he plucked at the hem of his rumpled jacket. 'Grand imaginings you say, *Herr* Stein?'

'That's all they are. Now come, for it is time to leave, Adolf.'

Chapter 1

May 10th, 1940
Wallonian-Ardennes Forest

The man didn't move.

Dressed in a heavy grey coat and with a fur cap pulled down to his ears, he was the same mundane hue as his surroundings: grey upon shades of grey.

The rain didn't trouble him, and neither did the cold. He merely sat there, appearing like any of the tombstones that jutted from the dark earth all around him. The drizzle pattered on his broad shoulders in a constant drum roll, but it was as if the rhythm helped lull him into this calm, unnatural state.

There was a grave just before him. He sat cross-legged at its edge, with his old Lee Enfield rifle, a relic of the last world war, resting across his knees. A blanket roll, bundled in a canvas tarp and tied off with rawhide was slung over one shoulder. He had a small satchel tied to his belt, but otherwise he had no other possessions, but for the clothes he sat in.

He was neither young nor old, but his face was craggy, weathered almost brown by the elements; both the scouring winds of his northern home and by the beating sun of the southerly climes he'd most recently known. Now, sat here in a graveyard in the Wallonian-Ardennes Forest, he looked out of place. His beard was longer than the fashion of hereabouts, unkempt and peppered with flecks of dirt. His hair was long as well, and worn in a plaited rope that hung between his shoulders. In another more ancient time he would not have looked out of place with a winged helmet upon his brow, but instead he wore only a goatskin cap. Some had taken him for a Norse man in the past, but he hailed from across the other side of the Baltic Sea, though Ludis Kristaps doubted he'd ever see his homeland again.

He just sat and stared at the grave and waited.

Distantly there was a roll of thunder.

Ludis finally shifted, but only to lower his chin and cock an ear to the sky.

The thunder made a steady roll, then was interspersed by the concussion of mortar shell detonations. Faintly he heard the screams of dying men. There was the chatter of machineguns. More screams.

People were killing and dying along the Maginot Line. The sound of strife was way off and of no immediate concern. Ludis went back to waiting.

Europe was on fire - as much of the world soon would be - but the war of those nations was not his concern. He had his own private war to contest and so long as he breathed he intended waging it. However, it was inevitable that both of their wars occasionally collided, and he must take care that he wasn't caught up in the conflict. By the sound of things, Hitler had sent his troops through Belgium to flank the French defenders and they were making steady progress through the forest, though many had originally thought it impenetrable. Here the Maginot Line was nowhere near as well constructed as further east along the French border. The German army were pushing back the French and the British Expeditionary Force, and before long soldiers would flood this area who would shoot first and ask questions later. Ludis did not call Germany his enemy yet – nor did he call any nation – but he could not allow anyone to stop him. Should a man come between him and his enemy, be he Nazi, Tommy or otherwise, Ludis would treat all of them the same.

There was a distant crackle of gunfire, the pounding of tank shells, yelling and screaming, but over it all he heard another sound.

Ludis stood, stretching his full frame to over six feet. In his thick coat and unkempt beard he looked like a grizzly bear, but for the rifle he gripped in his hands. Slowly he stepped backwards from the open grave, before turning and scouring the shadows around him with his fiery gaze. Nothing moved, but again he heard the soft snapping of branches as something shifted unerringly towards his position. Ludis dropped to one knee and brought up the Lee Enfield, working the bolt to send a .303 bullet into the breech. There he guarded the grave.

It was an open grave, but that was not how it should have been. Three days earlier, a young man who'd drowned in a nearby swollen river had been laid to rest there. For two nights his grave had gone unmolested, but on the third night, something had clawed aside the earth, splintered the lid of his plain wooden coffin and had gorged on the flesh of his upper torso. Ludis knew that the foul thing that had made a meal of the young man's corpse would return at dusk to finish its feast.

Rain trembled on his lashes and he slowly closed his left eye to better sight along the gun barrel. He held his position, waiting.

There was a rattle of branches and at the edge of the graveyard something stepped into view. From this distance it was little more than a smudge of black against the deepening grey of the landscape. Anyone else would have taken the shape for another man, but Ludis knew otherwise.

Once this creature had been human, and had died; but it had been a man of evil mind and worse intent and no sanctified grave could hold such a foul spirit. Now it had returned and its hunger for human flesh was voracious. This was no ravening beast though, but a cowardly, despicable fiend that preyed on the recent dead. Throughout the world these corpse eaters were known and in each nation they had different names. Ludis had recently conversed with an English soldier who he'd come across lying in a ditch. The soldier had been wounded – was most certainly only hours from death – and had been racked with fever and pain. He turned down Ludis' offer to carry him to a field hospital, and instead asked that Ludis only stop the *ghoul* from picking his bones clean. In the night, he said, a ghoul had crouched over him, waiting for him to die, poking him with fingernails cracked and filthy from digging through the earth, to check if life still pulsed within him. Only the rising of the sun had saved the soldier his terrible fate and the ghoul had retreated into the shadows. Ludis did not put the man's tale down to a fever-induced nightmare, for he knew that fiends did exist and that the war that was ripping apart the world had awakened such things and brought them forth.

He had waited until the man had passed, and then said a blessing over him. Ludis had then lifted up the man and carried him through the forest to a gigantic wall of stone, cut through by fissures and potholes formed by floodwaters of ancient times. He laid the soldier in a deep hole in the rock wall and then piled boulders over him, to foil the ghoul should it track the soldier by his scent. Ludis had then backtracked and found the spoor of the ghoul. Through the day he'd followed the trail but had lost it on some rocky ground nearby. Chance had brought him to the graveyard, and he'd discovered the grave of the drowned man and recognised the work of the fiend. And there he'd waited, unmoving throughout the remainder of the day.

But now it was here.

The ghoul.

Ludis watched the creature approach. It was tall and sinuous, and moved as a serpent would should it have limbs. Being an entity from beyond the earthly realm it was in contrast with everything around it, and though it was garbed in funereal black, it glowed with a weird non-light that reminded Ludis of candle smoke. It also flickered like a candle flame, insubstantial in one instant, solid the next. Ludis had no comprehension of how this should be, other than the ghoul strode through alternating dimensions, straddling both the earthly and astral planes and existing fully in neither for long. He had experienced such phenomena before, the Strigoi then being even less substantial than this creature: of late he'd noted that the monsters were becoming more physical, as though their power on this plane was growing. Soon, he suspected, the creatures of the night would become fully tangible and God help the world then.

He sighted along the rifle, vectoring in on the ghoul's head as it lifted its nostrils to the sky and inhaled. Since this thing died it had transformed, its shape altering so that it was better adjusted to hunting down and feasting on decaying matter. Its nostrils were flaring things now, its jaw grown under slung so that it jutted beyond the upper teeth. The eyes were large and slitted like a cat's: all the better to see in the night. An abomination, Ludis thought.

He watched as the ghoul sniffed the night air and then came forward. Ludis steadily increased the pressure on the trigger, allowing his pent up breath to ease between his lips. The ghoul halted, swaying like a dirty flame and its nostrils flared wide. Ludis had masked his natural odour, and he didn't like to think of how he'd taken handfuls of congealed blood from the corpse of the drowned man and smeared them over the front of his coat, but it seemed that the ghoul's heightened senses had detected something wrong with his scent.

Ludis squeezed the trigger.

The rifle cracked and spurted flame and Ludis saw the ghoul writhe with the impact of the bullet.

But then it twisted back again and its jaws opened in silent challenge.

It was cowardly and despicable, but like any cornered beast it was not beyond fighting back. The ghoul launched forward, lifting hands malformed into huge claw-ended spatulas.

Ludis had mistimed his first shot. The bullet had struck as it flickered beyond this plane of existence into another. Now it raced forward, flickering like a strobe, here one instant, gone the next. Ludis worked the bolt on his rifle, ejecting the spent shell and feeding a fresh one into the breech.

Crack!

The ghoul came on.

'Damn you.' The first words Ludis had uttered since conversing with the dying soldier.

Again he worked the rifle mechanism.

The ghoul was almost upon him, and his third shot wasn't primed.

Ludis came up from his knee, and he adjusted his grip on his rifle so that he could ram the barrel under the monster's chin. He held it off for a moment, as its claws reached past the gun and fastened on his heavy coat. Ludis grunted as he felt its ragged nails scour the flesh of his chest even through the thick fur lining of his coat. He couldn't allow the fiend further purchase on him. He reversed the rifle and slammed its skull with the butt. The ghoul was knocked aside and Ludis saw where he'd crushed its left cheekbone. Black ichor spilled from the wound. If it could be harmed, it could be killed, he knew.

Again the ghoul opened its jaws in silent challenge, and its baleful gaze burned into his psyche. The horrific warning in that look, he knew, would freeze some, but Ludis did not fear the foul thing. He worked the bolt, lifted his rifle and fired directly between the slit-pupil eyes.

Again his bullet flew in error.

The ghoul leapt at him.

Ludis stood steady and he jammed his rifle between their two bodies, allowing the momentum of the ghoul's charge to take them down and back. He powered his feet into its stomach and sent the ghoul in a somersault over the top of him. The ghoul fell into the open grave, landing on top of the splintered coffin with a crunch of bones.

Ludis sprang to his feet and swung to cover the grave. He worked the bolt. The fiend was lying on top of the drowned man's coffin; with the anti-tank stake Ludis had set there in preparation transfixing it. The ghoul writhed, still alive but unable to lift itself off the iron spike. Its mouth opened and closed, but no sound issued forth because the thing had no need for speech when devouring the dead. Ludis took careful aim, and this time his shot was true.

The ghoul's head exploded under the bullet's impact, spreading like an awful tide of gore over the walls of the grave. Ludis grunted at the stench, and stepped away.

He wasn't finished though.

He fetched a spade and began filling in the grave, and didn't stop until the earth was level once more.

The rain had continued unabated, but Ludis was filthy, and now the stink of the dead man's blood on his clothing was nauseating. He went to a stream to bathe, and was careful to set aside his blanket roll and satchel. Inside the bag was something that was very important to him and he could not allow it to get wet. It was the reason why he'd trekked here to the Ardennes.

Chapter 2

May 13 1940
Near Sedan, France

'That was a close one, Sarge,' William Green yelled as he tugged his Battle Bowler down about his ears. Clods of earth and splintered wood pattered down, an unnatural rainstorm. Green took a quick look over the rim of the trench, then twisted to search for gaps in the dense foliage. Through the canopy there were snatches of the indigo heavens allowing only the briefest of glimpses of the planes overhead.

Geoffrey Renyard, an infantry sergeant of the British Expeditionary Force squinted at Corporal Green. 'You're not kidding me. Keep your head down...Jerry will be taking another run.'

The continuous detonation of high explosives made talking almost impossible, so the soldiers' conversation was through shouts and hand gestures. For almost seven hours the German Luftwaffe had dominated the skies over the river Meuse, carpet bombing the French lines to force a way through for the 1st, 2nd and 10th Panzer Divisions. The bombardment was bad enough, but dive-bomber raids punctuated it where Stukas and Messerschmitts strafed the ground with a mixture of bombs and bullets. Around Renyard and Green the forest had been ripped apart, earth torn from the ground, bodies of their allies strewn everywhere.

'Where the hell are our fly boys?' Green yelled.

'They're still trying to bomb the bridges to halt the German advance over the river.' Sergeant Renyard grabbed at Green, pushing him down as an artillery round smashed through the trees nearby, obliterating hundred-year-old pines like they were kindling. The detonation sounded moments later, the sound wave compressing Renyard's eardrums. Green lifted his head, spitting dirt from between his teeth. Renyard didn't comprehend what Green said, but by the look on his face he didn't need to: it had to have been a curse.

His ears still buzzing, Renyard looked down the valley to the river. From his high vantage he should have been able to see the massing Panzer divisions but the air was full of smoke and fire. Somewhere out there was a bend in the river, sorely protected by the pillboxes and bunkers of the French that were ranged along the high ground behind him. The French forces of the 147 RIF had held out their positions most of the day, and had initially repulsed the advance of the 2nd and 10th Panzer divisions on their left and right, but, there at the river bend, tanks and the elite infantry regiment – Großdeutschland - had already broken through.

'We need air support, Sarge. Why is the RAF still trying for the bridges when the bloody Jerry just lays down pontoons?'

'It's all they can do,' Renyard grunted. 'They don't stand a chance against superior fighter planes. Those old planes of ours can't compete with their bloomin' Messerschmitt's.'

'Our Hawker Hurricanes are a match. So's the Dewoitines the Frogs have. But where the hell are they?'

'Protecting the bombers.'

'What about us blokes on the ground?'

Renyard thumbed back up the wooded slope. 'That's what the French artillery boys are doing.'

'You think so? Don't you think it's gone a little quiet behind us?'

Green had a point. The German attack had been so sustained, the noise so tumultuous, that Renyard hadn't given the sudden cessation of counter fire much notice until now. The French artillery batteries had either been routed or had fled from the advancing Großdeutschland infantry regiment. The main defence line troops of France's 55th Division couldn't hold back the Panzer tanks without the support of the batteries. No way.

'Tell the lads we're falling back, Corporal.'

'We're retreating?'

Renyard indicated a line of figures that had emerged from the smoke to their right. A ragged column of Frenchmen, some of them having already thrown away their equipment packs to make their flight quicker, were heading for a break in the ridge to the north. Some of them carried wounds; all of them had the desolate look of defeat in their hollow eyes.

'We're here to support *them*,' Renyard said with a nod towards the retreating French. 'It looks like they've given up. Do you want to stay here and wait for Jerry to arrive, or would you rather take the fight back to them another time?'

Green settled his helmet, tightened his chinstrap and wiped at the dirt on his face. 'This is bad, isn't it, Sarge? They're trying to break through, catch the allied forces in Belgium and force us back towards the Channel.'

'Looks like it. If we don't get moving we'll be rounded up as well. At least this way we can retreat further into France and not get stuck with the sea at our backs.'

Green flicked a salute of sorts. 'I'll tell the lads.'

Renyard watched the young corporal belly crawl away. The rest of the section was entrenched a dozen yards away, some with their Lee-Enfield rifles trained on the chaos in the river valley, two of them manning the tripod mounted Bren machinegun. Their serge-wool uniforms were covered in mud, their canvas webbing and boots slimy with must. His section weren't conscripts, urged to serve their nation through a moral obligation of duty. With conscripts, their training, like many of the French and Dutch fighters arranged against the German XIX Corps, had been rushed, and they were ill equipped. In comparison, Renyard's lads were riflemen of the King's Royal Rifle Corps, specifically trained as skirmishers whose skill with their weapons could upset the enemy's advance. Still, they were kids in Renyard's opinion, too green for this hellish war. He had already lost two of his lads, Rifleman Chiltern and Lance Corporal Hoskins who usually commanded the two men Bren gun team. Renyard was their sergeant and would do everything in his power to see the others safely home: despite the fighter planes tearing strips from the smoky sky, launching screaming death at them.

Green's question impinged upon him, concerning the lack of planes in the sky that the RAF Advanced Air Striking Force had launched earlier in the day. He'd tried to halt the corporal's concern with talk of how they were supporting the bombing raids on the three bridges spanning the Meuse in an effort at halting the German advance, but in reality he thought that the Luftwaffe had decisively routed them. With few sorties to fly against the Allied fighters and bombers, the German's now had an almost freehand to bomb and strafe the corridor they intended opening through the French lines.

'*Ils sont derrière nous. Les Panzers sont derrière nous!*'

Renyard heard the shout above the tumult of exploding bombs. The cry was harsh and accusing, tinged with fear. He had a schoolboy's grasp of the French language, but even he caught the meaning of the words of the French trooper rushing away from the scene of the conflict. The Panzers are behind us? How was that possible? The man had to be mistaken. The three Panzer divisions attempting to break through were bottled on the far side of the Meuse, and the intelligence reports had told of no other tanks in the region. Perhaps the terror of warfare had been too much for the Frenchman and had unhinged his mind. But if that was the case then hundreds of men must similarly be unhinged because all along the line of defence the shout was taken up. Mass-hysteria, Renyard realised, could shatter an army as easily as any enemy tanks.

'Is it true? They've somehow found a way to get behind us?'

Renyard was surprised to find Corporal Green back at his side. The young man's pale blue eyes flickered in time with the stutter of a nearby Bren gun.

'I can't see how they could do it,' Renyard grunted. 'But we're not hanging around to find out. Are the lads ready?'

'Awaiting your command, Sarge.'

'Then let's do it. Move them out, Corporal.'

The order went along the line, and the men of Renyard's section seemed relieved to be leaving as they crawled out of their dug outs and made a small column that moved up the slopes toward the crest above the valley. Renyard looked back the way they'd come, seeing other small groups of men in similar formations; a mass exodus was on the way. He couldn't help wonder if this was a turning point in the war and if France could withstand the German onslaught for much longer. Back home in England, it had been predicted that the war would not last until Christmas. Well, Christmas had come and gone over four months ago. But if France fell, then what would become of England then? The war would definitely be over by this coming Christmas, he decided, and the world would have a new master.

Yet even Renyard could not begin to guess at how foul a master had designs on the earth. Beside Him even Adolf Hitler would pale to insignificance.

Chapter 3

May 13 1940
Borderlands

Six miles from the French-German border Ludis Kristaps picked his way past the principle line of resistance erected after the Great War to repel the advance of German tanks through France. Metal rails – not unlike the one he'd utilised to finish the ghoul three days earlier – were planted vertically, their barbed tops extending almost chest height from the earth. In rows six deep they formed serried ranks as far as he could see through the forest. Only where the trees were too dense, or insurmountable terrain presented itself, was the ground spared the unnatural crop of metal spines. Behind the anti-tank obstacles dense rolls of barbed wire waited to ensnare the infantrymen. Ludis found he could make better progress beyond the defensive line, but he ran the risk of running into roaming bands of German soldiers, so chose to stay here where there was less chance of a fatal encounter.

Since leaving the graveyard he hadn't made much progress in his own mission, having been stalled by the ferocious fighting along the Maginot Line. However, this evening the bombardments had lessened as the battlefront shifted further to the north and east. Now the big man moved cat-footed between the anti-tank spikes, ears alert to ambush. He carried his old Lee-Enfield rifle by its strap over his shoulder. In his right hand he now held a Webley Mk IV revolver liberated from the corpse of a British soldier earlier in the day. From the pouches on the dead man's webbing Ludis had also taken a spare box of ammunition. It wouldn't help him should he again meet a creature the likes of the ghoul, but he knew now that the creatures of the night weren't his only enemies. The German invasion had thrown viciousness into the hearts of men and he could not allow anyone to hinder his progress.

He crouched by a row of anti-tank spikes, touching fingertips to the metal. The wind was blowing away from him. Even if he didn't hear the approach of tanks or marching groups of infantry the trembling of the ground would alert him. The metal was cold and still. He came up from his crouch and went on. Night was falling rapidly. Away to the north where the low clouds reflected the flames and explosions, the sky was a raw bruise. Here though in the forest everything was growing dark and impenetrable.

There were no animal sounds, which Ludis found odd. The fighting was many miles distant so that it echoed faintly through the forest like the rumble of thunder, but it wasn't so intrusive that it should send the creatures of the forest running for shelter. There wasn't even a birdcall, which struck Ludis as even stranger. With the plethora of corpses seeding the countryside, the crows and ravens were having a time of feast and plenty but here even the carrion eaters had fallen silent. Not a good sign. It meant that men were here...or worse.

Not for the first time, Ludis considered the growing number of supernatural fiends loose in the world. The death and destruction wrought by man had brought them forth, no doubt about it, but there was something else that empowered them, allowing them greater dominion over the earthly realms. He touched the small bag tied to his belt and wondered if there was any truth in the crazy woman's words. No it couldn't be. Surely the woman's ranting had been born of the strong liquor she was imbibing? So why had he listened to her and taken on the task she'd set him?

Crouching again, he checked for vibrations in the anti-tank spikes. Nothing. Without rising, he dipped his hand under the flap of his bag and touched the small item nestled in the bottom. It was warmer than metal should be: maybe the old crone wasn't so crazy after all.

Going forward, he was forced to clamber over a low mound of stones, slick with damp moss. He slid down the far side, where he hunkered like a wild thing as he listened for a sign that his clumsiness had alerted the hidden watchers to his presence. From his left came an indistinct shuffle, either a foot through a drift of pine needles or rough clothing against bark. Ludis lifted his Webley and trained it on the source of the noise. Should its perpetrator be one of the night things then the gun would slow it but not stop the foul thing, but at least it would give Ludis a few precious seconds of escape.

He didn't move. He waited as still as the rocks his back was pressed against. After a few minutes where the sound hadn't repeated itself he began to wonder if his ears had been playing tricks: had it merely been an echo of his own movement sent back to him from the near trees? Slowly he righted himself, but his finger never left the trigger of his revolver. Before setting off he dipped his free hand under his heavy fur collar and brought out a simple cross on a leather thong. He kissed the cross and then allowed it to slip back inside his coat. 'Walk beside me, dear God,' he whispered under his breath.

He took a step and his boots stirred the forest mulch.

To his left the sound was echoed.

Ludis turned and scanned the shadows.

To call out would be the death of him, he knew, for if the lurker was human then he'd be armed and would likely shoot first and ask questions later. If it was one of *the others* then Ludis invited certain death in a more horrific fashion.

Stock-still he waited, but again the forest fell silent. It must have been an echo, he decided. Nevertheless he waited a while longer. Finally satisfied that he was alone in the woods, he set off once more but his nerves were on edge, so much so that it felt like fire rode his veins. For every ten paces forward he stopped and listened intently.

The night was fully upon him by the time he reached a narrow stream running between rocky banks. He was thirsty and paused there to drink. The water was clear and smelled fine, but he'd no way of knowing if corpses further up stream contaminated it. Die of thirst or risk the plague later, he had single recourse. He crouched down over a small pool and cupped cool liquid to his lips. The rush of the stream was in his ears, splashing and tinkling over the stones, but above the noise he heard another more distinct sound: the thud of something landing heavily on the bank above him. Had a tree branch broken loose and fallen to the forest floor or was the sound something else? He continued to cup water from the stream with his left hand, while he held the right, and the Webley, hidden close to his belly.

Without warning Ludis spun around, bringing up the gun and aiming it at the top of the embankment.

He grunted into his beard.

There was nothing there but for a single tendril of mist rising from the water.

Gently he eased down on the hammer, and allowed the gun to dip.

But he continued to watch, probing the darkness with his sharp gaze. A shape, indistinguishable in the darkness, lowered itself a fraction, and it was all that Ludis could do to hold back the groan that bottled in his chest. He stood there watching, waiting, and finally the shape rose up an inch or two. He could not yet define the dark object against the darker night, but he knew it was no man. Yellow eyes, orbs of molten umber, opened in twin slits to regard him hungrily.

Ludis took a steady step back, allowing him a better angle of view up the embankment. The yellow eyes stared back at him. Ludis took another step and found he was standing in ankle deep water. He continued moving backwards, his gaze transfixed on that of the watcher. At the same time he cocked an ear, first left then right, listening intently. A soft thud rewarded him from further to his right, and it was followed a moment later by a similar sound from his left. Careful to keep the first unblinking eyes within his periphery, he glanced to each side and saw similar eyes peering back at him. Then he returned his gaze to the first watcher. He heard the escape of breath; it came at him in a series of short pants. Now when he looked the first watcher had risen higher and he could make out the pointed ears, the elongated muzzle, the teeth winking gently as a mouth opened and closed.

Despite his instinct to run, Ludis held himself in check. He continued backpedalling until he found the opposite bank and began moving up it. His gaze never left that of the first watcher, but he was conscious of the slinking shapes moving through the darkness to both sides. The Webley held six bullets: little good it would do him if the pack should come for him all at once because a quick tally told him there was at least twice that number of wolves stalking him.

He'd witnessed a pack bring down a reindeer once. They had used cunning and tactics to first stalk, and then pursue the frantic animal, before sending it into a trap launched by phalanxes that attacked from both sides as the tiring reindeer came within their sights. He didn't doubt that the same ploy was what the wolves had in mind for him now. Should he run, those at his heels would nip and tear at him, sending him into the jaws of those that had undoubtedly gone ahead to block his path.

Earlier he'd feared armed soldiers gunning him down, so too had he feared that one of the dreaded things released from the pit had come for him, but now he knew another kind of fear entirely. Men he could deal with, monsters he had a chance of surviving, but what of a pack of starving wolves?

He searched the trees above him. Could he clamber up a tree, wait the beasts out? No, for he would weaken before them, and likely fall asleep, crash down from the branches and offer them an easy meal. Not that any branch in sight looked capable of bearing his weight. The trees here were pine and fir, the branches densely packed but slim and full of sap and incapable of supporting him. Cornered and facing certain death he had singular recourse left to him. He lifted his voice in challenge and charged directly for the first watcher.

The wolf was startled by this unexpected turn of event, and its instinct was to turn away and take flight. Ludis didn't halt his charge, only changed direction, and before the wolf could get over the surprise he fled along the streambed, his heavy coat lifting on the wake of his passage. He knew he'd only earned himself a few seconds' respite, but had he done enough to show he was a more cunning prey than what the pack usually brought down? He put his head down and pumped his arms, driving with his powerful legs through the water. Thankfully it didn't get much deeper than his ankles and was no impediment, but that would not last forever.

He spun to check on the wolf pack. What he saw didn't garner much hope of an escape. The sleek bodies were loping along on either embankment less than ten paces behind him. Their muzzles were open in feral grins, pink tongues lolling. He'd be damned if they didn't look like they were enjoying the chase.

Let us see if you find this humorous? Ludis skidded to a halt, swung up the revolver and fired. On his left, the nearest wolf went down, rolling in a ball of fur and a spatter of escaping blood. The wolf didn't make as much as a yelp and Ludis knew that he'd hit it a fatal shot. But it seemed that the crack of the revolver and the subsequent slaying of one of the pack had an immediate effect. Now the wolves weren't loping along silently: their collective voices lifted in mournful howls, excited yipping and the occasional snarl. Ludis spun around and ran all the faster.

The streambed widened, the slopes on both sides becoming less steep. Not good, because it gave the wolves the opportunity to follow him down into the watercourse. Ludis kept pounding along, and didn't bother looking back because he could hear the foremost animal mere steps behind him. In the next instant something fixed on his coat tails, almost pulling him off balance. He yanked loose, swinging blindly with the barrel of his revolver. It struck something solid and a corresponding yelp rewarded him. Ludis flung himself forward, racing for a bend in the stream. On the right the bank grew steep again with large boulders jutting upwards and forming a cliff face that reminded him of how challenging some of the land hereabouts was. It was insurmountable for a lesser man than him but what about the wolves? He ran to the rock face and bounded up onto the first boulder. His wet boots skidded and he had to windmill his arms to keep from falling backwards. With his free hand he grabbed at the rock face, while twisting round to face his enemies. The pack was right there below him. One of the shaggy beasts, its thick grey fur matted with the blood of an earlier kill, leapt for him. The wolf was large, almost half his own weight, but it met his upraised boot and he pushed it back down into the milling pack. Ludis went up another boulder, and now he was well above their heads. He aimed and fired. The wolves twisted and turned, attempting to avoid his bullets, but he took one in the flank and another between its ribs. The first spun around, howling and nipping at its own haunches as the second one died without a sound. The rest of the pack swarmed about, incomprehension in their lupine faces as they surveyed the demise of their pack mates. Ludis could care less for their lack of understanding. He fired again, and took another of the howling creatures between its jaws. The wolf dropped in the stream, a pink cloud staining the frothy white water, evident to Ludis even in the darkness. He'd almost halved their number, for there wasn't as many of the creatures as he'd first approximated. Ten had started after him, but now three were dead and one was mortally wounded. He fired again, but this time his shot was rushed and he missed another of the sleek beasts as it ran in close to the rocks where he crouched.

'Back you mangy cur.'

Ludis kicked at the wolf but missed, but it was enough to make it bound backwards. The wolf stood in the stream, piercing him with its feral, ochre gaze. Ludis recognised the eyes as those of the first watcher. He had expected this to be the pack leader, the alpha male, but he saw now that this wolf was of slighter build than most of the others. Female, he realised. The deadliest of the species, he cautioned himself.

He brought up the gun and sighted along the barrel.

'Last chance,' he muttered towards the unheeding animal. 'Leave now or the next bullet's yours.'

The wolf growled deep in its chest, its shoulders hunching. Ludis knew it was preparing to spring for his throat. He allowed his lids to half close as he chose a spot between the she-wolf's eyes.

Without warning the wolf came at him. Its paws were tucked close to its body with the power of its leap, its jaws opening wide. Ludis caressed the trigger.

Click!

He'd only a split second to realise that the hammer had fallen on an empty chamber, and then the beast was upon him. Ludis wasn't exactly dismayed, since he had set off running he'd expected to die under the teeth of the pack. Not that he was about to go quietly. He dropped the revolver and it clattered down the rock face, even as he turned his elbow and rammed it into the open maw of the she-wolf. The jaws snapped down on his arm, and even if the thick fur and leather of his coat saved him from laceration he experienced the agony of teeth capable of grinding bones crunch down on him. The wolf gripped tight, scrabbling for purchase against his body with all four paws. Ludis roared in agony, but it was mixed with rage and the indomitable will of a man who'd fought and survived more desperate battles than this. His rifle was out of reach on his back, his revolver lost somewhere below him, but he still had weapons. He grabbed the wolf's head with his left hand, digging his thumb into an eye even as he bent to chew at one of the wolf's tufted ears. The wolf shook savagely, but then so did Ludis and now it was a battle to prove who was the most dominant killer.

Maybe Ludis would have vindicated himself, but for the other wolves. Firmly caught up in his battle with the she-wolf, he was unaware of the others coming up the rocks at him until they'd clamped their jaws around his boots. He kicked at them, but that was what they'd intended. Though he was not one for cursing, Ludis thought he'd be forgiven the guttural oath he spoke as he loosed his grip on the wolf's ear and slid in a jumble of writhing bodies towards the streambed.

His journey had taken him thousands of miles from his homeland on the shores of the Baltic Sea to the pitiless mountains of Eastern Europe, then back along the Mediterranean coast and hence north to this forest. But now, he thought, his journey was at an end. He only hoped that some other man would come across his eviscerated corpse and strip him of his belongings. His final wish was that it would be a learned man who'd recognise the item he carried in his bag and he would continue with Ludis' ill-fated quest. But he didn't think that there was any chance of that; in fact there was less chance than Ludis had of surviving more than a few seconds.

Chapter 4

13th May 1940
Bulson Ridge, France

Renyard directed his men to form a skirmish line, while sending Green and his two-man Bren gun team to their right. The corporal led Riflemen Cooper and McCoy along a winding path, through boulders, belly crawling their way to a niche between two large rocks from where they could offer supporting fire should the casement be less deserted than it initially appeared. What had began earlier as a trickle of men retreating from the front at the River Meuse had grown to a torrent, and though the French 295th Artillery Regiment should have held this final defensive line, they appeared to be long gone. That of course didn't mean that there was no one here: if the rumours were true and the Germans had already infiltrated this far behind the French lines then they could be in for a heated reception as they approached the artillery casement.

It wasn't so absurd a notion.

Earlier that day, Renyard had heard intelligence concerning the fall of Eben-Emael, a large fort controlling the junction of the Meuse and Albert Canal in Belgium. The Germans had overcome the fort's supposed impregnability by landing gliders on the roof from which they disgorged assault teams that destroyed the main gun cupolas with hollow charges, at the same time as the bridges over the canal were seized by German paratroopers. Renyard didn't think that such an operation would have been launched against this lesser fort, but he was no expert. So, while there was the slightest chance they might be greeted by a hostile party, he wouldn't walk his men in without checking out the casement first.

Rifleman James 'Winker' Watson was a severe-faced youth, his original dark greasy hair shaved short at the sides, his pointy nose jutting over protruding teeth. Winker reminded Renyard of a weasel, but only physically. There was nothing sneaky about the kid; in fact he was about the most self-controlled of the section and the best sharpshooter Renyard had met. He sent Winker to their left to find a higher vantage from which he could take out an enemy should he present himself. Winker headed out without comment, his rifle held tightly in his fist.

Allowing Winker and the Bren gun team time to get in position, Renyard held the others in check with an upraised hand. He caught a flash of a pale face as Green twisted from between the boulders: the corporal circled his thumb and forefinger, his other fingers spread in the universal sign that everything was fine. Renyard swept his hand forward, and led the remaining four soldiers up the hill. Over them loomed the concrete fort, its walls blackened from the smoke of indirect hits, showing pockmarks where the Junkers had strafed it. Its guns lay still, like the wilted limbs of dead men.

Renyard didn't like this, but he couldn't bypass the casement without checking it. They were in retreat, their ammunition and supplies growing low. They had passed other casements as they'd marched, but the fleeing Frenchmen had emptied them. This one was a larger structure, one of the double-decker casements. Renyard was familiar with its type and knew that the upper level would be the firing floor, armed with twin machineguns and 47 mm anti-tank guns, while the lower floor would provide the troops with rest and amenity areas. Inside there should be reserves of food, water, and ammunition: the things that he needed to keep his men alive. He glanced up at the two "cloches" or turrets at roof level, from which the silent guns protruded, watching for any sign of surveillance. The only thing that moved was a strip of cloth that fluttered from the leftmost turret.

'I don't like it, Sarge. It's too quiet.'

Renyard shot an admonishment at Rifleman Gerald White by way of a harsh glance. Young Whitey's head retracted into his thickset shoulders, so that it looked like his helmet was resting on the collar of his battledress jacket. Renyard felt immediately self-conscious, because the soldier had simply whispered the same concern he himself had. He winked at the young man, but placed a finger to his lips. He was sure that if it weren't so dark he'd see Whitey's ears glowing with embarrassment. Renyard turned his attention back to the casement, but nothing had changed.

As he walked up the slope, the slap of his entrenchment tool off his backside was a constant motivator to keep moving. The two-part spade, held now in a canvas sling at his lower back was an integral piece of equipment carried by all his section, as well as just about every Tommy in the theatre of war. It was valued not only for the purposes of digging in, but also as a weapon when the fighting became down and dirty. His had once saved Renyard's life when his sidearm had jammed as a German tried to bayonet him. The Jerry was incensed with battle lust and came at him like a wild animal: he quite literally lost his head.

For now though he wouldn't be wielding it like an axe. Renyard's SMLE with its ten round capacity magazine was his weapon of choice. He held it ready as he advanced. Spread out on one side of him was Whitey and Gary "Taff" Jones, and Paul "Blanco" Tyler and Leo Hughes to the other, and each of the men held their weapons with similar itchy fingers.

Without incident they approached the fortified walls of the casement. There should have been as many as thirty men inside, and whether friend or foe, Renyard believed they would have been challenged by now. He indicated that Blanco and Leo check out the far side of the armoured fortress while the others kneeled to offer cover for Winker and Green's Bren gun team as they came in. While he waited for the scouts to return he had to wonder if they'd find a way inside. When the French retreated, had they taken everything that could be carried with them, or had they sealed the casement? Either way they wouldn't find anything useful, because if it was the latter there was no way they'd get in without laying charges to blow the doors. If they did that, they'd alert anyone within earshot of the explosion, probably inviting discovery by the *Großdeutschland* infantry division that were sure to be hot on their heels.

Watson was the first to make it down from his position, walking in with his Lee-Enfield slung nonchalantly over his shoulder. He wore a face that said he was annoyed he didn't get the chance to practice his skills; Renyard on the other hand believed there'd be plenty opportunity in the next few days.

'There's no one here, Sarge,' Watson said with a nod towards the casement. 'Or, if there is, they're all deaf.'

Renyard studied the scars left by bullets and flames, but the walls were barely touched. The casement had been targeted during one of the Junker runs, but had held firm. He decided that the French troopers must have been infected with the same panic as everyone else and had retreated hours ago when the artillery batteries fell silent.

'Bloomin' Frogs,' Taff Jones said scornfully. 'They're the only soldiers I know who learn to march backwards.'

Renyard shook his head at the burly Welshman. The French were Britain's allies, but it seemed mistrust persisted in some of his countrymen. It was something that Renyard couldn't openly allow because his section had been dispatched here as reinforcements to fight alongside the French 55th Infantry Division. The 55th DI, as it was known, was a 'B' reserve division and required all the help it could get to try to stem the advance of the German war machine. You couldn't fight alongside men you didn't fully trust to cover your back.

'We'll have none of that talk around here, Taff,' he said.

'Sorry, Sarge.' Taff shouldered his rifle.

Corporal Green jogged over with Cooper and McCoy on his heels. Evidently they'd been close enough to hear the short discourse because McCoy, who had the Bren balanced over his shoulder, said, 'Hey, Taff. It's not the Frogs we have to worry about; it's those bloody Italians. You ask me, first chance he gets Mussolini will be kissing Hitler's arse for favours.'

'C'mon lads, you heard the sergeant. We'll be having none of that talk.' Corporal Green gave them the beady eye, but even he was chuckling under his breath. Renyard shook his head: he'd let the lads have their moment. What harm could come from it after all, and, if truth be told, he thought both Taff and McCoy were probably right.

Cooper had extra pouches fixed to his webbing, ammo for the Bren stuffed inside them, and he'd a spare barrel for the gun hanging between his shoulder blades. He was the biggest man in the section at six-foot three-inches and was best placed to carry the extra load. He rasped a hand over his unshaven chin, then pointed towards the left corner of the casement. Blanco Tyler looked to be stumbling as he rounded the concrete wall.

'Sarge,' Blanco said, his eyes wide. 'You'd better come and see this.'

Renyard preferred that the men establish their perimeter first, but he could tell by the shocked urgency in Blanco's features that it shouldn't be his first concern.

'Where's Hughes?'

'Watching the door,' Blanco said. 'Not that he needs to.'

'You've found a way inside and secured it? What do you mean "not that he needs to"?'

'Yeah, we found a door, Sarge. But there won't be anyone coming out of it...not alive any way.'

'What do you mean?'

'That's the thing, Sarge...uh, I think it's best that you come and take a look. I can't make any bleedin' sense of it.'

Renyard jerked his head at Green, no need for a spoken order. The corporal immediately set up a perimeter guard of Watson, Jones and Whitey, covering the three approaches to the casement. The others he led around the back, following in Renyard and Blanco's footsteps. He then told Cooper and McCoy to cover the back of the building before joining the sergeant at the door. Blanco Tyler held his Lee-Enfield braced against his hip, using the barrel to stab towards the blackness of the semi-open door. 'Leo's just inside, Sarge,' he said, but it didn't look like he was about to enter first.

Renyard glanced once at the young man's face. It was still long with shock, pale in the starlight. Renyard turned from him to regard the doorway. He was no coward, but neither was the sergeant a fool. He could feel there was something *wrong* about this and it gave him pause. Not that he suspected a trap, not in the usual sense, but he felt that if he stepped through that door then everything was about to change: most likely for the worse. It was as if something sentient and infinitely malignant peered back at him from the dark depths of the casement, some great arachnid drawing him into its web.

'Leo,' he called softly.

When he received no reply he glanced across at Green and saw that the corporal was as uneasy as he felt. Nevertheless, Green came forward and joined him at the door. A pace in front of him, Renyard stepped forward.

'Wait up, Sarge. You have to see this first.'

Before Renyard could stay him, Blanco moved past them both and gripped the edge of the heavy steel door. He tugged it wide and the door swung away from them. Blotches of liquid were splashed over the door; so dark it could be oil. Renyard caught the coppery waft, and being a veteran soldier, recognised it for what it was. Not oil but blood. He crinkled his brow as he leaned close to the door, studying the blotches. In the faint radiance of the stars he caught a thousand pinpricks of light, and moving closer he could differentiate one splash from another. There were gouts of blood splashed all over the door's inner surface. Not only that, but there was also myriad streaks, finger tracks through the blood, the flats of palms. Many hands had slammed and tore at the door in an attempt to escape bloody and violent death.

Renyard looked at the ground. Old boot prints stirred the dust, also the tracks of Hughes and Tyler as they'd come to investigate, but that was all. There was no trail of blood outside which he found strange, because if the men who'd bled all over the door had managed to get outside there should have been a swathe of gore leading away into the dark.

'Leo,' he called softly.

Again there was no reply and Renyard knew he'd no option but go in. His earlier feeling of foreboding was replaced by one of intense curiosity. He stepped inside, cat footed, expecting to find the dead strewn across the floor in front of him, but there was no one. He entered a short vestibule, with a staircase leading up to the artillery cloches above. Green swung his rifle to cover the stairs as Renyard proceeded inside, Blanco covering his rear.

Beneath his feet he could feel droplets of blood. They were fresh enough that they still smelled like corroded metal, but already they were coagulating, causing his soles to suck at them with each step. Other than the blood splatters there was no sign of the men they'd come from. Renyard frowned into the dark, but went on.

The casement was divided into various rooms, but none had doors. They could move from one to the next without hindrance. Still, they had to take it easy. Something evident had struck the sergeant: whoever had been wounded in here hadn't made it outside. That left a couple of mysteries. If they were still alive, then where were they? If they had died, then *where were they?*

They came into a barracks room and part of the answer presented itself. Recently - very recently judging by the stink of cordite hanging in the atmosphere - a gunfight had raged in here. Renyard could barely make out a couple of bunks nearby, geometric shapes in the amorphous darkness.

Turning to Blanco he whispered, 'We need some light. See if you can find a lamp or something.'

He continued forward slowly, sweeping the barrel of his rifle through the shadows. He bumped up against something on the floor and it clattered away from him with a metallic chatter. He paused, listening for a corresponding sound, but nothing except Blanco striking a match responded. A flame cast sombre ribbons of light across the nearest wall, and Renyard saw in the flickering light further evidence of a gunfight. Holes pocked the walls, dozens of them, perhaps hundreds. Fucking Jerry, he thought, had sneaked inside and slaughtered the French soldiers while they rested in their beds. His guess was only fleeting, and proven wrong in the next instant as Blanco touched flame to a wick in a lamp and more of the room came into relief.

'Jesus...'

The curse had slipped unbidden from Green's lips, but Renyard had thought much the same. He blinked around in incredulity at the bullet holes that marked practically every square inch inside the barracks. Not just the walls, but the ceiling, the floor, the beds and wardrobes. Bedding lay scattered over the floor, as well as boots, clothing, trinkets and oddments kept by the French soldiers. And there was more blood. Blood everywhere.

Renyard pivoted to take in the scene of carnage. In all his years he'd never seen anything like this. The walls and floors were painted with gouts of blood. Even the ceilings bled, drops of gore dripping like an ungodly rain.

'What the hell happened here?'

'Beats me, Sarge,' said Green, his voice a hoarse whisper. 'You think they were ambushed?'

Renyard shook his head, his Battle Bowler making a soft ringing noise in his ears. 'Judging by the number of bullet holes, it looks like the French weren't caught napping. They were fighting back.'

Using his rifle barrel to illustrate his point, Green aimed it several ways. 'Yes, but against how many? Jesus, Sarge, they were shooting in all directions.'

'There's blood everywhere.' Blanco was stating the obvious.

Renyard just looked at him.

Blanco lifted the lamp, casting luminance higher up the walls. Then down at the ground. 'With this much blood, they were hitting something. So where are all the bodies?'

Renyard shook his head. 'Maybe it's their own blood. This wild a fight they would've been in each other's arc of fire. They'd have been mowing down friend and foe alike.' But that was equally Blanco's point, and it was the sergeant who finished, 'So where are all the bodies?'

'All that blood at the door,' Green said. 'It looked like they were trying to get outside. Maybe they made it somehow and carried their wounded away with them.'

He was clutching at straws, and Renyard wasn't convinced. 'They wouldn't have carried the Jerry dead with them. Not only that, but if the Germans won, then they wouldn't have taken the Frenchies out either. So...where the hell are they? And where has Rifleman Hughes got to?'

'When we saw the blood on the door, I left him guarding it and came to fetch you, Sarge,' Blanco said. 'He should've been right there waiting for us.'

'You know Leo: he can't keep his nose out of mischief, that lad,' Green offered.

Renyard took one last look around the room. 'All right, we know he's not in here. Let's try those other rooms.'

From somewhere within the casement there was a clink of metal upon metal.

All three soldiers came to an immediate standstill, their rifles lifted.

From an adjacent room came the sound of soft footsteps. Renyard didn't need to give orders: Green went one way and Tyler the other. Renyard dropped to one knee, shouldering his weapon. Whoever came through that door would walk into three distinct lines of fire, with no hope of escape.

'Sarge?'

The whisper was in English and a voice they all recognised. Not that any of them were about to lower their guard just yet. They waited silently until Rifleman Cooper poked his head around the doorframe.

The bubble of expectancy went out of Renyard and he grunted in reflex. He allowed his gun to lower as Cooper took a stride into the room and then faltered. His gaze roamed the walls and the wreckage of the beds. His jaw hung open.

'What are you doing in here?' Green admonished him. 'I distinctly recall telling you to guard *the bleeding approaches.*'

'Uh, sorry, Corp.' Cooper came to attention, but it was a half-formed act as he was still enthralled by the sight of the blood-spattered room. Green stomped towards him, his tackety boots ringing on the concrete, the requirement to maintain stealth momentarily forgotten.

'Well?' Green demanded. 'What have you got to say for yourself?'

Renyard moved forward. 'Cooper. What?'

Cooper dragged his gaze away from the scene of carnage, and blinked down at the sergeant. 'Sarge, I, uh...well, what it is...'

'Out with it!' Green snapped.

'We've found Leo wandering about on the hillside.'

'He left his post?'

'Sarge,' Cooper said, directing his explanation at Renyard, 'I don't think he did it on purpose.'

'What the hell are you blathering about, Rifleman?'

'Come and see,' Cooper said, and his voice had dropped to little more than a whisper.

'Can't you see we're busy here-' Green began, but Renyard shook his head and the corporal clammed up.

'Lead the way, Cooper,' Renyard said.

Cooper took one last look at the room before slowly turning to lead them back through the anterooms to the vestibule. Rifleman McCoy was standing guard at the door, but not facing out as expected but within. He saw the small group of his companions approaching and visibly relaxed. Renyard thought he heard the young soldier mutter thanks to God.

'Where's Rifleman Hughes now?' Cooper asked him.

'Winker's looking after him.'

Renyard and Green shared a puzzled expression before pushing by. Green jabbed a nod at McCoy and Tyler to guard the door, but allowed Cooper to accompany them. They walked around the side of the casement and saw Rifleman Watson crouching in the dust. With his narrow back hunched and his pointed features he looked like a vulture investigating a corpse. But it was no dead body in front of him, but Leo Hughes. The rifleman was lying on his back, stretched out as if he was on a Red Cross litter, but his hands were folded over his face. As they approached, Renyard could hear soft sniffling. The lad was weeping.

Renyard came to a halt, looking down on the young man. Watson twisted up to return the sergeant's gaze, and his mouth was pulled into a tight grimace. He leaned in and prodded Hughes gently.

Hughes mewled like a cat.

'Come on, Leo. Sarge is here, mate.'

Leo took a second or so longer, but when he moved it was to roll onto his side and pull his knees to his chest.

'Hughes, get up off your arse,' Corporal Green hissed, 'instead of lying there, crying like a bloody coward.'

Watson, his face all angles in the darkness, glanced up at Green, and it was as if flames sparked behind his eyes. He said, 'Begging your pardon, Corporal Green, but do you mind *shutting your bleedin' gob for a minute*?'

Green bristled at the insubordination, but Renyard grabbed at him, shot him a warning glance. 'I'll handle this,' he said.

He crouched down, placing one knee in the dirt next to Hughes' head. He reached down and placed a hand on the young man's shoulder, shaking him gently. 'Leonard,' he said, choosing to use the soldier's given name. 'What is it? What's wrong?'

Without raising his head, Hughes moaned. 'They're all dead.'

'The French soldiers?'

'They're all dead.'

'You've seen them?'

Hughes finally struggled up, as though he barely had the strength to support himself on his elbows. He peered up at Renyard, his face covered in snot and tears. 'I've seen them.'

'You've seen dead men before...'

'Not like that,' Hughes said, and it was as if his voice came from some deep, dark haunted place. '*Never like that.*'

A shiver went through Renyard's body, leaving him cold. He'd heard an expression that described the sensation: someone had just walked over his grave. He turned to follow Hughes' horrified gaze, and stared up at the twin cloches at the top of the fort.

'They're up there?'

Hughes nodded, following it with a sob.

'Yes, Sarge. Every last one of them.'

Chapter 5

13th May 1940
Borderlands

Ludis Kristaps wasn't a man to curse his God, neither was he one to expect divine intervention. At birth, God gave Ludis free will, determination and a sturdy body, and it was down to Ludis to use them as best he chose. He could give in, succumb to the ravaging wolf pack, or he could fight with every breath left to him.

Ludis wasn't a quitter.

As the grey forms swarmed over him, their teeth clashing like yellow sparks against the forest, he roared with the same ferocity as the wolf pack. He was on his back, freezing water invading his clothes, with animals all over him. His thick coat spared him the superficial nips and bites, but other jaws had latched onto his legs and the pain was tortuous. Ludis had been raised in a tough land, where sometimes pain was all that told you that you were still alive. The agony galvanised him and he struck out with his fists at the beasts trying to find purchase on his throat. The wolves were supreme hunters, but never was Ludis prey and he tore at them with as much ferocity as they sent at him. One wolf, the Alpha-female, tore at the leather and fur over his stomach, attempting to disembowel him. Ludis latched onto its head with one hand, his thick fingers striving to crush its skull. With his other arm he batted at those trying to rip off his face. He kicked at one male that attempted to latch onto his genitals. The wolf howled and writhed on the floor and if Ludis had the time he'd have seen that he'd broken its jaw.

Brackish water splashed his face, and in the stream he could taste his own blood. Because of the water's icy touch his flesh was growing numb – or was that because he was bleeding out and fading quickly? No, because the blood raged in his skull and cast a red veil over his vision. If he was dying, he suspected that grey shadows would be flitting in his periphery. While he lived, he could kill. He struggled up to a sitting position, still grappling with the she-wolf's skull. In his other hand he lifted a smooth stone the size of a grapefruit from the streambed. Like a primeval warrior he held it hammer-like in his fist.

'Off me, bitch!'

He swung the rock in a vicious arc and felt the impact rebound up his arm and into his shoulder. Pain scorched him, but it was nothing to what the wolf must have experienced in the second before it fell unmoving at his side. Kicking and struggling up, Ludis raised his stone hammer again, his face brutish in his desire for killing. Water teemed from his clothing, while steam rose from his shoulders in wispy tendrils. He planted his feet in a wide stance, arms raised.

'Come on you bastards. What's wrong? Have you lost your taste for my flesh?'

Around him the remaining wolves circled, staying well out of range of his hammering blows. They slinked now, their haunches quivering, low growls and whines replacing the furious sounds of before.

'Cowards. I killed your queen and now you've lost the will to fight?'

His words were pointless, except he needed to rage against the pack. He intended to dominate them, strike fear into their hearts. He roared like a wounded bear and took a couple of running steps towards them. The nearest wolves tucked their tails and scampered away. Once beyond his reach, they turned back and snarled low threats of their own. This was not over by a long way. He'd destroyed their leader, but the wolves were not the base creatures he accused them of being. They were merely rallying, waiting for the opportune moment. He couldn't allow them to do that.

'Yaaaaah!' His scream was wordless and bestial. He swung at a nearby wolf, kicking out at its haunch. His boot slammed the beast's legs and knocked it sprawling. While it thrashed to find a way up, Ludis ran in and snatched the wolf up. It weighed half as much as he did, but it was also sodden with water and his blood. Nonetheless he hauled it up with one arm and grasped it against his chest. He had to drop his rock, but it was a fair trade, because in the next instant he caught at the wolf's throat with his free hand. The wolf snapped at his face but Ludis cared not: he lifted the wolf above his head and then hurled it at its pack members. The flying animal knocked down two of its kin, including the one with the shattered jaw.

He hoped to break its spine, but Ludis watched the beast struggle up and limp away. The two he'd knocked down also scurried off with their tails between their legs. He circled in the stream, expecting an attack from those behind him, but already the final couple were making off around the curve where the rocks towered. Ludis exhaled and weakness invaded his every pore. Almost going to his knees in the water, he fought the desire to collapse and staggered over to throw his back against the slick rocks. The wolves might try a second time and after his victory over them he had no intention of showing any sign of weakness now. Something glittered darkly in the water and he reached down and plucked out the Webley revolver he'd dropped earlier. The gun would require care if it was to ever fire again. He looked for his rifle, because some time during the battle it had slipped from his shoulder. He found the old gun in the stream next to the dead she-wolf, but one look told him that the gun was useless. His weight - and that of the wolf pack - had been on top of it and had shattered the stock. He let it lie in the stream.

Suddenly he slapped at the pack hanging at his waist and was relieved to find it in place. He quickly delved inside and felt the warm pulse of heat against his fingertips. 'Thank God,' he muttered under his breath. Despite his earlier doubts concerning divine intervention, he wondered now if something more than luck had kept the object safely on his person. Ha! It was a stupid and naive notion, for, if God had any hand in this, He'd have simply sent the wolves on another path and spared Ludis the battle. Unless, of course this was a trial, for Ludis knew that his God was a hard and pitiless divinity, one who'd tested Moses and Joshua of antiquity far more harshly than this. Ludis laughed at the absurdity: to compare himself to either man was supremely egotistical and a blasphemy in itself. Maybe it would be best that he pray to his uncaring God lest He strike him down.

Ludis shook his head. After what had happened to his wife and unborn child, God owed him leniency.

He looked at his hands. They still trembled from the ferociousness of the fight, shaking with the adrenalin pumping through his frame. There were myriad cuts and gouges in his flesh, the bleeding somewhat staunched by the chill of the water. Soon enough, he knew, the pain would come. He dipped his hands in the stream to clean his wounds, and, with no other option, had to shake the droplets off him for nothing he wore was dry. Luckily it was late spring: a month or two earlier and the cold would have killed him as surely as the ripping teeth of the wolf pack.

He waded from the water, watching the embankments around him for any sign that the pack had returned. He was rewarded by a mournful howl, but this carried from some distance. He smiled grimly, his teeth flashing in his beard. The wolves had fled, knowing that they'd met a more fearsome killer than them. As he stepped up onto the mossy bank he touched his face. There were gashes there – more scars to match those that already chequered his features. Thankfully none of his injuries were severe, his thick clothing saving him from the worst of them. His shins and ankles burned where teeth had scored him, but instinctively he knew that they were superficial cuts and bruises. They would slow him but never halt him. He patted the bag at his waist and set off again.

Clap.

Ludis went dead still.

Clap. Clap.

Leathery palms played a slow applause.

Clap. Clap. Clap.

'Who's there?' Ludis demanded.

The forest had fallen dark during his flight and subsequent battle and the trees rising around him now took on the forms of giant spectres swaying in the breeze. Ludis scanned from one to the next, searching for sign of the clapper. There was nothing he could see, but again he grew conscious of the uncanny stillness of the night, the hush that had preceded the wolf attack. Maybe he'd misread the reason then and it wasn't the feral animals that had brought silence to the forest. Maybe it was this secretive applauder all along.

'Show yourself.'

Ludis circled slowly and, even though it held no bullets, he lifted the Webley in threat.

The clapping came again, but the steep embankments made it difficult to pinpoint the source of the noise, throwing back echo after echo.

'Man or devil – or whatever you are - that's enough of your taunting. Show yourself.'

'*That was a titanic struggle, my friend. You are a worthy victor.*'

Ludis craned upward and there at the top of the rocks he'd recently scaled sat a small figure. In the dimness he could not make out any features, just a spindly form that seemed to have too many angles than a human should possess.

'You speak my tongue,' Ludis said.

'*I speak all tongues, yet I speak none.*'

'What madness is that? I understand you. Clearly you speak Latvian.'

The small figure tittered and the sound sent an uncomfortable shiver down Ludis' spine. *'Do I?'* the figure asked.

'Wait...' Ludis shook his head, as though clearing the water from his ears would help make more sense. 'You speak in *my voice!*'

'No, Ludis, you speak in your voice; I only return them so that you can understand me.'

'What deviltry is this? Foul thing, I will kill you.'

'Deviltry you say? You're sure about that?'

Ludis touched his fingers to his scalp and found his hat lost. He must have cracked his skull when he fell into the stream. That was it; this was some weird auditory hallucination brought on by a concussion.

'I'm no figment of your imagination.' Above him the oddly shaped man tittered again. The laughter was distinct in that it was emitted from the man's mouth and not directly in Ludis' ear. Ludis squinted up at him, wondering why the man was sitting there, why he hadn't struck while Ludis remained weakened from his battle with the wolves, for surely this was a creature of the night, another of the things that he must destroy?

'I see you're considering killing me? I wish you no ill, Ludis.'

The man's latest words staggered Ludis, for not only was the man mimicking his voice, but also it seemed he was anticipating Ludis' thoughts before they formed into words.

'Witch!' Ludis snapped. 'Keep out of my head.'

'You think me a witch. Aah, that explains all. "Thou shalt not suffer a witch to live." That is behind your reasoning for wishing to smite me, no?'

'Unclean thing...'

Again the laughter rang out. *'Have you taken a look at yourself lately? I'm glad that I'm upwind of you, Ludis, because I'm not sure I'd bear the stench otherwise.'*

'You have the temerity to mock me?'

'Hardly. I only state a fact. Sorry, Ludis, but how long is it since your clothing seen the administrations of a woman's touch?'

Ludis didn't reply. His stubborn refusal to answer was pointless for the small man seemed capable of reading everything inside his head.

'Ah! I apologise. I seem to have touched upon a raw spot. I am sorry about Galina. It was a truly shocking thing to have befallen your beloved wife.'

'Get out of my head, damn you. Do not sully my memories of Galina or our baby.'

On the rocks, the small man shifted. He rose up stiffly, supporting himself on some sort of staff or walking cane. When he'd risen, he had lost some of the weird shapes that the darkness had added, and Ludis could now see that he was simply a bent old man, albeit his spine was slightly humped. He used the staff to point at Ludis. 'Well, are you going to come up or do you expect me to clamber down these rocks like a goat?'

The first thing that struck Ludis was that the old man's voice, paper thin and scratchy like it had been ill used, no longer mimicked him, but was the man's own. Before he could comment the old man waved an arthritic hand at him. 'That mimicry thing is something I learned over the years, but it's only useful so far. I'm not incapable of speech, though it's been some time since I've conversed with another man. It's easier for me to throw a voice than it is form my own words.'

Ludis was still wary of the little man. 'It's some kind of trick? I have heard of men in sideshow acts who throw their voices...no, that isn't what you were doing. You were mimicking me, you knew my thoughts, and you knew my language. That is no trick, but black magic.'

The man shook his head, and Ludis heard a rattle of bones and twigs. 'Only the most ignorant of peasants would believe such.'

'You mocked me,' Ludis grunted. 'Now you would insult me?'

'Not my intention, my friend.'

'Twice you've called me friend, yet I doubt your sincerity.'

'Have I done anything to cause you such doubt?'

Ludis gestured in the general direction of the fleeing wolves. 'That was your doing, you sent the wolf pack against me.'

Tapping his walking stick on the rock at his feet, the old man appeared lost in thought. Finally he looked down at Ludis and it was as if his eyes shone with an inner light. 'I sent them. Yes. But it was not my intention that they harmed you. That was your own fault. When you ran, their base instinct to chase replaced my commands. Had you come along quietly, the wolves would've merely shepherded you to my hearth. You chose to fight and the wolves responded in kind.'

'You could have introduced yourself and asked me to join you at your fire.'

'The way in which you reacted to my wild friends, I'm glad that I didn't. Base instinct for Ludis Kristaps, it seems, is to fight. You might have brained me with a rock the way you did the she-wolf.'

'I might yet, old man.'

The chuckle that followed was dry and warm.

'No. I doubt that...now that we are friends. Trust me, Ludis: I mean you no harm.'

Ludis glanced once at the dead wolves arranged around him. 'Shame you didn't say so at the outset.'

The old man beckoned him upwards. 'Come, my friend, I'm at home in these woods, but even I would struggle on these slick boulders.'

'I'll come,' Ludis agreed, 'but only because my interest has been piqued. I wish to know how a man can converse with the wild things of the forest, and how he can learn a foreign tongue merely by anticipating the thoughts of another. But know that I don't trust you, little man. The first inkling that you're leading me into a trap, and you'll be sorry.'

'For one of the cloth, you have a poor grasp of showing tolerance to your fellow man.'

Ludis said, 'I am not of the cloth anymore. I am a man of flesh and bone, which is all. Right now, both my flesh and bones ache after what you put me through, and I've a mind to repay you some of that hurt...if you're deceiving me.'

'And if I'm not?'

'Then the warmth of your fire will suffice to put things right, little man.'

The old man chuckled again, then turned away and hobbled over the rocks. 'Then follow, friend. You might even be glad you met me, because I've more to offer you than a crackling hearth.'

Ludis considered for no more than a heartbeat. It was like he'd already said: his curiosity was piqued. But more than that, standing there in sodden clothing, stinking like a rutting warthog, the prospect of a warm fire and a dry place to lie down overrode any fear he had of walking into a trap. He reached up for the nearest boulders and hauled himself after the old man.

Chapter 6

13th May 1940
Bulson Ridge, France

Renyard considered himself a sergeant who led by example, and therefore not one to hang back while men under his command took all the risks. He led the way up the narrow stairwell into the gunroom, probing the darkness with the barrel of his SMLR. Rifleman Hughes had metaphorically tightened his chinstrap and was second in line on the stairs, carrying the lantern discovered in the lower rooms. Corporal Green and Watson brought up the rear, their earlier animosity to the other forgotten in the pressing urgency for moral support. Their boots came with metal studs, and it was a devil's game trying to mount the stairs in silence. Renyard didn't mind the scuffing sounds, because on this occasion it was best that anyone above would be alerted to their presence. Although Leo had been adamant that the entire French troop was dead, Renyard doubted it. The last he wanted was to poke his head through the hatch at the top and have a frightened Frenchman take it off.

'Hello. Is anyone there? We're British. Friends,' he called softly.

Watson, who spoke better French, translated his words, as they'd agreed before setting off up the stairs.

Neither language elicited a response.

'I told you, Sarge, they're all dead.'

Renyard ignored Hughes's words, choosing a number of his own. '*Bonjour, nous sommes amis et sont ici por vous aider.*' He wasn't sure if they would reassure any listener that they were friends and there to help, but it was all he could offer. Neither was he certain that his schoolboy French made sense, but a glance at Watson earned him a nod.

A metal door met them at the top, but it stood partially open, the way in which Hughes had left it after fleeing the chamber. Something that struck Renyard: all of that blood downstairs, yet not a speck here. If the French had been massacred down in the amenity areas, then carried up here by their killers, then why wasn't there a trail of blood to mark their progress? It was similar to the scene downstairs where a bloody swathe led all the way to the exit door before ending abruptly. It was uncanny. It gave him pause before entering the gun deck. He sucked in a deep breath, wavered, but curiosity got the better of him. He moved into the room.

During their initial retreat from the Meuse, the various casements they had passed came in different shapes and sizes, some with single firing rooms, others with two. Some had retracting turrets that could be lowered during heavy bombardment, while others – like this one here – had fixed cloches. This particular casement came armed with 47mm anti-tank guns and twin machineguns, and Renyard guessed that much of the space in the two firing areas would be dominated by the guns and stacked ammunition - as in all others he'd seen. Between the circular towers that supported the cloches, the usual layout was an open space where the soldiers manning the bunker toiled. This one was no different, he found.

Stepping into the workspace behind him, Hughes raised the lantern, casting jittering shadows to flee to the far corners. The light depicted a room just as Renyard expected, complete with a worktable where the officers would direct their men. Charts lay spread across the table, curling at their corners, and there were others tacked to the walls. Another table supported a boxy radio. A telephone handset dangled off the edge of the table, alongside the earphones the radio operator would have worn. Renyard found a light switch and flicked it on. These casements were self-sufficient, having their own electrical generators and back up systems to ensure their capacity for air and water filtration remained constant. Yet the lights didn't kick on, and it was probably because the generators had been sabotaged during the attack.

Renyard turned his gaze on Hughes. Though the young man had achieved some measure of control he was still showing signs of shock. His face was deathly pale, even under the yellow glow of the lantern. 'You said the Frenchmen were here...'

'They are. They're in there,' Hughes said, pointing a trembling finger to the firing room on their right. Because the turret was a target for enemy fighter planes and bombers, a steel door offered protection from a direct hit, forming a barrier between the officers and the men manning the guns. The door stood open a sliver. Renyard moved towards it, yet he couldn't shake the feeling that had earlier assailed him: by going through that door *everything* would change.

He was a rational person. Anyone who made his living as a fighting man had to be, because he needed his wits about him at all times.

Allowing flights of fancy to dominate him would only get him killed. Yet, here, in this place, he felt a trickle of unease that he couldn't explain. There was something wrong here. Something from beyond the bounds of everything he'd ever believed in before. Something *super*natural. For the briefest of time he felt afraid and his steps faltered.

He sensed Green move up to stand at his shoulder, could feel his presence hovering close by. It was enough to steel him, as though the closeness of another man fought back his urge to turn and run. His heart was beating twice its normal rate, and the blood buzzed in his veins, but a surge of endorphins also flooded through him, girding him against the fear. He readied his rifle and moved to the partially open door. He heard Hughes retreat slightly, but the young man was suddenly checked, and without looking Renyard assumed that Watson had taken hold of his friend. In the Great War, someone showing Hughes' reluctance to fight might have found himself in the sights of a firing squad. Things were more enlightened now, Renyard thought, but that wasn't why he forgave the young man his reluctance. If it was anything like what assailed Renyard now, he could fully understand the boy's terror.

Bodies, dozens of them, were jammed into the circular space. They were stacked like driftwood in a dam, one on top of the other, arms and legs comingling, heads squashed against chests, or between the legs of their comrades. There had been no care taken in the arrangement, no subtlety to it whatsoever. It was as if a giant hand had picked them up a dozen at a time and crammed and squeezed them into the structure, around the guns, among the stacked ordnance, against the walls. Stunned, Renyard stared at the mangled pile. Downstairs the floors, walls, the very ceilings, had been washed with gore. Here: not a drop. The nearest corpses he could see all carried horrendous wounds. Some skulls were split, chest cavities torn open, limbs ripped off yet...*there was no blood*. The wounds were ragged and should have dripped even now, even after coagulation must have set in. The blood downstairs had begun to discolour, but it was still wet, meaning that it had been spilled not long before their arrival at the casement. Renyard was familiar with death, had witnessed it enough to know that there was definitely something wrong about the entire scenario.

'They've been drained of blood,' Green whispered from Renyard's shoulder. 'Hung like pigs in a butcher's shop and their blood drained from them.'

Renyard nodded, for it was the exact thought that had gone through his head. What conclusion that offered didn't help. He said, 'And then they were stacked here.' He looked at the corporal and imagined his features were painted with the same dread as Green's were. 'Like meat stored in an ogre's larder.'

Green squinted at him, back at the stack of corpses. 'What else is missing, Sarge?'

Renyard didn't understand the question.

'Look at them,' Green went on, 'their injuries.'

Because his brain was struggling to make sense of the slaughter, it took Renyard another few seconds to arrive at the same conclusion as Green. 'They've been torn to bits. That's not the result of gunfire or even grenades.'

'Frigging Nazis...How could they do *this*? What kind of men are they?'

Now it was apparent that Green was the one playing catch up. Renyard shook his head, moving closer to one of the nearest dead men. 'Bring that lantern over here, Hughes,' he called.

The room brightened as the lantern was ushered closer, but when Renyard glanced up at its bearer he saw that Watson had taken charge of it. He checked for Hughes and saw the young man leaning against the doorframe, one hand on his face. Renyard swore internally: he'd intended forcing Hughes back in the saddle by making him face his fear, but it looked like his experiment had failed. He said, 'Leo. Get your arse back outside and watch for Jerry.'

Beneath his hand, Hughes nodded affirmative and then slipped away through the command room and down the stairs. Corporal Green grunted something unintelligible, but it didn't take too much guessing at whom his derision was aimed. Renyard didn't see it as cowardice; the young man was suffering from shock...and no wonder.

The corpse stared back at Renyard through eyes milky with cataracts, but in their depths, and the savage twist of the features, he could read abstract terror. The man had died screaming, and not because of a raid conducted by German paratroopers. Renyard watched as Watson swept the lantern over other faces in the mound. Every last face was stricken with the same ungodly fear. Tremulously, Renyard reached out with the tip of a finger and touched the nearest waxy face. It was cold, colder than it should have been even in death. These men had only perished in the last hour or so and yet they were almost icy to the touch. A similar chill went up Renyard's spine and he backed away.

'How many men are here?'

'Hard to say, Sarge, but at least two dozen,' Watson said.

'That's the same number of men that would've manned this bunker?'

'Pretty much,' Watson agreed.

'So what's over in the other turret?'

As a group the trio turned around and this far away the lantern did little to illuminate the entrance to the second gun cloche.

'Do we really want to find out?' Green said. It was as if his words hit him a blow, as if by muttering them he had attained the rank of a coward alongside Hughes. He dragged his britches up with one hand, while taking the first step towards the second cloche, attempting to re-establish his position in the troop. Renyard grabbed at his webbing and halted him.

'We're leaving now. There's nothing here for us.' Renyard didn't give a crap if his actions could be perceived as cowardly. Only an idiot – brave or otherwise – would go through that door. 'Get out now. Both of you.'

Watson opened his mouth to say something, but Renyard shook his head. 'We can debate this later. For now we have to get as far away from here as we can.' As an afterthought he added, 'If this is what the German's are capable of, I don't want any of the lads to be caught unawares.'

They moved across the command room, bunched together, and hit the stairs at a jog, each one moving faster than was prudent. Their boots made a clatter of noise, but Renyard didn't care. He had his troop to think of, and the best course of action was to get away. Not for one second did he think they were going to fall foul of a Nazi enemy, though, but something more despicable again. He didn't want to think of what his mind had conjured beyond the door to the second cloche. On his way in he'd experienced the feeling that some giant arachnid was beckoning him inside, and that was nightmarish enough, but his mind formed something even more terrible as they fled the casement.

Outside the night air was full of the stench of smoke from the fires burning in the valleys behind them, yet it tasted sweet to Renyard as he pushed out of the casement. Beside him, Green sucked in noisily, and Renyard realised he wasn't the only one that the tainted atmosphere inside had affected. He turned to look back at the doorway, half expecting to be overcome with the feeling of dread he'd earlier experienced, but his attention was taken by the fact Watson hadn't followed them out.

'Where's Winker?'

Green, his fists on his thighs as he continued to breathe deeply, gave him a confused look. 'He was right behind me on the stairs. He was carrying the lamp, maybe he had to put it down to collect his rifle.'

Renyard didn't think so. Watson and his rifle were never apart, and he could recall when Watson came forward to cast light on the mound of bodies that it was hanging over his shoulder. Renyard bit his lip with enough force that he felt pain. Small penance, he thought, for leaving a man behind.

'Green, round up the lads and have them ready to move out.' He looked again at the casement, dreading his decision but seeing nothing else for it. 'If I'm not back out of there in five minutes, lead them north-west. Try and hook up with our regiment. If that's not possible, try to find any of the Expeditionary Force and fall in with them.'

'You're going back inside?' Green straightened up. 'I'm coming with you, Sarge.'

'No, Corporal Green, I've just given you an order...obey it.'

Before the corporal could say anything else, Renyard lifted his rifle and headed back inside. Through his mind drifted a random line from a children's rhyme: come into my parlour said the spider to the fly. It couldn't have been more apt.

Chapter 7

May 13th, 1940
Borderlands

'Men approach from the north.'

The little man was squatting on a wooden stool, his legs and elbows bent at those strange angles that Ludis had found queer on first sighting him. It was, he understood now, an effect of the twist in the man's spine, where he had to sit thus to attain some comfort. In the woods, the old man had worn a cloak, and a necklace braded from bones and twigs, but he'd doffed both since coming inside and now sat in a tatty shirt and trousers. Ludis was on a similar stool, across the fire from him, his mouth watering as the juices from a roasting hare dripped into the fire pit. Ludis had also shrugged out of his wet coat, which now hung a safe distance from the flames. His attention was on the food, the first hot meal he would eat in days, so he didn't at first pay attention to the old man's statement.

'At least when I spoke in your voice you paid attention,' the man grumbled.

Ludis snapped out of his hunger-induced trance, looking up from the slowly turning hare. 'Forgive me. I was elsewhere for a moment.'

'You were thinking about your belly. Ha! Don't worry, I'm not reading your thoughts, it's painted for all to see in the drool on your beard.'

'I...I admit to being hungry.'

'After the battle you fought with the pack it's little wonder.' The old man used his walking stick to probe at two tin cups set in the ashes. He nodded his head, then, taking a rag from beside him, he picked up the nearest and leaned forward for Ludis to take it. 'Broth,' he said at Ludis' quizzical glance. 'Careful, it's hot. It will help heat up your bones.'

'It smells like no broth I've known before,' Ludis said, inspecting the brew in the tin cup.

'It's a concoction of my own. You might be pleasantly surprised. Yes it's as sweet smelling as a whore's armpit, but it is rather satisfying on the palate.'

A whore's armpit? Ludis was unfamiliar with such a scent, but he wasn't so sanctimonious that he couldn't conjure it. Perhaps the whores of France were different than the old doxy who'd serviced the unwed men of his fishing village: for there was nothing sweet about her odour. He'd never been within ten feet of her, but the waft of rancid sweat was enough to ensure he held fast to his marital vows. Such a glib thought, and yet his mind's eye suddenly flashed up a picture of Galina's pretty face. His wife had been very pretty, but she wasn't the last time he'd looked upon her. He closed his eyes, shook his head.

'You don't like it?' the old man said. 'Give it here, and I'll have it.'

Ludis didn't relinquish the cup. 'Sorry, I was elsewhere again.'

'You are such a melancholy brute,' the old man chuckled. 'How did one as dour as you ever gather a flock about them? Oh, yes, I get it. You put the *fear of God* into them no doubt?'

'I wasn't much of a preacher, that's for sure. I was a pastor in name, but not always in practice. Not that I have ever tasted of a whore's armpit.'

'Ha! See. You can be cheerful if you try.'

'I've nothing to be cheerful about.'

'You have a roof over your head, meat cooking on the spit and my joyous company. You have more to be thankful for than many other people this night.'

'I am thankful.'

'So paint a smile on your grizzled chops.'

'I'm not a man disposed to false humour. If I were to smile you would recognise it for a lie. Where would that leave us then?'

Across the fire the old man regarded him, his eyes twinkling as they reflected the flames. 'Then I shall smile for the two of us.'

'Yes, old man, that's a good idea. I cannot smile and drink your broth at the same time.'

'I should be thankful for small victories.' His comment caught another quizzical glance from Ludis. 'At least in your estimation I've moved on somewhat. Not so long ago I was a devil, a witch, now I'm just an old man. Pretty soon I'll have you calling me by name.'

'I've never learned it,' said Ludis.

'The time wasn't right to share it until now. Call me...' it was as though the man had to rack his memory, and was having the devil's own time recalling what he had once been called. Ludis thought that the old man had been out here in the woods, living alone with only the feral beasts as company, that it must have been years since he'd spoken his name out loud. The old man racked his brains a little longer. 'I've been known by so many names that I find it difficult to choose one.' He clicked his fingers, said, 'Borvo. You can call me Borvo.'

Ludis grunted.

'Is there something wrong with Borvo?'

'It sounds like the name of a jester or clown.'

Borvo squinted through the flames at him. 'I'm beginning to think your dour expression is a sham. You do have a witty side to you after all. Borvo is a good Gallic name. Once it was exalted...'

'Once?'

'A long time ago it was the name of a deity. A healer.'

It was now Ludis' turn to squint, taking in the malformed shape of the old man opposite him. 'A healer you say?'

Borvo winked at him, nodded at the cup in his hands. 'I am beyond healing, Ludis. But you enjoyed my broth I see. How are you feeling?'

Actually, Ludis was feeling much better than he had before. The aches and pains from his fight with the wolves had fled him and there was warmth spreading from his insides that made his flesh pulse with renewed vigour. He shook his head: no it was simply the result of being warm and comfortable for a change, nothing to do with old Borvo's broth, or his name's elusive connection to a forgotten god of healing.

'Better,' he said. He eyed the hare again. Fat sizzled on the hot rocks at the edge of the fire. 'I think I'll be better again with half that beast residing in my belly.'

'There isn't long to wait now, Ludis. A few minutes at most.' Borvo's eyes twinkled again. 'Just long enough for you to tell me your tale.'

'What tale would that be?'

'The one that brought you here, of course. The one that set you on your mission.'

'You tinkered about in my head earlier,' Ludis pointed out. 'Surely you gathered enough from my thoughts to save me the trouble now?'

Borvo chuckled. 'I wasn't reading your thoughts. I'm skilled in reading a person's reactions, that's all. It's something I studied a long time ago. A person's body language can offer much information, if only you know how to read it.'

'Have I my name tattooed on my forehead? You spoke my name without me giving it. You also mentioned my wife's name, and knew what happened to her.'

'I learned both your names from a different source. I admit I've learned of snatches of your past, but they are random, disjointed, and I can make little sense of them. I will tell you how after we have eaten.' Borvo poked at the roasting hare with a gnarled finger. He grunted, moved the spit handle round to reposition it. 'Maybe it'll take a little longer cooking than I first thought. Let's not sit in silence. Tell me your tale, Ludis, and then I'll tell you what you want to know. Then I'll tell you of the men approaching from the north.'

'What men?'

Borvo wagged a finger. 'You first, Ludis.'

His eyebrows fell like thunderheads, and Ludis gave the little man a stern look. 'There are some memories best left in the past. They trouble me, Borvo, and I do not like to dwell on them.'

Laughter sounded out of place as a precursor to Ludis' story, but Borvo chuckled anyhow. 'By the stern set of your face, it looks to me like you're thinking bad thoughts most of the time.'

Ludis grunted. His burly shoulders fell momentarily, but he straightened quickly, as though steeling himself for the task ahead. 'Maybe you'd best set the meat from the flames, because my tale might take longer to relate than even you can anticipate.'

Borvo winked at him. 'Don't worry about it; I can listen and turn a spit at the same time.'

'Maybe my story will spoil your appetite.'

'Then that will mean there's all the more for you.'

Ludis expelled another grunt, but this was tinged with humour. He gave the roasting meat one last fond glance, before putting it from his mind. Odd, he thought, that it was his need for meat that had brought him to this place and time. He wondered how things would have turned out if the larders had been full that day...

Chapter 8

Ludis Kristaps urged his horse down a wooded trail, the mud churned by troops fleeing east before the advancing guns of Germany's battalions. Already Hitler had annexed Austria, invaded Poland, and now his armies were pushing eastward. He saw signs of where shells had smashed holes through the forest. Deep craters pitted the ground like mouths opened in silent screams, the earth thrown far, along with the limbs and eviscerated bodies of Russian soldiers too slow in their retreat. He saw the ragged remnants of humanity tossed among the trees, some of them having already been feasted on by the creatures of the forest so that they were now as much bone as they were flesh. The stench of decay did not disturb him the way it bothered his horse: it was a stench he'd grown used to.

He was no soldier. Not in the conventional sense. Europe was reeling as The Third Reich pushed for dominance over the western world, and even now, from the west he could detect the distant pounding of mortars, the rattle of machine guns and the screams of the dying. He ignored it all. He was aloof to the war that was killing thousands, because he was engaged in a single-minded conflict of his own. The Nazis were a terrible foe for any nation, but their cruelty paled in comparison to that levied by his enemy.

Three months he'd been engaged in this personal battle. He had tracked his foe all the way from his Latvian village, down along the coast of the Baltic Sea until the trail turned south at the Gdansk Basin. Across the breadth of Poland he'd went, killing one horse with the urgency of his pace, and then through the Ukraine to this point in northern Romania. Always he was just a day or so behind his enemy, for he had discovered signs of his passing, and they were far more terrible than even the atrocities men committed upon each other.

Now, closer to his ancestral home his enemy had slowed in his flight. Perhaps he thought himself invulnerable here, where he was once more protected by his thralls, and surrounded by familiar terrain. Ludis was determined to show him that his confidence was as misguided as the night he'd visited unholy terror on an insignificant Latvian village.

A shadow flitting between the trees was too insubstantial for Ludis to fix his gaze on. It was there, then gone, and all that told of its passing was the settling of the branches it had pushed past. Without the evidence of the rattling fronds he would have believed the shadow a trick of his eyes, or of the shifting moonlight playing games. The clouds, a tattered stack of cumulus, had made the sky dark, and only occasionally did the eye of the jaundiced moon peep through.

Settling himself on his horse, Ludis allowed his hand to creep up his body. He ignored the stock of the pistol wedged in his belt, and instead felt for the crucifix hanging on the cord he'd slung round his neck. He held the small cross, with the effigy of the Lord racked in pain upon it, squeezing with the rough pads of index finger and thumb. The Christ's body was sharp-edged and dug painfully into his flesh: penance he accepted without comment.

The horse's flanks shivered, and Ludis leaned down and patted it comfortingly on its withers. 'Easy, girl,' he said. 'Not long now and you will be able to rest.' When he straightened and kicked the horse on, he rested his palm on the stock of his pistol.

Again, this time off to his right, where a jumble of crags thrust up from the earth like the rebirth of a giant escaping its tomb, the shadow moved again. Catching the movement in his periphery, Ludis grunted to himself, but refused to look at it. The wraith-like figure swayed just beyond the ability to focus on it. It moved like a snatch of lint floating on a breeze, or like the smoke from a campfire coiling amongst the tree trunks on a frosty winter's evening. Trying to look directly at it was pointless, he suspected the thing moved through other dimensions and could not be seen in the conventional manner. He knew that, should he indeed fix his gaze on it, he would see nothing. And that made the shadow-thing dangerous.

He cared not for the unclean thing. It was but a familiar of the one he'd come to kill, and therefore below his contempt. Though, he couldn't ignore it entirely. Should its master command it against him then he must be ready to defend himself. The Luger in his belt would be useless against the phantom-like thing, but he'd brought with him weapons far more potent even than his faith.

The shadow-thing went up the crags like an eel out of water. Ludis stoically kept his eyes to the front, watching the trail instead. Something scarlet, like twin sparks against the night, flashed once from where the thing peered back at him. It wasn't the first time he'd caught a glimpse of its eyes. The scarlet was the flames of hell, a reflection of the dimension on which the creature generally looked.

Ludis had seen the eyes before. And many like them...

He had been in the forest, had brought down a doe with his rifle, and had carried it back to the village, balanced on his wide shoulders. The following day was Mid-Winter's feast day, and being an able-bodied man, he had accepted the task of supplying the meat for the banquet. The hunt had been long, and it was after dusk by the time he came over the hillside and down into the cove on the rock-strewn shores of the Baltic.

The village was strangely silent. He expected merriment as the women and children prepared for tomorrow's feast; expected ribald song from the men as they started early on the vodka. The single street was deserted of villagers, and he'd walked between the rows of humble cottages with a feeling of dread gnawing at his insides. This was not right, it was...uncanny.

He'd placed the doe on the stoop outside Andris the cobbler's house. Then he ran the short distance to the small wooden cottage he'd only recently built, wherein his young wife should have been awaiting his return.

'Galina?' he called as he pressed open the door. 'Galina, it's me, Ludis. Where are you, my love?'

The house was empty. He did not have many rooms to check, only the living quarters, and the small bedroom at the side. Galina was in neither.

'Galina?' he called again.

Their baby wasn't due for another four months, but his beloved had been having a troubling time of late. The baby, she said, was lying close to her bladder and she had a constant urge to urinate. Ludis checked the closet, but it too was empty. He stepped back into the living room. Galina had been busy; she'd been making streamers to attach to the hitching rails to help decorate the village with bright colours. They were strewn across the floor as though a strong wind had gusted through the room. He picked one up, teasing it between his fingers. The ribbon felt icy-cold and he shuddered, allowing the snip of cloth to drift to the floor.

'Galina?'

Something moved and he turned his bearded face to follow it, but found nothing in the room. Out of the corner of his eye, he thought that something black and insubstantial writhed and coiled, then went up the chimney. He grunted to himself: must have been his own breath he'd seen condensing in the cold air.

He went back on to the stoop and searched the street. No movement.

A bell peeled: a single resonant tone that sent shivers running the length of his spine. He pulled his heavy fur-lined coat about him as he stepped down off the stoop and marched back towards the cobbler's house.

The doe he'd so recently left there had been torn to pieces and lay scattered across the road. The meat glistened redly, but otherwise there was no blood. Uncanny: the feeling struck him anew.

Again the bell peeled.

Ludis ignored the deer's sundered corpse, and reached for his rifle. It was a single shot, and better as a stave, so he held it by its barrel as he approached the chapel at the end of the village. There was no reason that he should approach the church armed like this, but for the fact he could feel the heat of evil pulsing from the building like it had become a sentient and devilish thing itself. The peel of its bell was a challenge to him to come ahead.

The shadows shifted, and this time he knew that the writhing, coiling things hadn't been his breath misting the air. The shadows swarmed, moving in the dark places between the cottages. Occasionally he caught sparks of fire as they turned baleful eyes on him. Ludis tried to put them out of his mind – they, he knew, weren't the greatest menace here – but it is a human reflex to search for the propagators of danger and he couldn't avoid a sideways glance. The shadows split and drifted apart, some disappearing under the cracks in doors, others through windows. Some even went up and over the rooftops.

As he progressed along the road, he noted that there were signs of disturbance. Here a barrel on its side, the spilled fluid darkening the ground; there an up-ended cart, some of the day's catch of fish ground underfoot by people rushing for the sanctuary of the chapel. His people weren't cowards, but they were superstitious and God-fearing people, and it was understandable that they'd seek safety in the house of their Lord. He gritted his teeth. He should have been there for them.

At the threshold of the chapel he paused, staring at the door through which he'd passed on so many occasions he could not begin to count. But, it had been some time since he'd been in the chapel. The day he met and had fallen for Galina, he knew that his Lord had slipped to second place in the measure of his love. From that day, he had been a self-exile from the church. Stepping forward meant accepting his mistake – perhaps his punishment.

Resolute, he pushed the door open with his burly shoulder, moved inside where the worshipers would normally gather. He breathed out a long, ragged sob at the defilement he found, and the rifle drooped in his fist and clattered on the rough planks.

'Dear God in Heaven,' he moaned. 'Why have You forsaken Your children?'

The strength went out of his sturdy frame, and he sank to his knees, his hands coming up to finger the crucifix at his throat. 'Why, Dear Lord? Why would You allow *this* to happen?'

There were bodies everywhere, semi-naked where the clothes had been ripped from them so that feasting mouths could adhere to their flesh. They were arranged in tortuous fashion, backs bent over the simple pews, over the font, over the altar from which the word of God was preached. Their bones had been splintered to get at the marrow within, and though many carcasses had been split asunder, they were bloodless. With uncomprehending eyes, Ludis stared, and for the briefest of time his mind threatened to close down completely. How could he look on this carnage without descending into insanity?

He stood, trembling in his boots: not from fear but from a rage he'd never known.

There, back stretched taut over the nearest pew was his beloved. Galina, who'd brought him from one path and onto another, had been opened from throat to navel. His unborn child had been ripped from her womb and it too had been feasted upon. No one in the village, man, woman child or foetus, had been spared the visitation of horror.

Ludis stumbled towards her, cradled Galina in his arms, and then stooped to catch up his child. The baby's face bore his strong features but his mother's golden hair. Ludis sobbed, held both his loved ones to his chest. Then he threw back his head and screamed in a mix of grief and torment at the figure of Christ on the cross above the altar. Then he drooped again, and it was all he could do to support his wife and child as he bore them out of the chapel and to their home. The bell peeled and Ludis knew that it was nothing earthly that pulled mockingly on the rope. Again the shadow-things were there, but they slunk away into the night like the insubstantial things that they were. Ludis laid out his wife and baby on the bed he'd fashioned with his bare hands.

There was laughter, and he brought up his head sharply. His shaggy hair hung over his eyes but he did not push it aside. It was as though the hair obscuring his vision helped block out the unholy sight of his slaughtered loved ones. He was pleased it had gone unshorn all these months. Then he turned slowly and looked to the open door and the thing that stood in the threshold.

No insubstantial thing this, but a creature of flesh and bone, albeit never in the sense that humanity would be judged. It was tall, taller even than Ludis who was considered tall among the village men. It was thin, like an eviscerated corpse, but its paunch bulged from its recent gorging on blood. Its skin was as pale as the dead, blue about the deep wrinkles around its eyes and the pucker of a mouth. The eyes themselves were like putrid flesh, gangrenous orbs that suppurated with evil. Sexless the creature disdained clothing, for what need was there to warm a body that was as cold as the grave? Long arms trailed talons, and its bare feet clawed at the threshold it could not enter.

Upir.

The word came unbidden to his mind, though Ludis had never believed in such a creature. Not before that night. He had always laughed at tales of these children of Satan, these blood-drinking fiends. These Upir.

He'd asked his God why? Why would He allow this to happen? But there was only one answer. It was punishment for walking away from his duty. He had chosen a woman over his calling. God had sent a plague upon his people of Old Testament proportions.

'No.' That was a lie born of the devil. His sweet God had conspired that he be sent to fetch meat for the feast. He'd been spared the slaughter in order to complete his service to his Lord. He should have been inside the chapel to protect them, but had he been, then he would have most assuredly perished along with his flock. Pastor Ludis had been spared the coming of the Upir in order that he took up both rod and staff in the name of his Lord. He'd been spared in order that he smite down this abomination.

Ludis met the monster's gaze and it was like a hot brand drilled into his skull.

'Get away monster. You cannot enter my home uninvited.'

The Upir tittered and the sound was a blasphemy against nature.

'Be gone. I see you are gorged and sated for now. Be gone foul beast. You are done here.' Ludis lifted the cross from about his neck and held it towards the fiend. 'In the name of our risen god, Jesus Christ, I command you. BE GONE!'

The Upir swayed where it stood, afraid not of the crucifix but wary of the man who bore it. It folded a clawed hand over its bulbous stomach, rubbed it contentedly, while it opened its puckered mouth. A solitary glob of drool dribbled down its sharp chin, black as congealed blood.

'*Christ Bearer*,' it challenged in its abominable voice. '*I am well fed. But I shall never be sated. My hunger knows no bounds. We will meet again.*'

Then it was like a giant invisible hand snatched the Upir away, and it dwindled in Ludis's vision, as though sucked backwards down an endless tunnel.

'Yes, Upir,' Ludis agreed. 'We *will* meet again.'

And thus began his journey and his personal war.

Ludis buried his wife and child, and said a prayer over their graves. The villagers he could offer no such tenderness, so instead the chapel became their pyre. Ludis packed the weapons he would need, then found a horse spared the slaughter and set off along the shores of the Baltic, following the ancestral trails of the ancient Lett tribe from whom he was descended.

'Christ Bearer' the demon had called him. A literal translation of his family name: Kristaps. But the foul thing should have taken note of his given name, for it meant 'War'. The warrior bearing Christ in his soul, a holy warrior: the bane of the Upir.

Through Poland he'd followed its trail. Always a step behind, too late to offer anything but a few words of prayer to the eviscerated corpses he discovered. Across the western Ukraine, where the creature had grown bolder and even attacked a troop of soldiers encamped in an abandoned farm, he went. Their bodies were nigh on obliterated by the Upir's ferociousness.

Ludis understood.

With men in conflict, with so many corpses scattered across the terrain, who could tell that their deaths had been anything other than the terrible consequence of war? Unwittingly, Hitler's invading forces had unleashed an evil even greater than themselves. Offered the cover of conflict, the Upir had travelled far from its ancient homeland to feast on fresh victims.

Here in these forests of northern Romania, he had finally caught up to the beast and its minions. He had forced them to retreat and the Upir to seek comfort in its deep hole: the grave from which it had risen.

Yesterday he'd come across an encampment of gypsy folk. Romanies, they called themselves, and to the elders he'd presented himself, and sought answers. One old woman, a crone who spoke in an ancient cant of the Indris valley, warned him that his quest was doomed to failure. No man could stand against the Strigoi, she said. No one could kill a Mullo – one who was already dead. The Nosferatu, the creeping spirits of evil men, awoken from Hell by the Strigoi's call, she warned, surrounded the Strigoi.

'I will kill this *Strigoi.*'

'No man can kill the *wampyr,*' she warned again. 'But you can banish it back to its resting place and ensure it never rises again.'

'Endless sleep is as good as dead,' Ludis said.

'There are others...'

'Others?'

'Creatures summoned from the pit,' she said. 'The wampyr might be the least of them.'

'Then I will send them all to their endless sleep,' Ludis growled. 'This I swear.'

'Then this is what you must do...'

Now, armed with knowledge, and a sack at his side, and the bullets in the Luger stripped from the corpse of a Nazi storm trooper, he guided the horse down the trail, aiming for the hidden valley to which the old crone had directed him. Whether he ever came out again, he cared not. So long as the Upir...the Strigoi...the *Vampire* remained there with him for all eternity.

Ahead of him the human war had raged. Trees had been pushed awry by advancing Panzer's, branches making tangled nets to snare those fleeing the machinegun fire and the shells of the tanks. Some of the dead, he saw, had become food for the Upir and his legion of Nosferatu thralls. Beyond the battleground, the hill fell away into a deep gulley, which was so deep, the old Romany woman swore, that the sun never reached the bottom. Ludis slid out of his saddle. He unstrapped the girth and allowed the saddle to fall to the churned-up ground. He loosed the bridle and reins and threw them away from him.

'You have served me well, girl,' he said to the horse. 'Now go. Take your freedom.'

He slapped the horse on its rump, and immediately the horse snorted, spun in a tight circle and galloped off the way they'd come. Ludis shouldered his sack, and approached the edge of the gulley, and at its lip he stared down into the endless depths as though peering into the Abyss. At first all he could see was impregnable darkness, but as he continued to stare, the black veil could not conceal things even blacker. The Nosferatu were massed against him, clinging to the walls of the ravine with their sharp claws. He didn't count the red eyes, but there were dozens.

'Stand aside,' Ludis called into the ravine. 'I am here to slay your master. Stand aside, unclean spirits or you shall perish alongside him.'

It sounded as though a multitude of voices were raised as one, the gurgling voices of creatures not fit for this earth. Hidden in darkness, feeling indomitable in their ancestral place, the Nosferatu surged up, ready to rend him apart with tooth and claw.

Ludis awaited them calmly.

They came scratch scratching up the rocky gulley walls, a steady stream of them intent on flaying his living hide from his bones as they supped on his life's blood. Their laughter was gloating.

Never had he seen one face-to-face until now. The insubstantial things coalesced into nightmare creatures like hybrids of man and bats. Their mouths opened showing scimitar-like fangs and tubular tongues like the proboscises of bloodletting insects. Their red eyes glowed, but this time it was with insatiable hunger.

They were almost upon him before Ludis snatched the sack from his shoulder, and upended its contents over them. The creatures howled in agony and tried to withdraw, but it was a pointless retreat as the sack's contents had already begun its work on them. Salt, the old Romany woman had said, was anathema to the Nosferatu, and Ludis was glad to find that she was as wise as her gypsy kin swore. He watched the Nosferatu burn under its cleansing influence, their bodies consumed from the inside by pale blue flames that scorched them with all God's righteous fury.

The Nosferatu tumbled downwards, their corpses now turning to ash and all they made was a dry rattle against the rocks. Ludis waited, saw the sparks dwindle, and knew that their evil souls had been ripped from the fabric of the earthly plane and back to where they'd come from.

Some of the salt had settled on his beard. Ludis licked his lips, grimacing, and could not understand how the foul creature he hunted could gorge on something even more sanguine.

He still had his gun and his crucifix, but now was time for a more potent weapon. His rage. 'Upir,' he screamed. 'I have come for you. I am Ludis Kristaps, and I have come to send you back to the Devil's Pit.'

He heard mocking laughter in return.

'Come, then, Christ Bearer. Your journey has been long and fraught with hardship. Let me put an end to your suffering.'

Setting his jaw, Ludis stepped down into the ravine. The sides were almost sheer, but he went down it almost as though he descended the trail depicted in the poems of Dante. There were no levels as Dante predicted: just this single cliff-side would bring him to Hell on Earth.

As he descended, the night fragmented with moments of moonlight, became as pitch. He could see nothing, but he was determined that the Upir would be sent back to its hole this night, and continued, more sure-footed than any man should have been. Ancient, gnarled trees hung to the side of the ravine. Boulders jutted, and some threatened to turn under his boots, but it was as if Ludis had been born to a lightless world. Each shadow he passed was like a looking glass into this dark and terrible place.

Finally he stood at the bottom of the gulley, his boots crunching the desiccated remains of the Nosferatu swarm underfoot. From his belt he drew the Luger, while he fisted his crucifix in his left and ripped the cord from around his neck. He held up the crucifix and from the way it tugged in his hand like a lodestone attracted to evil, he knew he was close to the beast. Following the almost-magnetic pull, he moved ahead, seeking the Upir's lair.

Plenty of indicators led the way. Down there in the chasm, his night-vision had intensified and he could now make out silhouettes against the deeper blackness. Corpses, so old they were mere racks of bone, ligament, and tatters of parchment flesh, were suspended on greased poles that had been forced through their living orifices. Men through their backsides, women their delicate feminine parts, children through their mouths so they hung suspended upside down. Ludis had heard of this practice, but had never thought he'd see anything so inhumane as impalement in this enlightened age. His last thought gave him pause. Dear, God! A war was raging where men were committing atrocities almost as horrific as this. The Upir was a child of Satan and had no command over the terrible acts it levied. Perhaps he should consider where the greater evil lay?

No! The devil was playing tricks again, attempting to sway him from his task. He had heard legends of the Upir. It was said they had the power to glamour a victim, playing with their minds from within.

'You murdered my beloved Galina. You tore from her womb my unborn child. You slaughtered my people and defiled my church. There is no argument, *no forgiveness*, for the crimes that you are guilty of.'

There was a clap of misshapen hands. The brusque sound of palm against palm resounded unnaturally.

Ludis came to a standstill as torches flared to life around him.

He was surprised to find that he'd walked into the entrance of an ancient cavern, but not perturbed. He had known that the Upir would dwell below ground, safe from the cleansing light of day.

Two men stood to either flank. They stood there like puppets suspended by slack string, drooling mouths hanging open, eyes transfixed on other planes. One wore the uniform of a Romanian soldier, the other a Nazi with lightning bolts on his black tunic. They were enemies in life, but now served one master. Human thralls this time, but equally as deadly as the Nosferatu if they got their hands on him.

'*Seize him,*' the Upir commanded from deeper in the cavern.

Both thralls turned and their gazes solidified on Ludis.

Ludis swerved quickly, avoiding groping fingers. Their nails were pitted, as though they had scrabbled in the dirt for scraps thrown to them by their master. As deplorable as they were, Ludis knew these poor souls had no control over their actions. Maybe they were men like him who'd come here for a reckoning with the monster but had been unable to deny the glamour. He must finish them kindly.

He snapped up the Luger.

A rifle he'd fired, but never a pistol like this. But it was a simple task to squeeze the trigger.

Bang! He took the Romanian between the eyes and the thrall dropped in a boneless heap.

The Nazi clutched at him, and Ludis grappled with him, his left hand grasping at the man's belt. He brought up the Luger, jamming it under the thrall's chin.

'Forgive me, brother,' he muttered as he blasted the top off the man's head.

As the Nazi collapsed backwards, Ludis tugged at the belt and freed the object he'd found there. He quickly secreted it in a coat pocket.

Again he was rewarded with the clapping of hands, but this time it wasn't a command for light, but applause.

'*Are you any different than I am? You kill indiscriminately. Tell me, Christ Bearer, did you feel the thrill as your enemies perished? Did you taste their blood on your lips as your heart beat with the excitement?*'

'No,' Ludis said. 'I am sickened. *You* sicken me fiend.'

Laughter was his only reply.

Clicking on rocks announced the Upir's approach; its long nails digging into the loose shale of the cavern floor.

Months ago when it had stood at the threshold of his home, he had the power to deny its approach. Had his kinfolk known, they could have commanded the foul thing away from them, but instead they'd sought sanctuary in their church. With no pastor there, to deny it entry, they did not have the power over the creature or its horde and had perished under their fangs. Here, in the demon's hole, Ludis had no ward against it. The Upir came on.

Standing firm, Ludis lifted the Luger to its keeled chest.

The Upir, taller than he believed, craned down so that it could look at the gun threatening it.

'*You bring Man's weapons against* me?' The Upir bubbled out a laugh. With one wicked talon, he slowly teased the gun barrel aside. '*If you think it will help, then fire your bullets, Christ Bearer.*'

Ludis returned the Luger to its starting point, directly before the creature's still heart.

'Thirty pieces of silver,' he said. 'The same number of coins that betrayed the Lord went to the forging of these bullets. Child of Judas, you should fear Man's weapons.'

Ludis fired. He kept on firing, and with each crack of the gun, the Upir took a step back, a fresh hole punched through its chest. With each hole, the Upir screamed.

The Romany woman had warned that you could not kill something already dead, but there were ways of slowing an Upir down.

It fell against a column of stone: some ancient stalagmite that had been the monster's perch. It folded its claws over the wounds in its chest, stemming the bilious ichor from flooding down its pale belly, and hissed.

For the first time, Ludis saw the Upir's fangs. They were long yellowed tusks, designed for rending flesh, not the delicate points depicted in folklore.

Ludis fired again, his final silver bullet, and shattered one fang. It also took out the back of the monster's skull.

The Upir fell to its knees. It crouched there shuddering. Ludis approached slowly. The Upir stretched up again, coming to its full height. Both chest and skull were whole, though the meat still swarmed as it knitted back to tendon and skin. The Upir let out a guttural laugh. *'Holy man, you have made a great and fatal mistake. You can not kill me.'*

'It is not I who is mistaken,' Ludis said, dropping the empty Luger on the ground. 'I *am* a husband and father, but I'm no longer a holy man. '

'Yet you bear the Christ's symbol?'

'I did not say I lacked faith.'

Ludis charged forward.

The Upir opened its jaws in silent challenge, its tusks whole again, and enfolded Ludis's shoulders with its great talons, drawing him into its lunge for his throat.

Ludis didn't fight the pull; he thrust at the monster's face with his left hand and drove the crucifix between its splayed teeth.

The Upir spat the cross away, but it had done its work; the fiend's tongue was on fire. It breathed hot fumes over Ludis and he felt his beard ignite.

Ignoring the pain, Ludis dug in his coat pocket and came out with the object he'd torn from the Nazi thrall's belt.

The Upir ripped through his thick coat, the talons shredding the meat of his shoulders. Ludis struggled with it, avoiding the snapping teeth, but at least the frantic movement doused the flames and his face was spared. In the next second it could be ripped off by either tooth or claw.

Ludis primed the object, reversed it and rammed the stick handle directly into the creature's heart.

The Upir screamed, thrust Ludis away from it and he went down on his back twenty feet away, his head ringing from the contact.

Dizzy, he looked up from his prone position.

The Upir was laughing, peering down on the impromptu stake.

'You fool! It must be a stake of wood to do me harm.'

'Do you think so?' Sitting up, Ludis's grin was feral. 'I think a German grenade will do the job nicely.'

The explosion threw Ludis on his back again. The noise was phenomenal, multiplied tenfold by the confines of the cavern, and his eardrums were compacted. He didn't hear the frustrated howl of the Upir in the moment before its body was ripped apart. He did feel the steaming chunks of its flesh rain down around him.

Rolling over, he pushed up on his forearms and came face to face with the beast.

It gnashed its jaws at him.

Ludis smiled.

The thing could do him no harm, being barely a skull rocking there on the stump of a neck.

Even its voice box was gone, so it could only scream silent curses at him as he stood and picked it up between his palms.

You can't kill a wampyr.

Its head still lived, and Ludis knew it was only a matter of time until the creature's recuperative powers pulled all of its parts from the far corners of the cavern and reassembled.

The skull twisted in his hands, the Upir attempting to fix a fang in his wrist. Ludis juggled the head in his grasp, gripping a gnarled ear in his left palm. He could already see the flesh knitting together at the stump, trachea and voice box reforming.

'You...can...not...kill...me...'

Ludis stared into the monster's eyes with disdain. 'No, but I can shut you up.'

From his pocket he dug a handful of salt scooped from out of the sack before arriving here.

'No...'

'Yes.' Ludis jammed the open jaws with salt.

He placed the flailing skull on the ground, and set about kicking a hole in the shale with his heels. He couldn't make a hole big enough, so bent to use his hands to scoop earth aside.

Finally, when he'd dug a deep enough trench, he picked up the skull by an ear. The Upir was still too busy trying to expel the burning salt from its mouth. Unceremoniously, Ludis dumped the head in the hole. All around, the fragments of the Upir's body twitched and squirmed, as they sought entirety, and Ludis knew that he wasn't finished. Kicking aside a couple of fingers crawling across the cavern floor, he stooped down and picked up the crucifix the beast had spat out earlier. Returning to the trench, he peered down at the Upir. It had managed to roll over so that it was peering back at him, its bilious eyes threatening him with all the curses of Hell.

'Galina gave me this the night we married,' Ludis said, and dropped the crucifix so that it landed on the Upir's forehead. The skin sizzled and the crucifix sank into the flesh and nestled there. All around the cavern the twitching, self-reanimating parts fell still as the lodestone of the creature's mind fell silent. Ludis said, 'I stepped away from my church for the love of a woman, but I did not step away from God who I also love. Galina said her crucifix would still serve me at times of darkness. She was right.'

He kicked rocks over the head, sprinkled them with the remainder of the salt from his pocket.

Returning to the dead Nazi, he pulled other stick-grenades from his belt.

These he arranged at the mouth of the cavern, pulling each primer one after the other.

He walked away, hearing the detonations and the crashing of boulders as the cavern collapsed, but he ignored the billow of dust that followed his trail.

His wounds would heal given time, he decided, but would the world?

War still raged, and, yes, there were other evils to contend with.

Ludis, whose name meant 'War', strode out.

Chapter 9

13th May 1940
Bulson Ridge, France

Renyard's small magazine Lee-Enfield rifle felt wholly inadequate a weapon as he eased back inside the casement, but he brought it up, settling the stock against his shoulder and his finger on the trigger. It was cold inside the bunker, colder than it should have been; yet sweat trickled from beneath his helmet and down the small of his back. The serge wool of his battledress trousers felt heavy, tugging on the braces that suspended them and chafing his shoulders. It was a small discomfort to contend with and he pushed it from his mind. He couldn't allow any distraction.

What the bloody hell had happened to Watson? Where had the intense young man disappeared? How had it been possible: he'd only been a step behind Renyard and Green on the stairs and neither man had heard a thing?

Renyard avoided calling out.

The air around him pulsed in his vision.

That was only a result of the blood racing through his system, the beat of his heart forcing endorphins through his body, readying him for the fight. Or to run for his life...whatever may be the case.

No. There'd be no running. Not before he found Watson and brought the soldier out of this devilish place.

Renyard frowned at his choice of word. Devilish: how else could he describe it? After discovering the signs of slaughter, and the way in which the victims had been crammed into the cloche upstairs, he knew that humanity had no hand in this place. Something - some *thing* - was responsible for the deaths of the Frenchmen. He wasn't normally prone to flights of fancy, was grounded in the real world, but this was like nothing he'd ever experienced before. This went beyond the horrors of war even, treading ground too infernal for his mind to understand. Not that he'd allow himself to turn away from it, not when one of his lads was in danger. He continued moving and found the first stair up to the firing rooms.

Each step was a mountain to climb, a mountain of doubt and insecurity, but he placed one foot after the other and came up onto the narrow landing outside the firing rooms. The lantern that Watson had earlier carried was there, sitting on the floor, its wick burned down so there was only a dim, oily light flickering from within. Without lowering his gun, he dipped at the knees and turned up the flame. Then, using the toe of his boot, he nudged the lantern inside the room. After a pause he followed, prodding the lamp before him. Perspiration poured down his face and he blinked stinging droplets from his vision. He could taste the salt on his lips. He could smell the charnel house reek coming from the right hand turret. His pulse pounded in his ears.

He ignored all sensory stimulus, turning to peer towards the door of the second turret, the one through which he was afraid to pass before. The door stood open a finger's breadth, beyond it the darkness so deep that it was a solid wedge of night. Yet the darkness appeared to move, to seethe and coil, alive with a malignancy of its own. Renyard doubted what his eyes were telling him, believed that the coiling shadows was an effect of the blood pressure within his skull. He took a single step forward.

'Don't move, Sarge...'

He heard the whisper, as insubstantial and dry as autumn leaves blown across the ground.

His eyes darting, he searched for the source of the voice. The lambent glow of the lantern did little to reach the corners of the room, but he was in such a heightened state that he immediately saw Watson hunkering in the shadows below the large table supporting the radio station. The young man's face appeared more severe than usual, the sharp planes of his cheekbones like razor blades, his hooked nose throwing a deep cleft of shadow over his top lip. His eyes shone with a mix of fear and excitement.

Renyard opened his mouth to speak, but Watson placed a finger to his lips, nodded towards the partly open door. Renyard slowly turned and looked back to the swirling darkness. Within the inkiness he was sure that something lurked, waiting for him to step past the threshold and into its clutches.

'I can hear it breathing,' Watson said, his voice barely discernible.

Renyard listened but could detect nothing but the rush of blood through his inner ears. He glanced again at Watson and saw that the young man's attention was rapt on the doorway. Renyard followed his gaze, inspecting the blast-proof door, and saw exactly what he was hoping for. To the young soldier he mouthed a quick order: cover me.

Then he threw his shoulder forward against the door, pushing hard with his feet and the door slammed, the crash reverberating through the casement. His SMLR hampered him slightly and he had to swing it under one arm so he could use both hands on the large bolt he'd noticed. He grabbed at the bolt, scraping his knuckles raw on the abrasive metal of the door, but, ignoring the hot pain that rushed up his arm, he threw it. Just as the bolt slipped into the retaining bracket a corresponding crash sounded from the other side and the door juddered in its frame. Renyard took a step back, bringing up his rifle as the door was slammed again. Dust sifted from the lintels. His breath caught in his throat. That door was designed to halt a direct hit from a mortar and yet whatever was behind it almost lifted door and frame from the wall.

'Get out now,' he yelled.

Watson came from under the table, his boots striking sparks from the concrete floor. He ran without as much as a look back for the exit door leading to the stairs. Renyard backed away from the door, his gun readied as once again something immensely strong threw its weight against the steel barrier. Renyard saw the metal buckle slightly. What in Gods name was behind it, he wondered, a charging rhinoceros? Continuing to backpedal, he watched more dust sift down, this time from a crack that widened in the ceiling. Whatever was assaulting the door it went way beyond anything he'd ever imagined before. There was a rending of metal, a high-pitched squeal of tortured steel and he realised that the thing beyond the door was now exerting steady pressure. The bolt was beginning to bend in its bracket.

Renyard turned to run.

There was a metallic spang! The broken bolt flew across the room and cracked against the wall to Renyard's right. His reaction was to duck to avoid the ricocheting metal and he almost went down on his knees. Fighting to keep to his feet he stumbled towards the exit door, just as something huge burst from out of the firing room. He heard the door thrown open and slam the wall, then the heavy tread of the thing as it bounded out into the operations room after him. Renyard twisted, bringing up his gun, and without attaining a target fired at the shifting shadows that seemed to swirl over him. He couldn't quite bring anything to bear in his vision, was too confused by the speed of the thing, its bulk looming over him. He caught a glimpse of black, chitinous plates, large limbs that appeared to be covered in tough scaly hide, flashing yellow teeth that were as long as his thumbs.

Suddenly Renyard was down on his back, and good job that he was because a huge clawed hand swept the space where his head had been an instant before. Despite himself, Renyard's eyes screwed tight, expecting the claws to next pluck him from the floor and rend him apart in the same way as it had the Frenchmen.

He felt something bump against him, and then a hand hooked into his webbing, dragging him away. He opened his eyes, but still he could make no sense of the thing looming over him. In the next instant he heard Watson's exclamation as he hurled something at the monstrous thing. Flame almost seared Renyard's vision, and he turned his head aside. Yet he couldn't turn away for long and twisted round to look. Watson had hurled the lantern at the thing, and it had burst on its chest, spattering it with paraffin, which had ignited in a small explosion. Renyard saw the huge form behind the flames, but still could make no sense of it. It was bipedal, almost man-like in shape, but for its size and the horny protuberances on its hide. Nevertheless it was moving too fast for him to get a fix on it for more than a split-second, and then the room was filling with smoke and obscuring his vision even more.

Watson was still tugging at his webbing, and Renyard fought to stand up as both of them clattered onto the head of the stairs. Renyard was both embarrassed and relieved at the same time, and it was the former that won out. He'd come in here to save Watson, not have the lad save his miserable life. He managed to get his feet under him and stood up. Miraculously he found he still had hold of his rifle and he brought it up. Watson too brought up his rifle and together they fired a succession of rounds at the burning monstrosity. They were rewarded with a roar of rage and frustration, but thankfully it leapt away from them and through the doorway into the firing room.

Renyard and Watson shared a glance. Both had the stupefied expressions of idiots, and under any other circumstance they might have grinned, but not now. Renyard realised immediately...

'The armament is stacked in there. Let's get out of here, Watson.'

They went down the stairs three and four steps at a time, both men bumping shoulders in their haste to get out. They burst from the stairwell, across the corridor that was still slimed with coagulating blood and towards the outside door. Green was blinking back at them as they caromed from the shadows, and, without explanation, Renyard grabbed at the corporal and dragged him away from the casement.

The trio went down on their bellies, hands coming over their ears, and none too soon. The explosion that rocked the casement blew the leftmost turret apart, sending chunks of concrete and metal flying in the night sky. There was a momentary roar, animalistic, demonic, but it was drowned by a secondary detonation, which was even more catastrophic than the first. Huge slabs of concrete rained down, digging furrows in the hillside all around them. A fist-sized rock smacked the earth next to Renyard's head and out of reaction he rolled away from it, bumping hard into Green's prone body. Then came the rain; the smaller bits of debris that clattered off their helmets and bodies. Some of the rain was wet and sticky, some of it steaming chunks of flesh.

Renyard's ears were ringing with the concussions, could barely make sense of the shouts all around him, and he was dizzy as he came to his feet and ran from under the casement's shadow. Beside him came Watson and Green, both men as stunned as him. Others of the section met them but in his confused state the sergeant couldn't place a name alongside a face. It was enough that the figures were human and that they listened as he shouted at them to move out. They fled over the ridgeline and down the other side, caring less that their flight might take them into the sights of a troop of German paratroopers: after what he'd just lived through, Renyard welcomed a wholesome fight against human enemies.

Chapter 10

14th May 1940
Borderlands

Borvo studied the large man who was sleeping next to the fire pit in his small hut. The broth he'd had the big Latvian sup had done its trick and had sent Ludis into a deep, dreamless sleep. Borvo thought back to the battle he'd witnessed, at how Ludis had fought with animal-like ferocity against the pack and knew that, should he wish the man harm, now was his only opportunity to do so. Not that he wished ill on the dour brute, quite the opposite in fact. He hoped only for a fast recovery and knew that his broth would have the big man back on his feet and fit for the task ahead in no time.

The carcass of the hare was stripped, even some of the bones having been gnawed upon. Give Ludis his due, he had eaten only his fair share of the meat and had not taken liberties with Borvo's kindness. Borvo had saved some of the meat from the hindquarters, because Ludis would require breakfast and his cupboards were almost bare. Instead, Borvo had chewed on a crust of flatbread he'd baked the day before, nibbled at some cheese he'd found left for him on the flat rock near the river. Some of the locals who lived at the fringes of the forest saw Borvo as a tad strange – and well that they should – but their curiosity about the hermit's life meant they didn't mind sharing their food with him now and again. Once or twice a week he'd walk to the flat rock and retrieve the gifts left for him there. Long ago the flat rock had been a shrine of some sort, a place where offerings were made to the woodland spirits, and Borvo fancied that some of the backward folks thought of him as such. Despite his archaic name, his odd appearance and his uncanny ability to read thoughts, Borvo was a man and nothing else. Still, it helped for the superstitious locals to think that they might have a demi-god in their midst and offer tribute in the way of food and drink. Since the war had began, though, the number of food parcels he received had dwindled. He wasn't sure, but he thought that with the threat of German invasion, many of his neighbours had fled the borderlands, while others had decided their need for food outweighed his in the weeks and months to come.

He stoked the fire, adding logs to bring it back to life. Ludis' coat steamed slightly, giving off a pungent stink. Borvo frowned, but what could he say? He doubted he smelled so wholesome himself, and couldn't recall the last time he'd bathed with soap and hot water. Ludis had journeyed far, that was evident even without having heard his fantastic story, and it was some time since the big man had shaved or had shorn his hair. Borvo was often called a wild thing, a creature of the woods, but he thought the description more apt for the grizzled man lying on his pallet. He suspected that - since the horrendous murder of his wife and unborn child – Ludis' mind had been set on other things and personal hygiene would have been the least of his concerns.

He considered the tale of Ludis' *Upir*, and, though it was fantastical, a spooky story to be told in hushed whispers around a campfire, Borvo accepted it for what it was. He did not doubt that the man had tracked the beast to its lair and slew it, even if before meeting the big man he'd believed vampires were figments of ignorant minds. He did not count Ludis as ignorant, and believed his tale. There were strange rumours circulating these days: although he kept primarily to himself, Borvo was not above eavesdropping from the fringes of nearby villages. There were whispers; stories going around that Adolf Hitler had annexed Austria for no other reason than to ensure the Lance of Longinus fell into his hands. The lance, the Spear of Destiny as it was often called, was a powerful icon. Previous wielders of the lance had been great and mighty rulers, whereas the Nazi was a despot and tyrant: Borvo could only guess at how the power of the lance could be twisted to such a man's nefarious ends. Legend said that the lance had the power to raise the dead, and maybe the legends were true. There were other whispers; there were things stalking the night, creatures *not of this earth*, and Borvo had to wonder now what other ungodly creatures could be brought forth by the power of the lance. Ludis had spoken of the Nosferatu thralls and how they'd been insubstantial beings, so too had he told of fighting a ghoul and how it flitted between dimensions. The ghoul, though not yet fully materialised in this world, sounded like it was more firmly entrenched here than in the one from which it came. Was the influence of the lance growing, was it bringing forth creatures more solidly formed to blight the world? More importantly than that: how many of the fiends were out there?

Resting on his walking stick, the old man hobbled to the rear of his hut. A canvas sheet obscured a chest he had long put to the back of his mind. He pulled back the sheet, a billow of accumulated dust reminding him of just how long it was. He avoided hacking out a cough, mindful of waking Ludis. He stood, staring down on the large wooden chest, cautious of opening it because to do so would herald in the future.

Once, many years ago, Borvo had been known by another name. Then he'd been Francois Borvoise, and he'd lived a more civilised life than he did these days. Back then he'd been a scholar, and his studies had taken him between Paris, London and Vienna. He recalled the first time he'd seen the Lance, displayed alongside the Hapsburg Treasures at the Hofburg Museum. On viewing it he'd doubted its legend, or that it was the spear that the roman centurion, Longinus, reputedly used to skewer Christ on the cross. It was said that from Christ's side had flown, not blood, but water, proving his divinity to the world. Borvo had always believed the story to be allegorical, but then that was before he'd studied the legends behind the lance.

He had always wondered about the spear that the alleged centurion thrust into the Messiah's side: why for instance that particular soldier and more importantly that particular weapon should be imbued with power and why it should be exalted as an immensely powerful icon.

He unsnapped the hasp on his box and hauled open the lid. Within was a small stack of books, protected from the damp woodland atmosphere by a second sheet of tarpaulin. The books contained the sum total of Borvo's notes he'd carried with him when retiring here all those years ago. Really he had no need to paw through the tomes, because all was coming back to him, but it did no harm to crosscheck the jumbled references in his mind.

Much of the lance's history was shrouded in myth and misinformation, and to this day there were varying claims to the validity of the actual spear grasped by Hitler as being the real item. Borvo recalled the tales, that the original spearhead was crafted by the seventh generation grandson of Adam, a metalworker who forged the iron from a meteor fallen from heaven as a gift from God. Imbued with the power of the angry God of the Old Testament, the spearhead was destined to be the one that pierced the Christ's side at his crucifixion. It was believed that at the slaying of the Christ – itself a supposed kindness by Longinus to spare him having his legs broken in the act of *crurifragium*, a practice to hasten death on the cross – the power of the lance was somehow corrupted, imbuing it instead with an Unholy Spirit that some believed to be the anti-Christ.

These perversions of the story did not deter great leaders from desiring the spear, and it was said that Constantine, Rome's first Christian Caesar, and Charlemagne, who ruled the Holy Roman Empire by *Divine Right*, owed their success to having wielded the lance. Borvo had also heard that the corrupted power of the lance came with two-fold promise: the power to rule the world, but immediate death should its bearer ever lose his grip on the spear. Perhaps, he concurred, it would be a good thing for the lance to be spirited away from Hitler. He glanced over his shoulder at the sleeping man, saw that he was deep in slumber, and turned back to his books.

Purportedly, following the Persian conquest of Jerusalem, when the lance was on display alongside the Christ's Crown of Thorns at the basilica of Mount Zion, the spearhead was snapped. Allegedly the point was set into an icon and, via Constantinople and many centuries, was later transferred to Sainte Chappelle in France, and thus to the Bibliotheque Nationale in Paris. From there the whereabouts of the tip was a mystery to all as it subsequently disappeared during the French Revolution.

This tale always caused Borvo to frown, because the Spear he'd seen in Vienna, the same one subsequently taken by Hitler to Nuremburg was complete. Attestation was that the spear in the Hapsburg Treasury was indeed the lance carried by Constantine the Great, but that it contained only a slither of metal from the original lance, alongside a nail from the crucifixion. Borvo accepted the word of the ancient chroniclers of the Vienna Spear, and thought that along the way both lances had attained much power. What did that then make of the tip broken from the original blade? He suspected that the tip – the part that skewered the side of the Lord – must be the greatest of all icons, for on it would be traces of Christ's blood. Would it be corrupted like the other blades, or, more rightly, would it be a balance against the unholy uses to that which Hitler – or worse, Heinrich Himmler – was supposedly putting the Vienna Spear to?

Borvo put away his books, for in them he could find no answer. Having wrapped them again, and settled the lid on his box, he turned and spied Ludis' sleeping form. His gaze tracked the broad shoulders down to the man's lower back to where a leather belt cinched his trousers about his waist. There hung a small leather satchel.

Nightly - over the preceding seven nights - Borvo had dreamed an identical dream. In his dream a Northman had strode out of the forest and he'd the blood of creatures on his hands. The Northman had opened a pouch on his belt and pulled from it a faintly glowing shard of metal. The shard had spoken to Borvo, whispering in the recesses of his mind, telling him the man's name, his sad history, and the future task he must accomplish. It was the reason why Borvo had waited patiently at the riverside, at the scene of Ludis' subsequent battle with the wolf pack, because the shard commanded him to. While he had waited, he had practiced the man's language, copying the northerner's voice from his dream to attain the correct accent and inflection: as a young man, Borvo's studies had included many languages that included those of both western and eastern Europe. It was no easy task recalling a language he hadn't spoken in many decades, but gladly he'd accepted his charge. He understood that he must be able to communicate with Ludis if he expected to look upon the fragment he carried. Borvo stared at the small satchel, and believed he could feel warmth radiating from it. It was warmth different from, and more statically charged, than that from his hearth-fire.

Was it true?

Did Ludis really carry the icon lost during the Revolution?

Stiff-legged, he approached the sleeping man. His gaze would not allow itself to drift from the satchel. Borvo laid down his walking staff, for his hands desired to touch that which lay within the pouch. He crouched, his arthritic knees protesting loudly, and with tremulous hands he reached out. His fingers trembled as he touched the flap.

Ludis snapped a huge hand over both Borvo's wrists.

The big man rolled over to face him, fully awake. Borvo guessed the Latvian had been faking slumber for some time now, expecting something like this.

'You drugged me, you old devil,' Ludis snarled, his voice hoarse from disappointment. 'You lulled me with the glib tongue of friendship in order to *rob me*?'

Chapter 11

14ᵗʰ May 1940
Bulson, France

Throughout the early morning German armour and anti-tank units rushed across the River Meuse, repulsing a counterattack launched by French tank battalions on the bridgeheads they'd taken the evening before. Infantry from the reserve regiment that Renyard's section had previously bolstered fought in the subsequent battle, but the British soldiers were not involved. Since their horrifying discovery at the casement on Bulson Ridge, Renyard had pushed them through the night, keeping them marching. He had no immediate destination in mind, only somewhere far away from the hellish place where his belief system had so drastically changed.

By the time that the sun was a hand's span above the eastern horizon they were at the verge of wide fields, dotted in the distance by abandoned farm buildings. Renyard called a halt just within the treeline of a small copse of trees and the men sank down wearily, before Corporal Green had a chance to set sentries. Renyard sat down with his back against a tree trunk and pulled off his helmet. He dropped it beside him to wipe sweat from his short fair hair. His hands still trembled as he finger combed the strands flat. The upright collar of his shirt was stiff with grime, and far from the colour it had set out. Under the flaps of his pockets he found the brass buttons on his '37 battledress jacket were tarnished, green with verdigris. Ordinarily the unkempt state of his uniform would have concerned him, but right then, right there, it was the least of his concerns. He glanced around the small gathering of his section and noted that all of his men were in a similar dishevelled state. Even 'Blanco' Tyler, normally immaculate, looked as if he'd been dragged a couple miles along a muddy track. Blanco had attained his nickname from his almost fanatical use of the substance of the same name used to preserve the life of their webbing. In powder or block form the Blanco was applied to the wetted canvas with a brush, lengthening the life of the canvas and making it smarter in appearance. Some of the lads joked that Blanco really got his name from sniffing the damn stuff, that he got a kick out of the high. Renyard wondered if they'd all been sniffing Blanco and had suffered hallucinations. He'd no other explanation for what they'd witnessed the night before.

All through the night the events within the casement had rolled through his mind on an endless loop. Whatever way he looked at it, he could not come up with an explanation that satisfied his normally sceptical outlook. He had wondered if some sort of gas or chemical had been loosed within the casement, and it had been responsible for conjuring in his mind the monstrous beast they'd fought, but each time he even considered it, he shook the thought loose. He had not been suffering from hallucinations, no more than had Watson or Green or Hughes. They'd all witnessed things that were unbelievable but all too real. No. He had to admit that there, in the French casement, something monstrous and *inhuman* had attacked them.

As he sat there, his eyelids drooped, before snapping open immediately. In his mind's eye had raged the immense scaled form of the beast, its claws ripping the space he'd just vacated. Renyard had lived the life of a soldier for some years now and had faced death on more occasions than he cared to remember, but none had come as close as those rending claws last night. His life and career had been built on certain beliefs, and none of them included the existence of monsters, but now that all his beliefs were shattered, he realised that he was a changed man. How could anyone look into the face of the beast and come away unchanged? He suspected that henceforth – at the very least - he would always be a little unhinged from reality.

Green had doffed his helmet, carrying it by its chinstrap. He had regained some order and was busy setting sentries. Renyard watched the corporal with a strange sense of distraction. Green hadn't seen the monster, only Renyard and Watson had, and was still performing his duties on the surmise that all was well with the world: as well as it could be when nations were at war. Renyard shook himself mentally. He had to get a grip on his senses. All right, he'd witnessed events difficult to believe, but he still had men under his command relying on him to lead them safely back to their regiment. Ordinarily, a section came under the remit of a lance corporal only, so the men were fortunate to have both Green and Renyard along with them. It was unusual, but then these were unusual times. The troop that Renyard commanded had been splintered, some dispatched to other duties as the threat of German invasion had grown. Renyard, Green and the eight remaining lads of the section had been sent to bolster the defences at the Meuse, and now – having lost all radio contact – Renyard had no idea where the rest of his regiment, let alone his troop, were.

He struggled up, feeling the effects of the long march in his muscles, but determined to reinstate order in both his mind and in his men. The boys all looked hollowed out, their faces drawn with weariness and fear. Staying within the treeline he searched across the fields to where he could see a couple of agricultural buildings. The sheds would offer cover from aerial attack, but would most likely draw the attention of any infantry troops passing through: the woods was still their best option for catching some rest before moving on.

Moving to stand inside the loose ring of men squatting among the trees, he told them to break out their rations. There wasn't much left, but the men fell to with gusto. Cooper and McCoy set up the Bren gun so that they had a wide arch of fire across the fields, then that done they also broke out their supplies. Whitey dug in the pockets of his jacket and pulled out a pouch containing the makings of his cigarettes.

'Is it all right to light up, Sarge?' he asked.

Renyard could smell smoke on the wind and thought it would do them no harm. 'Go on,' he said. 'If any of you other lads want a cig, go ahead.'

Green and Taff Jones took up the offer. After a few seconds, Renyard himself tugged out his makings and lit up. Hell, after the night they'd been through, he wouldn't deny any of them a calming smoke. Leo Hughes was sitting with his back against a fallen log, with his rifle braced across his thighs. His elbows rested on the gun, his hands hanging as limp as his head did on his chest. Renyard moved over and eased down beside the young man. During their forced march here, Hughes had had very little to say and had merely moved along like an automaton with its spring half-wound. He looked up at his sergeant and his face burned with shame.

Renyard offered him a cigarette, but the young man refused politely.

'How are you doing, Leo?'

'Embarrassed, Sarge,' he admitted.

'There's nothing to be embarrassed about,' Renyard reassured him.

'I was like a cry baby back there.'

'Not surprisingly. To be honest, I felt like crying myself.'

'Begging your pardon, Sarge, but I doubt that.'

If only he knew the truth, Renyard thought.

Leo stirred slightly, taking his gun in both hands. 'Sarge, am I going to be brought up on a charge?'

'Why would you be?'

'Well...the way I acted.'

'You had a shock, that's all, Leo. We all did.'

'Yeah, but I was the only one who couldn't take it.'

'You took it. You're here now. I think that's proof enough.'

'The other lads might think I'm a coward. I'm not, Sarge. I swear to God, if the enemy was *human* then...'

It was as if Hughes had just realised what he'd implied, and that he was sinking himself into a deeper hole.

Renyard turned to fully appraise him. 'You're not crazy, Leo, and you're not a coward. So you can stop thinking like that right now.'

'But, but, all I wanted to do was to get out of there.'

'So did I, son. So did I.'

'Winker told me about the demon,' Hughes said conspiratorially.

Renyard hadn't told the troop anything about the monstrous thing that had come close to killing him and Watson. Too demoralising, he'd decided. He had hinted that the thing that had attacked them had been a man, albeit insane with what he'd witnessed. Not one amongst the troop believed his story: after all, following the explosion that had ripped apart the casement, they'd seen parts of the creature raining out of the sky. Even men gone insane didn't grow scales or horns.

Renyard considered Hughes' words. What other description was there for a creature that had single-handedly ripped apart thirty French soldiers and then stored them in its larder for feeding on? *Demon* fit the bill, he had to admit. Not that he was prepared to mouth the word. Renyard had never considered himself a religious man. Sure, he was raised in the Church of England faith, and observed the rules when he could – Christmas, Easter, occasional Sunday services – but that was all. He didn't exactly believe in God, but then again he feared not to in case he was wrong. There were more devout Christians in his troop, some Catholics, and it would be easier for them to accept the existence of God and His angels, and therefore the parallel existence of Satan and his devils. Even having seen the foul thing in the cloche, Renyard wouldn't accept the supernatural explanation. He admitted that the thing had been a monster, but he believed its origins were still of this earth. He didn't buy into the religious dogma, so the thing that he'd fought had to have been created by something – someone – grounded in his world. He only had one answer for that: Nazis.

Renyard stood up and ground his cigarette beneath his heel.

'Winker,' he said to Hughes, 'doesn't know what he's talking about.'

Chapter 12

14th May 1940
Wewelsburg, Germany

The small convoy winding up the narrow road towards the castle appeared out of place this far from the front line, consisting as it did of a large Mercedes-Benz staff car protected front and back by armoured vehicles, a troop wagon containing a dozen soldiers, and outriders on motorbikes and sidecars. Having taken Rotterdam, troops of the *Leibstandarte SS* were currently moving towards The Hague as they spearheaded the German invasion of the Netherlands, while the *SS Totenkopf* pushed into France. As *Reichsführer* of *Schutzstaffel-Verfügungstruppe*, known as SS-VT, the bespectacled man sitting in the rear of the Mercedes-Benz was a long way from where was expected at this important juncture in the war, however his mission here was important to both him and his Führer, and therefore took precedence.

The castle was as incongruous as was Heinrich Himmler's presence here. It was unlike any other castle in the Wewelsburg district, more a fortified chateau. In the last few years, major reconstruction had adapted the castle, walls erected in three concentric circles around the original building. It was plain to anyone looking on the castle that the walls were not designed to stave off an attack from without, but that they'd been built for the express purpose of keeping something in. As overseer of the concentration camps, Himmler was familiar with the concept of imprisonment, but even he would agree that there was nothing like this castle anywhere else. Looking upon the foreboding blank grey walls, the inward facing towers arranged around the outer circle, he experienced a thrill of anticipation tempered only by the trickle of anger he'd carried here during his trek from Nuremburg.

The small convoy swept along the approaches to the castle, startling the crows gathered in the trees and causing a wild flurry of movement and raucous cries. At the last moment the front armoured car and motorbikes peeled out to allow the Mercedes-Benz to approach the massive iron gates first. As his driver steered the car to a halt, Himmler straightened the silver cuff band of his black uniform. It was an unconscious habit, one born of his anger. He waited for his driver to step out and to open the rear door for him. The dozen *Leibstandarte* clambered from the troop carrier and fanned out, forming a protective wall behind the staff car; their dark grey uniforms a match for the castle walls. They faced outward, alert for any attack and Himmler frowned. The danger – if it presented itself - would come from within the walls, not the surrounding woodlands.

Stepping from the car, Himmler settled his peaked cap on his narrow skull. Without the uniform and regalia he would look like a genial man, a man of letters or numbers, but here he struck the epitome of terror. He was pleased with the image, and had always aspired to live up to his father's idealism. As a small boy, his father had once called him a 'born criminal' and had declared as such with pride. Young Himmler had taken the declaration as an honorific, meaning he was *one to be feared*, and now he truly believed in his father's vision. He could see the effect that his presence had on the men awaiting his arrival at the gate, and yes, fear was the overriding emotion on their waxy features.

He strode forward, earning salutes from the trio who had come to meet him. He shot out his stiff-armed response, muttering the desired retort. These weren't low ranking soldiers. Before him was Oberst Wilhelm Kumm, the equivalent of a *standartenführer* or colonel, of the Wehrmacht regular army. The other two, *sturmbahnführers* or majors of SS-VT, were Otto Hartmann and Ewald von Seid. Himmler was dismissive of Oberst Kumm and appraised the two majors answerable directly to him. 'Where is Klein?'

Hartmann, tall and slim, with a face to match the skull on his cap, blinked slowly, his Adam's apple bobbing before forming a reply. Himmler leaned close, peering into the man's visage. Saving him, von Seid elected to answer. 'Klein remains inside, Reichsführer.'

'He does not deem my arrival worthy of his presence?'

'He begs apology, but also asked that I inform you he dare not abandon the inner chamber for fear that the fools beneath him make another error.'

'He seeks to lay blame then, casting the *error* on his underlings?' Himmler snorted, and pressed by Hartmann and von Seid. This was not the first time that Himmler had visited the castle and had no need of a guide through its passages. Unseen watchers within the castle worked mechanisms that opened the iron doors. They split at the centre, opening like the unfolding wings of a vulture. As they widened to allow him entry Himmler noted the geometrical diagrams on the inner surfaces of the gates. Once the gates closed behind him, the symbols would interlock to form a giant pentagram, circled by thirteen seals, each a representation of the anti-Christ and the twelve most powerful demons of Hell, the antithesis of Jesus and his disciples. Himmler glanced at them scornfully. Little good the wards had done if the urgent messages dispatched to the Führer were true.

His boot heels rang on the cobblestones of the first inner courtyard, reverberating back at him like gunshots. The three officers following in his wake walked with care for fear they fell out of rhythm. Approaching the second defensive wall, levers were thrown and a gate similar to the first – but if anything even larger – began to open. The diagrams on the inner surface here were in a language older again than the medieval satanic glyphs of the outer door: ancient Hebrew, despite Hitler's hatred of the Jew. Himmler knew that these ancient symbols predated the birth of Christ, for even before the Messiah people feared the devil. As he approached the final door he slowed. The gate stood ajar, but not in anticipation of his arrival. It hung slightly askew on its hinges, as if something immensely powerful had wrenched the doors apart to make a clear passage. There was no evidence that the gates had taken a hit from a bomb because there was no scorching or fatigue marks. There were four horizontal slashes dug inches deep into the iron, as though a bear with titanium claws had taken a swipe at it. Himmler paused to study the rips, frowning as he rocked back and forth on his heels. He stepped through the gateway and immediately turned, causing the trio following to halt. He studied the symbols, a whimsical smile on his face. Here the seals were more ancient than even he gave credence to. The writing was reputedly that of men from the dawn civilisations of Atlantis, Thule and Lemuria, but Himmler lay as little credibility in any of those lands as he did the existence of Santa Claus *der Weihnachtsmann*. Little wonder such mumbo-jumbo had failed to keep their prisoners from escaping.

He turned away without comment: best he didn't allow his doubts to be overheard for he did not wish the ire of Hitler to fall upon him. The Führer believed in the teachings of his spiritual mentor, Dietrich Eckhart, a central figure in the Occult Thule Society to which Hitler had been indoctrinated early on during the formation of the Nazi party. Eckhart, a dedicated Satanist and occultist, was responsible for Hitler's fascination in black magic and it was through his influence that this nameless castle had been erected. On his deathbed, Eckhart was reputedly heard to say, 'Follow Hitler. He will dance but it is I who has called the tune. I have initiated him into the *secret doctrine*, opened his vision and given him the means to communicate with the *Powers*.' Then, just before slipping into death, he'd finished, 'Do not mourn for me. I shall have influenced history more than any other German.' Yes, Himmler thought, you have done that, Eckhart. And if I don't put right your meddling, then perhaps your legend should be as having influenced history more than any other *man*.

Tight-lipped he continued his walk, coming at last to the entrance to the castle proper. Who was he to say that Eckhart, and, by proxy, Adolf Hitler, were wrong for believing in the ancient magic of a mythical age? After all, he had witnessed first hand the results of Eckhart's other prodigy, Artur Klein, since Hitler had entrusted to him the safe keeping of the Lance of Longinus. As difficult as it was to believe, Himmler had been present when first the necromancer had performed arcane rights over the spear, and had used the powerful talisman to unlock the doorways to parallel worlds. Nazi scientists had hypothesised that ours was but one of multiple dimensions, and that Heaven, Earth and Hell were but dogmatic terms for realms coexistent in the same space. They said that should the key to unlocking the doorway between the worlds ever be found then powers beyond belief would be at Hitler's disposal. Thinking to harness these powers, and to use them in service of the Third Reich against its enemies, the Führer had ordered the doorways opened. Fanciful as it sounded, Himmler had seen the opening of one door, and had watched insubstantial black wraiths spill from out of a rent in the very air before him. At first these wraiths had been formless, mist-like, flickering in and out of existence, but the longer they remained on this plane, the stronger and more tangible they became. Evidently the doorway that was opened did not lead to Heaven for the creatures that grew from the mist were vile horrors. Before Klein was able to close the doorway, countless of these beings had streamed through the rift and had escaped the castle. Since then Himmler had heard tales of monstrous things stalking the lands, and the terrible things cared not whom they preyed upon, German or otherwise. Vampires, werewolves, imps and ghouls: he'd heard whispers that they ravaged the lands. And there were other creatures not easily labelled by the terms known in folklore, for they had no precedent in myth or legend. Singularly these fiends were not a major problem to the ambitions of the Nazi party, and, despite having formed a team of crack troops to find and dispatch the creatures, Hitler had decided to allow them some free rein, for their vicious attacks helped demoralise those they preyed upon and helped throw discord into the hearts of his enemies. Hitler had of course demanded that the doorway be sealed evermore, for he had recognised his error in attempting to harness such devils.

The doorway had been closed.

But that had all changed.

It was the reason why Himmler had come here at the cusp of the invasion of France, to discover and report back to Hitler *what* had come through this time.

Chapter 13

14th May 1940
Borderlands

'You're sure that they'll come, these men that you spoke of?'
'Positive.'
'Based only on words spoken in a dream?'
'You turned up didn't you, Ludis?'

Ludis Kristaps stood outside Borvo's little shack in the woods staring north. He couldn't see beyond a few hundred yards due to the dense trees, but it didn't matter. He was imagining what lay beyond the forest, and he didn't like what he was conjuring in his mind's eye. Behind him, old Borvo stood in the doorway, cowed after Ludis had grabbed him as he tried to touch the icon in his satchel. Borvo had begged release and Ludis had recognised in the man a genuine regret at having tried to rifle through his belongings. Borvo explained his fascination with the legends surrounding the Spear of Destiny, and how he only desired to see – and touch – the icon that Ludis carried with him.

'I still don't see how you could have dreamed of my coming, or of these men you speak of. You say you are no magician, and do not possess the power of precognition, and yet you know more about me and my mission than I like.'

Borvo still leaned against the doorframe, his gaze on the big Latvian's broad back. 'I can't explain it. All the years I've lived here in the wild woods, I have studied and practiced, and have attained a modicum of success when it comes to pre-empting the thoughts and actions of others.' He held out a hand, though Ludis couldn't see it. 'Before you say anything about that, my ability has nothing to do with magic. We all have the ability, varying levels of it at least, an ability left over from an earlier age when the necessity to commune with everything in nature was a required prerequisite for survival.'

Ludis scowled, turning to appraise the small man.

'I know it sounds ridiculous, but tell me Ludis, haven't you ever experienced the feeling of eyes of unseen watchers on your back, or anticipated the words of someone as they come to greet you?'

'Instinct and chance,' Ludis said.

'Instinct definitely,' Borvo said, 'but chance? I think not.'

'So what are you saying? Your dream was actually a subconscious prompt, that you had anticipated the coming events? Sounds a little farfetched if you ask me.'

'Yet I say again; you arrived, Ludis.'

'I've only your word on that. For all I know you dreamed of a one-legged Spaniard carrying a piglet, and now you twist your dream – and my showing up - to suit.'

'And you think it no more than a coincidence that you happen to be the bearer of the tip of the lance, and I was once a scholar of it?'

Ludis placed his palm flat against the satchel, and even through the material could feel the warm pulse of the object within. The man had a point: circumstances went way beyond mere coincidence. 'So you're saying that we have both been led to this meeting, that some outside force is guiding our actions?'

'Ludis...you are a man of God. You must believe that a higher power could indeed be guiding us all?'

'I *was* a man of God.'

'You still are, regardless if you are ordained or not.'

'True. I still have my faith, but I want to make it clear that I am no longer a pastor. Why would God guide one who has fallen from the wayside?'

'I don't think that God's hand is in this.'

Ludis walked back to stand over the little man. 'I do not like what that implies, Borvo. Explain yourself.'

Laughing nervously, Borvo said, 'I wasn't suggesting that the devil is guiding you, Ludis. I meant...' He nodded down at the satchel.

Ludis pursed his lips. He again touched the warmth seeping through the satchel, experiencing a tickle like a mild electric charge through his palm. 'You mean that the shard itself is my guide. If that is true then it would have to be sentient, and again do not like what that might suggest.'

'Your name is "Kristaps". It translates as "Christ Bearer", does it not?'

Rearing back, rage building in his chest, Ludis rebelled at the man's suggestion. 'You are insane, Borvo. Do not say such a thing again, or I'll...'

'You'll what? Strike me down like a sick dog?'

'Just do not say such a thing again.' Ludis' eyes burned.

Borvo indicated the satchel, and the item it concealed. 'If my suspicions are correct and what you carry there is indeed the tip broken from the Lance of Longinus, then it stands to reason that-'

'That *what*, Borvo?' Ludis almost snarled the words. 'The blood of Christ has imbued it with His spirit? That is sacrilegious. Don't even utter such words.'

Borvo shrugged, his twisted spine causing the gesture to shake his entire frame. He leaned on his staff and looked up at the looming figure over him. 'Whatever the case, it is a very powerful icon. Guard it well, Ludis.'

'I intend to.'

'Do you intend following the directions I gave to you?'

Borvo had related the story of his entire dream: after the huge northerner had held out the icon to him, a voice had whispered instructions to him. The voice said that the icon had a predetermined destiny, and that Ludis must deliver it to a certain person if it was to turn back the tide of horror launched by the Nazis. Secluded as he was out here in the wilds, the name of the man destined to take charge of the shard meant nothing to Borvo. Ludis seemed unfamiliar with it too, and he'd frowned at the knowledge that he must travel to a foreign land.

'I've only your word on this,' Ludis said.

'Is that not enough? Before you met me you were wandering without direction; without any knowledge of where your feet were leading you.' Borvo angled his staff to indicate the satchel. 'I think it spoke to me because I was able to hear it. Open your ears, Ludis. Open your heart and mind and maybe you will hear it as well. Then you won't have to rely on the guidance of a crazy old woodsman.'

His final words were meant as sincere, but Ludis found humour in them. He grunted out a laugh, but it had a calming effect on him, and his attitude to the old man. He hung his head, slightly ashamed now having been rude to someone who'd shown nothing but kindness to him. Ludis delved in the satchel and pulled out a small item shrouded in cloth. Unbeknown to Borvo, the cloth was a strip taken from Galina's dress, and meant as much – perhaps more – to Ludis than the icon it protected. Gently Ludis unwound the cloth that was his only reminder of his deceased wife. He folded it and placed it back in the satchel before holding out the small piece of metal. 'What does it say now, old man?'

Borvo's mouth slipped open, showing discoloured teeth as yellow as his rheumy eyes. Leaning on his staff with one hand, he extended the other, his fingers trembling visibly. More than anything he wanted to touch it, to trace its sharp edges with the tips of his fingers, to experience the warmth that Ludis had told him resided in the shard of blade. Yet he allowed his fingers to drop away. He shook his head slowly. 'For now it is silent,' he said. The spear tip had spoken to him all that it was going to, and only in his dreams. Now it would speak only to the man that carried it, or ultimately to the one to which it would be delivered.

Ludis offered the shard to Borvo again, but the old man merely shook his head and turned away. 'Put it away, Ludis. Take it to the person I told you about. The men coming from the north will help you, and will direct you to him.'

Ludis didn't reply. It would be right that he thank Borvo for his kindness and aid, but already the old man had moved back inside his hut. The door closed slowly, leaving Ludis to stare at the warped planks. He took the cloth from his satchel and wound it around the shard, then placed both back in his satchel. His pack roll and weapons were laid out on a log bench beside the hut and he lifted them and hung them about his body. That done, there was nothing left to keep him there and he set out, heading north to intercept these mystery men.

Chapter 14

14ᵗʰ May 1940
Wewelsburg, Germany

Artur Klein was a small, bird-like man, his receding hair slicked back and accentuating the swoop of his forehead down to his hooked nose. He had beady eyes that were unnaturally tinted a yellowish shade, but that could have been an affect of the guttering torches arranged around the pit. Klein was standing with his hands clenched in the small of his back as he bent to peer down into the stygian depths below him. So rapt on what lay beneath, he did not hear Himmler and his entourage entering the inner chamber.

'Klein!' Ewald von Seid snapped.

Without looking, the small man waved dismissively and went back to his studies.

'Klein. Turn around.' This time von Seid strode forward and tugged at Klein's shoulder.

'I haven't the time for you right now,' Klein said harshly, without taking his eyes off the dark hole in the ground.

'Oh? Do you have time for the *Reichsführer* of *Schutzstaffel-Verfügungstruppe*, Klein?'

Klein spun about, his gaze tracking from von Seid to Himmler. He visibly swallowed, an effect of an over large Adam's apple. 'Forgive me, Herr Himmler. I was totally engrossed in my duties.'

Himmler elected not to answer, but walked over to stand beside the small man. He adopted the same pose as Klein had earlier, clasping his hands behind him to peer into the hole in the ground. He stared into the blackness. 'Fascinating,' he said.

Missing the sarcasm, Klein nodded in agreement. He was dressed unlike any necromancer from popular fiction, in a grey suit and waistcoat, a white shirt with tightly knotted tie pinched at his throat. A pin brooch at his breast pocket was the only sign of his loyalty to the Nazi party: a black swastika edged in red. His skin, Himmler noted on entering, was pallid, as if the man didn't get out in the fresh air often enough. Klein leaned forward, striking the same pose as Himmler. Together they stood thus in silence, peering down into the pit. Finally, Himmler reared back and took a couple steps away.

'What exactly are we looking for?' he demanded.

Klein tore his attention from the pit. He fiddled with the buttons on this waistcoat. 'We are checking that the seal is intact, Herr Himmler.'

Himmler perused the chamber. It was a simple square room, the walls bare masonry with no frippery or embellishments. After viewing the imposing glyphs on the outer gates, one would imagine this room to be dominated with such. 'How can we tell? I see no sign of wards here.'

Klein pointed downwards. 'I inserted the seal below, to cap the doorway.'

Himmler frowned. The last time he'd been here there had been no pit, and the interdimensional doorway had opened directly in the air before him. 'Who dug this well?'

'The pit has always been here, sir,' von Seid interjected from behind them.

Himmler and Klein turned to regard the SS major.

Von Seid was immaculate in his dress uniform. Tall, powerful of build, with blond hair and blue eyes, he epitomised Hitler's Aryan blueprint for all men. Himmler despised the man with a passion, but had to admit that he was the only officer in the room worth his salt. Both Otto Hartmann and Wilhelm Kumm were below Himmler's contempt.

'Explain,' Himmler said.

Klein was crestfallen that he'd been brushed aside, but knew to keep his peace. Himmler suspected that there was a power play going on within these walls, and that he'd just offered von Seid a step up the ladder.

Von Seid blinked languidly before beginning. 'As you are aware, *Reichsführer*, the experiments conducted by Herr Klein and his acolytes achieved *mixed results*.' He waited until Himmler nodded, happy that he'd stressed his final words and cast sufficient aspersion on Klein. 'As a result of the ensuing problems Klein's experiments brought forth, orders from the *Führer* were that the doorway be sealed forever. The door *was* closed and sealed and held for some time. However, two nights ago there was a shifting of the land – an earthquake – and it was discovered that the floor here had collapsed. Investigation has shown that the castle was erected on an ancient site, where once another fort or castle stood atop this well.'

Himmler studied the lip of the sinkhole. It was perfectly circular, and edged in interlocking flagstones. 'This does not appear the result of natural subsidence.'

Von Seid inclined his head in agreement. 'Yes, it's very strange indeed. I have visited this chamber on many occasions and had not noticed the make up of the floor. However, the hole must have been capped and a false floor laid over it. Following the earthquake, and the well's subsequent discovery, it was surprising to find that the rest of the room was untouched by the collapse.'

Himmler took a couple of steps away from the pit. 'The floor has been checked for stability, I assume?'

'Perfectly sound,' von Seid said. As if to prove his theory he stamped a heel on the floor, the resulting sound as sharp as a gunshot. 'In fact, if you look at the sides of the pit they are cut from the solid bedrock. It was only the cap itself that failed and fell into the pit.'

'You have an idea of its depth?'

Klein had stood to one side too long in his estimation. He cleared his throat, stepping forward. 'Oberst Kumm has been of great assistance, Herr Himmler. He supplied men to conduct an investigation of the pit.'

Von Seid snorted. 'Little good that achieved.'

'Do you care to explain your outburst, von Seid?' Himmler adjusted his spectacles, and it was as if his scrutiny of the SS officer had intensified.

Straightening under Himmler's gaze, von Seid said, 'It was a waste of men in my opinion. With ropes, five soldiers were lowered into the pit. Only one came out again.'

'The ropes failed?'

'The survivor cut his comrades away.'

'What?'

Oberst Kumm, squat and barrel-chested, sporting the waxed moustache of a previous era, understood that Himmler believed the Wehrmacht inferior to his own crack troops. Discovering that one of his men might be perceived to be a coward, and a murderer to boot, he decided that damage limitation was in order. 'My man had no choice in the matter. He had to cut away his companions or perish. If that had happened then we'd have had no idea what he had discovered.'

Himmler appraised the colonel as if perusing something distasteful. 'And what exactly was it that he discovered?'

'Hell.'

Himmler sniffed in disdain.

'Not literally,' Kumm went on. 'But that tunnel...it leads to a place as cursed as Satan's lair.'

Himmler turned back to the pit. This time he fearlessly strode to its very edge. Below him was only a yawning gulf, where the lamplight failed to penetrate more than a few arm lengths. 'Tunnel you say? Not a well, then?'

Klein came forward. 'It drops directly down for three hundred feet, then branches horizontally to the right. Oberst Kumm's men reached the branch and set out to discover what lay beyond. From up here we heard machinegun fire and then the screams of the men. We tried to drag them to safety as they were still roped together, but we were at first thwarted. As the screams continued the rope suddenly slackened and we were able to heave the remaining soldier to safety. He did not admit to cutting the rope, but it was snapped cleanly and there could be no other explanation.'

Himmler grunted. There were many alternatives for how the rope could have been cut, but all were immaterial.

'Where is this man now? I would speak with him.'

'Under guard,' Kumm said.

'He's been imprisoned?'

'No, Herr Himmler, he is watched to ensure his own safety.'

'You give a suspected coward favourable treatment?'

'No, sir, it's not like that. I fear that should he be left alone he would do himself harm. When we dragged him from the tunnel he was trying to tear off his own face, to pluck out his eyes. If he was left unrestrained, I fear he would complete the task.'

'He has gone insane?'

'If what he witnessed is true, then I would challenge any man to retain his sanity.'

'Any man, Oberst Kumm?' Himmler eyed the Wehrmacht colonel, inviting him to right his inconsiderate slip of the tongue.

'*Any* man,' Kumm reiterated.

The air grew palpable as Himmler and Kumm considered their interplay. Perhaps there was more than one power struggle going on here at this unnamed castle in Wewelsburg. Artur Klein broke the atmosphere with a wave of his hand. He returned to the lip of the pit and again looked down. 'You received our last report, I take it?'

Turning his attention from the upstart colonel to the necromancer, Himmler couldn't decide which of the men he hated most. Next to Hitler, he was the most powerful man in Nazi Germany, yet here were men who would talk to him like he was their underling. 'I received it, read it, and came directly here. I have seen the evidence of the gate. Something escaped, you said.'

'Yes. But since then I have laid wards at the base of the tunnel, nothing else can come through.'

'You said as such last time,' Himmler reminded him.

'We were unaware of this doorway then. The spear opened a rift directly above this door. It was intangible and easily sealed, but it seems here we have a direct route into *some other place.*'

'Hell, if Oberst Kumm's man is to be believed.' Himmler laughed at the absurdity of his statement, but it was for show. 'This thing that escaped: tell me about it. Was it like the others?'

'The *others* were base creatures: ghouls, vampires, and other such fiends. No, Herr Himmler, this was something else entirely. And, if you forgive my forthrightness, I can only agree with Herr Kumm.' He pointed downwards. 'This is a direct route from hell and the thing that came through it must surely be very powerful. The seals were no object to it and had no effect whatsoever. You said you witnessed the damage to the gate on your way in. The beast swatted it like it was mere straw and twine. What you did not see were the dozen or so men it slaughtered on its way out. They were crack infantry; they may as well have been children armed with toy guns the little good they did.'

'They were conscripted men,' von Seid said disdainfully. 'Had I a troop of *Leibstandarte SS* to hand it would have been an entirely different outcome.'

Himmler snapped von Seid a glance, demanding silence. Returning his attention to Klein, he said, 'The first things to come through were wraith-like and had little substance on this plane. I have heard reports that they are becoming more substantial the longer they exist here but it has taken time. Yet, this latest atrocity to come through, from what I gather from your excitable tale, is that it is already fully formed. Is that so?'

'Yes, Herr Himmler.'

'And yet you still have not described it to me. Come, Klein. Tell me what this powerful creature is: an ogre or giant perhaps?'

Klein shook his head slowly.

'Well?' Himmler demanded.

'It looks like...uh...well, it looks like a man.'

'A man? That is all?'

'No,' Klein looked down into the pit as if continuing his studies, but it was really so he didn't have to look Himmler in the eye. 'Not just any man. He was the most beautiful and perfect being, *Reichsführer*.'

'He does not sound so horrible then. I expected a devil, a horned monstrosity with hooves and a tail. Beautiful, you say?'

'Yes, Herr Himmler, and he's all the more terrible because of that.'

Chapter 15

Evening, 14ᵗʰ May, 1940
Borderlands

The forest thinned at the crest of a ridge, replaced by undulating waves of earth and tufted grass that levelled out to form the banks of a broad, slow moving river. Ludis did not know the river's name but thought that it must be a tributary of the Meuse that lay somewhere east of his position. The invading army had not come this far yet, but there were signs that much traffic had passed through recently: either the French as they went to bolster the defences along the Maginot Line or those same soldiers as they retreated again.

Crouching in the tree line, Ludis scanned the broad valley for movement. Birds circled in the sky on the far side of the river, but they were the only indication of life. He could detect the rumble of machinery on the breeze and thought that any wildlife would have long fled the place as men and their war machine's advanced. Perhaps the wild creatures had more sense than him. He should retreat into the forest and find another place to cross the river only that would throw him off course. Borvo had been specific in the directions he had given and should Ludis deviate from his path then in all likelihood he would miss the men he was seeking. That was supposing the men existed and Borvo wasn't merely a crazy old man who'd spun him a weird and fantastical tale. Ludis had thought hard about his meeting with the woodsman, and his uncanny ability to pre-empt his thoughts. A year ago, before Galina was murdered, and Ludis was but a simple man living a simple life, he'd have scoffed at the notion of precognition, the likes of which Borvo exhibited. To him, fortune telling was a fabricated skill possessed only of fakers ensconced in tents at the fringes of a circus. However, having now experienced more than his fair share of the weird and unusual, he believed that the supernatural world was as real as that which he strode through. If he could accept the existence of vampires and ghouls, then a man who could predict the future was the least fanciful notion he should accept. Yet his doubts persisted.

He wasn't sure if he trusted Borvo, or if indeed he should.

Much of what he had set out to do was based on an unquantifiable trust, he supposed.

After slaying the Upir in its lair he had partly achieved his quest to revenge his wife, his child, and his neighbours. But he had known then, as he'd stepped out from the vampire's cavern, that there was much still to do to rid the world of similar unholy creatures. He had accepted the task without argument, seeing his fight against the demonic as his duty, and that his decision to do so had been guided in his trust of God. To trust in God was unquantifiable, and was based primarily on faith. Had he similar faith in Borvo's words? The simple truth was that no, he didn't.

Still, he had already set out on his journey prior to meeting the man, so it wasn't as if any of this was new to him. He had accepted the duty of carrying the shard north with no real idea of where he must take it or to whom he must deliver it, only that he must. He hadn't shirked from the task, trusting that signposts along the way would send him to the correct recipient and that God would steer him right. Maybe his meeting with Borvo had been engineered after all. God moves in mysterious ways, it had been preached, and his acceptance that He had had a hand in sending Ludis away from the village that fateful day was no different than if He had sent Ludis to Borvo's home in the woods.

Such decisions had tested Ludis' faith. If he had been chosen to complete this great service, then why must his journey be so difficult? If God wanted him to take the shard to its rightful owner, then surely He could smooth his path along the way. There was a simple answer: trial and tribulation were aspects of God's mysterious ways. Take the fatal trials levied on Samson or that of Abraham being commanded to sacrifice his son, Isaac, and God's way of testing a man's faith were both cruel and unusual. Well, Ludis thought that his task was of no comparison to theirs, so he should get on with it.

First he had to cross the river before him, but to do so would place him in great danger. It wouldn't matter which army was approaching, he ran the risk of being gunned down with impunity. Unless God truly wanted him to succeed and would throw a bulletproof shell around him, he thought with dark mirth.

Moving from the security of the trees he remained at a crouch until he could place one of the hummocks of earth between him and anyone approaching alongside the river. The folds in the land were the result of erosion over many thousands of years. The river had grown, taken different routes, cutting its way through the land, leaving behind ghosts of its past routes as it diminished and grew again along a different track. Tumultuous in past incarnations it was now broad and shallow, strewn with rocks stripped from the hillsides or carried here from distant places on floodwaters. If he were lucky there would be ample stepping-stones to allow him to cross the river without a soaking.

Midway to the river he paused. The sounds of machines were louder now, and he was certain that the tumult of indistinct noises carried along with them were the tread of marching infantry, the rattle of their equipment and low-pitched conversation. Judging by the way the earth trembled beneath him there were many tanks and men approaching. It was best that he get a move on and cross the river before they arrived.

He moved out from the slopes, jogging across ground springy with water seeping from the river, using tufts of reed as stepping-stones. His boots still sank ankle deep in the mud, the ground sucking at him as though attempting to slow him down. Then he was in the shallows and he sought larger boulders by which he could cross the river without a drenching. He made it part of the way across before the rocks gave out and he'd no option but to forge his way through a trench of deeper water. Holding his bedroll and revolver out of harms way he stepped down off his latest perch and the water swirled up around his hips. He grunted at the pervasive chill – it was spring, but the river still held the chill of the mountains where it was born. Clenching his teeth he set off for the far bank, and was momentarily distracted by his discomfort, so at first the keening in his ears was but a soundtrack for his misery.

He snapped around, his gaze zoning in on the source of the new sound. Over the ridge from which he'd come two darting black shapes ripped the sky. Twin Stukas – the sirens built into their nose cones emitting the soul-sapping wail – swooped low into the valley. At first Ludis believed that he was their target, but the Luftwaffe wouldn't waste their time on such an insubstantial target as he. The two planes banked, and then straightened as they followed the river to the west. The roar of their engines now competed with the shriek of their sirens, and out of reflex Ludis ducked as they blasted overhead. More water invaded his clothing, but he barely noticed it as he followed the flight of the two planes. Moments later they disgorged their payloads and he watched black flecks become raging fireballs as they impacted with the ground. At least he knew who the advancing army was now: the French come to counterattack the invaders. They had been nearer than he'd suspected judging by how close by the Stukas had dropped their bombs. With a fresh sense of urgency he powered through the water, seeking solace in the forest on the far bank. The last thing he needed now was to be caught up in the battle set to rage here in the valley.

More planes dotted the sky.

Bombs detonated with solid *whumps!*

His eardrums compacting to the enormous detonations, Ludis threw himself at the far bank.

Machineguns rattled death among the French as the Luftwaffe streaked over them. Return fire was mounted, tracer rounds sparkling in the sky. The tracer rounds had a downside, because they worked both ways: the Luftwaffe pilots zoned in on the guns, tracking the fiery arches of phosphorous to their sources. Another salvo of bombs rocked the earth and some of the French guns were silenced: some - but not all. The French weren't going down without a fight, and their response was immediate and deafening. One of the Stuka was ripped apart by the French anti-aircraft guns and exploded into a flaming ball of wreckage that rained from the sky.

Kicking foamy water before him, Ludis surged from the river and raced across the swampy ground for the far side of the valley. The battle raging less than quarter a mile away threatened to reach him sooner than he would the trees. His ears popped, and the sounds of carnage hit him like a blast of hot wind, almost sending him sprawling. He righted himself, unconsciously grabbing at the satchel fixed to his belt and kept running. He heard shouts and even without Borvo's ability to absorb and then speak foreign languages knew that the order was directed at him to stop. He ignored the shouts, and pushed hard for the cover of the trees.

Bullets churned the ground to his rear, encouraging further speed from him. There were more shouts, then more bullets. This time the ground erupted in front of him, but there was no way that he was going to surrender to the men in grey uniforms that he caught in his periphery. He vaulted the torn ground as if it would make any difference to the bullets churning the air around him. Something tugged at his coat, but without the searing impact of metal through his body, he realised he hadn't been wounded. He kept running. Finally he found a fold in the land and threw himself behind the low mound of dirt. He couldn't stay there. The German soldiers advancing on the French would come upon him in seconds and this time he could expect no warning. He scrambled forward on his hands and knees, heading again for the trees.

Longer grass offered further concealment and he swarmed through it on his belly like a lizard, grabbing periodically at his belt to check the shard was secure in its bag. Then he came upon a fallen log and threw his shoulders against it, scrunching down in the grass with his arms and legs spread to make a lower profile. Nearby he heard the scuff of running men, soldiers searching for him. In the next second their guns were crackling as they found other targets further along the riverside. Return fire earned a volley of cries and the occasional scream as men were cut down. Using this to his advantage, Ludis rolled away from the log and came to his feet. Without looking in either direction he fled towards the forest.

The first lines of trees were sparse and widely spread and didn't offer concealment, but they were better than nothing. Ludis put his back to a trunk and for the first time took stock of the numbers of men moving on each other. The Stukas were the vanguard but it appeared that infantry in grey uniforms were the order of the day. There were dozens, no hundreds, of them advancing along the river valley towards the French position. Some of the German soldiers were also within the treeline, moving forward in an attempt at flanking the French. Ludis realised that he was in a very bad place, because not only were there men between him and the river, but now there were others beyond him in the woods.

What to do? Hunker down there at the tree and hope that he went undiscovered or to try for a sudden burst for the deeper woods? Ludis was never one for hiding. He made a rapid decision, and with it he sprang out from concealment and charged up the slope.

'Halt! Halt!'

He didn't obey the screamed command, he kept running. Guns cracked but thankfully from a distance. The trees took the brunt of the gunfire, bark and splinters shredding from the trunks he dashed behind. Other rounds were spent digging into the earth, while others were lost in the branches over his head. His breathing was harsh and blood pounded in his head from the sudden exertion, but there was no way he'd willingly stop to rest. *Willingly* being the operative word, he realised, when directly in front of him two grey-clad soldiers stepped out to stop him. Their guns were coming up, and their fingers were on the triggers, and there was nothing that Ludis could do to save himself except follow his headlong course.

He pounded towards them, his voice rising in a shout of challenge. Dressed, as he was, his hair and beard as wild as his expression, the soldiers were momentarily stunned as they tried to make sense of the creature bearing down on them. To date Ludis had no ill will towards Germans – any more than any other race – but now by virtue of this moment they had become his mortal enemies. He was upon them in seconds, batting at their guns to knock aside their aim even as he crashed into them. All three went to the ground in a bundle of limbs. One man's gun went off, and it was only then that Ludis realised that the German was armed with a machinegun. Bullets churned the trees around them, and Ludis could feel their heat but all missed him. The second German lost his grip on his gun, but he was a fighting man and immediately went for the dagger on his belt. Machinegun or knife, either weapon could kill Ludis as quickly as the other, but he was more concerned about the gun than the blade. Ludis grabbed at the gunman and pulling him towards him he butted the man in the face. The man's helmet caught the side of Ludis' skull, but not half as sorely as Ludis' forehead did the German's nose. Ludis rolled sideways, pulling the swooning man with him, just as the second man swung at him with the dagger. The knife buried itself to the hilt in the first German's body and his fingers went limp on his gun. Ludis grabbed at the weapon even as he disentangled from the dying man. He continued rolling and used the momentum to bring him up onto one knee. Unfamiliar with the machinegun, he utilised it as a more primitive weapon. Holding the hot barrel in one hand, he swung the stock down on the second German as he tried to loosen his blade from his comrade. The machinegun struck the man's helmet with enough force to strike stars in the man's vision but not enough to stop him. Grunting words in his own language the German grabbed at his fallen gun, but Ludis was already moving in on him, and this time he struck at the man's collarbone. The sickening crunch of breaking bone elicited another word from the man, this time a curse in any language. The soldier wasn't finished though, not by a long way, and he tried again to bring his gun to bear. Ludis snapped a hand down to his revolver and brought it up.

'Don't,' he said.

The German didn't understand, or if he did he was too full of battle lust to obey. He continued bringing round his rifle. Ludis fired first and his bullet took the man below his heart. The German sank down, his gun falling from lifeless fingers before he pitched face first onto the dirt.

Ludis knelt there over him, his face open with shock.

Ludis had killed before. An Upir, a ghoul, numerous Nosferatu, half a pack of wolves and two reanimated corpses were some tally, but this was the first time he had killed another human being. The first soldier died under the blade of his friend, but there was no denying the second German died solely by Ludis' hand. It was not a feeling that sat well with him. He was once a man of God, a pastor; now look where he had ended up. A murderer!

No, he shook his head. It was a man's first right to defend his life. The German soldier intended killing him, so where was the guilt in killing him first? It was a moral dilemma, and one that would trouble Ludis for some time to come, but this was neither the time nor the place to dwell upon it. He spoke a quick prayer over both dead soldiers then came up to his feet. His revolver he shoved back into his belt, and then he stooped to retrieve another weapon. He didn't go for the machinegun, but rather lifted the rifle that would replace the one he'd lost when fighting the pack yesterday. He'd thought earlier that God was both cruel and unusual in his testing of man's faith, but his God could also be benign: maybe the next time he used the rifle it would be on something that he intended eating. Or it would be on another of the fiends he was determined to send back to hell.

The fight had lasted moments, but the tide of battle had shifted somewhat. The men moving adjacent to him were now much further along the riverbanks, joining in close quarter conflict with the French defenders. The racket was horrendous. Tanks exchanged rounds, machineguns competed, but dominating the sky – and the tumult of sound – was the wailing sirens of the Stuka bombers as they dived again. There were a handful of planes up there now but none of them French or British. Ludis heard one of them streaking down to send another volley of death among the Frenchmen, but then he heard a rattle of anti-aircraft fire and the Stuka engine sputtered then went silent. The sudden cessation of its siren was like a herald of doom riding on the wind. Ludis snapped his gaze beyond the treetops searching for the stricken airplane. He couldn't see it and that was a bad thing. He began running.

Seconds later the Stuka crashed among the trees so close by that Ludis felt himself lifted and thrown through the air by the corresponding explosion. Disoriented, his limbs flailing around, he spun head over heels and was lucky not to smash his spine on a tree trunk. He landed flat on his belly with nauseating force as chunks of burning shrapnel ripped through the air above him. Smoke and flame surged over him and Ludis scrunched his face into the forest mulch, his arms over his head, to avoid his flesh and hair burning away. There was no oxygen and he couldn't breathe. Blackness billowed at the edges of his consciousness.

No!

After all that he'd done and all he'd endured he would not die like this.

But it seemed he had little say in his fate because the dark clouds enveloped him and Ludis' mind went blank. Somewhere, it seemed, his cruel God must be laughing at him.

Chapter 16

Late evening, 14th May 1940
Southwest of Bulson, France

'What now?' Corporal Green asked.

'Keep the lads moving.'

'The same direction, Sarge?'

'Where else?'

Renyard knew that he must take his section north and re-join his regiment, or even another of the British Expeditionary Force. The problem being the BEF were still engaged in a running battle in Belgium and already several Panzer and motorised infantry divisions had cut a swathe into France effectively cutting off a safe route through. Not normally one for running from a battle, Renyard couldn't see another option. First and foremost in his mind was the safety of the boys under his command. They could try to fight their way through the German forces but he knew how that would end. No, he decided that they were better served heading southwest, moving at speed and trying to find a way back to the north ahead of the advancing Wehrmacht.

Currently they were moving through arable land, dotted here and there with abandoned farms and hamlets. Far off the droning of aircraft had occasionally split the night, but all was quiet now and the landscape was predominantly deserted – but the enemy was out there. The day had been long and they hadn't traversed as far as Renyard would have liked. It had been a game of cat and mouse, where they had moved in short but hurried bursts, avoiding the Wehrmacht fighters as best they could. On one occasion they had to fight their way through a roadblock, and had been extremely lucky that the enemy comprised only of six soldiers whose armoured car had been stuck in the mud at the side of the road. More fortuitous was that the German's hadn't been expecting an attack from behind, and once Winker Watson had put his sniping skills to good use, taking out two of the German's in seconds, the others had fled into nearby woodlands. Scavenging what they could from the armoured car, they'd replaced some of their depleted ammunition reserve, as well as found food rations that would sustain their march a day or two yet. One soldier killed by Winker had been an *oberscharführer*, or lance sergeant, and his sidearm was a prized trophy. Renyard had turned down the Luger and allowed Winker to claim it – he felt the act of stripping the dead more heinous than he'd like to admit, but kept his peace when Winker tucked the gun into his pack. His reason for hating the act of trophy taking was irrational in one sense, for there'd always been an acceptance that to the victor goes the spoils of war, but, as he'd looked down on the dead Nazi, he saw in the man a reflection of himself. The man was of similar rank to him, and though he was of the despised SS-VT, who was Renyard to judge him personally? The Nazi had been a man following orders, whose desire was probably the same as his own; to ensure the lads under his command made their way through the war safely. The Nazi had failed his mission and Renyard felt that he could end up the same way, lying there with a bullet drilled through his skull: maybe in the days ahead some German would pick over his corpse for a similar trophy.

Corporal Green moved ahead of Renyard now, urging the troop along. McCoy and Cooper were the rear guards; ready to lay down supporting fire with the Bren gun should an attack come from behind. Renyard glanced back at the two riflemen, seeing indistinct shapes trudging through the darkness. They looked mismatched, McCoy being short and stringy of build, while Cooper towered over him. The lads had the most difficult task of all, hefting along the heavy gun and ammo bags, but they did so without complaint. Ahead of him, Whitey, Taff, Blanco and Leo were strung out in a loose line, while somewhere further on Winker played scout. Renyard felt the gaps in their line like a dull weight in his heart. He kept expecting to see Lance Corporal Hoskins back there with the Bren gun team, and Chiltern up front swapping jibes with Taff Jones. They were two of his lads that had already fallen to the enemy, and Renyard carried their loss along with him, a burden heavier than the Bren balanced across Cooper's broad shoulders. Losing Chiltern and Hoskins was hard to reconcile in his mind, but of late – and it was no coincidence that his thoughts had swung this direction with the deepening darkness – he had begun to ponder again the events of last night. The more he thought of the monstrous thing that had made a lair in the French casement, the more he thought he should be worrying not about his lads' physical wellbeing but that of their mortal souls.

He'd disregarded all natural explanations for the creature – the effects of gas or chemicals, mass hallucination induced by panic, even the state of his own mental health – and could find only one answer. He didn't like to admit it because demons were the bogeymen that haunted more God fearing men than he. But what else could it have been? Now, as they struck out through the fields, he was looking for more than enemy soldiers in the darkness, for he felt that the monster in the casement was not unique. If he could believe in one demon, then why not believe in legions of the terrifying things?

Perhaps it was this admittedly crazy notion that conjured a monster out of the night. Off to their right were two red pinpricks of flame and in his vivid imagination they were the flashing eyes of a devil. The breath caught in his throat and he came to a standstill. Sweat broke out along his hairline, even as the short hairs of his scalp stood on end. Behind him, Cooper and McCoy recognised his sudden halt and they also became statues. The men in front however had no way of knowing they were in danger. They kept on going, following Green's earlier order to double-time their efforts. The sound of their boots through the grass, the rhythmical pat of their entrenchment shovels off their backsides, sounded like a stampede to Renyard. If he could hear them, then the beast out there surely would as well.

Mouth open, Renyard peered back at the devilish eyes. He was struck momentarily with the same horror that had assailed him in the moments before Watson had come to his aid with the lamp and had doused the monster with burning fuel. Feeling useless, he could only go for his sidearm and hope he could slow the beast until his men could flee. He was drawing his revolver, bringing it up when the creature's eyes jerked and one of them drifted to the ground and winked out.

What the hell?

It took Renyard all of a second to realise his over-wrought imagination had indeed conjured an hallucinatory beast and that what he was actually seeing were the embers of two cigarettes – one recently thrown to the ground and stamped underfoot. Even as realisation hit him, the second cigarette was doused in quick fashion. There was only one reason that the smokers had relinquished their cigarettes so rapidly: they had heard Renyard's lads out here in the fields.

Were they French or German soldiers?

It wouldn't matter, because under the cover of darkness and the way in which the smoking sentries had just reacted, he didn't expect a peaceful challenge.

'Take cover,' he said, loud enough for the nearest men to hear him.

Before any but Cooper and McCoy could react a shout split the air. It was a yell in the guttural tongue of the enemy and Renyard knew then that all attempts at sneaking away was beyond them. He brought up his revolver and fired towards the source of the voice.

His gunshot had an immediate effect, and he was glad to note that his warning of a moment before now coalesced into an efficient response from all his men. They hit the ground and brought their weapons to play within seconds. None of them – particularly Renyard – had any idea of the strength of numbers they faced, but all he could hope for was that their volley of fire did enough damage to the enemy to throw them into retreat.

He found that his hopes were ill founded as from across the fields came a return volley of fire. Muzzle flashes indicated more than twenty guns, more than double their strength. Add to that that the German's were encamped within a copse of trees while they were out on the open ground and the fight would appear a little one-sided. Then came something that brought even more disdain to Renyard's mind: the cranking of an engine. The German's had some kind of vehicle out there, and Renyard had heard enough tanks recently to distinguish the roar of the engine that followed.

'Go, go, go,' he shouted as he came to his feet and ran in the direction his men were spread out. Quickly he searched for some kind of cover, but everything was flat black every direction he looked. Nevertheless he waved his men up and away, sending them across the fields at an oblique angle from where the roar of the tank sounded. Their best course of action now was to get as far away and as quickly as they possibly could. Thankfully the darkness was in their favour and even the tank guns would do them no harm if they were firing in the wrong direction.

Lights cut through the night.

Renyard swore angrily, watching as searchlights flickered on along the German line.

In contrast to his earlier command he yelled, 'Get down!'

In the second or so it took him to follow his own advice there was a whump! He felt the air over him disrupted by the shell then from somewhere across the fields came the corresponding explosion. Earth and small stones clattered down on him. Someone was shouting nearby and he prayed that the explosion had injured none of the lads. Renyard lifted his head marginally and saw the searchlight sweep the field before him. Up to now the German's still hadn't got a bead on him or the others and were shooting blind. Tracer fire went over his head.

Renyard fired back, emptying his revolver at the lights. It was a pointless exercise because in the back of his mind he knew they were out of range of his handgun. Plus his muzzle flashes had made a target of him. The nearest searchlight swept over him, the glare causing him to blink. In the next seconds instinct kicked in and he rolled sideways, putting himself out of the beam of the light. Bullets churned the earth where he'd been lying moments before.

The tank engine roared and the feared Panzer pushed out from the cover of the trees. Renyard caught a glimpse of the metal behemoth as one of his men fired at it. Sparks jumped from the turret but did no harm. Shooting at a tank with a Lee-Enfield rifle would get them nowhere.

'The searchlights,' he bawled. 'Go for the searchlights.'

Someone – most probably Watson – had come to that same conclusion. A searchlight shattered and went dark. There were still more than a handful of others, and they criss-crossed the fields seeking targets. Renyard glanced to his right and saw that McCoy and Cooper had set up the Bren. Lying prone, Cooper targeted while McCoy had the more dangerous task of feeding the gun with ammo. The heavy rattle of gunfire cut across the fields and there was a pause in the German assault as they realised the battle wasn't all going their way. Renyard thought he heard screaming from the German lines but could feel no satisfaction from the sound.

The tank was still moving forwards, and it reminded them all with another blast. Again the explosion that followed was from behind Renyard's men, but it would be mere moments before the German gunners recalculated and placed a shell directly among them. They had two options that Renyard could see: run or stay and fight. No, that wasn't particularly true. Either of those would probably end with his entire troop dead. There was a third option: take the fight to the enemy. He shouted orders to "fix your swords" that was passed down the line, and he watched as the men prepared themselves. Exempt from his plan were the Bren gunners and Watson who were of better use offering their own brand of warfare to support the rest. Even as he rose up, Renyard saw Watson gain another direct hit and take down a second searchlight. Renyard charged forward, his SMLR now in hand, and his bayonet fixed.

Leo, Taff, Blanco, Whitey and Corporal Green joined the charge forward. Six of them against twenty or more – plus a tank – Renyard didn't fancy their chances, but when he considered the alternatives he'd rather they took some of their enemies with them than be torn to pieces out in the open.

Running hard Renyard led his small group across the fields. It was spring and time for tilling the fields, but the sowing of the ground had been put aside this year. The grass had not started to grow yet, and was short and stubby underfoot. The ground beneath was hard packed but a soft spot – and a resulting twisted ankle – was a very real possibility. Still, forward momentum, and fearlessness in the face of the enemy was their best bet. Renyard knew there was little likelihood of defeating the German force, but that wasn't his intention. All he wanted from this exchange was to disrupt the German assault, and then find room for him and his men to slip away.

The Panzer fired again, and Renyard realised that if he hadn't led the charge when he did the shell would have impacted directly where they had been lying. Over the rattle of guns he could hear Leo Hughes' boots pounding the dirt alongside him, his breath short and sharp and almost as rapid a beat as that made by his feet. Renyard had no doubt that Hughes had shaken off the unnatural terror he'd experienced at the casement, and that the lad was eager to prove his courage now that they faced the more common enemy. It made him proud to be at the head of these boys...no he must stop calling them boys; they were men and proven warriors.

Bullets cut the night all around them, and Hughes swore loudly. His anger was evident, and told Renyard that he hadn't been hit, but that it had been a close call. Behind at their right the Bren gun roared and, now that they were approaching the German line, Renyard saw sparks flying as the bullets found a metallic target. A truck was parked beneath the trees but a camouflage net had been thrown over it to disrupt its shape. Men were taking cover behind it. Beneath the distinctive shape of the German helmet, the enemy faces looked wan in the pale glow of gunfire. Still running, Renyard fired at them, but if he hit any of the targets he'd be lucky. The heads drew back behind the truck, but popped out a moment later and return fire lit the night.

Safe from the Panzer's cannon now, but not from its machineguns, Renyard went down on his belly. Lying prone, he fired off another couple of rounds, but didn't choose his targets: he was too busy looking for the tank. It was a little to his left now and had ground to a halt as its crew realised that the enemy was now much closer. It would be difficult for the tank to fire on them without putting the German's in danger as well.

An explosion rocked the scene, and Renyard watched the front end of the Panzer lift a full hand's span off the earth. Ten yards in front of it Blanco Tyler was lying in the dirt with his hands covering his ears. It had to have been Blanco who threw the grenade. Then the fire of the explosion was gone and Blanco lost to the night again. Renyard scanned the tank, hoping that the grenade had done some damage, but it looked unaffected, and even as he watched, the tank pivoted and the gun turret swung towards Blanco's position. Guns blazed and Renyard could only hope that Blanco had got out of there under the blanket of darkness.

'Sarge! Look out!'

Renyard twisted around.

Three figures burst from the darkness, running towards him. One of them had his arm cocked, and in his fist was the distinctive shape of a stick grenade. It seemed the German's had thought to pay Blanco back in kind. Beside Renyard, Leo was down on one knee. He sighted on the grenade thrower and loosed a bullet into the man's chest. It knocked the man down, but not before his arm had arched forward. Lost in the dark Renyard had no idea of the grenade's trajectory. He buried his face in the earth. His ears pulsed to the sudden silence, and then came the ear-searing bang as the grenade detonated. Something hot snatched at Renyard's left thigh as shrapnel tore through his serge trousers. Thankfully that was all that hit him, and even then with no damage to his limb. Renyard scrambled up, bringing up his rifle.

The other two German soldiers were still coming on, their mouths open in challenge. Renyard fired, but knew that he'd missed. The two soldiers bore down on him, ten feet away. Suddenly Leo was up and between Renyard and his would-be killers. He fired point blank at one soldier, and then turned and the fighting was too close for gunfire. He rammed at the remaining German with his bayonet. The German responded in kind, and suddenly the battle was more reminiscent of one from an earlier epoch, where blade against blade was the order of warfare.

Leo and the German were caught in a deadly duel, their bayonets jabbing in and out, and then their bodies crashed together and the men's rifles became jammed. Their boots scuffed in the dirt, their grunts were animalistic and savage. Now Renyard was up, and though it irked him to do so, he did the ignoble thing and speared the German's spine with his bayonet. As the man arched backwards in agony, Leo fought his rifle free and then jammed his bayonet deep under the man's chin. Renyard and Leo shared a glance of appreciation, but that was all they had time for. Bullets singed the air around them.

Renyard charged forward again, and reaching the trees he threw his back against a trunk. He scanned round, seeking enemies, but also checking on his men's progress. To the extreme right, Rifleman White yelled as he fired. It was an act of desperation and Renyard wanted to go to the man's aid. Half a dozen guns from the treeline assailed him and only his instinct to keep moving was keeping him alive. Corporal Green was his nearest assistance, but he could do only so much with his Lee-Enfield. What Renyard's section could achieve if they had fully automated machineguns...but that was a pointless thought. Renyard brought up his rifle and fired along the line of trees, hopeful of hitting the men targeting Whitey but with little chance of success.

Somewhere out there was Watson, and he was employing his sniper skills to better effect. Another of the searchlights went out.

A grenade exploded off the side of the tank, again with little effect.

Guns spat fire and death and the sound was tumultuous. Smoke now drifted on the breeze, stinking of cordite and the fear of men.

Another searchlight went off, then another and another. The lights were going down with the rapidity of a heartbeat, and Renyard's pulse was racing just then. What was going on? Even Watson wasn't that accomplished a sniper.

It was about then that the screaming began. All along the German lines men were roaring in agony. As full of battle confusion as he was, even Renyard understood that his small handful of men weren't the reason that so many of the enemy were dying. He was very close to one small group of soldiers clustered among the trees. He swung his rifle on them, but even as he did so he noted that their attention was no longer on him or his men. They were – to a man – staring up into the trees. Renyard followed their gaze, expecting to see a British or French fighter plane soaring overhead, but no. Their attention wasn't on the sky, but on the tree limbs directly above them.

Renyard shook his head.

It was crazy enough leading his men against the better armed and positioned enemy, but nothing was as insane as what he witnessed now. Things – he could not bring himself to think of them as anything else – were dropping from the branches directly onto the German soldiers. They were small, no taller than a ten year old child, but they had the broad shoulders, sturdy arms and heads set low on thick necks common to apes. But these were no chimpanzees leaping down on the German's because no chimp Renyard had ever heard of had scaly hides or claws easily as long as his fingers.

He recalled his earlier misgivings about the falling darkness and knew now that his nightmares were coming true. The creature in the casement had not been unique: there were legions of the devils. And they were here now.

A rattle of fronds overhead brought up his gaze and he tracked along the tree trunk's sweeping length to where the boughs spread over him. Blinking down on him were eyes like twin orbs of fire. They widened perceptively as the thing's gaze alighted upon him. They grew even larger as the thing dropped towards him.

Chapter 17

Morning, 15th May 1940
Borderlands

His first waking thought was one of mild disgruntlement.

When the downed Stuka crashed through the forest, the fuselage ripping apart and the wings disintegrating among the trees, the resulting explosion had knocked the senses out of Ludis. However, there was one small part of his brain that still functioned, and it told him he was about to die. As he'd succumbed to the comfortable wings of unconsciousness folding around him, he relished the idea, because more than anything he longed to be reunited with his dead loved ones. His faith promised that he would once again see his wife and child when he joined them in the afterlife; therefore he had no fear of death. So, when he finally awoke, rolling over onto his back and dislodging the dead weight of a fallen soldier from where he'd lain over Ludis' back, he swore softly under his breath. His reaction was barely momentary because – though he had no fear for his mortality – neither did he wish to die this way. Not while he still had a task to complete. When his reunion with Galina and their baby happened he wanted it to be one of joy and undying love, not one tarnished by his failures. He even doubted that he would be allowed a place in heaven if he failed to complete the task levied upon him. That thought struck more terror into his heart than anything, and motivated him to shake off the doldrums and get about what needed doing.

Clambering to his feet, he tested his limbs for injuries and found them to be in working order. His coat was somewhat scorched by flames and had even been torn in places, but mostly it was still serviceable. The corpse of the soldier who had fallen over Ludis had served him two fold: it had spared him much of the brunt of the explosion, while also offering camouflage to him as he lay oblivious to the fight raging around him. Soldiers from both sides must have passed him by during the night, but they would have seen the eviscerated corpse of the soldier and assumed that Ludis was as dead as he was.

He thought that the battle must have been ferocious and none engaged in it had time to gather up their fallen, because he could still see the two men that he had fought lying nearby. There were others too. Men in grey uniforms, but he suspected that the corpses further down the valley would be mainly French. He had no idea who had won this confrontation, but was thankful that the victors had moved on. It didn't matter to him whose flag flew today, swastika or tricolour, because neither side would look on him in friendly fashion. To both sides, speaking a strange language and having an odd bearing, they'd believe him a spy for the other side. French or German bullet: either would kill him as swiftly.

Birds moved in the treetops. He could hear the dawn chorus as the woodlands came alive. It was a good sign because it meant that the men who had so recently fought here had moved on. He suspected that they would have gone further to the west rather than back towards the Meuse, for no other reason than he believed that the French had little chance standing against the might of the Nazi war machine. How soon would it be until all of France was under the iron fist of Adolf Hitler? If that were to happen – which he believed undoubtedly – then it would make his journey all the more difficult, and the longer he remained here the worse it would get.

He checked the soldier's kit and took with him a water canteen and a partly eaten block of chocolate. The dark, waxy chocolate was poor substitute for a hearty breakfast but he wasn't going to complain. He washed down the bitter taste with lukewarm water from the canteen as he went. He felt no guilt at taking the man's belongings because where the German had gone there was no need for earthly sustenance. Yet the act troubled him in another way: if he had gone through the man's things, then who was to say that others hadn't gone through his? He quickly pulled his satchel up so he could delve into it. Relief washed him as he felt the familiar shape of the metal shard wrapped in cloth. He pondered taking the shard out and inspecting it, maybe even to lift it to his ear and listen for the voice that Borvo spoke of. He didn't though; he put the satchel back at his hip and checked that the strings were securely tied to his belt.

This time yesterday he had set off from Borvo's hut in the deep woods. It seemed like an age ago, and more for the fact that he hadn't eaten a decent meal in the past twenty-four hours. It was not the first time he'd gone so long without nourishment, his upbringing on the shores of the Baltic Sea had been tough at times, particularly when the fishing boats failed to bring a catch home. But, as Bonaparte had extolled "an army marches on its stomach", and that was as true for one warrior as it was for many. Ludis laughed at the absurdity of the notion. He, Ludis Kristaps, once a man of the cloth, had now become a warrior. He had no formal training, and until the day that he'd taken up his fight with the Upir had no real concept of battle. As a boy he'd scrapped his way to adulthood, but that was about all the experience he had of fighting. He thought of all those that he'd killed - monster and human alike - and decided that perhaps he had an aptitude for warfare. Either that or he'd been exceedingly lucky to date.

With no firm destination in mind he continued heading north. The rising sun was over his right shoulder and as long as he kept it behind him he shouldn't err from his path too far. The woods and the clouds made seeing the sun difficult at times, but part of him, some instinct inherited from ancient times, told him where it was at all times. So long as he continued to adjust his direction as the sun made its arch through the heavens he should stay on a line that should bring him to the men that Borvo spoke of. Not that he knew who these men were or to whom they would lead him. Borvo had mentioned the name of the final link in his journey but it had meant nothing to Ludis, and was not a name that he was familiar with. He had of course been out of the loop for the past year, had not kept up with world news, so the man could have recently come to power for all he knew. He would just have to wait and see, he decided, supposing that he was successful in his journey.

He carried with him snares to trap rabbits, but setting snares and waiting for them to do their work was time he couldn't spare. It was best that he continued on and tried to find food in a less conventional manner. There would be abandoned homes ahead of him where he could perhaps find a few scraps left behind as their owners fled the advancing Germans. Stealing behoved him, but scavenging did not. Anything left behind by the displaced French were fair game, considering it would only spoil, or fall into the clutches of the invaders. All he had to do was find a farm of cottage that had gone unmolested.

It was hours before he found such a place.

He discovered a small farm where the primary crop raised appeared to be too seasonal to be any good to him. Orchards surrounded the farm, fields laid out to rows of apple and pear trees. The problem was that it was far too early in the year to reap fruit from the trees: in fact, they had barely begun to blossom let alone bare anything edible. Nevertheless he thought that he might find some stores left over from last autumn's crop. As he moved through the rows of trees he spied the farm buildings, trying to decide if their occupants had indeed fled. A farmer with an itchy finger might take him for an invader and exert his right to protect his property. A gut full of buckshot wasn't the way he intended filling his belly.

The farmhouse was typical of the region, small and squat, brick walls topped by a peaked roof and dominated by a chimneystack at one corner. The chimney was cold, but not a definite sign that the occupants had left. It was warm enough that a fire might not have been lit. Abutting the house were a row of stone sheds with rickety wooden doors that could do with some care and attention. A tractor with iron wheels and an exhaust pipe that stood eight feet in the air was parked alongside the far end of the outbuildings. A simple glance told Ludis that the tractor had been abandoned to the elements some years before, as the grass grew long among its wheels, as did a patch of brambles. It was doubtful that the machine was serviceable otherwise it would have been taken when the farmer and his family left.

Ludis came to a wooden fence that separated the orchard from the farmyard and he crouched there, spying towards the house. Curtains were hung at the windows, all closed. Odd that they should be drawn during the daytime, but the family could have left during the night and simply neglected to open them. He listened. The apple trees creaked with a mournful song of their own, as if they bemoaned their abandonment, but it was only the effect of the breeze tugging at their branches. From the farm there was no sound that hinted of occupation. The air smelled dusty and didn't carry the odours of cooking or anything else. There were no animals left behind. A place like this should have horses at least, but they had likely been drafted into service to carry the family and their belongings away. Happy that the farm was deserted, Ludis climbed over the fence and walked towards the outbuildings. Anything edible in the house was probably packed up and taken away but something could have been missed in the barns. As he approached the furthest building, he pulled out his revolver and thumbed back the hammer. It wasn't that he'd use the weapon on anyone with a right to be here, but he suspected that he wasn't the only traveller on the roads these days and some may be desperate enough to protect a cache of food with lethal force.

The door was formed of warped planks, supported by a roller mechanism that ran in tracks above it. There were cracks between the planks and Ludis found one large enough to peer through. The interior of the barn was exceptionally dark and he stood there for some time trying to determine the unusual shapes within the gloom. He held his breath, listening for movement. There was none, and finally he gripped the edge of the door and drew it aside. The roller mechanism squealed in protest and the door juddered open wide enough for him to slip inside. A quick glance showed him he had wasted his time here. The room was a single square block, its walls unpainted. The floor was hard-packed dirt, strewn with bits and pieces of farm equipment that would be better smelted down for the value of the iron. Old sacks were stacked in one corner, and if any of them had held fruit from last year's crop they would now be shrivelled and beyond edible. With a pointless care, Ludis closed the door firmly behind him and moved onto the next door. The second building was similar to the first in construction but inside he found benches and a worktable. There were some tools in a wooden box. On a shelf there were clay pots and he took one down. The contents of the pot made his eyes water, and he couldn't determine what the paste inside it was, but he didn't fancy tasting it, suspecting it would kill him more quickly than starvation would. He found a string of onions hanging from a beam. They were withered brown but he still pulled them down and cracked away the outer skins of the largest. The heart of the onion was shiny and moist, and if nothing would cut up and make the basis of a broth if needs be. He pulled the string of onions apart and pushed the healthiest deep into his pockets. In another box on one of the benches he discovered some carrots. They too had seen better days, and were almost flaccid as he tested them. The firmest of the bunch was rotting at its tip, but he broke off and discarded that bit. The carrot had some crunch when he bit into it, but that could have easily been the dirt adhering to the skin, as it was the freshness of the vegetable. It tasted all right, though, and he moved from the room chewing on the mulch, thankful to taste anything at all. Again he closed the door behind him and moved on to the final outbuilding.

The doors were similar to the others, expect here they were hung on hinges and opened down the middle. A simple iron hook held them shut. He flicked the catch over and eased open the doors. This was where the dray beasts slept, he assumed, because he found a couple of stalls with straw on the floors and in the hakes. The animals were gone but mounds of manure showed him that the stalls had been deserted only a short time before. The smell from the droppings was rich and they still glistened with moisture. He supposed that it made sense that the farm had only recently been deserted, because even though Germany had been threatening to invade for some months now, the move to do so had only begun days earlier. Farmers were a hardy type and would not have abandoned their land or livelihoods until the last second. Judging by the freshness of the animal droppings it could have been as recent as last night when they had finally made off. A few dried up onions and a carrot wasn't much of a haul, and hoping that in their rush to evade invasion the family had left behind something more nourishing, Ludis decided it was time that he check the house.

Holding the gun by his side he walked the short distance to the nearest window. The glass was dusty, like the rest of the place. He put his face close to the glass, cupping a hand around his eyes to cut out the sunlight. The windows were tightly closed and he couldn't see inside. Abandoning the window, he went to the front door. Something tickled his subconscious and he found himself looking back at the window and the tightly closed drapes. He shook the thought away and pressed the fingers of his left hand to the door. Soundlessly it swung inward on oiled hinges. Whereas the farm buildings were utilitarian and didn't get the treatment they deserved, the house at least had seen some administration lately. Perhaps it was because the sheds were the domains of the man, while the house was purely that of his wife and she had more exacting standards. He poked his head inside, considering calling out a greeting. His French was limited, but he was sure he could achieve a simple *bonjour*. He remained silent. He listened. Inside was neat but simple. He was looking directly into a living space, complete with upholstered chairs, table, a couple of dressers with trinkets arranged on top. A radio and a separate gramophone were set up at one end of the room, and in the opposite corner was an old upright piano that had been polished to a high sheen. Whoever lived here had an appreciation for music and leaving these belongings behind must have brought pangs of regret. On the piano lid were doilies, hand-made by the look of things, and more of the lace coverings had been spread over the table and the arms of the chairs. The doilies added femininity to the living quarters that reminded Ludis of how Galina had attempted to spruce up their simple home with ribbons and flowers. That thought had an immediate souring affect on him, because it brought to mind the day he'd returned home and found the room strewn with ribbons. That discovery had led him minutes later to the church and to the scene of the slaughter of his loved ones. He nipped his bottom lip with an eyetooth as he turned away and headed for the door that led – he surmised – to a separate kitchen area.

He had guessed correctly. The kitchen had been recently cleaned and there was an underlying smell of detergent. He smiled: even as the farmer's wife had prepared to leave she had not wanted her home to be found in disarray either. When the German army marched through, she wanted it known that she had kept a good and clean home and it should not be soiled by their presence. The woman had a similar spirit to Galina, proud and determined. The likelihood that she'd left anything to spoil in her cupboards was pretty slim, he thought.

He found the larder and peered inside. It was empty but for some glass containers with handwritten labels adhered to the outside. He lifted down one of the jars and tried to make sense of the writing. The scrawl was mostly illegible to him, so instead he flipped off the lid and scrutinised more of the pasty substance he'd seen in similar jars in the outbuildings. He sniffed and caught a vinegary tang. Pickles of some kind, he realised. He dug into the paste with a finger and put it to his lips. Yes, definitely pickled, but he had no idea of the vegetable used. It tasted none too bad and he dug a larger dollop out. Happy that the paste was a conserve of some type – and not something used for greasing the axles of a cart – he sucked his finger clean and then dug out some more. But then he set the jar aside, because he suspected too much of the acidic conserve would sour his stomach and cause him to throw up. He checked other jars, and in one found stewed apple. This was more to his liking and he found a spoon in a drawer next to the sink and set to half emptying the jar.

He sat at the table, thinking about the people who usually filled this space and for a moment felt like an unwelcome interloper. He was sitting where the man of the house would normally sit, at the head of the table, and he could imagine the man's wife serving him from the other end. Perhaps a couple of tousle-haired children would have sat either side, eagerly awaiting the go-ahead to eat. The image conjured the life he'd imagined for himself, and a wave of melancholy fell over him. Suddenly he lost his appetite for the mildly sour applesauce and he left it unfinished. He stood up, intending washing his spoon in the sink, but then thought how pointless an exercise that was. He pushed the lid back in place on the jar and shoved the spoon, licked clean, into his pocket alongside the onions. He was considering going to fetch one of the empty sacks from the shed to carry the jars and few vegetables in when he heard a faint sound. Old houses were prone to noise, he understood, but he'd bet his life's worth that that was the creak of a floorboard underfoot. He came dead still and listened. Sure enough, a few seconds later, the sound repeated itself as someone in the attic bedroom took another step.

The kitchen floor was tiled, and made little sound underfoot as Ludis made his way back towards the living room. At the far end of the living space he'd noted the fireplace, but also a doorway set a step up that he now believed to lead to a staircase to the attic. Someone was up there. That they'd heard him was undeniable, otherwise why would they now be walking so stealthily? He had no desire to bring trouble to the farmer or his wife and thought to leave immediately, without taking the food he'd found with him. But he was reminded of the feeling he'd had when noting the tightly drawn curtains and recognised that the same unconscious feeling of dread hadn't left him the entire time he'd been in the house. The farm – though abandoned – hadn't been done so by choice. No one left their home in such a pristine manner, despite his earlier thoughts about proud wives and their housekeeping standards. No, if the family had fled, then they would have taken their treasures with them: the ornaments, the radio, the gramophone, and the piano even. Also, the doilies so lovingly woven would have been bundled up and packed away. The family hadn't left he understood now, they had been displaced.

In the living room he looked again at the curtains. Not only were they closed, but he saw now that nails had been driven through their hems and into the sills, to avoid them being opened at all. Some one with a disliking of the sun had moved in, causing the family to flee.

He thought immediately of the Upir hiding in its darkened cave, with a hatred of the sunlight that had the ability to scorch its hide and a tremor of hatred ran through him. It was followed immediately by the sense to get out of the house immediately. When facing the Upir in its lair he had gone prepared with salt and crucifix, not to mention a grenade that had blown the thing to pieces and given him time to deal with it before it could regenerate; this time he had no such tools. Safety lay outside in the cleansing light of day where the Upir could not follow. All he had to do was slip outside and he was safe. But his feet refused to move for the exit door. When Ludis had set out to avenge Galina it was not on a task to rid the world of one unholy terror but from all. If there was another such beast lurking up there in the attic rooms it was his duty to cleanse the house of its infernal presence.

Pulling free the replacement cross he'd fashioned and attached to a thong about his throat, he held it between thumb and forefinger of his left hand. His right was clenched tightly round the butt of his revolver. He stood at the centre of the room waiting, counting the steps down from the attic as whatever foul monster approached alighted each stair and steadied its weight on the next.

How many stairs could there be in such a small house?

The wait was interminable.

Before the creaking stopped, perspiration was streaming out of Ludis' hairline and trickling down his face. The sweat was cold and as viscous as oil. Come on, come on, he thought, just show your hideous face and let me get this done.

Now there was another subtle creak, but this one was from the small door set adjacent to the fireplace. The door opened a crack and Ludis looked into darkness more solid than anything he believed he'd seen before. He aimed the Webley at the darkness, tracking the crack upwards to where an eye blinked as it peered back at him. Mirroring Ludis' reaction, the watcher from the stairwell took an involuntary jerk back. Decisions were formed in the space of a heartbeat and Ludis took a step forward, his finger tightening on the trigger of his gun even as the door was thrust open and his nemesis stepped forward.

Chapter 18

Mid-day, 15th May, 1940
Southwest of Bulson, France

Sergeant Renyard could barely credit what had happened and, despite the saying that you shouldn't look a gift horse in the mouth, he couldn't bring himself to believe that the fortuitous attack of the beasts was lucky, but a dire warning of future events.

The creatures, so vicious and blood thirsty, had undoubtedly saved him and his section from the overwhelming odds they faced, but also their intervention had come at a price he wasn't happy to pay. Losing any of his men hurt him, but this particular one more than most. Renyard had talked with the youth so recently, and it was the promise made that had brought about the boy's untimely death.

As Renyard had stood beneath the trees, watching as the simian-like beasts dropped on the German soldiers, he'd been careless and allowed one of them to creep overhead. Seeing it at the final moment he had barely time to get his gun up and fire. But that had not been enough to save him.

The creature came on and Renyard thanked God and all the saints that he'd had the presence of mind to fix his bayonet before taking the battle to the Germans. His upraised rifle had halted the monster's descent with jarring finality as it was skewered through the chest by his blade. The thing didn't die immediately; it clawed at him with hands and feet, its claws tearing strips from his battledress uniform, and some of the skin beneath. His helmet had kept its claws from his face as Renyard forced the beast to the floor. He ripped out his bayonet and immediately plunged in again, stabbing the beast directly through an eye and into its brain. Even then it took time to die, and in a frenzy of loathing Renyard stabbed again and again.

The screams of the dying made a background chorus to his assault on the beast's carcass and it took him a time to realise that his scream had joined theirs. He finally staggered away from the corpse and looked for his men. Out in the darkness they might not yet be aware of what it was they faced and it was down to him to warn them. The tide of battle had changed, because now the German's didn't have a mind to fight their usual enemies but had instead turned their thoughts to surviving the attack of another foe. Now they were shooting into the trees or grappling with the creatures swarming among them on the ground. Renyard had led the charge towards the copse of trees, now he had a mind to run in the opposite direction.

He began running towards where he'd last seen his men, mindless of the bullets still cutting the air around him. Now the guns were targeting randomly, but a stray round was as dangerous as any other. 'To me!' he shouted. 'To me, men!'

Suddenly from out of the night ran a figure. The man was burly, and the distinctive shape of his helmet made him look like an urn on legs. The man was swearing gutturally as he plunged towards Renyard. The German must have depleted the ammunition in his gun because he was coming with his bayonet leading his charge. Renyard yelled, but that was all he managed before the German bore down on him. Something rammed Renyard and he went down hard on his side. Stunned by the blow, it took him seconds to roll back and bring up his gun. Over him stood Leo Hughes, and he was jabbing his own bayonet remorselessly over the top of the German's arms and into his throat. The German died with a low hiss of escaping breath and he slumped back. Leo bent over him, continuing to stab the life out of the man who had so nearly skewered his sergeant. Renyard struggled up, using the stock of his SMLR to lean on. When Leo had knocked him aside he'd also taken some of the wind out of him. Not that he would complain. He was grateful: the young man's action had definitely saved his life.

He put a hand on Leo's shoulder. 'He's finished, Leo. You've done enough.'

The young man gave the German one final prod of his bayonet, then, with the blade jammed through his body, he stood there, leaning on his gun like it was a crutch. He was wheezing with the exertion of killing, but that wasn't all. Renyard saw now that the only reason that Leo was still standing was that he was propped on the end of the German's rifle. The stock end had dug into the earth while its muzzle was pushed tightly under Leo's sternum. Renyard moaned as he saw the end of the German's bayonet protruding from between Leo's shoulder blades. It had gone unnoticed at first because it was hidden by the kitbag on Leo's back, and it was only as he slumped over the dead German that the bayonet had pushed out from under the pack. The bayonet had taken him through the heart and Renyard was stunned that it hadn't killed the lad immediately, only some intense presence of will could have kept him alive long enough to kill his foe. Leo was undoubtedly dead, there was no mistake, but Renyard dropped his rifle and caught the boy by the shoulders. He tugged him off the German's bayonet. He was respectful as he pulled the lad away, taking care not to yank him off the steel, as if it made any difference now. Leo had been so intent on proving his bravery, and that his actions in the casement had been an anomaly, that he had carelessly thrown himself in the way of the German's bayonet. His selfless act had saved Renyard and there was no way that he would repay Leo's sacrifice by being any less than tender with him now. He laid Leo down on the ground and crouched over him. He checked for a pulse, even though he knew it was pointless, and then gently used his thumbs to close the lad's eyelids.

'The other lads might think I'm a coward. I'm not, Sarge. I swear to God, if the enemy was human *then...'*

Renyard recalled Leo's words, and knew that his promise had been binding. He had intended saying that he would give his life for any of them. He had done that all right and Renyard was sickened that it was for him that Leo had died. Even now, twelve hours and many miles distant, he couldn't shake the feeling that Leo's selfless sacrifice was spent on one as undeserving as he. A boy of eighteen years should not have died in the place of a grown man responsible for *his* life.

Renyard marched in desultory fashion. His boots were heavy with mud, which didn't help, but it was the weight of Leo's death that forced the slump into his shoulders. Corporal Green had tried talking to him but Renyard had sent him away, telling him to keep the section moving. He wasn't in a mood for conversation, and especially didn't want to share his burden with Green. In the casement it had partly been Green's attitude to Leo's terror that had troubled the boy so much. In some way, Leo had died because of Green's admonishments. The corporal had simply been performing his duty, and there was nothing personal in his anger at Leo, so Renyard would not blame him, but he could tell that Green was feeling guilty. In sadistic fashion, Renyard wanted the corporal to suffer remorse a while yet. It didn't help soothe his own guilt any, but both Renyard and Green had a responsibility to these young men and it was good for the survivors' moral to see that their superiors cared about them.

126

Renyard replayed the scene through his mind, seeing again Leo standing over him like a guardian angel, his blade sliding in and out of the German soldier's body. Then came the moment he had drawn Leo off the bayonet and laid him out on the ground. Looking into the boy's eyes he had seen relief even as the cataracts of death paled them. He could not bear to look and had gently closed the lids. The last thing he wished for was to recall those eyes every time he closed his own. The battle had still been raging around them, but now the tank was of no concern. Some of the creatures had swarmed the Panzer, gained entry and taken care of the men inside. Renyard had gripped Leo by his webbing and dragged him across the field, away from the on-going slaughter. Rifleman White had materialised from out of the darkness and lent a hand and together they had carried the corpse of their friend out of harm's way. They could not take Leo with them, but Renyard was adamant that he was not going to allow the lad's body to be feasted on by the creatures, and between them they had carried him a mile or so to the south. The men had collapsed down in exhaustion, the recent battle having leached them of all strength, but Renyard had snapped at them and got them moving. Using their entrenchment tools they had fashioned a shallow grave on the top of a hillock, well away from any overhanging boughs. Whitey had brought Leo's rifle, and using it as a marker they had placed his battle bowler on top of it. It made a forlorn sight silhouetted against the night sky when they walked away, with Renyard pocketing the boy's dog tags. They went into the same pocket already containing those of Chiltern and Hoskins.

They had continued marching at a steady pace, until just after dawn where they had sank down and rested. Renyard had been too engrossed in his own pain to see the haggard looks of desolation in the faces of his young companions. After a brief breakfast of reconstituted rations they set off again. Renyard would rather stay in the open after what had happened among the trees last night, but that was madness. He had sent the men along the fringes of a forest instead, with instructions to take cover within the trees only on his command. Until now that hadn't been necessary. The only sign of the German invaders they had seen in the last few hours had been a squadron of airplanes flying west, but they had been a couple of miles from their position and no threat to them.

Rifleman Watson was somewhere ahead of them, scouting the terrain. He had been given the responsibility of plotting a route back to the north and Renyard hoped to see the man soon. Their trek had taken them sufficiently ahead of the German advance and he thought it was about time they tried to cut ahead of it and re-join the rest of the British Expeditionary Force. Earlier they had perused a map and taken compass bearings from nearby landmarks. Watson was currently seeking a track that would take them north, bypassing the city of Reims and – hopefully - all the way to the channel port of Calais where they could forge east again into Belgium. It was a trek of more than a hundred miles, so another task set for the young scout was to find some kind of appropriate transport that would take them there in less than the week that the march would.

Renyard hoped for the best but expected the worst. He wasn't that optimistic that everything would be as easy as that. Not after what had befallen them last night. It was one thing out-marching the Wehrmacht advance, but what of the other things that were spreading across the countryside like a plague? The sun was high in the sky now, but very soon it would dip towards the shoulder of the earth: Renyard did not relish meeting whatever the next nightfall heralded in.

Chapter 19

15th May 1940
Borderlands

'It's all right. You needn't fear me. I am a friend. *Je suis...uh...amis. Oui?*' When Ludis received no reply he racked his brain, trying to trawl up the little knowledge of the French language he possessed. '*Je suis votre amis?* I am *your* friend. *Ne comprenez-vous?*'

The boy still had not stepped down from the stairwell to the attic, but stood there with his hands raised as if to ward off the interloper in his home. Until now he had made only low moaning sounds, deep down in his throat, and Ludis wondered if the boy was so terrified of him that he'd lost the power of speech or even comprehension.

'*Mon ami, je suis un ami.*'

Ludis had no idea if he was speaking clearly in the French tongue, but he thought that if he repeated the phrase enough times it would eventually sink in. '*N'ayez pas...peur.* Don't be afraid, boy. *N'ayez pas peur, mon garçon.*'

The boy continued to moan, but his gaze had become centred now. Ludis squinted at the lad, taking him for a farm boy, judging by his rough clothing and mud plastered boots. The boy's hair was dirty, dull with dust and there was an equally dusty cobweb matted to his forehead, barely concealing a small but vivid bruise. Ludis thought that the family might not have fled as he'd assumed but had taken refuge in the attic, hoping that they would go undiscovered when the invaders passed through. He thought that it was a stupid plan – or it was desperate – because the German's would scavenge this place far more thoroughly than he had. They would have easily found the family and then the Lord knows what they would have done with them.

'Your mother and father, boy, are they here?'

The boy's moaning diminished, but his stare was growing more intent. Ludis found the boy's attention disconcerting; there was something lascivious in the way it lingered on Ludis' throat. Ludis placed his free hand there and found the cross he'd fashioned and realised that the boy wasn't as interested in his skin as he was the icon. Ludis held the cross forward, as if its very presence would help him soothe and therefore communicate with the farm boy. The boy's eyes followed the cross, and he stepped down from the stairs, alighting in the living room with a soft crunch of dirt beneath his boots. His finger that he'd earlier held out as if warding Ludis away now began twitching, as if he desired to touch the cross but was nervous of doing so.

'You are a Christian, boy? Christian? You have no need to fear this.' Ludis unsnapped the cord from his neck and held out the cross to the boy. '*N'ayez pas peur de la croix.*'

The boy's fingertips were pitted with dirt, and his nails chewed to the quick, dirty and soiled. It seemed to Ludis that the boy had been digging recently, and he didn't think it was through a task necessary for the running of the farm.

'Here, *mon garçon.*' Ludis tossed the cross to him and the boy snatched it out of the air, closing his fist tightly around it.

Ludis watched the boy's features, waiting for the first sign of pain, but the only change to his features was in a softening of his eyes. Was he remembering something, a fond memory perhaps?

When the cross wasn't dashed to the floor, the boy's hand erupting into flames, Ludis relaxed a little. His test had been uncouth, but it had assured him that the boy wasn't the unclean spirit he feared. He recalled the result his first crucifix had had on the Upir, and had thought that this would achieve similar results here. So, the boy wasn't the spawn of a vampire, as he'd feared, just a boy. One who was frightened and dirty and looked a little hungry.

Actually, on second perusal, the boy was more than hungry; he looked positively starved.

Ludis' assessment was forced to change in the next instant. The boy opened his fist and allowed the cross to fall to the floor. He had crushed it, broken the cross beam away from the upright. He smiled up at Ludis, his face glowing with pride. His mouth opened and a string of drool oozed between his teeth. His laughter came like a slow heartbeat. Ha-ha. Ha-ha. Ha-ha.

Was the boy insane? That was the easiest way to explain the look that had come over him. Ludis now wondered if the family had indeed fled their home, but had left behind the boy who must be a burden upon them. Had the boy been abandoned to his fate because of the infirmness of his mind? Ludis found the notion despicable, but he also understood that it was a practice of many in some parts of the world. He noted the bruise on the boy's forehead, and, thinking that the boy could have recently been knocked out, he wondered if he was still confused from concussion. He glanced from the boy to the destroyed cross and frowned. No, that wasn't it.

'You're no Christian,' he said.

He understood then that he had been clutching at hope. Despite his promise to slay every one of the fiends that had escaped from Hell, he had not anticipated coming across one in the guise of a child. He knew now that it was only a disguise, worn like a cloak thrown over the true devil to camouflage its evil intent. Dressed in innocence, the beast beneath would be able to get close to its prey before it struck with devastating finality.

Ludis brought up the Webley and placed it directly between the boy's brows, on the spot where his skin was marked. The boy's eyes rolled up, as if he was trying to focus on the cold muzzle pressing into his flesh. He laughed again, but now it was more like a whine. Ludis sighed, his finger tightening on the trigger.

No.

He allowed the gun to drop away.

What if he was wrong? What if this was some feeble-minded child abandoned by his parents? He could not kill the boy without firm proof.

The cross had shown no effect on the boy. But what if Ludis was correct and the body stolen by the devil had belonged to one of another faith? A Jew for instance would have no fear of the cross, and there were many others upon the face of the earth who followed other teachings. There would be people out there who neither recognised the significance of the cross nor even knew of the man who had died upon it to save their souls. He lifted the gun again, and was greeted by another soft titter from the boy. Then again, should not the fiend understand and be repulsed: despite the beliefs of its host body, the wicked thing should still recognise the cross as anathema to its kind.

Ludis had found the killing of the German soldier difficult to take, and he had been trying to kill Ludis at the time. To coldly shoot this boy was no easy task. In fact, the truth be told, Ludis wasn't sure he could do so even if his suspicions were proven if the boy went for his throat. He began to backpedal away. The farm boy watched him, his expression now that of what Ludis had originally thought: extreme hunger.

The drapes were closed, nailed to the frames for a reason. The boy was dirty because he had lain amongst soil gathered by his own hands.

Yet he did not exhibit the signs that he was a vampire. He did not bear the bloodless skin, or the vicious fangs of the Upir. But Ludis recalled that the Upir he'd slain was an ancient devil, one that had probably existed for many centuries and had become the creature it had over the intervening years. What if this boy was recently changed and still bore the look of humanity, as he'd not yet had time to alter? Was there a period of metamorphosis, like the one he'd witnessed in the ghoul? When the ghoul had died, then raised again, physiological changes had occurred to make it more accustomed to its task of eating on the flesh of the recent dead. Maybe the same was true of vampires...and of the many other forms that the devil-infested took.

All was speculation, and did not mean much, not when Ludis' priority was to leave this damned place. He took another step back, and was perturbed to see the boy follow him.

'Come no closer, boy. I don't wish to harm you but...I will.' He raised the gun, but as before the boy showed it as little fear as he had the cross.

From Ludis' right there was a click.

He snatched a glance that way but saw nothing.

Was it the creak of a loose floorboard or something moving in a breeze from the partly open door?

The creak came again.

Ludis was loath to take his aim from the boy, but he couldn't leave his flank uncovered. He tried to watch both ways at once, his gaze flicking back and forth. Movement caught in the corner of his eye. Not to his side, but from the floor. He took a quick look down and saw the planks rising, and understood that he had missed a trapdoor in the floor. Beneath his feet was some kind of storage cellar. Now the door was being lifted with no thought of stealth and Ludis realised he'd walked directly into a trap. Coming out from under him were three figures: a wizened man, a skinny woman, and an older youth. They were as filthy and unkempt as was the boy, their foreheads marked with identical bruises, and had the same look of starvation upon them. These were the family he'd imagined sitting down to eat around the kitchen table, but their hunger would never be sated by food raised on this land. It was apparent from the drool flooding from their lips that they desired *other* sustenance. They desired him.

They came up from the floor and spread out, aiming to block his escape route through the door or via the kitchen. They opened their mouths, and he saw their teeth champing down in eagerness to taste his flesh. He had not noticed it before, but now that he saw the ring of bodies helming him in, they each carried the same ravenous need in their features of a drug addict. Only flesh and blood would satisfy the cravings racking their bodies. He should have recognised it when first he saw the boy who came down from the attic. These were not vampires. They did not fear the light of day or crosses because they were mindless. That wasn't true: they could think but it was merely at the base level of a maggot seeking food. The hammering of the drapes must have been an act performed by the family prior to their turning, before they died and rose again as the walking dead. Maybe they thought to keep something out and had shored up their home, seeking solace in the comfort of the enfolding darkness. Whatever the case it had made no difference. They had died, and whatever creeping evil had invaded the lands had resurrected them, charging them with the need to feed their endless hunger lest they rot to shuffling carcasses.

Beside the small bruise, Ludis had seen no wounds on the boy, but on the parents were signs that they had been shot. A hole was punched through the man's chest, while part of the woman's skull was missing just above her left eyebrow. The youth's shirt was bloody, but hid his fatal wound: a stab to the heart by all appearances. Ludis turned to the boy and wondered how that poor soul had perished. The boy had moved on him silently as was bending low, aiming to take a bite out of Ludis' thigh. Ludis pushed the boy down and held him there under his boot. The boy squirmed, but had no chance of biting him face down on the planks. Ludis shuddered as he spied the boy's wound. The back of his skull was opened, and, inside the open vessel, his brain showed grey and pink. The blood that had spilled down the nape of his neck had coagulated to a sickening black sheet.

Once these had been good, hard-working people, but now their bodies were simply the shells carrying a voracious plague, a parasitic life form that had reanimated them and forced them to feed it. Ludis would have no qualms about squishing a mosquito or leech, and to him that's all these people should now represent. Yet there was something in their forlorn demise, and subsequent resurrection that irked him to cause them further harm. This ravenous hunger was not of their doing, and harming them went against the grain somewhat.

Yet he could not allow this plague to persist. He told himself he had to forget that these were once god fearing people, that now they were vessels of evil. He fired point blank into the face of the farmer. The man went down on his back, twitched a few times, his hands making claws, and then he rose again. In the faces of the man's wife and oldest son there was no emotion. They cared not for their loved one, they were of only one thought and that was to feed on Ludis' body. Even the boy on the floor had twisted so he could claw at the boot holding him to the ground.

Ludis jumped away and watched as the boy rolled over onto all fours. The boy came at him, reminding Ludis of an arachnid with some of its limbs amputated. As loath as he was to do so, Ludis booted the boy with all his might, knocking him sprawling in front of his mother and brother.

His bullets were useless here. They would not kill the autonomous creatures, and to shoot would be to waste the few rounds he had left. Ludis shoved his gun away and turned instead for a nearby chest of drawers. The furniture was heavy, stout and formed of the land as its owners had once been, but Ludis was a big man and strong with it. He hauled the drawers up to his chest, before striding forward, using them like a ram to batter the family members backwards. Over the top of the chest they raked at him with their dirty hands, but he kept well clear of their teeth. He suspected he should be safe, so long as none of them got their teeth into his flesh, for this plague was most likely spread by their saliva or other bodily fluids.

Ludis had the mother and oldest son pinned with the drawers. The smaller boy was at his feet, and easily enough kicked backwards. Only the father posed any threat because he was slightly to one side and was even now clawing his way past the drawers to come at Ludis. Ludis gave the drawers one final shove and the woman and youth fell back into the cellar from which they'd come. Ludis threw the chest down on them, then stooped and grabbed the boy. Closing his eyes momentarily, he pitched the boy down into the darkness and heard the crunch of his bones as he landed on top of the chest. Down there, all three would be trying to regain their footing and to come after him again. Ludis had to trust that he'd have time to deal with the farmer before that happened. He felt the man snag his heavy coat, and could detect the pressure of the grinding teeth munching down on his shoulder, but wasn't immediately concerned. It would take teeth sharper than the farmer's to break through cloth that had resisted a wolf pack. Ludis twisted and caught the farmer by his hair and tore the head away. The farmer's eyes had grown bilious, something green and rotting invading their depths. He snapped his teeth at Ludis' hands and the big man propelled the farmer away from him. The man crashed against a wall, rebounded off, and came immediately back at him.

Reflex made Ludis grab at the gramophone. He twisted and came away with the copper horn in his hands. As the farmer leaned in, aiming to bite at Ludis' face, he met the open end of the horn instead. Cupping the back of his head with one hand, Ludis forced the man's face deep into the horn, and now the man's teeth, and the threat of infection, were nulled. Pivoting, Ludis swung the man around, just as the youth popped his head up from the cellar with a triumphant grin. Then the youth was gone back below, his father on top of him as Ludis threw him down. Ludis stood over them all and could see their faces tilted up at him. Their only emotion was still that gut-burning hunger and he knew that they would come again, and continue coming until they picked the meat from his bones. He slammed down the trap door. That wouldn't hold them more than a few seconds, so Ludis acted quickly. He rushed over to the upright piano, pressed his shoulder to it and forced it to the centre of the room. Then he heaved it over and it hit the floor with a dull chime, sealing the cellar.

The fact that the family's love of music had been his saving grace was not lost on Ludis. If their instruments had not been there, then he would have found another way to defeat them, but still there was an irony to the situation that he couldn't shake. He promised that he would sing a song of lament for them all. But first he had another task to see to.

While they were entombed, it did not mean they would perish. Yes, they would deteriorate, their flesh and ligaments decomposing, but still they would pose a threat to anyone else coming upon this house in the orchards. Curiosity would make a visitor shove away the piano, to see what it concealed, and perhaps they wouldn't be as lucky as Ludis was at evading the biting teeth. He could not allow this plague to spread – even among the invaders.

He looked around and found a lamp containing paraffin. He splashed it over the piano, the surrounding floor and the drapes, and even the doilies so lovingly woven by the hands of the woman now sealed down below. He found matches in the kitchen and returned to stand over the piano. The family – no, their bodies were now inhabited by something ungodly – tried to push up on the trap door. The piano chimed with each rattle. It was not sweet music.

Fetching one paraffin-soaked doily, Ludis struck a match and waited until the fire bloomed. He tossed the doily on to the piano and flames immediately burst forth. Next he strode through the room, touching the still burning match to the other places he'd fuelled. Smoke filled the room, blue flames writhing up the walls. Perhaps the risen dead could know fear after all, because their attempts at shifting the piano grew wilder and from their throats came sounds that again sounded like the low moaning he'd first heard from the boy.

Hating himself, Ludis stepped outside.

He had no desire to watch and ensure the flames did their work; he had full faith in them. He strode away, angling around the farmhouse to pick up his route north, and forbade himself to look back.

As he strode out, he lamented the lives of those taken within that house, singing in a voice surprisingly sweeter than any would expect from such a gruff man.

Chapter 20

16ᵗʰ May 1940
Wewelsburg, Germany

While the ruined house in the orchard smouldered hundreds of miles away, a much larger structure made a far more impressive pyre for those trapped beneath it. Heinrich Himmler stood on a promontory of limestone a mile from the nameless castle near Wewelsburg, a tic jumping along his jawline. Already he'd adjusted his spectacles to ensure a clear view but such was the conflagration that oily black smoke drifted this far and laid a greasy deposit on the lenses. It didn't matter to him that he saw the entire structure burn to the ground, it was enough to know that the charges had detonated, brought the countless tons of stone down on top of the mouth of the well, and sealed it so that no other creatures from the other side could find a way through. A short while earlier, he'd ordered von Seid to call in bombers to complete the work. The Luftwaffe had come through, pinpointing the castle with an accuracy that pleased Himmler and all that now remained was a jumble of boulders and timber to mark the castle's location. The bombs dropped upon it contained phosphorous, the ghost lights of their blinding white explosions even now swirling across his retinas. Artur Klein stood behind him, but Himmler did not need to look to know that the man was wringing his hands as he too observed the destruction. The necromancer was probably picturing his future and feverishly plotting ways to avoid a firing squad. Himmler smiled to himself: there was no way out for a man responsible for such a disaster as this.

Part of a wall collapsed in on the ruins sending up a great waft of sparks and smoke and Himmler took it as a sign that he'd seen quite enough. He had taken off his leather gloves earlier, but now he slapped them against his thigh in agitation and began the short walk down from the promontory to where his staff car waited. Klein fell in behind him, muttering something under his breath. Himmler thought that the man was praying: whom would he beseech for help at a time like this?

Both *sturmbahnführers* waited beside the car, Hartmann as grim as ever, while the Aryan poster boy, von Seid, was his usual smug self. They gave the ubiquitous salute and in perfunctory fashion Himmler replied. 'Heil Hitler,' he said, wishing that they dispensed with the silly practice. They had no need to confirm their allegiance every time he re-joined them, for he knew that they feared him too much to be anything but one hundred per cent loyal at all times. Perhaps they feared a similar fate that was on the cards for Klein and they felt the need to win favour with him and the Führer. Oberst Wilhelm Kumm was another matter entirely. As commander of the operation at the castle, there was much favour for that man to reinstall if he was to avoid execution. Himmler had spoken on the telephone with Hitler a few hours earlier, when the decision to destroy the castle and seal the portal was made, and Hitler had been more enraged than he had ever heard him – and that was saying something. His fury had been directed at the ineptitude of both Klein and Kumm, and if Himmler could feel pity he'd experienced it on both men's behalf. His concern was only fleeting, because he was not a man who'd attained such heights caring about the welfare of others, and now he anticipated seeing the men sacrificed as scapegoats. Their deaths would mean his sheet would remain clean. It was known only to a select few, and only at the highest echelons of the Nazi party, that Himmler himself was overseeing the entire project here in Wewelsburg, and if the blame for its failure could be laid on the heads of two dead men then who was he to complain?

If he were to be killed now, questions would be asked about Kumm. He had men under his command, he had a family and associates, and his assassination would have to be handled correctly to avoid suspicion. Kumm had received orders to lead his men to the front, and already a team of SS-VT killers were awaiting their arrival, disguised in the uniforms of British Tommy's. Kumm would die in the line of duty, and be hailed a martyr of the German cause. For Klein, though, there was little need of deception: the only ones who knew of his part here were men who despised him and any one of them would volunteer to join his firing squad. That was not necessary of course, because Himmler had already briefed his executioners.

Klein would have to be handled carefully, because wretched as he was, he was not without resources at his command. As a top tier wizard of the Thule Society he could call upon the protection of his brothers and even Hitler did not have the authority to supersede their decisions should they intervene on Klein's behalf. Unknown to most, Hitler had risen to supreme power in Germany through the influence of the Thule Society. He was initiated to the cult many years earlier, under the auspices of Dietrich Eckhart, and had won favour among their numbers, but should he be seen to do harm to any of their people he was not beyond removal, to be replaced by another Society initiate. Hitler, despite his faults, was much preferred to whichever man should replace him.

Von Seid opened the rear door of the staff car, and Himmler slid inside.

'Come, Herr Klein, sit with me,' he said, showing the man his open palm. The offer was less an invitation than it was a thinly veiled order. Klein nodded and squirmed on to the bench seat next to him. Ordinarily Himmler travelled with a driver who doubled as his bodyguard, as well as a contingent of outriders. The driver – not to mention Himmler's retinue - was conspicuous by his absence. *Sturmbahnführer* Otto Hartmann was the driver this day, while von Seid took a position in the front passenger seat. As they drove away, following a trail into the deep woods, Klein's gaze flickered over the two men, before he closed his lids slowly. He was no fool and understood the reason for his travelling companions.

'The lance is safely en route?' Himmler already knew the answer to his question, having seen it escorted away from the castle before the demolition began.

'It is in the hands of my most trusted people,' Klein replied, equally aware that his answer was rhetorical. 'They will protect it with their lives. As would I…given the opportunity.'

Himmler took a cleaning cloth from his uniform jacket and busied himself by cleaning his spectacles. When he replaced them he turned to regard Klein and his eyes were brighter and harder than the augmentation of the lenses warranted. 'You know what must be done, Herr Klein?'

Himmler always thought the man to be a snivelling wretch, and was surprised that Klein returned his look with features set equally as tough. 'I argued against putting the lance to such use, I cautioned that we were wielding powers too great to understand and asked for more time for study of the icon. This was not my fault, *Reichsführer*, as well *you* know. I opened the gate, yes, but it was under your orders. As you recall, I advised against such impatience, and warned that we were not yet ready to control the forces that would be unleashed.'

Himmler snorted. 'What you say is true, Klein. But let me ask you this: had the opening of the gate been successful and you had harnessed the powers in servitude of our nation, then who would now be accepting the accolades and the gratitude of the *Führer*? You would have happily accepted the praise lauded upon you, and yet you balk at punishment when you have so obviously failed in your task.'

'I am still of value to you and to Hitler, and what you intend is both ill-advised and a waste of my talents.'

'In your opinion, yes.' Himmler smiled, but there was little warmth in the gesture. 'I do not value you or your skills, Klein, and neither does *Mein Führer*. Before you offer your talents in finding the latest escapee, forget it. I already have other arrangements in place. You, Klein, are worthless and an embarrassment.'

From his side Himmler lifted a dagger. It was long and tapering with a cross guard formed of an eagle with spread wings. A swastika was embossed upon the Eagle's chest. Himmler buried the blade as deep as the symbol in Klein's side.

Klein coughed on blood that flooded his mouth. The dagger had slid neatly between his ribs, piercing a lung. He would not die immediately, but he would struggle to breath and experience intense agony with each intake. The man's torture pleased Himmler. It was one thing ordering the murder of others, quite something else when yours was the hand that delivered death. It had been some time since he had been offered an opportunity to slake his thirst for pain. Drawing out the blade, he held it up and inspected the blood caught in the furrow down the centre of the dagger. He had thought the blood would be anything but the glistening red it was: yellow, he'd supposed.

Klein turned to face his slayer. 'You're wrong if you think you can stop it. I only wish I was around to see your failure, *Reichsführer*, and be the one to plunge a dagger into your chest.'

Himmler laughed at the dying man's bravado. He tapped Otto Hartmann on the shoulder. 'There: that clearing in the woods. It suits our purposes. Hurry, man, before this…this *vermin* bleeds all over my car.'

Hartmann pulled off the road, bumping over mounds of grassy earth, but the car was sturdy enough to handle the mistreatment. He had no sooner stopped than von Seid was out and had tugged open the rear passenger door to manhandle Klein into the centre of the clearing. Klein had no strength to resist, and von Seid took great delight in dragging him like a bundle of rags. There was a natural depression in the ground and von Seid threw Klein into it. Klein struggled up to his knees. He looked up at his would-be executioner. 'If you have any pity, von Seid, do…it…quickly.'

Von Seid sneered at him. 'You expect pity from me? You're asking the wrong man.'

Von Seid drew his Luger.

Himmler and Hartmann loomed into view, both men drawing their own sidearms. Himmler pointed his gun at Klein's gut. 'To deter suspicion we must make this look like an ambush, Herr Klein. I'm sure you understand.'

Klein closed his eyes, and bit his lips, determined not to cry out.

Shots – too many to be a clean execution – rang through the woods. Before they stopped, Klein was screaming.

Then all was silent again until a car engine burst to life and then diminished into the distance.

Chapter 21

18th May 1940
Reims, France

The section had ensconced themselves in a barn outside the town of Reims, thankful of somewhere warm to rest and regain some of the strength expended while marching for the past two days. Daytime stops had been kept to the minimum, and Sergeant Renyard had pushed them through most of the first and second night. Thankfully his fears of creatures preying on them during the hours of darkness hadn't come about, yet there were other dangers that could prove equally fatal to them all. On a couple of occasions they had seen troop movement, always from a distance, and always wearing the wrong coloured uniforms to be their allies. At one point a fighter plane had buzzed them, but they had recognised the insignia as being that of the French Armée de l'Air, and it was a relief that the pilot recognised them as British, so no bullets were exchanged. The fighter plane flew on, its pilot's mission unknown to them, but the section had cheered him anyway. At that time they had no clue that France had almost given up the fight against the invaders, or that their Prime Minister, Paul Reynaud, had already telephoned the new Prime Minister of the United Kingdom to declare France had lost the battle. As a result, Churchill had flown to Paris and found the French government burning its archives and preparing to evacuate the capital. Churchill had tried to console the French, reminding them of how the German's had been repelled under similar circumstances during the First World War, and as a result the hastily formed 4th DCR, under Colonel Charles de Gaulle, had mounted an attack from the south, intending cutting off the Wehrmacht advance on Paris. Yesterday, de Gaulle's attack had seen a measure of success, but it was nothing when compared to the relative accomplishments of the various German divisions. As they now languished in the barn outside Reims, Rommel's Panzer Corps had just taken Cambrai merely by feinting an armoured attack on the city, and things were looking equally as desperate for the Allied Forces throughout the continent.

Renyard was conscious that, without communication with the British Expeditionary Force, he had no way of knowing where he should lead his men. He was considering reconnoitring the nearby city and finding a working telephone. Out here in the sticks there were no such mod cons. He shouldn't be ungrateful, he supposed, because they had shelter, and soft straw to lie down on, and at least *most* of his section was still alive. That vagrant thought brought Rifleman Hughes to mind, and the lad's sacrifice. He had died on behalf of his friends, and his bravery was a clear lesson for Renyard. For two nights now he had been running scared, and that was not good for a man with the lives of others to consider. With no clear idea of *where* to go next, he was beginning to mull over *what* he should do. His section had been chosen to bolster the forces protecting the Meuse for a specific reason. They were proven fighters, their bailiwick being that of skirmishers. They were secreted among the French troops for the purpose that – should an invasion be inevitable – they utilise their special skills to throw disarray among the German's. They were to use stealth, coupled with hit-and-run assaults, to inflict harm on their enemies. Up until now, he could only claim two attacks against the German army and neither of them had been planned, but spur of the moment necessity. It was about time he got the men down to business.

'Listen up,' he said.

The men were spread throughout the barn, two of them lying down, two sitting, while Watson and Blanco had been stationed outside as sentries. Green was up in the loft area, also keeping an eye out through a hatch where straw bales were loaded via a winch mechanism. The corporal heard Renyard and came forward, peering down from the upper level. 'Do you want me down there, Sarge?'

'As long as you can hear me, you're fine where you are.'

The other men – Cooper, Whitey, Taff and McCoy – pulled themselves up and came to stand in a ragged line in front of Renyard. By now their battledress was dishevelled, their faces and hands streaked with dirt. Whitey, who had helped carry Hughes away, had dried blood on his jerkin, brown and stale now. They didn't look capable of the type of action that Renyard had decided on, but he only had to look into their features to see otherwise. Each one of them had aged over the past few days: not in the normal fashion but in wisdom. They had grown from boys to men, and he could read their determination – their readiness – to do more than run.

'We're turning back,' he said.

His announcement didn't elicit much of a response, all he received were nods of acknowledgement. He glanced up at Green and saw the corporal dip his head, but there was a faint smile on his lips, as if – finally – he was glad that Renyard had come to his senses.

'We could continue on our current path, but what will that achieve?' Renyard went on. 'Sooner or later we would get caught, and probably shipped off with the other POWs: that's if we weren't stood in front of a firing squad. I take it none of you are happy about that idea?'

He received a round of negatives from all the men.

'My plan is to take the fight back to the enemy.'

'Here! Here!' McCoy said, and there were affirmatives from the others this time.

'If we are careful, and avoid detection, we can slow their advance into France. My best guess is that Hitler intends pressing our lads back towards the Channel, but to do that he first needs to push deeper into France in order to block the BEFs retreat this way. We are going to do our best to give our lads a way out the back door, right? We do what we do best: hit them hard and fast, slow the buggers down, disrupt their supply lines, do anything we can to stop them here.'

'Eight of us against the Wehrmacht?' Cooper wasn't complaining, he wasn't even stating the obvious, he was actually proud at the prospect of confronting overwhelming odds.

'If we don't do this and our lads get stuck with their backs to the sea, Germany will annihilate our forces, and you all know what their next step will be.' An assault on the British mainland was a real threat now, and should the BEF be caught in the trap there would be nothing left standing between Germany and its plan to dominate the world: a fact that was lost on none of them. Even if they did manage to traverse the country without losing their lives what would be left to go home to? Renyard understood that the little effect they had against their enemies wouldn't make that much difference to the outcome of the war, but he sure as hell was going to do *something*. 'We're here to do a job, lads. I say we get on with it.'

All the men had witnessed the attack on the German troop, when the creatures had swarmed on them from out of the trees. Whitey was the only one with the balls to bring the subject up, though. 'Sarge, those *other* things?'

'What about them?'

'Well, the first time…you know, back at the casement?'

'Like I said, Rifleman White: "What about them?"'

'Back then we all thought the thing that killed the Frenchies was some sort of German weapon, like a super soldier or something. Y'know, like a man that'd been *experimented* on. Well…apparently it wasn't.'

'Considering the way that the others attacked the Germans, I'd agree with you. Not unless they had their wires crossed and went for the wrong target.'

'They didn't care who they slaughtered,' Taff Jones put in.

'So what if we come across any more of them?' Whitey asked.

'What're the chances?' Renyard said. 'We left them two days south of here. They'll have moved on by now.'

'I know, Sarge.' Whitey glanced round as if every shadow inside the barn concealed something infernal. 'What if they followed us here?'

Renyard sighed. 'If they did, I think we would've known about it by now. Forget those other things. If we're going to help our lads we have to concentrate on the job at hand. We have to slow the Wehrmacht.'

Whitey nodded, but he wasn't fully convinced. 'Maybe the Wehrmacht isn't the worst enemy we have out there, Sarge. That's all I'm saying.'

'What do you suggest, Whitey?' Green leaned over the parapet so he could be seen clearly, and his stern features could better display his anger. 'We ask the bleedin' Germans to help us deal with the common threat? Jesus!'

'All right, leave it alone, Corporal,' Renyard grunted. 'Whitey has a point. Those things are a danger to us all, but nowhere near as big a problem as the Germans destroying our army. I think we were just amazingly unlucky to come across them twice,' he said to appease Whitey, 'but what are the chances of it happening again? There are thousands of men out there, all of them fighting for their lives, all of them as likely to attract the bastards before we do again.'

As Whitey acquiesced, Renyard thought: Yeah, what are the chances of it happening again?

If the truth was told he didn't like the odds.

A faint whistle came from outside, a low-pitched signal from one of the sentries. Next second Blanco poked his head inside the door. 'Someone's out there,' was all he said. In a rush, the men all brought up their guns, moving rapidly to positions of concealment in the barn. Jesus, are the chances stacked so heavily against us? Renyard thought.

Renyard scooted over to join Blanco, who had now come inside and was spying out through a crack between the closed doors.

'You get a look at him?' Renyard whispered.

'No, Sarge, it was Winker. He spotted someone spying on the barn and sent me to warn you. Winker's going to try and capture him before he makes his move.'

If anyone was capable of ambushing the spy, then it was Winker Watson. Renyard nodded to the others, a silent order to ready themselves for action, in case Watson required the backup. There was a flurry of soft rattles as the section readied their rifles.

Chapter 22

18th May 1940
Eastern France

In the three days since he had discovered the family at the house in the orchard Ludis had concentrated on moving north as quickly as possibly. Along the way he had witnessed the aftermath of battles, coming across the remains of destroyed tanks and troop wagons, and the corpses of those that had travelled within them. The indigenous wildlife was having a field day, feasting on the flesh, but there was no sign that anything unnatural was reaping the bounty of food. He was torn by the discovery, because – even though his mission was to deliver the shard to its rightful recipient – he had set himself his own trial of destroying the unholy things stalking Europe. He had to caution himself from deviating from his path, as he was certain that out there among the dead were those he hunted, and stick to his route. He felt like a ghoul himself, prowling through the battlefields, stripping from the corpses the necessary items to help him survive. The few vegetables he'd taken with him from the farm had been consumed the following day, and seeing as the jugs of conserves had been left to the fire, he required nourishment. Unlike the ghouls he would not touch the flesh of the corpses he found, but among their possessions were the occasional food items. Also he was able to scavenge enough ammunition to replenish his Webley revolver, and he found an updated Lee-Enfield rifle to replace the one broken when he'd fought the wolf pack far to the south. Also, stick grenades that he'd found so useful against the Upir, he took them from German soldiers and loaded them into his belt. He left the German machineguns were they lay, having no familiarity with them, and no desire to employ them against his fellow men.

On one occasion he had come across a convoy of evacuees heading towards Paris. They were folk forced from their lands, hoping to find shelter and protection in the capital, but Ludis suspected they were on a fool's errand. Paris, like the rest of France was destined to fall. Even he who had no real understanding of the strategies of war could see that the German Wehrmacht was wholly outmanoeuvring the Allies. He gave Paris a few more days of freedom, and then it would fall under the might of the Third Reich.

Yesterday he was offered succour by a small band of travellers. At first they had treated him with suspicion, based mainly on the fact that he was so outlandish, but once they had all sat around a small fire and shared liquor and food they had relaxed somewhat. From them, Ludis discovered that the British Expeditionary Force was currently retreating towards the Scheldt River, and the general consensus was that the British were being thrashed as soundly as the French were. The German Luftwaffe was the terror of the skies that the British were struggling to contend with. A Panzer division led by an impetuous man named Erwin Rommel had began to distinguish themselves, destroying the French 5th Motorised Infantry Division who had intended blocking them. Rommel had moved faster than the French had expected and surprised the 5th Division while they were refuelling. They had completely trounced the French, overrun their position and taken around ten thousand prisoners. The travellers spoke of Rommel with equal levels of hatred and grudging respect. They spoke also of a colonel rising to distinction in their own army, Charles de Gaulle, who was having similar success in his battles, as was Rommel. Ludis remained silent on his opinion: if de Gaulle was achieving such amazing victories then why wasn't the German war machine stalled here in the borderlands?

There was an air of impending defeat among the folk gathered around the campfire, their hopes of de Gaulle saving France was somewhat leavened by the proof around them. They were not yet ready to give up, though, and thought that the German's would never take Paris. Many such thousands of refugees were heading for the capital, while Ludis suspected that there would be a similar exodus of people fleeing the city to the wide interior of the country. He considered advising this small group to make different plans, and to perhaps lose themselves in the wilds. Then again, he thought morosely, out there they could fall prey to the other things waging war on mankind. Instead he thanked them for their generosity and waved them off as he took up his journey north once more. He was saddened that this extended family group might not survive very long, but then there were other families who did not have the same opportunity at escape that they had. He thought of the farmer and his family and how, once the shadow of Lucifer had moved over them, they had no chance whatsoever. The only thing that stopped him succumbing to a deep depression was the hope that his slaying of them had at least spared their immortal souls from further servitude to the devil.

He had journeyed through yesterday evening, and then through the night, and this morning had found a hollow tree where he'd managed to scramble inside and catch a few hours sleep. Waking up, he'd washed himself in a stream. In the cool water he had caught sight of his reflection and it was no wonder that the good folk in the refugee camp had at first met him with distrust and, yes, not a little fear. If Galina were here she would scold him for allowing himself to deteriorate so much. His beard was wild and matted and his moustache was stained about his lips. His hair – once worn in a neat braid – was now a tangled mane that hung over his brows and onto his shoulders. His thick coat and trousers were torn and filthy. He had lost many pounds and was skinnier than he could remember. Around his eyes were deep furrows, but they were unavoidable considering what he had witnessed in the past year or so. He peered down at his reflection, and saw a stranger frowning back at him. Back when he had hunted the Upir, hygiene had never been an issue, as he had never expected to survive the encounter, yet since then months had passed. Traversing the frozen mountains, then trekking through the hot climates of the south, his hair and beard had offered some protection from the elements. Here though, there was no need for a thick hirsute in this gentler environment. He'd made a decision.

His blanket roll doubled as a pack in which he'd folded his meagre belongings. Among their contents was a razor and strop. He set about sharpening the blade that had gone unused for so long that it had lost its edge. Soap would have come in handy, as would warmer water than the stream afforded, but he didn't complain. Using the still water at the side of the stream as a mirror, he set about scraping away the wild growths of facial hair. Never again would he look like the wholesome young man that Galina fell in love with, but when he again checked his reflection, he saw someone more akin to her lover. He had aged somewhat, his cheekbones looked more pronounced and his eyes had sunk deeper within the sockets, but at least he no longer looked like a wild beast. Taking a handful of hair at the back, he hacked it off. It made little difference, so he continued with the task. On the banks of the stream there looked to be enough hair to gather up and stuff a mattress, and briefly it was something that he considered doing. When next he looked at the face in the stream he was surprised by the transformation. With his hair now cropped close to his scalp, his ruddy skin glowing, he looked and felt more vital than he had in a long time.

With his renewed look came a fresh vigour for the journey ahead, and he had pushed on with nary a glance back. Somewhere over the horizon there was a battle going on and he headed for it. Not that he was looking for a fight, but hoped that it had moved on before he reached it. Having no idea of the landscape hereabouts, and with no access to a map, he thought it best that he continue due north and, if the battle still raged, he would find a way round it and then pick up his route once more.

He had assumed that the battle was only a few miles away, yet he marched for a couple of hours before reaching the crest of a low hill and could at last see the conflicting armies in the valley below him. From his vantage point, he was slightly to the rear of a German infantry division who were advancing through the wide valley. Six tanks augmented their forces, but they had fallen already to the French "Matilda" tanks arranged at the other end of the valley. Nevertheless, the German's were in superior numbers and were outflanking their enemies and forcing them back. Ludis wondered if the vaunted de Gaulle commanded the French tanks, or if it was some less successful colonel at their helm. Having neglected to pick a side to support yet, Ludis should have been nonplussed by the apparent German supremacy, but the more he seen and heard about Hitler, and the actions of some of his men, the more he felt inclined to rush down into the valley and do what he could do to spare some of the French fighters. No, this was not his battle. He turned further east, and then crept through the loose encampments of soldiers waiting to move forward once their way through the valley was cleared. As he did so, Ludis ensured he went unobserved. The travellers he'd shared the camp with last night said that the German's had taken more than ten thousand prisoners: well, one more man sent to the prison camps wouldn't mean much to them, but would spoil everything for him.

Once he was beyond the valley, and moving through pastoral lands he paralleled a dirt track. The going would have been easier on the road itself but also heightened the risk of meeting someone. He ensured that he could see where the road went but that it was a good two or three hundred yards from his position: far enough away that he would see anyone moving along it but that he would go unobserved. The early season made it more difficult to find appropriate cover as the grass and crops had not yet began to grow, but there were enough fences and irrigation channels he could conceal himself behind or in to suffice. Following the track he finally came to a main road, this one paved and seemingly well travelled under normal circumstances. Now it appeared deserted, but he couldn't count on it as an easy route to the town that now poked its higher towers above a treeline to the north. He approached the road, crouched at its verge while he listened for traffic and then sprinted across and slid down an embankment at the far side. Coming to his feet, he set off again, heading into a small copse of trees that showed the first bloom of spring. As he moved among them, blossom fluttered down on him, loosened from the branches by a wind that was stirring. At the far side of the small wood he again paused. The sky was growing darker by the minute, and a haze had settled over the horizon that he recognised as rain falling distantly. Before long the shower would reach him. He spied across fields, eyeing a small range of hills that partially blocked his view of the town beyond. Glancing again at the approaching rain he had no desire to sleep under the sky again tonight and made a decision. The town had until now avoided the conflict ranging all around them, but how long would it go unmolested? He hoped that it would be spared this night at least, because the prospect of lying down somewhere dry was a fine thought. Not that he would be as impetuous as approaching the town without first reconnoitring it. He moved out across the fields, but angled his path so that it took him towards the crest of the highest hill. From there he thought he would be able to spy on the town and determine who were its masters. If the German's had taken it, then he would have no option but move on and hope that the rain didn't fall as steadily as the clouds threatened.

A quarter of an hour later he was crouching on the top of the hill. Beside him was a jumble of boulders, and dressed in the dour colours that he was, they offered camouflage to him. So long as he didn't stand up he would de indistinguishable from the rocks to anyone below. Searching the streets of the small town he could see none of its inhabitants out and about. He found it odd, even in this time of uncertainty, for approaching evening he would have expected many people to be making their way home to have their evening meal, or to settle their children for bed. He could not see a living soul. The only movement came from birds clustered along the rooflines, and from a lone dog scavenging for a morsel of food next to an upended barrel. Something else that struck him as unusual: the chimney stacks of the fifty or so houses clustered round a church and small general store were cold. He had expected to see fires lit in hearths to ward off the coming chill of the rainstorm but there was not a single column of smoke anywhere. Perhaps the villagers had already evacuated, fleeing the impending invasion? That was what he had assumed back at the farm in the orchard and he couldn't have been more wrong. A shudder ran the length of his spine: what if the entire village had been infected by the evil creeping across the lands, and everyone who lived here had become like the deathless things he'd killed back at the farm? He suddenly had no desire to investigate the town, the prospect of falling foul of a town full of the walking dead outweighing another uncomfortable night under the elements. Sighing deeply he rested his back against the boulders, deciding that he'd rest here a while, then move on past the town under the cover of the rainstorm.

As the wind kicked in, he pulled up the collar of his coat. Maybe shearing away his hair and beard hadn't been such a good idea after all. The boulders afforded a little shelter, but could do nothing to halt the patter of rain on his head. Stoically he took the chill, thinking now on the task that had brought him here; direction from a mad woman, not to mention the questions left unanswered that he was loath to ask.

Chapter 23

After his hunt for the Upir, Ludis' trek had taken him west through the southern Slavic lands to the coast of the Adriatic Sea, where he'd wandered across the northern expanse of Italy at the feet of the Dolomites and into southern France. His journey had been uneventful as regards meeting any of the unholy things he knew were abroad, and he had arrived in a small coastal village perched in the natural 'V' between towering cliffs with a sense that his feet had led him adrift. The rumblings of war had resonated that far south and the villagers who mistook his language for German/Prussian greeted him with distrust and he was in danger of being stoned to death. A peddler called Hector – himself a stranger in town – had offered a welcoming hand, and Ludis had joined him as a travelling companion, taking a seat on the Spaniard's cart. The fee for his passage came at a price of course: Hector had taken one look at Ludis' stature and deemed him a useful companion to have at his side during those turbulent times. Ludis hadn't thought that he would take employment, and especially not as a guard protecting a traders wares, but it was not a job he objected to. Hector's caveat had gone unspoken, but Ludis had read the man's glance as he'd spied the rifle over his shoulder, and chose to make the man none the wiser. If he had been travelling the road alone he might have had to protect himself, so extending protection to the peddler was a price he'd gladly pay.

Two days on the road had brought them to Hector's next stop. The village was called Ancienne, and Ludis had to agree that the name suited it well. It was a simple town of decrepit mud and wattle abodes, clustered around a central chapel. The chapel had to be a thousand years old – ancient by anyone's standards – and Ludis guessed this was from where the town took its name. The chapel was small in comparison to some he'd seen on his travels, and was even smaller than the one he had ministered over back home. Like the other buildings it was built of mud brick, with an outer skin of adobe that was as cracked and weathered as a crone's face. A small tower reared at one end, flat-roofed as opposed to the spire familiar in the north. Ludis was confused by the symbol embossed upon the lintel over the main door. Here was a golden sun, rather than the cross he expected. He wondered if different races had used this chapel over the years; perhaps the Moors had converted it to their use; or the symbol was Christian but from a time before the cross was the supreme symbol of his faith. As Hector had set out his wares, then began calling forward the villagers to trade, Ludis had thought the man safe enough from attack and had approached the chapel. Pushing open the creaking doors he had stepped into cool darkness, a relief from the burning sunlight outside. There were no lamps burning, no votive candles, no sources of light whatsoever, yet the church was small enough that the rays entering the doorway were enough to illuminate a frieze on the back wall. There were paintings that preceded the medieval art of many churches, but still he recognised some of the saints depicted upon the walls. There were – to his surprise – no pictures of Christ or of the Virgin Mother. What did dominate the frieze was another symbol of the sun. No, that wasn't entirely true. When he looked closer the sun had a fiery tail and appeared to be falling to earth. It was in fact a comet or shooting star. He had seen no such symbolism in any church before, and moved closer, making his way between rows of rough-hewn pews.

'*Vous avez enfin venu.*'

Startled by the reedy voice so close to his ear, Ludis had jerked away, and unconsciously his hands had formed fists. He would have sworn that the ancient crone sitting on the pew beside him must have heard the creaking of his ligaments as he unclenched his fists, but for the fact she looked so infirm that her hearing must be as feeble as her body. The old woman was unconcerned by his aggressive stance though, being more intent on a flask she tipped to her lips.

'*Excusez-moi, dame,*' Ludis croaked out, offering the old woman his poor grasp of the language in halting fashion. '*Je n'ai…*uh…*pas vous y voir.*'

'*Vous ne m'avez pas vu?*' The old woman cackled as if his words were a joke: all he'd said was that he had not seen her there. '*Il y a beaucoup de vous ne connaissent pas, gros homme. Bien des choses que vous devez ouvrir vos yeux - et le cœur - de si vous êtes pour accomplir votre mission.*'

Coupled with the rat-a-tat delivery, and unaided by the alcohol that was thickening her tongue, Ludis had no comprehension of her words. '*Pardonnez-moi. Je ne comprends pas.* I do not understand.'

The old woman cackled again. She shifted her weight on the pew, lifting the flask to punctuate her point. 'You are of the cold north: it is lucky I travelled there in my youth. But, though it was a long time ago, my memory of your language serves me well. Better than your French does you, eh?'

The crone was speaking in a dialect particular to his Lithuanian neighbours, but was much easier for him to follow than her French.

'I admit my French is poor. I've been in this land only a short time and my only source of conversation has been with a peddler who thinks everyone should speak Catalan.'

Again the woman laughed – a little too loudly than his jest warranted. He studied her a little closer and noticed that her rheumy eyes were not fixed upon him, but on a spot somewhere over his head. She was feeble of eyesight and, judging by her over-excessive laughter, of mind as well. Or maybe it was simply that she'd supped too much of the alcohol from her flask.

She surprised him in the next moment, her gaze drifting down to settle on him. Because of the heat he had doffed his heavy coat and wore only a canvas shirt, open at the collar. The cross he'd fashioned was nestled among the hairs of his upper chest. 'I see you outwardly proclaim your faith. That is good, big man. It tells me that you are the one I have been expecting.'

'You have been expecting me? What are you, old woman: a prophet?' he had tempered his tone to reassure her that he was making light of his words. Nevertheless, she laughed maniacally once more. In a shapeless blue dress, a chequered apron tied around her middle, and her wispy white hair held back in a knotted handkerchief, she did not look like any priestess or nun he'd come across. He wasn't even sure if she was an official of this church, but the village drunkard who'd crept inside looking for somewhere she could sup undisturbed.

Once she'd settled down, she said, 'It's like I said earlier: there is much you are unaware of, big man. Much that you must open your eyes - and heart - to if you are to complete your mission.'

'What do you know of my mission?'

'Only that it is doomed to failure without the guidance of one more knowledgeable than you are.'

'And this knowledgeable person…that would be you, I take it?' Ludis snorted into his beard. He did not mean to insult the old woman, for it was apparent to him now that she was not only drunk but also crazy. But it was not in his nature to accept the ravings of fools gladly. Even when he was ministering to the simple folk in his chapel he had been both blunt and to the point in his teachings. The woman raised the flask, but it was in acknowledgement, and she did not appear insulted. Ludis shook his head, turning away so she did not see the smile forming on his lips. Typical, he thought, that the first person in an age he could converse with clearly was as mad as a springtime hare. 'Tell me, then, wise woman: what is this place?' He nodded at the mural and the flaming comet burning its way to earth.

'Why,' the old woman said, pausing to take a plug from the flask, 'it is a church, of course.'

'I know that, but it is unlike any church I've been in.'

The old woman struggled to stand, and Ludis offered her his arm. She either didn't see it or was too proud – or too drunk – to accept it. She hobbled past him without a word and approached the far wall. She stood beneath the frieze, dead centre, and reached up to caress the image of the comet with fingers that were swollen and crooked with arthritis.

'Our religion is much older than Christ,' she said in a matter-of-fact fashion, as she lowered her hand.

Having moved to stand behind her, Ludis could see over the top of her head, his face on a level with the burning comet. 'I am familiar with the Old Testament. I am, however, unaware of a falling star having any significance within its pages.'

'That all depends on which version of the Bible you've been indoctrinated in to.' The old woman waved down any objections of heresy. 'If you are so well read, you must know of the *Apocrypha*?'

Ludis was aware of what she was talking about. *Apocrypha* quite literally meant 'hidden things' in Greek, and it was the term used for texts of a Biblical nature that had never formed part of the canonical version of the Book, or had at some time been taken out, due, he'd been taught, for textual issues. Now the old woman was suggesting the real reason for their lack of inclusion was because of doctrinal issues. He would have taken umbrage at her words, had he not often suspected a similar reason. He nodded slowly for her to continue, but she wasn't looking at him, or - even if she was - her eyesight might be so poor that she missed the gesture. 'Go on,' he said.

'In the *Apocrypha* it tells of the great, great grandsons of Adam, who at that time, more than seven thousand years ago, lived in an area southwest of the Black Sea, in the lands later ruled by the Assyrian Tibareni. These brothers were the founders of several industries necessary to the development of man, one of them being the first metallurgist. In one of the lost books it tells that God sent a falling star from the heavens and into the hands of this man, teaching him, the first blacksmith, the value of the metal he took from the heart of the star. Being of the line of Cain, this man thought first to fashion an object true to his nature: a weapon. Angered by the misuse of his gift, God cursed the weapon and bade the smith conceal it in the wilderness. The smith did as he was commanded, but, being of the violent nature of his grandfather, the smith coveted the weapon above all the things that he later forged, and, lest it be lost forever, whispered the secret hiding place to his sons, and they to theirs and so on. Through thousands of years the weapon remained hidden away, but in the time of the first Christian Caesar, the weapon was unearthed and carried by him as a symbol of divine might.'

'That's quite a tale, but nothing more than a myth, surely?'

'A myth? No not a myth but a legend, and in all legends there is a grain of truth.'

'I've heard of this story. You speak of the Spear of Destiny?'

The old woman laughed, but this time there was little humour in the sound. 'I speak of another weapon entirely. I speak of something far more powerful than any Roman lance.'

'Did not Constantine, the first Christian Caesar, wield the spear then?'

'Yes, but the Spear of which you speak is not the one I refer to, neither is it that carried by Constantine The Great.'

Ludis grunted. 'I am confused.'

The old woman shook the flask at him. 'Would you like a slurp? It will help clear your mind.'

Ludis shook his head. Perhaps the old woman wasn't as blind as he'd thought, because she merely walked away. 'Come then, and I'll show you.'

'Show me the weapon?'

She turned and regarded him as if he was a dolt.

'Is it not obvious to you that this shrine is dedicated to the weapon? Are not the signs all around you?' She gestured towards the frieze and its shining image. 'Before you ask: yes, this is the very place on which the shooting star fell.'

'This far from Assyria?' he said scornfully. 'How did the smith make it all the way here?'

'The smith had a good guide, lest you forget.'

Ludis grunted. He found that the woman elicited such a reaction from him with most of her words. Still, he followed her to the front of the church. The old woman tapped her heel and Ludis heard the stone ring hollow beneath her. 'Lend a hand,' she said, 'I am not capable of lifting the trap these days.'

There was a seam in the floor, one that allowed Ludis to hook his fingertips under it and lever up a large slab of stone. He had expected to find a stairwell leading into a cellar, but all that was disgorged was a trough dug from the bare earth. Nestled in the bottom was a plain wooden box. It looked like it wasn't big enough to hold a child's toy, let alone any weapon he knew of.

'Go on and lift it out. Or would you make an old woman bend her back in your place?'

Frowning, Ludis crouched down and grasped the small box. He lifted it up. The box was old, maybe a century or so, but he didn't believe that it could be the vessel of something many thousands of years in age. It was as if the woman understood his doubt. 'The box isn't important. It is simply the container the weapon was transported in when smuggled here to safety during the Revolution. It's what's inside you need to see. Go on, open it.'

Ludis felt a trickle of trepidation creep through him. Though he doubted the old woman, thinking she was quite mad, he couldn't deny that some primordial memory was flitting through his skull. It was as if he had known of this item all of his life, and that something had guided him here in order that he take command of the thing in the box. If he had to pinpoint where the memory surfaced from he could not, but it was there nonetheless. Was there such a thing as preordained fate? As a Christian pastor he would have said no, but as a man whose imagination went much further than his teachings he accepted that mere coincidence did not explain his arrival here. He teased up the lid of the box.

'Wait!'

'What is it,' he asked.

'Before you look upon it. Remember that it is not yours to keep.'

'Don't worry, old woman, I'm no thief.'

'Oh, gladly I'll give you it, big man. But what I mean is that I give you it with one promise from you.'

'And what would that be?'

'That you take it to its rightful destination. You take it and give it to the one who needs it most.'

'Who? Who is the person you speak of?'

The old woman shrugged her shoulders. 'I don't know who it is, but you will when you meet him.'

Frowning at her, thinking she had lost her mind fully, he levered the lid open.

Lying in the bottom of the box among crumpled rags of silk was a triangle of metal no longer than his thumb. It was unremarkable, tarnished almost black and its surface pitted with indentations. 'An arrowhead?' he said.

'It's not an arrowhead you idiot. It is the tip broken from a longer blade.'

'Yes, I see that now.' Ludis could indeed tell that the bottom of the triangle was less tarnished than the rest, with faint stress marks along the edge were it had broken off. He poked at it with his finger, and almost dropped the box and the shard of blade. A charge not unlike static electricity had shot up his arm. Involuntarily he had yelped. The old woman laughed at him.

'Be careful; sometimes it grows hot,' she chuckled.

He looked at her dumbfounded. If the shard was empowered by God or not, it didn't matter. Whatever was the case, it was a remarkable thing. In that moment nothing else meant a thing to him. His overriding need was to touch the shard without being repelled.

The old woman tut-tutted at him. 'First you must promise to do as I asked of you.'

Without pause, he said, 'I promise.'

'That is not enough. You must give your solemn word to God.'

'Then I do that,' said Ludis, crossing himself.

'Good, for if you didn't the shard would strike you down. It is a powerful weapon. as I said.'

Ludis didn't doubt that the metal held some charge, but he was not yet sure that it had anything to do with God. He had found there were other items that could gather static electricity from the atmosphere, which gave quite a kick if you touched them. 'How is it used?'

'That is not for you to know, big man, but for its rightful heir. All you must know is that unless it is delivered in time, the fate of the world is in balance.'

He laughed. 'This thing will decide the outcome of the war, will it?'

'Perhaps. Remember, the Almighty supposedly cursed the original weapon, but that was because it was an evil thing. God's power reversed its potency. There is another such weapon out there and it is being put to a use even the original smith would never have conceived of. This shard could be used to counter it, but time grows short and you have many days of travel ahead of you.'

'Where is it I must go?'

'Follow your nose,' she said.

'Can't you be more specific than that?'

'The stench of warfare shall lead you. You have heard of the rumours of war in the north? Go that way.'

'How will I know when I find the right person to give it to?'

The old woman tipped the flask to her mouth and took a long swig. She wiped her lips on the sleeve of her dress. Then she turned from him and hobbled away, as if she was done with him. Yet, she still had one more piece of advice: 'You will know.'

Chapter 24

18th May 1940
Reims, France

The man that Rifleman Watson led to the barn wasn't quite what any of them had expected. In fact, it was true to say, Renyard hadn't formed any opinion, but had almost expected that the figure spotted lurking out in the shadows was not a man at all but one of the horrible creatures that had plagued their movements for the last few days. He was therefore nonplussed when the slim man, wearing clothes obviously scavenged from a bigger person, was ushered through the door at the point of Watson's bayonet. The man was generally mundane, neither tall nor short, with pale hair cut short to his scalp, and colourless eyes like snow melt. He wore no jewellery, and there was no insignia on his rough clothing, consisting of a black wool button-up jacket over blue coveralls and muddy work boots. Immediately, the sergeant took him for a local, a farm worker, and therefore not worthy of concern. Of course, that was a cavalier attitude for any leader, and he knew that he had to deal with the man very carefully. Without a doubt there would be spies abroad, and this could very well be a German who had come to infiltrate their ranks. Their mission was to sabotage and disrupt the enemy, and it was obvious that the Wehrmacht would have similar agents in the field.

He indicated that Watson move the man to the rear of the barn, where he was to sit down with his back to a beam supporting the upper deck. Watson nudged the man forward, pressing him in the small of the back with the butt of his rifle. Without complaint, the man shuffled to the indicated point, looking abashed more than anything. Renyard wondered if he was a poorly trained agent, and one that was ashamed by his ineptitude. The man placed his back to the beam, using it for support as he slid down. He was weary judging by the way he thumped loosely onto his backside. He immediately pulled his knees up and tucked his arms around them. He sat, looking up at Renyard, his cheeks hollow and his eyelids drooping. Something about those colourless eyes shook Renyard and he didn't know why. It was like looking into a still pool, beneath which lurked a poisonous serpent. Angry with himself, Renyard shook the thought loose. God damn it all, if he wasn't giving in to the fear that had gripped his soul. He'd only recently taken charge again, decided on pro-action, and already he was allowing himself to sink back into the doldrums.

'Watch him,' he said to the other men, who had not yet lowered their weapons. He jerked his head at Watson. 'With me, rifleman: I'd like a word.'

Watson followed him to the front of the barn, far enough away that the man would be unable to hear their conversation, as long as it was at a whisper.

'Tell me about your prisoner.'

'There isn't much to tell, Sarge. I was alerted to him only because I heard him cough. If he hadn't done so, I don't think I'd have noticed him, he was sitting there so still.'

'You didn't see him approach.'

'No, Sarge. Like I said, I only noticed him when he coughed.'

'So it's likely he was there since before we arrived?'

'That's my guess.'

'Then why didn't he make off?'

'Perhaps we surprised him and caught him out. Once we were here he just sat there, hoping for an opportunity to make a getaway. I'm guessing that, if he'd have moved, I'd have seen him, so he thought it best to sit there and wait until he got an opportunity to sneak away.'

'So he sat there for hours, totally still and in silence?'

'Looks that way.'

'And then he makes the mistake of coughing?'

'Maybe he had grown lax, or he'd started to doze off or something. I'm sure he would've covered the cough if he could have.'

'Or he coughed on purpose,' Renyard pointed out, 'to let you know he was there.'

'There's always that,' Watson concurred. 'What do you think, Sarge? He wanted in here to hear our plans?'

Renyard pursed his lips. He wasn't sure what he believed.

'What has he had to say for himself?'

'Nothing.'

'He didn't speak, or he didn't mention anything important?'

'Didn't speak: not one word. He just sat there with his hands on top of his head when I challenged him. He didn't give me any trouble whatsoever.'

'Which enforces my idea that he wanted you to take him prisoner. You searched him for weapons, I take it?'

'Nothing. No other belongings I could find, either.'

'What do you make of him, Watson?'

'I think he's a refugee, and he's hungry and cold and thinks we might be his best bet for a free meal.'

'Not much chance of that is there?' Renyard said ruefully, because there was very little to sustain the section either.

Conspiratorially the two men turned to look the man over. He was sitting as they'd left him, hugging his knees to his chest. His head was down now, as though he found something interesting in the dirty straw beneath his boots.

Renyard nodded at his decision. 'Come on, we'll get to know more if we go ask him. I'll need you to translate for me.'

They approached the prisoner, the others making way for them, but still holding their weapons ready, as if they expected the man to leap up and attack at any second. Corporal Green was overseeing the scene from his high perch, and Blanco Tyler had found an excuse to stay inside by guarding the stranger. Renyard knocked Whitey and Taff Jones' elbows. 'Sentry duty is all yours, lads.'

The two riflemen looked a tad annoyed that they had to give up the relative comfort of the barn, as well as the chance to watch the interrogation of the prisoner. Talk about fishwives, Renyard thought, there's no one as nosy as a bloody soldier. They slipped outside, with jealous glances directed at their mates remaining inside. Cooper, McCoy and Blanco took a few steps away, allowing Renyard and Watson to stand over the man. Taking the hint also, Green sidled back to where he'd been watching the countryside through the hatch.

Silence is sometimes the best tool in an interrogation, and Renyard waited, allowing the man to grow conscious of his closeness, to order his words and to offer explanation. The man said nothing, but he did lift his head and regard the sergeant. His expression was still one of shame, or perhaps sadness?

'Ask him who he is,' Renyard finally directed Watson.

'*Quel est votre nom?*'

The man didn't reply.

'Again.'

'*Quel est votre nom?*'

The stranger looked confused.

'He is French, isn't he?'

'*Êtes-vous français? Où voulez-vous venir?*' Watson asked, demanding also to know where he came from.

The stranger shook his head.

'*Allemand?* Do you speak German? *Parlez-vous allemande?*' Realising the stupidity of his question, Watson rephrased it in the proper language. '*Sprechen sie Deutch?*'

The man shook his head slowly.

'You don't speak English by any chance, do you?' Watson tried, but again to a blank look. 'Polska? Russkii? Shit, Sarge, I don't know what else to try.'

Renyard considered the conundrum. There weren't too many languages spoken in the near vicinity that the man shouldn't have recognized one of them. Either he was from much further afield, or a damn liar. Suddenly a third explanation struck Renyard. He crouched down, to meet the man eye to eye. Reaching out, he touched the man's shoulder, and then brought his finger to his own chest. Slowly, enunciating his words clearly he said, 'I am British. My name is Sergeant Renyard. Who are you?'

The stranger shook his head, indicated incomprehension at the foreign words. But then nodded, cupped both his hands over his ears.

Renyard stood up. 'He's deaf.'

'Isn't that just a little too handy?' Watson asked. 'For a spy, I mean. What better way to overhear someone's plans than pretend you can't hear a bloody thing?'

'Yeah,' Renyard admitted, straightening up. 'We can't take the chance. Take him outside and shoot him.'

'Uh?'

Renyard wasn't listening for a comeback from the coldly delivered order; he was too busy studying the stranger for a response. Even a disciplined spy, feigning deafness, couldn't help a reaction of some kind. There was not a hint of a flinch, or even an involuntary widening of the eyelids. Renyard was certain that the man had heard nothing of what he'd said. He was a damn poor spy if he was stone deaf, and Renyard doubted that he'd been drafted into any army. Chances were he was exactly what Watson had assumed already: a refugee seeking warmth and sustenance.

Watson and Renyard shared a glance, and there was relief in the young man's face, having realised that the Sergeant had been playing a trick. Renyard offered a faint smile, then crouched down in front of the man again. He touched the man's shoulder, establishing contact and then pointed at the man before motioning towards his mouth. He mimed eating.

The man nodded enthusiastically, and from his throat came a moan of pleasure that was almost animalistic. Poor sod, Renyard thought, he's deaf *and* dumb.

'We're going to feed him?' Watson asked. 'Are you sure he's not pulling the wool over our eyes, Sarge?'

Renyard shrugged. The trouble was he wasn't sure about anything, but maybe if they were kind to the man then – if he was playing a part – something would give him away when his guard was relaxed. Perhaps Renyard had played his hand too early with the man, because a clever spy might have anticipated the bluff about taking him outside to shoot him, so Renyard thought he'd try again later. In the meantime, he hoped everyone would keep their lips sealed and mention nothing about their plans.

'He might come in handy,' Renyard announced. 'For when we move from here.' He'd couched his words so that the men were aware for a need for caution around the stranger. The arrival of the refugee had somewhat stalled his plan to get moving, but it might turn out a boon if the man was what he appeared to be. Someone with knowledge of the surrounding countryside could come in very handy to their mission. 'Someone find the bloke something to eat: he'll be no good to any of us if he collapses from starvation.'

'He's my prisoner,' Watson pointed out. 'I'll see to it.'

'No,' Renyard said. 'You're the best scout we have, I think it's better that you aren't tied down to him. Rifleman McCoy, you get something for him.'

McCoy grunted an affirmative, then went to root in their packs for something left over from their previous meal – which wasn't much to start with.

'You want me to go back outside and keep watch?' Watson asked.

'No…not yet. Try to get some rest: you deserve it.' Renyard moved in close to whisper: 'We'll be moving out soon, so long as nothing else happens.'

His words proved too prophetic than he would have liked, for in the next moment he heard a soft thud from outside, followed by the yelp of a man. Renyard recognized the voice. The sound of pain wouldn't mean an awful lot under other circumstances, because Taff Jones was clumsy at the best of times and regularly elicited such noises, but even he should find it difficult hurting himself when standing sentry duty. Renyard spun to the entry door just as a shout rang out and there followed the burp of a machinegun.

Without warning there was a flash and corresponding bang and splintered timbers ripped through the interior of the barn. If Renyard had been a few feet closer to the doors the flying debris would have torn him apart. As it was, the shock of the exploding grenade picked him up and threw him backwards to the floor. He hit hard, bouncing and rolling, his hearing numbed by the concussion. He staggered up, movement all around him as the men sought protection from the incoming armament. Distantly he could hear Corporal Green yelling for the gunners, while a cacophony of panic spread among the others. From outside came a rattle of gunfire, and Whitey shouting a redundant warning that they were under attack.

Shivering with adrenalin – and maybe a little fear – Renyard ran to conceal himself behind slotted beams that formed an animal pen. Readying his SMLR, he worked his jaw to regain full hearing, and in the next moment wished that he hadn't. Rounds punctured the walls of the barn, making hissing and popping sounds as they cut through the aged wood. Inside the barn there was an occasional metal implement and when the bullets struck them the sounds were much louder and more terrifying. But nothing was as horrible as the *thwack* of bullets through flesh, and Renyard heard these too. McCoy, who had been bent over, delving in the packs for scraps of food, had been the last to react to the attack and, having dumped what he was carrying, he had struggled to pull his weapon off his shoulder. He was still out in the open. Bullets tore through him, lifting him on his toes and holding him there like a dancing marionette. Then it was as if the strings had been cut and he flopped to the earth, and there was no way Renyard believed he'd rise up again. The death of another of his lads, plus that of Taff Jones outside, hit Renyard like a battering ram. But this time, instead of striking him with depression, it charged him like a dynamo.

He roared orders, preparing the section to repel the assault on the barn that was sure to follow this initial surprise attack. He took stock of who was left: Cooper, Watson, Whitey and Corporal Green. Outside, he hoped that Blanco had avoided the sneak attack that had taken out Taff. Then his gaze fell on the stranger.

He was supposed to be deaf: but an inability to hear anything would mean nothing when surrounded by this chaos. Renyard blinked at the man, trying to make sense of what he witnessed.

Calmly the man had stood up, and Renyard watched as he stripped out of his cumbersome jacket and stood bare-chested. He held his hands at his sides, and then slowly raised them, palms out, while bending back his head, and he opened his mouth to issue a strange howl that wasn't so much animalistic as it was bestial. Then the stranger lowered his face and fixed his gaze on the shattered remains of the doors. He grinned, savage and feral, and it was as if colour flooded his pale eyes. It could have been the flash of gunfire, but Renyard would swear that the man's eyes glowed like lambent flames.

Who were the German attackers seeking to kill here?

Us, Renyard wondered, or *him*?

Chapter 25

18th May 1940
Eastern France

After recalling the events that took place in Ancienne all those weeks ago, Ludis could not rouse himself to approach the small town below him. He'd remained where he'd sat, his back against the boulders as rain pattered down. His mind was too full of memories of how he'd said a brief goodbye to his travelling companion, Hector, and then strode out, accepting the mission set for him by the crazy woman. He wondered now if there was more to that old crone than met the eye and if she had somehow mesmerized him, employing mind tricks to send him off on a hazily described quest without as much as an argument from him. There were many questions left unanswered, and it struck him now, how he'd so readily accepted the woman's fanciful story of cursed artefacts and the necessity to deliver a chunk of metal to an unnamed recipient, where to fail might mean the end of the world. He had been played, all right. But he had to question whom it was that had set all of this in motion. He had mulled the problem over on many occasions before this and had come to the same conclusion each time: God had directed him. Even after Galina was murdered, he had chosen to believe that God had sent him on an errand in order that he was spared the attack of the Upir and his Nosferatu thralls on the village. Ludis had believed that it was to allow him to then avenge his people, send the devil back to hell, and reinstate the equilibrium between this world and the next. Had he not left the village that day, and the hunt for the deer taken him many miles and hours away, he would not be sitting here now, guardian of a cursed shard of metal. Had that been God's plan all along? Had he been prodded and poked across the war-torn lands, first to the Upir's lair, then on to Ancienne and the crazy woman, and hence to Borvo's hut in the wild woods by the hand of his God? He would not believe that. God, despite His cruel and vengeful disposition, would not punish His servant so. No, something else was behind this scheme, and he only had one answer. Borvo had said that the shard spoke to him. Ludis had thought the man as touched in the head as the old crone who'd given him the shard was, but now he wasn't so sure. Perhaps the shard had been speaking to Ludis all along, in the subconscious quarters of his brain that forbade him from denying its influence, and it was the force bending him to its will. The crone told him that God cursed the weapon: well, what if it was the evil within this shard that was tugging at the strings of fate and propelling him on this journey?

He had taken out the shard, still wrapped in its protective cloth, and held it in his hand. He had sat there, the rain growing steadier, and listened closely. He couldn't hear a thing except the pitter-patter of rain on his skull. The warmth from the shard had increased marginally but that was all. Confused by it all, he'd put it away again and secured the satchel on his belt. Whatever, whoever, was behind everything, he would only be happy when he handed over the damned thing to its *rightful heir*. He only wished he had a clue who the men were that Borvo spoke of, because without any idea of who they were, then how was he meant to find them? He supposed that – if the more than coincidental meetings with the crone and Borvo had been engineered – then he could simply sit there on the hill and they would find their way to him. But that wasn't going to happen. Ludis wasn't the type to shirk his duty, and if he had ended up here at the bequest of his God or otherwise, then he was not about to change his ways now.

He had stood up, shouldered his new rifle, and made his way down from the hilltop. He had skirted the silent village, for nothing in it tugged at him, the way it would if he was supposed to go there, and he'd marched into the next valley and followed a stream towards a deeper river whose banks were wooded and offered some refuge from the rain. The woodland also made him invisible to the troop movement he could hear through the rain, and he was able to progress a few miles north without seeing another human being. At a bend in the river, where it twisted south and took him off his route, he looked for somewhere to cross, and this time, instead of having to rely on algae-slick steppingstones, he found an arching stone bridge. Checking that he was unobserved, he jogged over the bridge and then immediately lost himself in the woods on the northern side. These woods were ancient, with thick gnarled trunks and branches that bent almost to the ground. In the summer, the foliage would be so thick that there would have been no easy route, but now, with only buds on the branches, he found he could squeeze through. Despite that, the going was slow and he considered finding his way back to the road, and forging ahead with little to impede him.

The rain stopped, but it was little blessing. Moisture now hung in the night air, wraithlike bands of fog drifting between the tree trunks. The swirling fog reminded Ludis of the shadowy things that had served the Upir and set his teeth on edge. He was pleased when he found the far edge of the wood and came out into tilled fields again. The fog was still here, but it reminded him now of nothing but the mist rolling in from the Baltic Sea during the autumn months.

Now, instead of causing him illogical fear, the fog was his friend, because it meant he could travel at speed with little worry of discovery. High up in the night sky a squadron of German bombers headed for parts unknown to him and he stopped for a moment to watch their droning black shapes cutting through the clouds. Unconsciously he rubbed at his beard, and was surprised to find the unfamiliar touch of skin on skin. He'd worn the beard so long now that it had become a part of him, and was missed like an old friend. He thought that it had been the correct decision to shave, though, as it was to cut off his hair, because he wanted to be greeted as a civilized man and not a wild beast when finally he met the mystery men.

That thought started him moving again, and he trudged through more fields sown to crops that he suspected would go without harvest this year. What a waste of food it would be, he lamented. The thought of food had the usual effect: his stomach began to growl, reminding him that he'd eaten nothing substantial in days. The onion broth he'd concocted was both bland and with little nutritional value, and he now felt a real desire to sink his teeth into a solid hunk of meat. There were no animals out in the fields, though, and he did not have the time or inclination to lay snares to catch a rabbit. He pushed on, watching for signs of habitation where he could perhaps forage for more succulent pickings than a few withered vegetables.

The fields were dotted by small copses of trees. He avoided them now, trusting to the fog to conceal him from any observer, and began to jog. The activity helped his body to warm, and now there were similar tendrils of mist rising from his shoulders as the rainwater evaporated from his clothing. He continued at a steady pace, holding his rifle tight to his body to avoid making any noise that might carry far. The soft thud of his boots through loose earth wouldn't travel more than a few yards in the cloaking fog. The ground began to rise, and he crested a hilltop. The fog banks were beneath him, looking like lakes in the hollows of the land, and he could see other peaks that reared from the fog like islands in a pale sea. Outlined on the hill he was in danger of being seen, but he also had a good view out across the land and could discern no movement. Despite the apparent abandonment of the area, he trusted that others were moving through the landscape, so he was quick to descend into the cover of the fog once more.

He travelled another couple of miles, cresting and descending the folds in the land, and again found a road. In all likelihood it was the same one by which he'd crossed the river earlier, but, whereas he'd had to follow the contours of the hills, this road had taken a more direct route through the countryside. He could see a weathered milestone, and crouched down to wipe away the grit adhering to it. A broad cross was depicted upon it, and the single word REIMS etched into the stone. It was a cathedral town, he guessed, from the Christian emblem, and lay only a handful of miles away. He had no desire to visit a town, though, so turned from it and plunged from the road and back into fields. Again he found a stand of trees bordering another wide swathe of land set to crops. The fog had cleared here, and he could see a good distance now that the moonlight had found egress through the broken clouds. At the end of a triangular plot of land, its boundaries marked by a picket fence, he could make out a cluster of farm buildings, dominated by a large barn. He eyed the barn keenly, imagining a soft bed of hay, and perhaps a lamb or piglet its owners might not miss. Much as he was loath to stoop to thievery, he was desperate enough that he'd take what he needed and beg God for forgiveness afterwards. If God were behind his quest, then maybe He'd allow the minor slip when it came to obeying His commandments, because, after all, theft was one of the lesser sins man was guilty of these days.

Ludis took a step forward. Then he halted, becoming motionless.

Figures were moving through the darkness on the far side of the field from which he stood. They were swathed in black uniforms; even their features were concealed behind hoods beneath their Romanesque-shaped helmets. The group, approximately a dozen in all were doing their best to advance on the farm with care. Ludis knew that if he moved quickly he would be seen, so very gently he lowered himself down to a crouch, watching as the mystery men advanced towards the barn. Ludis peered that way now, wondering who were the targets of these men's stealthy approach, and he saw a figure step momentarily out from the edge of the barn. Even at this distance Ludis saw and recognised the bowl shape and flaring rim of the British soldier's helmet.

Ludis did not owe allegiance to either side. However, on hearing of Nazi depravities from the refugees he'd camped with, his sympathies lay firmly in the British court. Yet this was not his fight. If he tried to warn the British soldier about those creeping up on him, then it would bring the German soldiers down on him. The German's wore different uniforms than those he'd witnessed to date, and judging by the skill with which they were moving on the farm, he took them to be a crack troop of some sort. Having them chasing him through the French countryside would only end one way. It would be best if he sneaked away while they were otherwise engaged and continue with his own quest. Let fate decide the outcome of the battle here: if God wanted the British to win, then that would be the outcome…without Ludis risking his skin. The thought irked him: was he allowing cowardice to creep into his soul? He was – or at least used to be – a minister of the Christian faith; he could not turn his back and walk away and allow cold-blooded murder. Not when a simple signal from him would be enough to put the British on their guard, and on a much better footing.

He was still crouching there, formulating a plan to alert the British sentry when he realised his mistake. The German's had moved in on the barn, not only from this direction but from simultaneous sides all at once. He caught a sudden movement to the left of the sentry, and even in the darkness, recognised it as a man coming up from the ground and pouncing towards him. Ludis opened his mouth to shout a warning, but it was too late. In the German's hand was a knife, and he had grabbed the sentry from behind, tugged back his head and swiped the blade across his throat before the words built in Ludis' mouth. The sentry emitted a yelp of pain, but that was all he managed. His killer released him and he fell, his shoulder bouncing off the wall of the barn.

Ludis shuddered at the man's death. His inability to take action sooner had allowed a gruesome murder. Well, he would not allow the same thing to happen to anyone else.

His determination proved redundant again.

A second British sentry, more alert than the first, came from the opposite corner of the barn, just as the German troopers in the field began a run towards it. He bellowed a warning to his colleagues, who must have been inside. At a run a German fired his machinegun at the sentry, but Ludis saw that the man had already dropped to the floor and was levelling his rifle to shoot. More machineguns joined the first, but the sentry seemed to have found a dip in the earth and he was able to weather the attack and return fire. Not that Ludis gave him much chance at survival, because his was one gun against many.

Fire lit the scene as a grenade was thrown against the front doors of the barn. Ludis jerked back out of instinct, but he was too far away to fear the flying debris. When next he looked, the sentry appeared to have crawled away – or he was dead – because there was no counter fire from his position. All the bullets now were from German guns.

While the fight progressed Ludis should take the opportunity to sneak away. In essence it was no different from how he'd attempted to escape the battle between the French and German troops in the river valley a few days earlier. Except this time it felt different: on that occasion the armies had been well matched, whereas here, those in the barn were sitting ducks. The Germans had the element of surprise on their side, as well as overwhelming forces. Guilt assailed Ludis, telling him he should at least *try* to do something to help the cornered British. But what could he do?

He decided he wasn't going to run away. He began moving forward, on a parallel line, albeit a healthy distance to the rear, of the German's moving towards the barn through the field. Beyond the barn, others had taken up the fight, and muzzle flash lit up the far side of the farm. From within the wooden structure the British tried to return fire, but they had no real targets and their shooting was random and ineffective. One German trooper ran almost to the door, and then unloaded a magazine full of bullets through the gap caused by the explosion. Others making a skirmish line moved forward, and they too began unloading on the barn. Ludis thought that it must be hell inside the structure by now, with no escape for those trapped there. He gripped his rifle firmly, thought to offer them a chance at escape by bringing down their attackers from behind. He went to one knee, bringing the rifle stock to his shoulder and sighted along the barrel. He had a German in his sights, but he couldn't pull the trigger. He could not shoot a man in the back. Face to face might be a different issue altogether but not like this. He began to rise up again, but something strange forced him back to his knee.

There were three German soldiers moving in on the barn, and they did not carry rifles or machineguns. Two of them lugged large poles with a trio of barbed tips on the end. They were unlike tridents, or pitchforks, because these three points were arranged almost akin to the legs of a tripod. The third soldier had a different type of pole, this one supporting a noose and rope that the soldier held in his other hand. Back in Ludis' village, the local rat catcher had employed a similar contraption when hunting vermin, but this was much larger. The three implements were strange enough, but it was the fact that they shone silver in the night that had caused Ludis pause. The tools – or weapons – looked archaic to an extreme and had no place in this modern field of war, and Ludis couldn't fathom their use. He was still wondering when another grenade detonated against the barn door, bursting the remains inwards, and some of the German soldiers rushed in. Guns exchanged thunder, and Ludis thought that it was a pointless exercise offering assistance to those within the barn now. More German's approached the front of the barn, and the shooting stopped, but now shouted challenges were raised. Ludis saw the trio of men rush into the structure, their strange weapons extended before them.

Still unsure of what to do, Ludis continued to crouch there in the field, listening as men's voices rose and fell in pitch. Then he heard something else. Someone was howling and at first he believed it was the death cries of many dying men, but then he realised that the voice was born of one throat. At much the same time, he felt something stir at his hip, and, dumbfounded, he slapped a hand down on his satchel. Inside it, the sliver of metal was vibrating, the tremors rising in speed and agitation, as if the shard was responding to the pitch of the growing howl.

Ludis snapped his gaze back towards the barn.

Who was inside? Were the British defenders the men from the north that Borvo had sent him to meet? Was the howling man the one he'd been seeking: the shard's rightful heir? It seemed there was no doubt that the shard and he shared some sort of common bond, otherwise why would it react so?

One thing that Ludis couldn't do now was retreat. He must do all that he could to ensure that the German's failed to capture the British soldiers. He stood up, and feeling the shaking of the shard pass through his entire frame, he strode forward. If God truly ordained his quest then what else could he do but face it head-on?

Chapter 26

18th May 1940
Reims, France

Sergeant Renyard was seeing red – literally. The blood was
pounding through his veins with such force that the capillaries in his
retinas were swollen and tingeing his vision. In his ears there was a hush,
like wind heard from beyond heavily shuttered windows. Only the
sharpest of sounds impinged in his mind, usually being the cries of his
men, or the impact of bullets caroming off the metal farm implements
nearby. He was in full battle mode, and his vision had tunnelled tight, so
that he was seeing only things directly in front of him but with stark
clarity, and it seemed everything around him moved in slow motion. He
thought that he would be able to track the course of each individual
bullet as it tumbled past him, reach out and snatch the projectile from
the air. The only problem was that he also seemed to be moving as
slowly as everything else.

Seconds had passed since he'd turned from the crumpled form of
Rifleman McCoy, his attention falling on the stranger and his odd antics.
It was as though Renyard was wading through soup as he twisted from
the man to the front door, bringing up his rifle. Shadows swarmed
beyond the flames left over from the grenade, indistinct, but obviously
the forms of the enemy firing indiscriminately through the walls of the
barn. Renyard acted on instinct, shooting back at them. Others of the
section were shooting too, and in some dim recess of his mind, Renyard
could hear Corporal Green yelling for the Bren gun. Over everything
rose the keening pitch of the stranger's howl, a challenge to the Germans
that was at once exultant and demanding.

Despite the necessity to pinpoint the enemy, and to cut them down,
Renyard found his attention drifting to the man behind him.

The stranger had stripped down to his trousers. He was slim, almost
to a point of absurdity, but Renyard noted that it wasn't through
malnutrition. The man's physicality was unlike anything the sergeant had
seen before. His skin – once pale and soft - looked almost leather-like
now, and muscles bulged and pulsed beneath it, ligaments and tendons
standing out like ropes. His skeletal make-up just wasn't right, either, as
if he possessed too many bones than a human body could contain.

Given the time to ponder the strange metamorphosis, Renyard would have also said that the man appeared to have grown a full foot in height, and his shoulders broadened in stature. It was almost as if his form was malleable, that he'd been stretched and pressed and his body reformed by the hand of a demented sculptor.

Renyard shook his head. The transformation had to be a trick of his over-active mind. Just as time seemed to have slowed, and his hearing had muffled, this weird sight must be a product of the adrenalin pulsing through his body. Whereas some of his senses were compounded, others had been heightened, and that must have been what he was experiencing now. The man's size and shape had to be a product of the fact Renyard was close to the floor, looking up and back from a skewed perspective. Yes. That had to be it, because anything else was beyond belief.

Another grenade exploded and Renyard was forced down, his arms covering his head. Before the debris had settled, he groped for where he'd dropped his SMLR but all his fingers found was hard-packed dirt. He scrabbled around, searching for the revolver on his hip now. By the time he'd grabbed his sidearm and pulled it free from its holster the tide of battle had changed for the worse. Figures were rushing in now, their machineguns blazing. Renyard heard the harsh curses of one of his men, but could not determine which over the rising howl of the stranger. Then there was a tumult of sound, interspersed by flashes and sparks, and the angry shouts of men intent on killing.

Chaos reigned.

Remarkably, Renyard found that he'd managed to crawl away from the stall where he'd taken cover and was now lying under a cart, his gun extended between the spokes of a wheel whose tyres had deteriorated and the rims had buried themselves in the dirt. He was still shooting but the hammer was falling on empty chambers. Around him the guns of his section had fallen silent as well, but then, so had the guns of the Germans.

Renyard had only an impression of their attackers, men swathed in jet uniforms, and whose only insignia was silver lightning bolts on their stiff collars. They wore the distinctive helmets synonymous with the Wehrmacht, but even these had been painted black, and the men hid their faces behind dark hoods. Only their eyes could be seen. Renyard searched their gazes for signs of mercy, but they were fixated. They weren't interested in Renyard or the others; to a man they were all staring at the howling stranger. When Renyard searched for the faces of his men, he found that they had all turned to regard their prisoner as well. Shaking confusion from his mind, Renyard followed their stares, straining round to where he'd last seen the supposed refugee.

His scream had not diminished any, in fact, it had grown louder and more needy than before, but the man had crouched down, and his hands were now clasped between his bent knees. Hunched as he was his skull projected forward, and his mouth hung wide, teeth as white as snow. But it was his eyes that caught and held Renyard's attention. There was no muzzle flash now, and the small flames around the shattered door were concealed behind the Germans clustered inside, so it couldn't be either that gave the orbs the look of hot coals this time. Renyard had seen similar eyes before: once in the casement, once more in the faces of the simian-like creatures that had attacked from the trees. But, if eyes were the mirrors of the soul, and levels of malevolence could be measured in them, then those other creatures paled in significance next to the evil radiating from the stranger.

There was a clatter from the front door and Renyard spared a glance that way, before returning his gaze to the stranger. Busy trying to make sense of what was happening, the arrival of more German soldiers wasn't enough to tear his attention from him. Then the unconventional weapons wielded by the newcomers struck him and he turned again to regard the soldiers. Two of them carried long poles tipped with a trio of barbed points, while the third had a pole with a noose attached. Those weren't weapons of war, but more akin to implements carried by slavers in previous centuries. Yet no slaver had ever hefted tools such as these, because Renyard knew that they were solid silver: even the rope noose was woven from silver thread. Neither Renyard nor his section was the target here, and pure bad luck had brought them into conflict with the German troop. That wasn't to say that the Germans wouldn't kill them all to get at their main quarry.

The stranger was rising up to his feet. Renyard saw the Germans stiffen; their heads tilt to follow his progress. Renyard swung back to watch him. The stranger stood tall and proud, but his gaze had fallen on the strange tools, and unless Renyard was mistaken the timbre of the man's howl had changed. Was that wariness edging its way into the sound?

Renyard felt a prod in his leg. Looking up he saw a German standing over him. The soldier's gun was pointing directly at his face, but Renyard was unconcerned: the German merely used the gun to direct him out of the way. Across the barn he saw that his men were also being ushered to a far corner. Their guards didn't bother to strip their weapons, or even keep an eye on them. Every one of the German troopers was too enrapt in the single figure they had come to capture. Renyard recognised a chance of escape, and, without argument, he rolled from under the cart and scrambled over to the trio of men huddled in the corner, collecting his dropped rifle on the way. As he approached, the lads were full of unspoken questions, but Renyard shook his head, commanding silence from them. Up above them all Corporal Green had slipped away from the edge of the upper floor, and so long as he didn't make too much noise, he would continue to go unnoticed by their enemies. Then again, the corporal could be screaming blue murder and he would receive as little notice as the rest of them.

In the few seconds that his back was turned, things had changed irrevocably. Soldiers had fanned out, making a semi-circle around the bare-chested stranger, and they held him under threat of their machineguns. The stranger seemed little concerned about the guns, but he was watching the advance of the trio with the poles with new intensity. His mute status was now a thing of the past, because now he was making a series of low hisses, and interspersed between the sibilance was definable syllables, but not in a language that Renyard understood. The Germans also were talking, but their language was also lost on Renyard, though he took their low murmurs to be warnings to the three men with the poles. The trio was now almost in range of the stranger, and the two with the tri-pronged spears moved to close on him, their poles levelled like halberds. The third soldier loosened his rope, making the noose hang wider: enough to encircle both head and shoulders.

Before the trident men could advance further, the stranger moved. He had stood so calmly, egging them towards him with his taunting words, that he had momentarily lulled them into expecting an easy capture. Now he moved with shocking abruptness. He stooped and shot forward at an angle so that he passed beneath the trident of the man on the left. Shouts rang out as the man tried to bring round his weapon. Too late: the warning fell on deaf ears. Before the man could recognise the feint, the stranger dodged back the way he'd come and grabbed the rim of the soldier's helmet with one hand, while his other stiffened hand speared in and out. It was as though his braced fingers was a blade of iron, the way they pierced the man's chest. When they pulled out they glistened with blood. The soldier was mortally wounded, but his would-be slayer wasn't finished yet. He tore back and up on the helmet, breaking free the chin strap, but not before the soldier's neck was violently twisted and broke with an audible *crack!*

Machineguns opened fire. Bullets punched into the stranger, knocking him back on his heels. He shuddered at the impact, but that was as much as the hurt extended. The bullets – though they struck him and the force was enough to stagger him – did not pierce his skin. But that was not the purpose of the shooting, Renyard realised. The Germans were only firing at him to give another of them an opportunity to snatch up the discarded pole. The stranger was pushed back and he braced his spine against the upright beam where he'd earlier sat. He swung his arms as if batting aside the spray of bullets striking him. The second pole-wielder rushed in and jammed the three barbs into his midriff. The stranger roared, and even from the far corner of the barn, Renyard saw bilious smoke rise from his flesh and the stench of charred meat filled the place. The noose-man edged forward and tried to lasso the stranger's head. Yet his actions weren't as determined as they needed to be. The stranger tore loose from the trident and swung away so that the beam was between him and his tormentor. Then he snapped down a hand and grabbed at the pole jabbing towards him. More smoke peeled from his clenched fist, but he withstood the agony and wrenched free the second trident pole. He threw it behind him like the reviled thing it was. The noose-man tried to rush in, looping a coil of silver rope over the stranger's head. Again he wasn't quick enough and the loop missed. In a blur the stranger sprang at the soldier, and he grasped hand and pole together. He wrenched up and away, and the pole came free – along with the arm ripped clean from its socket.

There was a moment of panic among the soldiers inside the barn: orders were screamed now, and men scrambled to retrieve the silver poles, but it wasn't as slick or as confident a manoeuvre as had been their initial assault on the barn. Renyard knew that this was their best opportunity for escape. The German troopers were too engrossed in the task at hand to bother about their prisoners; the British were mere men while they faced a monster. Renyard gave the order and the section broke for the front door, the sergeant taking the rear and covering them with his rifle. A couple of the Germans glanced their way, undecided in what they should do, but each turned quickly back to the on-going fight with the stranger. Renyard watched as Blanco made it to the door, Watson and Cooper hot on his heels, but he was too astounded by what he'd already witnessed not to take another look at the stranger. A couple of Germans had retrieved the trident poles and were prodding him back; the way lion tamers controlled a big cat with chairs. Others continued firing their guns at the figure and the noise was tremendous. While they had him moving away, another man picked up the noose pole, but had to prize free the arm of its original handler before he could bring it to use. In that moment the lack of attention was the death of the soldier. The stranger swiped the edge of his hand across the man's throat and head and helmet went flying in gouts of blood.

Renyard blinked in horror, shook himself and turned to follow his men out the door.

He caromed against a huge figure, rebounded and went down on his backside in the dirty straw.

Dear God, Renyard thought, what new horror has come for us now?

Chapter 27

18th May 1940
Reims, France

The sound of battle should have been enough to send any wise man scuttling in search of a hiding place where he would continue to go unnoticed. By the number of bullets discharged, the screams of dying or injured men, there was a bloodbath underway, and no way possible that one man could do a thing to change the outcome. Yet, Ludis didn't turn away. He continued trotting towards the barn, his approach undetected by any of the German soldiers still yet to enter the barn. Between the ill-fitting planks of the building's walls, the flash of gunfire made a strobe effect, causing static objects to stutter as their shadows were cast in dozens of directions. Either the British were offering superhuman resistance, or their slayers believed in overkill. The howling sound had stopped at least, but now it had been replaced by the screams of the dying. Ludis wasn't sure which noise was the more perturbing.

As he ran, he was conscious of the vibrating coming from the shard in his satchel. Heat emanated from it, all the way through the fabric of the bag, the tails of his coat and his trousers, and before long he believed his skin would be seared. He ignored the burning and the vibration, accepting that this was a sign that he had indeed found the men he'd been seeking, and therefore there was no need to ponder the shard further. He was in slight flux nonetheless: which group of men was its recipient? At first he'd thought it had to be the British soldiers, because the name whispered to him by Borvo had been English, but having seen the tools carried by the Germans he now understood that they too were on a mission to contain the horrors stalking the land. It was evident now that the howling man was no man at all, but the thing that they sought. Instinct made him deny the notion that the Germans were allies in his fight: he would not seek friendship from men who committed the kind of brutality they were engaged in. Even if they were on a mission from God, he would defy them. He had to help the British soldiers, or he would die trying.

Not all of the Germans had gone inside yet. Those that had advanced on the barn from the far side were still to enter, having only just come forward to secure the perimeter. Thankfully their attention was on what was happening beyond those walls, and Ludis was able to advance almost to the front doors. He looked to the left and saw the corpse of the British sentry whose throat had been cut at the outset. There was nothing that Ludis could do for him; even prayer would make no difference now. He looked for the second Tommy who had come under fire, but there was no sign of him. Ludis hoped the man had survived and had crept off somewhere to hide until the fighting was over. Two German soldiers were standing directly ahead of him. Again their uniforms struck Ludis as odd. They were unlike anything he'd seen – or even heard of – and he could only assume that they had been designed specifically for this crack squad whose mission was of a different purpose than any other Nazi. The lightning bolts on their collars were the only distinguishing marks he could discern, but they were enough to send a shudder of hatred through Ludis. According to the travellers with whom he'd shared a campfire, it was these SS who were behind the mass murders and genocide ordered by their *Führer*. Driven by righteous fury Ludis hefted his rifle like a club.

One German heard him coming, and glanced round. Perhaps he was expecting another of his murderous friends, because he didn't react as though he was facing an enemy. With his face swathed in a hood it was difficult to make out his reaction when he saw he was mistaken. By the time he'd opened his mouth to call a warning to his friend Ludis had brought the rifle down. Ludis avoided hitting the helmet, aiming instead for the side of the man's neck. The thud was muffled as the stock slammed down into flesh, and the man dropped unconscious to the floor, but it was still enough to bring around the other soldier. Ludis was already moving, bringing around the rifle in a backswing, and he rammed the stock into the man's jaw. The soldier let out a croak of pain, brought up his machinegun and fired. Thankfully he was already verging on unconsciousness and his aim went high and over the top of Ludis' head. Ludis struck him again for good measure and the man went down on his back. Nearby, other soldiers alerted by the unexpected gunfire shouted questions, and Ludis rushed forward for the barn door before they could get him in their sights. Going inside so soon was never on his agenda, but there was nothing for it now.

As he made the shattered remains of the door, he was about to duck inside when a trio of figures came out at a run. His instinct was to bring round his rifle, and he stood like a Neanderthal threatening the three men with a club. One of them, backlit so that he was no more than a silhouette, brought up his rifle in response. Neither man fired. Maybe the soldier had recognised Ludis for what he was and not the enemy, the same way in which Ludis noted the outline of the man's helmet and understood that he was British and therefore a friend. Ludis had some English in his repertoire of words, and speaking recently to the soldier hunted by the ghoul, he'd had some practice. He grabbed at the slim man, got a handful of his serge jacket and dragged him down. 'Stay low,' he hissed in command.

The other two soldiers followed his direction without argument, dropping quickly to the floor and crawling past him. Ludis paused only for a second or two, listening for gunfire from the Germans outside, but none came yet. He had done what he could for them, and it was down to the British soldiers to find cover for themselves; he had to check for anyone left inside. Decision made, he stepped around the doorframe and into a scene torn from the fabric of hell.

Ludis had only the briefest of seconds to take in the figure at the far side of the barn, the men swarming around it, prodding and jabbing with their archaic tools, the torn and dismembered bodies scattered in front of it. Then another figure slammed into him, rebounded from his sturdier frame and went down on its back in the blood-spattered earth. The collision was enough that Ludis' rifle was knocked from his hands, but he let it lie as he bent over the downed man. He noted the stripes on the uniform, the shock and terror in the man's features, and knew that this man was momentarily beyond commanding his own men to safety. The soldier scrambled back from Ludis, and he was trying to bring round a handgun to shoot. Ludis stepped on the sergeant's gun hand, plucked the revolver from him before panic made him slay his saviour. Bending closer still, Ludis rasped, 'I'm here to help you.'

The sergeant blinked at him in confusion, and still terror etched his features, but Ludis knew he'd got through the man's feverish mind and he'd recognised the words for what they were. Before panic or confusion could set in again, Ludis hauled the man up to his feet and jammed the pistol back into his hand. 'The others are outside, but there are other Nazis too. Take cover when you leave. I want you alive when I leave this hellish place.'

'Who are you?' the sergeant asked, his voice a dry croak.

'I'm here to help.'

That was all that Ludis would allow, because suddenly the tide of the battle had shifted and there only remained seconds before it was directed his way. He propelled the sergeant out the door, and then turned quickly back. The figure he'd noted on entering the barn was in the middle of tearing a soldier apart, great gouts of blood fanning in the air, tendrils of intestine coiling like ropes around him. Of the German's still alive, they were now engaged in a different battle than the one they'd started. Overwhelming numbers, modern weapons, even the archaic tools they'd brought could not help them ensnare the figure. Now it was almost languid in its slaughter of the remaining few left standing. One desperate soldier still tried to control it, prodding it with his three-pronged spear, but the bare-chested figure seemed mindless of its burning touch. The figure was drenched in blood that glistened on its hide, but Ludis suspected that none of it belonged to the monstrous thing. To think he'd considered that the shard was destined for the hands of this thing. The shard wasn't vibrating because it had found its rightful heir. No, it had found something that it was designed to destroy.

No sooner had the thought tumbled through his mind than the vibrations fell still.

Also, the blood-splashed figure turned and regarded Ludis as if he was the last man left on earth.

Around the figure the remaining soldiers were forgotten as it lifted a hand and beckoned to Ludis. COME HERE, the gesture ordered. Despite himself, Ludis felt a tug at his heart, and he took a faltering step forward.

What would have happened next he couldn't say, because the gesture had been so compelling that he could not have defied it. Likely he would have marched forward, offered up the shard to the foul creature, and in the next second he would have also offered his throat to its rending claws. But that didn't happen. Seeing the creature distracted, the Nazi with the spear rammed it into the creature's chest and threw all of his weight behind it to force his prisoner back against the far wall. Another soldier, blood marking his uniform from an earlier wound, joined his colleague. He snatched up the noosed pole and managed to loop it around one of the creature's wrists. He pulled the noose tight, snaring the arm and pulling it to the wall where he jammed it in place. The creature roared in agony, but its baleful gaze never left Ludis. Ludis mentally shook himself, freeing himself from the compulsion set upon him by the demon. He knew what he had to do. He dipped his hand into his satchel and pulled out the shard. He quickly unwrapped it from its silk coverings, held it tightly in his fist so the point protruded. A tingle of power ran up his arm, but it was unlike the time he'd first touched the shard at Ancienne: this time the charge flowing through him was energizing.

He started forward.

The tip of the metal began to glow and heat up, but Ludis found he could bear the burning sensation.

One look at the trapped creature told him that it would not.

Its fiery eyes appeared to dim, as if water had been thrown over hot coals. It hissed at him. Stoically Ludis continued forward, and he raised his arm, ready to hammer the shard into the monster's skull.

There was a roar of gunfire.

Ludis threw himself to one side, and he tripped and sprawled over the corpse of a soldier. He hit the ground and was assailed by a sickening sense of failure. A few seconds more and he would have slain the beast, but now the intervention of a desperate man had ruined everything. A British soldier, one that Ludis and the Germans had all missed had clambered midway down a ladder from the hayloft. In his free arm he held a huge machinegun that he'd braced between the rungs. The man pulled on the trigger while shouting vulgar curses and his bullets were indiscriminate. To the soldier, everyone inside the place was an enemy to destroy. His bullets tore through the soldiers controlling the beast; they also pounded into the creature itself, but with little effect. The last remaining Nazi survivors were cut to pieces. Only the fact that Ludis had fallen behind the corpse saved him from being targeted by the bullets. That did not mean he was safe. Freed now from its captors the beast ripped the noose from round its wrist, pushed aside the tri-headed spear, and lunged towards Ludis' prone body.

Ludis twisted around onto his back, bringing up his hand. The feeling of the shard was still there, but one glance showed him it was a ghost sensation as his fist was empty. The creature was coming for him, its hands outstretched and dripping with the blood of its previous victims. Ludis cast about, trying to find where the shard had been knocked from his hand as he fell. He could almost feel the rending claws sinking into his spine, the monster must be so close now. He saw the shard glowing faintly, partly covered by dirty straw. He scrambled towards it, knowing that he was too late.

The machinegun roared again.

Ludis twisted round and saw the creature being knocked back a step at a time as spent rounds compacted against its flesh. With each impact there was a corresponding hiss, but they were of frustration rather than pain. Bullets wouldn't kill this thing: no weapon designed by modern man would. But they would slow it. Ludis recalled stripping weapons from the soldiers he'd come across during his travels and he dug for one of the stick grenades he'd carried ever since. Blindly, he primed it, thinking of how he'd used the same type of weapon to bring down the Upir. Rolling onto his back, he lobbed the grenade and it hit the creature in its chest, before clattering to the floor. He did not know how many seconds was on the fuse, but evidently he'd thrown it too soon. Too soon to detonate on the creature at least, but enough time for him to grab at the dead soldier on the floor and haul the corpse over his body.

The detonation was tremendous.

Ludis felt the body ripped from his grip, then he was tumbling across the floor, his limbs feeling like loose rags as he was twisted over and over. He slammed into something hard, and then timber rained down on him, smacking his body with the power of punches thrown by trained pugilists. Then there was a solid impact against his head and everything went dark.

Chapter 28

Evening, 19th May, 1940
Northeast France

Ludis awoke with a start.

He sat up too quickly and his head swam, threatening to throw him back into the pitch-black sea upon which he'd been adrift. He couldn't allow himself the escape to oblivion again because that would allow his enemy time to recoup and come at him again. He had to retrieve the shard and finish the foul thing while it was still reeling from the explosion. He cast his gaze around, searching for the shard, seeking its faint glow against the shadows. He couldn't see it, and instead checked for the creature. Smoke must still billow, he thought, because he couldn't see anything clearly. For a second panic assailed him. How close was the fiend? Was it already stealing up on him, ready to rend him apart the way it had the Nazis? He shook his head. Bad idea: it didn't clear his vision only set off a pounding headache behind his ears. He screwed his eyelids tight, then forced them open, but still he could see nothing but a veil of blackness. Fresh panic struck him. Had the explosion blinded him?

He struggled to raise himself. Even blind he would not give in to the creature, not when he was still physically able to fight. He was unable to get up. He croaked out a moan of despair. He was blind *and* incapacitated. He shook his head again and pain flared in his skull. He bit down on his bottom lip, wrenched about, determined to get moving.

'Hold still, damn you.'

Ludis jerked at the words, twisting round in an attempt to locate their source.

'I told you to hold still. Do as I say before you hurt yourself.'

Ludis wasn't sure if he was relieved or not. The voice spoke in English, at least, and he was certain it did not issue from the beast he'd been fighting. Even though the command was gruff, it held compassion. What irked him was that he was evidently a prisoner. He wasn't paralysed, as he'd feared: the reason he could not rise was because of the cords tied around his ankles and arms. His blindness was due to a rag wound tightly about his face.

'Is this the way the English treat their friends?' Ludis asked, his voice raspy.

'When they're thrashing around so much that they're a danger to themselves? Yes, I'd say it is.'

Ludis considered the words. He grunted. 'How long have I been unconscious?'

'Since we dragged you out of the barn.'

Ludis grunted again. 'How long, I asked?'

'Best part of a day, I'd say.'

'What of the fiend?'

'I take it you're referring to the stranger?'

'The fiend,' Ludis said, although they had to be talking about one and the same. 'You must have realised that he was more than a man?'

'See…that's my problem,' said the Englishman. 'Nothing is what it seems anymore. I'm looking at you and can't make up my mind what you are either. Who are you?'

'I'm the person that saved your life.' Ludis adjusted his frame so that he was looking directly at the source of the voice, despite the blindfold.

'We were doing all right before you arrived. We were already on the way out, to make our escape. You didn't save me.'

'You were in no state to save yourself. I'd to drag you off the floor remember.'

'Only because you bloody well knocked me down in the first place.'

Ludis laughed. He'd assumed that his captor was the British sergeant; due to the fact he'd want to be the one to first talk to Ludis when he woke up. The man had confirmed his theory. 'You know I'm not your enemy, Sergeant. Is it necessary to keep me bound and blindfolded like this?'

'Like I already said, you were tied up so you didn't hurt yourself. The fever…'

'Has passed,' Ludis said. 'Even if it hadn't, I don't know how a blindfold would make a difference.'

'Your face was burned. It's not a blindfold. It's a bandage.'

Again Ludis grunted. He tested his eyelids, could feel his lashes flicking off material. Now that he'd come round he could make out movement beyond the veil and guessed that they were in a room somewhere, lit by a lantern or such. 'I feel no pain in my eyes, I'm sure I will see if you take it off.'

'In a while.'

'I'd rather know now.'

'In a while I said.'

'So I am your prisoner, not your patient as you would have me believe?'

'Like I told you: nothing's as it seems. I haven't made my mind up about you yet. There are things I need to know before I release you.'

'Let me talk to you like a free man, and I will explain.'

'I'm not going to make the same mistake twice,' the sergeant said. 'Last time I showed a stranger pity it proved fatal. I lost two good men back there. I won't lose another to you.'

'I have no reason to hurt any of you. I helped if you remember.'

'You didn't help. You had your own agenda. You were after the stranger. The same way the Germans were. How do I know you weren't working with them? You say that you saved me…I'm wondering if you only wanted me out of the way.'

'As you fled the barn, did you not see the Nazis I knocked cold?' The silence told Ludis that the sergeant had indeed seen the two German's he'd clubbed. 'Would I have done so if I was their ally?'

'Who knows what you would do?'

'I'm not your enemy, Sergeant,' Ludis repeated. 'I think you know that.'

There was a shifting of the shadows beyond the blindfold, a scuff of boots on hardwood, dulled a moment later on softer flooring. Fingers gripped the edge of the cloth and Ludis braced himself for the blindfold tearing away. Surprisingly it was teased up. Perhaps it was a bandage, after all. The glare of the lantern tore at his pupils and Ludis screwed his lids tight, averting his face. Slowly, he opened his eyes, allowing his focus to stabilize. When next he looked up, the sergeant was standing over him, the bandage in one hand, and a metallic object in the other. Gun, Ludis assumed, until the sergeant held it out to him and his vision focused on a tin cup.

'Drink,' the sergeant said. 'It's only water, but it's all we have.'

Ludis dipped his mouth over the cup and it was tilted towards him. The water was tepid and tasted of rust, but it was like nectar to his parched tongue. He slurped greedily. When he sat back, he said, 'My thanks.'

The sergeant wasn't beyond grunting either. He turned away. Ludis watched the man walk away, heading for what looked like a lady's dressing table, replete with a huge mirror. The lantern was on the dresser, the mirror helping to reflect and strengthen the light. Behind the mirror, drapes had been pulled tight and they were heavy enough that they would conceal the glow from anyone outside. Ludis continued his perusal of the room. He was lying on a metal bed frame, but if there had ever been a mattress then it had been removed. Ludis was on the bare springs and they had sagged under his weight so that he was touching the floor beneath. His arms were tied to his body, with the trailing cords attached to the bedframe. His ankles also were tied to the frame at the bottom end. A threadbare carpet failed to reach the corners of the room, and the boards there were scuffed and stained, and dotted with mouse droppings. The dressing table was an anomaly – possibly an item of furniture discarded by its original owner and brought here by one who cared less for matching decor. It was a poor room, in a poor house, with the concession that the walls were solid and the roof intact. And it was warm. Ludis had spent more uncomfortable nights than this.

'My name is Geoff Renyard, I'm a sergeant with the King's Royal Rifle Corps, under command of Lieutenant Colonel Euan Miller of the British Expeditionary Force.'

'I am Ludis Kristaps.'

'That's it?'

'It's who I am, I have no need of fancy titles.'

'Who do you fight for? Your accent…it's Russian?'

'Latvian,' Ludis corrected. 'I fight for myself and for God.'

Sergeant Renyard returned to stand over the bedframe. He had his hands clasped as he stared down at his prisoner. 'Kristaps. That means…?'

'In your language? Christ Bearer.'

'Pretty apt for a holy man, I'd say.' Renyard frowned at the bullish figure, the rugged features and hard eyes of the man staring back at him. 'Unusual for a fighting man, though.'

'Why do you take me for a holy man?' Since the undead boy had destroyed his cross, there was nothing about him to suggest his faith.

'When you were under the fever, you talked incessantly. No. Not talked. You quoted scripture.'

Ludis was surprised by this discovery. He had no memory whatsoever of the hours between the fight in the barn and waking here, a full day later. It surprised him more that he would have been reciting the Good Book; because it was a practice he'd fallen from the day that he turned his back on his church and took Galina to his heart. 'You understand Latvian? No: otherwise you would have known I was not Russian.'

'You spoke Latin,' Renyard corrected him. 'I don't understand it, but I've heard enough sermons to recognise the most commonly used prayers.'

'I do not understand Latin either,' Ludis smiled. "I only repeat what I have learned by rote.'

'You also spoke of *this*.'

Renyard brought both hands forward as though requesting benediction with a gift. Across both palms was a strip of cloth, and lying dead centre on it was the shard. 'One of my men, he understood enough to hear you repeat the same phrase over and over. *Žebērklis*. It means spear, doesn't it?'

'Near enough,' Ludis conceded.

'It doesn't look like much of a spear to me,' Renyard said.

'It is the tip only. And it is of *The Spear*.'

Renyard had no clue about the Spear of Destiny or any other spear for that matter, but he was no fool. He knew there was something about this chunk of metal that transcended its appearance.

'When you threw me out of the barn back there, I didn't leave immediately,' Renyard said. 'I still had a man inside and came back to bring him out. You were holding this thing and it was glowing like a star. The stranger could see it too…and he was afraid of it. I saw what you intended doing with it.'

Ludis didn't reply. He was intent on the shard, and was conscious that – in the sergeant's hands – it was merely a cold hunk of iron.

'It's a weapon,' Renyard continued. 'And I'm not just talking in the conventional sense. That thing – the fiend as you call him – our weapons could not touch him, and yet…'

Ludis nodded. 'The shard would have done so. Had your man held his fire, I'd have slain it.'

'Corporal Green probably saved *your* life. If he hadn't fired when he did the fiend would have had you.'

'That's…how would you say it? Debatable? Had he not killed the Nazis holding the fiend, I would have got to it first.'

'The bloody Nazis were our enemies! They had just murdered two of my men…*don't dare* criticize my man for avenging them.'

'I'm criticizing nobody, merely putting the record straight. The Nazis had the fiend under their control and I would have slain it. Now, reading between the lines, I take it that the foul thing escaped.'

Renyard nodded sharply. 'The grenade you threw slowed it down, but it was relatively unharmed. However, the back end of the barn collapsed and it made its escape through the wreckage. What was left of the SS troop gave chase, but I don't fancy their chances. Not without those weird silver poles.'

'They left them behind?'

'Both tridents were damaged, only the catch-pole was in one piece, but it was buried under the wreckage.'

'You brought it with you I hope?'

'For the one tied up, you ask a lot of questions.'

Ludis flickered a smile that didn't extend to his eyes.

'Yes, we brought it,' Renyard said, returning the non-committal smile. 'Its monetary value alone would be worth the effort. But before you start preaching, we're not idiots. We brought it having seen its power against the fiend.' He lifted the shard. 'The same reason we brought this. Just in case we cross paths again.'

'I don't think it is a case of chance. We are all destined to meet the fiend once more.'

Renyard shook his head. 'We've a mission to fulfil, and it doesn't include chasing some sort of inhuman monster all over the continent. It looks like the SS are already doing that and they're welcome to the task. I'll be happy if we never see it or its likes again.'

'You've seen others?'

Renyard didn't reply. He didn't have to; the slump of his shoulders confirmed it.

'Then you know that there are worse enemies than the Nazi to contend with. Your mission has changed Sergeant Renyard.' Ludis nodded at the shard. 'It changed the moment you picked that up.'

Renyard studied the spear tip, before folding it inside its protective cloth and shoving it into a breast pocket of his jerkin. Ludis nodded up at him. 'Keep it safe, Sergeant. It is now yours to deliver: that is your mission, and one you must succeed in if the world is not to fall into evil hands.'

Renyard snorted, his thoughts tracking to the complete disarray of the allied forces. 'I think that we're already a too late for that.'

'No. There is time yet. As long as the shard goes to its rightful heir.'

'Sounds like mumbo-jumbo to me,' Renyard said scornfully, but the tone was as faux as his tough stance. He had witnessed the evil first hand, knew that there were things he did not comprehend in this world, and that there was something magical about the shard he'd taken possession of. Not that he'd ever admit it to anyone, but he had heard it whispering to him while he'd stood vigil over his prisoner, and Ludis had just repeated its instructions verbatim.

'I do not know the man personally to whom it must be delivered, but I was told his name,' Ludis said.

Renyard felt an impending wave of déjà vu. He had heard the name too, whispered to him by the voice of the shard, and he had recognised it immediately.

Ludis confirmed everything, naming the recipient.

It was the name of the newly sworn in Prime Minister of the United Kingdom: Winston Churchill.

Chapter 29

Evening, 21st May, 1940
Northern France

The King's Royal Rifle Corps were famed infantrymen, who it was said could move faster than any other British regiment, due to their ability to march one hundred and forty steps per minute, compared to the hundred and twenty maintained by regular troops. Even under the circumstances that they now found themselves in, Renyard's section lived up to the legend.

Since the terrible events that occurred outside Reims, where the weight of Taff Jones and McCoy were added to the burden resting on Renyard's shoulders, the section had moved with speed to a deserted cottage further north, despite carrying with them the burly form of Ludis Kristaps. After that one stop, Renyard had released the man's feet and the going had been easier on his few remaining riflemen. Cooper and Whitey being the strongest of the section had been tasked with bearing their prisoner from the barn to the cottage, but even their strength had been tasked. With the big Latvian now able to walk under his own power, Cooper had taken charge of the Bren gun once more, but it was something he was used to and didn't slow him down. McCoy was sorely missed by the big gunner, and not because he had carried the spare ammunition and parts. Corporal Green had taken on that task.

They passed through countryside that was devoid of the enemy, but also of the local inhabitants. The rush to sanctuary in Paris was still on, but most of the refugees had fled this part of the country before now. They marched through terrain desolate and eerie, the only indication that a war raged being the distant rumble of gunfire somewhere over the eastern horizon. Occasionally they came across pockets of destruction, where brief battles had flared. Unable to find a mode of transportation, they were at least able to scavenge food, water, and ammunition. The men marched without complaint, as their training dictated, but Renyard knew that they all had unspoken questions that deserved answers.

He had shared Ludis Kristaps' story with Corporal Green, and had expected ridicule. Green had been there, seen what Ludis' fiend was capable of, and acquiesced to Renyard's plan to make haste for the Channel ports. They did not know that Lieutenant Colonel Miller and their regiment were currently tasked with defending Calais, or that there were whispers of an impending mass evacuation of the British Expeditionary Force. They only saw a quick march for the coast their best opportunity for hooking up with their own side and seeing the shard safely delivered to the British Isles. Ten days ago, had anyone told Renyard or Green what their mission would entail, both men would have laughed in their face. Tales of ancient talismans and unholy fiends weren't the fare of fighting men, and for long enough they had both resisted the proof shown them by their experiences. As foul an idea as it was, Renyard had hoped that the monsters he'd fought were the results of Nazi experimentation, that the creatures were simply the warped bodies of men and animals, but after the events in the barn, there was no explanation other than the diabolical. Even then his rational mind would have rebelled, and within a short time he would have convinced himself that all was not what it seemed. But, with the arrival of Ludis and the glowing shard – *the shard that talked to him inside his head* – he had no option but believe. Yes, it was insane, or he was. But that meant that the other five survivors of his section must be as equally crazy, because not a man among them argued against their new mission. Renyard wondered if the shard was influencing them as well, that they heard it too, but he was loath to raise the question. Maybe they followed him out of duty, or respect, but would they be so ready to do so if they discovered he was following voices in his head?

On the first night after their departure from the cottage, they had camped next to a river, on a bend where a high clay embankment offered cover from the elements, as well as discovery. There they had sat, and Ludis had told Renyard what he had learned of the spear tip, and also the legends behind it. Apparently there were a number of spears purported to be the one that skewered Christ on the cross, and that one of them had fallen into the clutches of Hitler on the day he annexed Austria. It was apparent to Ludis that Hitler had employed the spear to open a gateway to hell, the only explanation behind the monsters stalking the lands, but had lost control of the fiends he'd loosed and was now in a battle to send them back to where they'd come. Proof of that was the presence of the SS troop, and the magical tools they had carried. From what Ludis had come to understand, Hitler's spear was not the only talisman to hold great power, and it actually paled in significance alongside the one from which the shard had been broken. The big

Latvian had said the shard was from the first metal weapon forged by the hand of man, and such was the force of his belief that Renyard was carried along with it. Hitler's spear carried a legend. It was said that whosoever should wield it would rule the world. Well, it was starting to look like the story held validity judging by the way his forces were totally overwhelming all opposition. But, Ludis said, the shard would balance Hitler's dominance, and give Britain a fighting chance if it went to its rightful heir. But Renyard had to question facets of the big man's tale. Hitler's talisman was charged with a nail taken from Christ's crucifixion and bound into the spearhead; Ludis' weapon was broken from a blade supposedly cursed at the beginning of time by God – therefore which of the two would be the most potent weapon for good? Hitler's was sanctified by divine blood, Ludis' cursed. Ludis had brooded over the quandary, and had come to a conclusion other than that offered by the crone at Ancienne. By Hitler employing his spear for evil intent, it must have reversed the polarity of the spears, and the weapon that was once cursed was now blessed. His argument didn't hold water, but for one thing: the shard was anathema to evil. The way in which the fiend reacted to it went some way to prove that. Renyard had not told Ludis everything that had occurred after the detonation of the grenade. Ludis, caught in the shock wave, had been knocked unconscious. The fiend had barely been touched by the explosion and had advanced on Ludis, ready to tear him apart. Renyard had seen where the shard had fallen and scrambled for it, even as Green had emptied another magazine of bullets against the monster's chest. Then, as the Bren had run dry, and the fiend again loped towards Ludis, Renyard had sprang at it and slashed at its face with the metal blade. The fiend had recoiled, black ichor bubbling from the rent in its flesh, and it had screamed with all the fury of hell as it had backpedalled and then sprang out of the hole in the collapsed wall. The scream had been one of agony, but also of terror. The fiend had thought it was invincible…but it wasn't.

Renyard had wanted to know more about the shard, and for that reason had commanded his men to lift Ludis out of the rubble and carry him away with them. It was during their first stop at the cottage that the shard had begun whispering to him, and while they sat at the riverside, Renyard told the Latvian so. Ludis wasn't surprised, and he told the sergeant of a strange old man who had command over the beasts of the forest who also swore that the shard had spoken to him. Through this man, Borvo, it was the shard that had sent Ludis north to his rendezvous with Renyard. When Renyard asked if the shard spoke to him, Ludis had shook his head. Ludis replied that he must not be important enough in God's scheme to hear His voice.

After that, Renyard had loosened Ludis' hands, and gave him back his weapons. 'Maybe it's because you are the most important that He spares you the doubt that it's His voice,' Renyard had pointed out.

The next day they travelled as allies, and Ludis proved as able a scout as Watson was, and both men took turn about to lead the section north. And the famed marching skills of the King's Royal Rifle Corps were put to the test and proven. Arriving outside a small hamlet braced between a canal and marshland, Renyard had finally called a welcome halt. As much as the men needed rest and food, he required further answers from Ludis, and it wasn't something he'd had opportunity for during the forced march. Before they could make camp, other questions presented themselves though. Watson, who had been scouting ahead, had already made a brief reconnoitre of the small village. He returned with a look of shock and weariness unbecoming of the man. After all that they had witnessed and overcome, Renyard dreaded to think what could have shaken Watson like this.

The young rifleman had pointed towards the hamlet.

'Not even the Nazis are capable of *that*,' he said.

Chapter 30

Evening, 21st May, 1940
Northern France

'In the name of God!'

'God has no hand in this.'

Truer words had never been spoken.

Renyard and Ludis stood side by side, looking up at the trees that circled the small hamlet. The soldier's face was lengthened by shock, whereas Ludis held his flat and emotionless. He did not feel the ache of sorrow any less than his companion, but, since losing Galina and his babe, he'd been inured somewhat to the despicable acts perpetrated by the evil ones.

There were men hanging from the trees. Worse than that there were women and small children. Such a sight would be awful enough to behold, but ropes had not hanged them. The very branches had skewered their bodies, rammed through their torsos so that they were actually held in space by the tree limbs. Some of the thicker limbs held more than one corpse, sometimes what amounted to an entire family group. The slaughter had occurred not too long ago, but already the birds and wildlife had begun to feast and most skulls were without their eyes and parts of the softer flesh. Coagulating blood made streamers that drooped from the bodies, like garlands, some of them swaying in the evening breeze. At their arrival, crows and ravens had lifted into the sky, their raucous cries mocking and taunting of the living men below them, for they knew that when the soldiers moved on they could reclaim their feast. They circled in the greyness overhead, biding their time.

The others of the section were crouching in the road behind Renyard and Ludis, their guns trained on the small town, but all eyes were on the horrific crop. More than one of them had already vomited, but again the sounds of retching could be heard. Renyard waved them forward distractedly, and the men rose up, thankful for something to occupy their minds other than *this*. He sent them into the village. 'There may be survivors,' he croaked.

Ludis doubted that anyone had been spared. Recalling the slaughter of his own village folk, not a man, woman, child – or unborn baby – had escaped. Here, as well, he believed there'd be no exception.

'What do you think is responsible for doing this?" Renyard turned to his newfound expert on the supernatural. 'I told you about the ape-like things that attacked the Wehrmacht troop…'

'Not them.' Ludis nodded up at the nearest corpse, a young man with a shock of unruly hair and wearing overalls. 'Those things were driven by hunger. They feasted on the men they killed, you said. These people are untouched.'

Apart from the pecking of birds, Ludis was correct. The young man appeared to have been lifted, slammed onto the branch, then left to die in agony.

'All that I have fought before now have killed for meat, or for blood,' Ludis went on, 'ghouls, Strigoi, the walking dead, but this is different. These poor souls perished through wanton slaughter. That or rage.'

'You're talking about *him*, aren't you? The fiend.'

'He is different than the others,' Ludis replied.

'They're all monsters.'

'Yes.'

'But you think he is different?'

'With the exception of the Upir, himself a higher demon, the others were all lower denizens of hell. Base creatures with no intelligence to speak of. Like I said, they are driven by hunger and think only of their next meal of human flesh. The fiend, as we've come to call him, is much more than that, much more than the Upir even, more than the imps and gargoyles and devils that serve Satan.'

'He's a demon.'

'No.' Ludis grimaced before delivering his next thought. 'He is an angel.'

'What? But I thought that angels were good.'

'Forget not that Satan was an angel,' Ludis said. 'Before Michael banished him to the lower regions he stood at the throne of God. Surely you are familiar with the tale?'

Renyard exhaled, his shoulders drooping. He kicked at the dirt in futility. 'How are we supposed to take on Satan himself?'

Ludis barked a humourless laugh. 'He is not Satan. Do you think any of us would have made it out of that barn alive if the Great Deceiver was present?'

'But you said…'

'I said that the fiend was an angel, not that he was the Black Angel himself. When Satan, or Lucifer - dependent on your teachings - rebelled against God he was not alone. He had his supporters: other angels that were enraged that God had set Man above them in His favour. War raged in heaven, until Satan and his cohorts were expelled and fell into the flames of Hell. If Satan is the emperor of the lower realms, then the other angels also took positions of servitude beneath him. But forget not that kings and princes serve emperors. Our fiend is a mighty enemy, whichever way we look at him.

'Does he have a name?'

'I'm sure he has, but what it is I couldn't tell you. Men have attempted to name the fallen ones, and to give them designations, but it is all supposition. It is enough to know *what* he is as it is to know his name.'

'An angel.'

'Demon if you prefer.'

'Angels are supposed to be shining beings with wings, demons horn-headed with cloven hooves. He looks like neither of the traditional descriptions.'

'Traditional images are just that. Pictures conjured by the minds of men to suit their own needs. I suspect that we could not look upon their true forms, so they appear to man in ways we can understand. The man we saw, that is not the fiend's true likeness. I believe that he can take any form that he wishes.'

'So how in hell do we find him?'

Ludis touched the sergeant's breast pocket.

'The spear tip will lead us to him?'

Shaking his head, Ludis said. 'The fiend will find it. You said that it realised that there was something on the earthly plane that could challenge its invincibility. The demon will not rest until it finds the shard and destroys it: all the more reason why we must press on and put it in the hands of its rightful heir. Luckily we have weapons to fight him with. The shard and the catch-pole.'

'The pole can hold it. I've been wondering why...if it's such a powerful demon.'

'Silver is one of the most pure of all elements, and it has been long held that it has unparalleled cleansing properties. To something with the foul heart of a devil, its touch burns like acid. Also, silver holds great significance in Bible tradition. Forget not what Judas was paid for his betrayal. No ungodly creature can bare its touch. We are lucky to have the pole to hand.'

'I've a feeling our task won't be as easy as that. For a start, it looks like the BEF are on the verge of defeat, that the Wehrmacht is corralling them back towards the coast. We've the full might of Hitler's forces to get through before we can find a way home. A catch pole will do us no good against machineguns or tanks.'

'Taking on the entire German army will be nothing compared to defeating an angel,' Ludis grunted.

'That's an inspiring thought.' For the first time in many days Renyard allowed himself a smile. After a moment the gravitas went out of Ludis' features and he too smiled. Then, it was as if both men realised their humour was misplaced in front of their audience. They both lapsed into silence. After a while, Renyard asked, 'Is there nothing we can do for them?'

'We could pray for their immortal souls.'

'That's your job, isn't it? Being a holy man?'

A few days ago, Ludis would have disagreed. He had believed he'd no right to think of himself as a minister of God's word, but what had he become once more if not a servant of the Highest Power?

'I will pray for them,' he concurred.

'Me too,' Renyard said, and he meant it.

Ludis faced the sergeant. 'And then we will avenge them. But first we must get the shard to your leader.'

'Aye.' Renyard touched the object in his pocket. He was sure he felt a faint vibration, but wasn't sure. Perhaps it was simply the jitters of excitement Ludis' words had inspired in him.

Ludis stood in silence, his hands steepled in front of him, his mouth working in silence. He gesticulated, forming the sign of the cross, offering it to the four points of the compass. Beside him, Renyard merely stood. Externally he gave no sign, but he too was making peace with the Lord and asking that He take the souls of the murdered to His heart. Also he begged for protection for the lads under his command, but he could not bring himself to ask for clemency for his own life. He felt undeserving of that.

A murmur of excitement broke the moment. The two unlikely allies moved from under the trees, heading towards the source of the voices, wondering what had happened now. Anything had to be better than standing witness to the bodies hanging in the trees. They moved between wattle-and-daub houses, with small well-tended gardens, down a central avenue that was little more than a cart track and came across Corporal Green, Whitey and Blanco all chattering over their discovery. Cooper and Watson had not yet joined the party, but already they were heading in from the opposite end of town.

'What's all the fuss about? I could hear you all the way from the edge of the village.' Renyard had no real reason to ask, because it was evident that the trio was discussing the truck that sat in the central square, its engine grumbling. The truck – to Renyard's surprise – was a Bedford OYD, the standard troop transport truck of the BEF. He wondered how a British Army vehicle had come to be here, but it was apparent to him that his wouldn't be the only displaced troop since the flash invasion of France and Belgium. His next thought was where the soldiers were now, but again the answer was conclusive. There were many trees on the far side of the village, and likely they bore strange fruit too. Before they left the village, Renyard swore he'd find the British and take them down from the trees, but then recoiled from the idea. If the fiend – Ludis' fallen angel – had slaughtered the villagers with such impunity, what would it have done to the bodies of soldiers reminiscent of its newest enemies? Maybe it was best they didn't find out: let their prayers be enough to honour the dead.

'I'm just explaining that we can move more quietly on foot, and in this bruiser we'd be sitting ducks to the Jerry.' Corporal Green looked to Renyard for support.

'You're right,' Renyard said. His next words brought sighs of relief from Whitey and Blanco. 'But I'd prefer to take the chance. We have to make speed for the Channel and this truck is exactly what we need.'

Green shrugged, but Renyard could tell he wasn't happy about the decision. Not that Green would argue: Renyard's word was to be followed to the letter in his opinion.

Cooper and Watson jogged up.

'Sarge,' Cooper said. 'No sign of survivors, but the village is pretty much untouched. I've been in a couple of the houses and found food and stuff. There's even a pub down the road…'

He wasn't suggesting that they plunder the cellar, but that taking food from a business premises was morally acceptable to him whereas burgling houses wasn't.

'I don't understand. Everywhere we've been, the people have fled their homes and headed for Paris. Why didn't these people leave?' Renyard offered the question to all of the men, but they all looked to Ludis for an answer.

Feeling mildly uncomfortable under their scrutiny, Ludis gave them the first thought that came to mind. 'Perhaps they didn't want to leave their homes and preferred to greet the invaders rather than fight.'

His suggestion set off a few grumbles among the men – he heard the word "cowards" repeated more than once.

'There's nothing cowardly in it,' he growled. 'Maybe they realised that they had no hope of defending their town and that they were safer allowing the German's to roll on through.'

'Collaborators.' One of the soldiers spat.

'Not collaborators: men and women with children and elderly parents to protect. If this were your village and your people, would you take up arms if the enemy intended you no harm?'

'In a second,' said Green. 'I'd fight them tooth and nail.'

'I take it you are childless?' Ludis looked at him and saw the corporal sway nervously from foot to foot and knew that he'd struck a chord. Ludis spat between his feet. 'If you knew the enemy intended harm, that would be different, but these people had no reason to fear attack.'

'It still happened to them, though,' Cooper pointed out.

'Not from the Germans,' Ludis said.

Renyard interjected before the discussion got out of hand. Their politics might be different, but his troop had the same objective as the Latvian, and he didn't want a moral argument to split them. He ordered Cooper and Watson to return to the tavern and retrieve any food they could find. 'And no supping from the barrels,' he added as an afterthought. Green, Whitey and Blanco he told to load their equipment onto the truck. He wanted to be away from this village before nightfall. The last he wanted was to still be here when darkness fell, in full knowledge that the dead still surrounded them. Ludis had told him of the un-dead family he'd discovered in a farm to the south and he had no wish to relive history if the dead here should return. He visualised their corpses twitching and squirming as they attempted to extricate themselves from their skewers, and was glad he had not eaten a full meal lately.

Ludis was the only man without a job to get on with. Renyard did not feel as if he had the right to command him so allowed the big man a moment of silent reflection. Renyard guessed that the man was thinking of another village, where the folk there had also fallen into the sights of a devil. He wondered how the man would have reacted that day, had he been in the village and suspected the arrival of an enemy. It was different of course, because the Germans – for all the tales of depravity whispered about them – were simply men, but Renyard suspected that Ludis would have still fought tooth and nail, however benign the enemy was, despite his argument to the contrary.

Soon Cooper and Watson were back, lugging hessian sacks bulging with produce. They lifted them to Blanco who was on the back of the truck. Blanco and Whitey had already stacked all their equipment at the front of the truck, up against the front board behind the cab and had unfurled the canvas sheet that would keep the elements out. Jerry cans filled with diesel fuel were arranged opposite the stack of kit. Looking out of place was the silver catchpole that was propped in one corner. Wooden benches were fixed to both sides, giving ample space for the men to stretch out upon. There was room in front for three of them and Renyard was considering seating arrangements when Ludis came over and clambered up into the back. That sorted things for Renyard, and he told Green to get in the cab with him. Cooper was best served in the back where he could wield the Bren if necessary, and Whitey could serve as his second. Watson was their crack shot, and again best in back for rapid deployment. That left Blanco Tyler with driving duties. The young man grinned as he accepted the order, and clambered up into the seat like a kid with a new bicycle. He was a little heavy-footed on the throttle as they set off, and he tugged on the gear stick like he was stirring porridge in a cauldron, but Renyard allowed him his moment.

Green was perched in the middle and Renyard had taken the position next to the passenger door so that he could quickly get out of the truck if needs be. He had a good view of the large wing mirrors, but he avoided looking into them as they passed beneath the trees. He wasn't the only one who kept their eyes forward until they were over the crest of a hill and the silent hamlet was lost behind them. The steady grumble of the engine lulled Renyard and he began to doze, but the road was so uneven that he was occasionally jolted to wakefulness. Beside him, Green slept. Blanco's initial delight at being awarded driving duties had now been replaced by the realisation that he couldn't join his corporal in dreamland. He now chewed at his bottom lip, his eyebrows set like thunderheads. Renyard squirmed deeper in the seat, settling his head next to the window, but the vibration wouldn't allow any rest. Instead, he peered out the dusty windscreen, watching the night gathering about the truck. His thoughts were now turned to the road ahead of them, and what exactly they would find. He hoped that things would get better, but doubted it. Ludis said that the demon would target them, to destroy the weapon Renyard now carried, but he thought that Ludis was wrong. The creature wasn't following them: it was leading the way. He wondered if they all had a similar destination in mind, and the thought made him shudder. There was no way he would sleep now.

Chapter 31

23rd May 1940
Rastenburg, Germany

Adolf Hitler walked the grounds of "The Wolf's Lair" – his headquarters of strategic command – shadowed to right and left by Heinrich Himmler and a second SS-VT officer whose face was marked by duelling scars, picked up during his university days. Hitler's demeanour was dourer than his recent successes should suggest. Only this morning he'd received news that a detachment of the BEF under Major-General Harold Franklyn had been forced back to Vimy Ridge, after attempting to halt Rommel's Panzer division at Arras the day before. The overwhelming might of the British Matilda tanks had looked impregnable to Rommel's 37mm anti-tank guns, but not to the anti-aircraft and field guns employed by the inspired German commander. A rush of Wehrmacht reinforcements had bolstered the German lines and pushed back the British. To the east of Arras, a subsequent attack by the French was also foiled by the arrival of the German 32nd Infantry Division. This morning, Hitler's High Command had regained such confidence that they had ordered General Heinz Guderain's 19th Panzer Corps to press on to the ports of Calais and Boulogne, to successfully trap the British and Allied forces. It was too early for celebration, but soon, they felt, cigars and cognac would be passed round.

Turning abruptly, Hitler signalled the scarred man. 'I would speak with *Reichsführer* Himmler alone.'

The scarred man was Hitler's personal bodyguard, and it was his duty to ensure the *Führer's* safety, but that was never an issue here at the heart of

Die Wolfsschanze. Clicking his heels, saluting, he strode away and took up position out of earshot. Hitler gestured the *Reichsführer* to walk beside him and they continued through the grounds, the scarred man matching them step for step at a distance.

They came to a sunken fountain, surrounded by a tiered garden, a place where the younger Hitler would have found inspiration for his artwork. Now the garden looked grey and featureless, despite the spring daylight. Hitler supposed it was the frame of his mind that coloured things so. They sat at the edge of the well, obscured from sight to anyone above, and Hitler trusted his bodyguard to deter anyone from coming within hearing distance.

Without preamble, Hitler looked at the bespectacled man. 'Update me.'

He was not enquiring about war plans.

Already, Himmler had confirmed the destruction of the castle at Wewelsburg and the sealing of the physical gateway that had been opened by Klein's poor control of The Spear, and that the magician had paid dearly for his ineptitude. However, a concise report from the specialist team Himmler had sent after the 'escapee' had only recently fell on his ears.

'Things are proving more difficult than we ever imagined,' Himmler said. '*Der Schwarze Reiter* caught up with *Graue Teufel* at a farm near to the French town of Reims. However, there were complications and the demon escaped.'

'*Complications* sounds like an excuse for incompetence, Heinrich. Explain.'

'It seems that the Grey Devil was in the company of a troop of British soldiers: they fought even though our men showed them leniency and the devil escaped.'

'That was a mistake. These British…they knew what they were consorting with?'

'It's unlikely, for the devil had taken the form of a peasant. It appeared that they were fooled by his benign image.'

'So they were merely misguided, and retaliated out of hatred for us?'

'Or the fact that the Black Troopers were indiscriminate as they launched the assault to corral the devil. Some of the British were killed in the attack.'

'Your Black Troopers – handpicked for their fearlessness and superb fighting skills – could not take on one troop of Englishmen? I am disappointed.'

'As am I: but let's not forget that their priority was to capture the Grey Devil. The English struck while they were engaged with the beast. A cowardly attack by all accounts, even after the survivors had been shown clemency.'

Hitler laughed scornfully. 'They would have known their fate was a firing squad. I do not blame them for their actions; any man would have fought for their survival. *Der Schwarze Reiter* should have killed them all at the onset and avoided their subsequent failure.'

'I agree, *Mein Führer*, and had not their officer been slaughtered during the battle he would have been punished accordingly. In their defence, the Black Troopers were assailed on more than one front.'

'There were others involved?'

Himmler looked down at his boots, checking for imaginary scuffs in the highly polished leather. 'There was one at least, but he proved a considerable foe.'

Hitler stood up sharply, slapping at his thigh as though he held a riding crop. 'One man? Your crack troop could not take on one man?'

'This was no ordinary man…'

'Another *escapee*?'

Himmler cautioned his commander, for his raised voice would travel to ears not open to this conversation. Hitler snorted and sat down once more. His jaw set, he glared at Himmler, catching his reflection in the man's spectacle lenses.

Himmler said, 'He wasn't an escapee. He was a man, but unlike the British. He is reported as being a giant, with wild eyes and a wilder demeanour.'

'But still vulnerable to a German bullet, I take it?'

'No one took a shot at him. The man appeared to know what he was facing, and attempted to kill the Grey Devil.'

Hitler scowled. 'That is…unfortunate. I hoped that nobody but the Inner Circle were aware that a devil was loose in the world. This man…did he survive the encounter?'

'It's unknown, I'm afraid. He detonated a grenade that brought down the building they were in and the Grey Devil escaped. *Der Schwarze Reiter* gave immediate chase, as was their mission – at least those that lived did. We lost two-thirds of our strength in that one battle.'

'Send others.'

'I have arranged as such.'

'If he lives I also want this wild man brought here. Find him and deliver him to me.'

Himmler nodded. 'It shall be done.'

Hitler stood, finished for now, but was surprised to find that Himmler did not echo his salute. Only the *Reichsführer* of *Schutzstaffel*-

Verfügungstruppe would get away with the slip in etiquette. 'There is something yet to report?'

'There is,' Himmler said. He stood slowly, straightening his uniform. 'The man carried a weapon: one that the Grey Devil feared. I have consulted with Eckhart's necromancers and it appears that this man – whoever he is – was in possession of the *original* spear.'

Stunned, Hitler could only stand there, his eyelids twitching as he considered this news. A greater threat to his power he couldn't bring to mind. Finally, he looked up at Himmler, and his lips were tight across his teeth. 'The Holy Lance is supposedly enshrined under the dome of Saint Peter's Basilica in Rome. How does a wild man come to have it in his possession?'

'I wondered the same thing. I have had our people in Rome check that the relic is still there and they have confirmed as such. But, as you know, our experts already conducted a thorough inspection of that spear and found it to be an inert chunk of metal. It seems to have been robbed of its potency when the tip was broken off during the taking of Jerusalem in the seventh century by the Persian king, Khosrau II.'

'I am in no need of a history lesson, Heinrich. I know all the legends of the various spears. Get to the point.'

Himmler smiled at Hitler's ill-chosen words. 'Then you will recall that some scholars believe that the power imbued in the Holy Lance of Rome wasn't destroyed when the lance was snapped, but that it all transferred to the tip itself.'

'The tip of the lance has not been seen or heard of since it was smuggled from the Bibliotheque Nationale during the French Revolution, despite all our efforts to discover its whereabouts.'

'That's the point,' Himmler said, with an unusual show of brevity. 'It appears to have turned up…in the hands of this wild man.'

'Then it is all the more important that you bring him to me.'

'I fear that our military successes might compound the search for him. All the allied forces are being shepherded against the coastline. If he loses himself among them he may end up just another casualty. The spear tip could be lost…again.'

Hitler snorted. 'Then I shall slow our advance and allow your men the time to find him.'

'Even if that means allowing time for the BEF to evacuate?'

'It's a small price to pay considering the alternative.' Hitler was dismissive at the best of times, but his decision still came as a surprise to the *Reichsführer*.

'Forgive me, *Führer*, but such action could be a decisive error on our part. I must counsel a different plan of action.'

Hitler was scornful of the suggestion, attested by the growl he issued. 'Do you forget, Heinrich? With the Spear of Destiny *and* the tip of the Holy Lance in our grasp, Nazi Germany will be invincible. Who cares if the damned British escape, when in a very short time we will follow them to their island and crush them? I will hold fear of no man, or any weapon. I will rule the world and all in it. Let even the Grey Devil come for me and I will vanquish it!'

'Of course, *Führer*.'

'Of Course.' Hitler dismissed him.

This time Himmler was careful to follow protocol, saluting and calling Heil Hitler! The *Führer* strode away, calling for his scarred retainer. Himmler watched him go before he too climbed the steps from the sunken garden. He stood at the rim of the garden, watching Hitler march away with all the pomp of a gilded cockerel. Egotistical maniac, Himmler thought. When he laid hands on the spear tip, he would ensure it did not fall into the hands of that moustachioed madman. Then *Mein Führer* would see who was the invincible one.

Chapter 32

24th May 1940
Flanders, France

It had been a tortuous journey through the hinterlands of war for the last two days. A distance that should have been achievable in half a day had been multiplied, and then multiplied again, due to the diversionary tactics taken to ensure they did not fall into the sights of the invaders. Main roads had been barricaded or bombed, making access even more difficult, so farm tracks and back roads had to be employed to take them north. Along the way they had met refugees who told them that Calais had fallen despite the valiant efforts of the 30th Infantry Brigade, and turned instead for the nearby port of Dunkirk where the BEF was still holding out. Although some of the regiments they skirted were of the Allied Forces, Renyard made the decision to avoid them: if they approached any of them they would be caught up in their battle plans and that would severely hinder their own.

Yesterday afternoon, almost a full day since leaving the silent hamlet, they caught another sign that the demon had passed that way. A body was strewn across the road, ripped limb from limb and his skull crushed. Looking at the corpse anyone would decide that the man had fallen victim to a grenade but there was no sign of a detonation, no crater or damage to the trees to either side of the track. On inspection, they found remains of the soldier's uniform, and it was the dull grey of the Wehrmacht regular. Though the man was an enemy to them, the sight of him was enough to stir greater hatreds in the men of the King's Royal Rifle Corps. Ludis had made a further discovery. Clenched between the man's teeth was a strip of cloth torn from his tunic, and teasing it out, found it to be an insignia patch from the uniform. The swastika – though adopted and subverted by Nazi Germany – was an ancient symbol of peace: it appeared the fallen angel found it distasteful and had rammed it into the German's gullet. They could not determine if the man had been alive at the time. They hoped he hadn't.

This morning another sign had presented itself: and though the body there hadn't been eviscerated to the same extent, the sight proved equally as shocking. They had come across a village, passing beyond its boundary and into the main square with little hint of the small cluster of houses until they were among them. The village lay obscured by the hilly terrain, erected along the banks of a rock-strewn riverbed. It looked like a ford had once been situated there, replaced now by an arching stone bridge, and various dwellings and workshops had sprung up to service those using the crossing. A church stood alone at the end of the main square, the road forking around it and its tiny walled cemetery. The villagers had fled days ago, but the priest had chosen to stay. Perhaps he thought he'd be immune to the invaders, but he could not have guessed at the kind of enemy he would meet. They found him transfixed to the front door of the church. Metal rods had been driven through his wrists and ankles, suspending him upside down in mockery of Christ's crucifixion at Calgary. His cassock hung open, displaying a terrible wound in his chest: no one wanted to delve, but it appeared that his heart had been ripped from its cavity. It would have taken them days to take down all the corpses from the trees surrounding the silent hamlet, but Ludis refused to continue until the travesty here was rectified, and they buried the priest in his own graveyard.

It was not lost on any of them what might have been the outcome, had the SS troop and Ludis not chosen that moment to make their appearance at the barn. The devil was a king of deceit and had been biding his time, but they knew what fate he had had in mind for them.

Or had it? Renyard wondered. Was the devil's reason for coming to that barn pre-ordained, the same way in which he and Ludis had been drawn together? Had it come to the barn not to slaughter Renyard's section but await the arrival of the shard? The fact that their meandering journey north should continue to intersect with that of the devil was no coincidence in his opinion. Was the damned thing waiting for them to arrive at Dunkirk?

The answer now promised to be revealed, because the port lay only a few miles distant and if they could make it through their own lines unchallenged they should be there in a short while. Of course, it wasn't only the BEF they had to worry about. The Luftwaffe had mobilised their forces against the town and even from here they could hear the explosions and see the defenders' tracer fire arching into the sky in search of the elusive bombers. For some reason unknown to them, Panzer divisions stood idle along the banks of a canal, but Renyard thought they were likely holding off for one final crushing attack once the bombing raids softened the BEF. They had no hope of making it through the arrayed German forces in the Bedford truck, so Renyard ordered that they abandon it. By now Corporal Green was at the wheel and it was with certain satisfaction that he pulled off the road and into a ploughed field: he felt that his judgement had been severely damaged having travelled this far in the truck undetected, and the sergeant's latest decision went to vindicate his earlier warning that they should stay on foot. As the others clambered out, hoisting along their kitbags with them, Green had plans for the truck.

'No way we should leave it for the Germans to take,' he said, as he splashed fuel from one of the diesel canisters over the canvas awning.

Renyard watched the young corporal. He wondered about the logic of it – the smoke could attract the enemy – but in the end allowed Green his moment. This small pall of smoke was only one of hundreds dotting the countryside. Plus, he would rather the truck burned than be drafted into use by the Wehrmacht. He turned from the truck, Green now with the bonnet up and pulling loose the wires and draining the oil to seize the engine, doing as much damage as possible to the truck. The others had already begun to walk towards the gate, settling their packs in place. Only Ludis stood alone, and as well as his rifle and bedroll, he'd slung the silver catchpole over one shoulder. Renyard moved towards him even as there was a dull whump from behind him, followed by the thud of boots in the soft earth as Green escaped the heat of the fire.

'Are you ready?' Renyard asked.

'I'm worried,' Ludis admitted.

'I'll vouch for you, don't worry about that.'

'I don't mean about being accepted by your people. I'm worried that I will be refused an audience with your prime minister.'

There was little hope of that happening, but Renyard wasn't about to say so. More likely he'd have to work his way up the chain of command, and they'd be lucky to speak with Lieutenant Colonel Miller, let alone Churchill. Ludis studied him, and his features were grim.

'We must deliver the shard directly into Churchill's hand. We cannot take the chance it gets lost along the way...or worse, it is cast aside by some doubter before it reaches him.'

Pushed, Renyard would admit that he too was concerned. Who in their right mind would believe their story of devils and counter-charms? He thought that when he raised the subject he'd be diagnosed as suffering from shell shock and hospitalised at the first opportunity. It would be prudent to remain candid about why he needed to speak to his commanding officer, he guessed. 'We'll worry about that when we get to town,' he said, and wasn't sure which of them he was reassuring.

From nearby came the grinding of heavy machinery and the two looked across the field to a low ridgeline. Over the crest of the hill came an armoured behemoth that Renyard immediately identified as a Czech manufactured PZ 38t tank, the black on white German cross on its flank. Renyard feared that Green's injudicious burning of the truck had brought the enemy down on them, but the turret didn't swing their way and the tank continued its slow progress across the field, heading in the general direction of the port. Renyard and Ludis ducked low, then scuttled towards the gate and placed the hedgerow between them and the tank crew. Green had already brought the remaining few men of the section to a halt, and they were all lying in the grass at the side of the road, peering through the hedges at the tank.

From further away came the roaring of more engines as an entire battery of tanks approached the town. It looked like things were going to grow even hotter in Dunkirk before long. However, to their surprise, the pitch of engines changed and the trundling of the metal tracks diminished, and – like those they'd witnessed earlier – the tanks halted their advance. They had come so close that should they peer through their binoculars the tank commanders would be able to see the spires of the town's churches...and yet they had stopped. If not for the continued assault by the Luftwaffe bombers and fighters, the BEF might have known a slight reprieve.

'Why aren't they attacking?' Blanco Tyler wondered for them all. 'They could wipe every last defender from the beaches.'

He'd be damned if he knew, but Renyard wasn't about to miss an opportunity. 'Maybe Hitler's had a change of heart,' he said, though his humour sounded forced, 'and has decided to fight fairly instead.'

'You're talking about a man who opened the gates of hell...he does not know what fairness is.' Ludis' face was set in stone.

And you obviously don't understand the concept of irony, Renyard thought. British humour was often misinterpreted: most often, the sergeant found, by dour Eastern Europeans and ballsy Yanks. 'Whatever has happened, it's a good opportunity for us. Let's get moving before their infantry arrives and finds us.'

'You heard the sergeant,' Green broke in. 'Get your arses in gear, lads.'

The section moved out, keeping a low profile so that the hedgerows continued to conceal them from the tank crews across the field. Watson took point, and jogged away along the road, seeking passage through the arrayed enemy ranks. The Germans were spread widely at this time, and the real problem would be from their own side. Soldiers with itchy fingers might shoot first and ask questions later, so it was imperative they made a careful approach.

As they progressed towards the town, proof of the Luftwaffe assaults became more evident. Here at the hinterland of the port were clusters of industrial buildings, but practically all had been torn apart by previous bombing raids. Collapsed walls, splintered roofing beams, smoke and dust marked their route. They had no concept of how dire the situation was for the BEF defenders, or that tens of thousands of soldiers had been forced to a narrow strip of land along the beachfront, stretching almost eighteen miles along the coast. From this close, though, they were beginning to get the idea. The sounds of conflict were muted by the babble of thousands of voices, the clinks and bangs of men engaged in more mundane tasks. The buildings in town had been commandeered for shelter and concealment, but there were frankly too many men for even a large city to contain. Tents and shelters had been erected, soldiers had dug in, sandbags their only defence against the armament of the attackers, and on the beaches themselves thousands of soldiers had no other recourse than huddle in groupings: the shoal mentality where numbers lessened your odds of being the one that caught a bullet.

The English Channel was close by, but there was no hint of it yet, the salty-breeze overladen with the acrid tang of smoke, the sea beyond the low curve of the horizon. The sky to the north was overcast, pockmarked with donut rings of darker smoke where anti-aircraft shells had burst. Lightning strobes danced up and down, accompanied by the chatter of machineguns. There were the louder detonations of Luftwaffe bombs, but the overriding clamour continued to be that of thousands of men shouting orders…or dying in pain.

They were advancing towards hell on earth, but there was nothing else to do if they were to stop the image becoming literal.

Green suddenly raised a hand, then gesticulated frantically, causing all of the men – Ludis included – to hit the dirt. They were exposed to anyone advancing along the road, but the men that Green spotted were on the swell of a hill to their right. Crawling on his belly, Renyard pushed forward so that he was lying in the grass at the side of the trail. Gaps in the foliage allowed a view through the hedge and up the mound. He was about to ask Green if the men had seen them, but he didn't have to. An officer in a peaked cap had his binoculars to his eyes, and they were trained the section's way.

'Ready your swords,' he hissed. The men had been fastidious about their bayonets, and they fixed the gleaming lengths of steel to their rifles with practiced urgency. Bolts were worked to chamber rounds in their guns. Even at this desperate time Renyard was mildly proud of the efficiency of the men. After all that they'd been through together, it was good to know that the lads' training was more natural to them than the desire to run for it. Not that their rifles or bayonets would save them this time. There was upward of a hundred men encamped on the mound, alongside artillery cannons and an armoured car, on which was mounted a heavy machine gun. The overwhelming odds were bad enough, but even as Renyard watched the Wehrmacht officer watching him, he saw a man next to the officer on a radio. The cranking of a tank turret split the air from behind the section, and an engine roared. One of the PZ 38t tanks was coming to investigate.

The road to Dunkirk remained open to them – but only for half a minute or so before the tank could roar ahead and cut them off. They had to move now or be caught between the German guns.

Waving them up, Renyard sent his men down the road at a gallop. A short flurry of bullets followed, cutting through the foliage around them, but Renyard was surprised at the lacklustre Wehrmacht response to their presence. Maybe they had seen many British soldiers flooding back to join their companions beyond the cordon, and meeting them in face to face combat wasn't necessary when the tanks and planes could easily finish everyone off. A handful of soldiers were dispatched from the main group and they jogged down from the mound, following closely, but they made no attempt to shoot yet. While still running Whitey fired off a round, but it was spent in the earth many yards ahead of the advancing Germans.

'Conserve your ammunition, rifleman,' Renyard yelled at him. Every bullet would count before they made it into the safety of the BEF lines.

Ludis Kristaps clumped along at Renyard's shoulder, his heavy boots slapping on the hard-packed dirt. Slung on his back, the silver pole shimmered in response to the roll of his shoulders, a sparkling signpost for a bullet. In his right hand he clenched his Webley revolver, his chin set, his deep-set eyes twinkling with fierce determination, and yet again it wasn't lost on Renyard what an aberration the big man was. Right then and there, nothing about him suggested a peaceful minister but a warrior. Renyard shook loose the thought: better that he had another fighting man at his side than someone prepared to offer up his last rights.

Rifles crackled, but once more the shots were undetermined and came nowhere near hitting them.

'They're corralling us,' Ludis grunted.

'Looks that way.' The tank powered across the fields on their left, crushing its way over hedges and ditches, bouncing over the uneven ground.

'Where though?' Ludis asked.

Renyard thought a more pertinent question was why?

A hundred yards ahead there was a crossroad, and in the fields beyond that another tank approached, called in to halt their forward progress. Trees marked the junction, but they were no defence against a couple of tanks. Renyard scanned the area to their right, where the slope of the hill held by the Germans met the road and saw an abandoned factory of sorts. A large brick chimney raised to the heavens, untouched as yet by the bombing raids, and adjacent to it a squat brick-built oblong with dingy windows and shuttered doors. The factory could be the very location the Germans were pushing them towards, but it also offered a place of concealment from where they could defend themselves. The way things looked, the Germans had no intention of simply mowing them down, so the buildings were unlikely to be shelled if they intended taking Renyard and his section alive. As they pounded towards the crossroad a figure emerged from the trees. James Watson waved, urging them to join him. As the men charged up to his position, he quickly turned and led the way towards the factory. The soldiers in the field adjusted their trajectory, coming quicker now. Maybe their orders had changed now that they saw their quarry heading for potential shelter. The gunfire intensified, and Blanco Tyler yelped. He kept running but there was a distinct gait to his loping now.

The factory had been a hive of activity until recent events had forced the workers away. The courtyard was piled high with mounds of clay tiles manufactured but never delivered to their recipients. Reclaimed oil drums and pallets held an assortment of other wares: all unimportant to the men who charged past them, looking for a way inside the building. Machineguns were indiscriminate weapons at best, but most of their loads were wasted in impact against the clutter in the yard. Some bullets did find fleshy targets and both Green and Whitey were knocked sprawling in the dirt. Cooper grabbed up the corporal and dragged him towards a large wooden door, painted bottle green, with the business owner's name hand-painted upon its surface in elaborate red and gold script. The burly soldier showed no regard for the painstaking work of the artist and simply booted the door open, smashing boards under his boots. Green moaned in pain, but he struggled to right himself and not be a burden. Behind them Ludis and Renyard hooked Whitey's armpits with their elbows and dragged him backwards towards safety. Watson and Tyler used the stacks of tiles, concealing themselves from the enemy as they fired off rounds at the pursuing infantrymen. As was his wont, Watson took a man with each shot, but Blanco wasn't so skilled: nonetheless his bullets forced the Germans to throw themselves aside to avoid dying. One tank came trundling along the roadway, but halted outside the gates, while, judging by the roar of its engine, the second one made its way round powering through a low wall at the back to cut off a retreat.

With Green and Whitey safely deposited inside, Renyard returned to the door, lifting his rifle and seeking targets. Men moved beyond the stacks, but he didn't have a clear view of any of them. For good measure he put a single round above their heads, then watched as Watson and Blanco surged up, running to join him in the building. Blanco's trousers were dark with blood and his limp had intensified. Shouts followed them, but surprisingly no bullets sought them out. They came sliding up to the door, ducking low so as not to impede Renyard's aim.

Once they were inside, Watson swung round to replace the sergeant at the door, but Renyard shook his head and pressed the young man inside. The door smashed in by Cooper was little deterrent to an all out attack, but Renyard shoved the remains of it to. He ran into a workshop area wherein long trestles were laid the length of the dusty room. Tools and machinery had been abandoned, and along the walls there were more stacks of tiles, these ones more elaborately decorated than the plain roofing tiles outside.

'Get those tables up against the windows and doors,' he yelled, 'and pile as much junk as you can to hold them in place.' No way would the flimsy barricades halt the tanks but it would impede an assault by the foot soldiers. The men responded to his command, but some were more able-bodied than others, and Whitey almost collapsed as he tried to rise. Corporal Green didn't look much better, his face as pale as a fish's underbelly, and as clammy. Blanco had been hit in his left thigh and was bleeding badly, but he had already fastened a rudimentary bandage in place and had struggled up to help Watson and Cooper. No way could the three of them perform the task as quickly as Renyard hoped so he jumped into the task, pulling over one long trestle and then pushing it up to the wall overlooking the courtyard. He searched round frantically, looking for anything else that he could throw onto the barricade. That was when he saw Ludis Kristaps walk determinedly for the door he'd recently closed to.

'Ludis. Get away from there and come help me.'

Ludis ignored him, and instead opened the door and stepped outside.

'What is that crazy man up to?' Renyard hollered as he ran to the door. From outside there was a volley of gunfire, and the sergeant threw himself out of the line of fire as bullets spent themselves against the brickwork to either side of the door. He cringed, thinking of the hailstorm of hot metal that Ludis had to suffer.

Then the door opened and the big Latvian stepped back inside.

Renyard and the others gawped at him – he was intact, not a sign of an injury on him.

'What the hell?' Renyard screamed at him. 'Are you totally insane. What is it, you believe all of this fate crap so much that you think you'll be spared a bullet in the skull?'

Ludis shrugged his burly shoulders.

'I was testing a theory,' he said.

'What, that you're bloody superhuman?'

'No,' Ludis said, 'that they aren't trying to kill us. They had the opportunity just then but aimed to miss. They were only interested in getting me back inside and safely out of the way.'

Blanco laughed, sounding slightly hysterical. He indicated his wounded leg, the poor state of Green and Whitey. 'If they don't want to kill us they have a funny way of showing it!'

'I think you were all hit by accident. They want us in here; that is obvious to me. Out of the way where they aren't forced to use extreme force to stop us escaping.'

Renyard had to admit that the big man had a point. At any time the Germans could simply tear the factory to pieces with their guns and grenades, or the tanks could push their way through the walls and allow the infantrymen to spill inside. But, it appeared they were willing to wait it out without engaging the section in combat. 'Why do it?' he wondered.

'They're holding us,' Ludis said, 'until someone else can arrive and deal with us properly.'

Chapter 33

25th May 1940
Flanders, France

Though he had the capacity to do so without complaint, and for a long time, Ludis hated waiting.

More than once in the five plus hours since they'd taken refuge in the abandoned tile factory, he'd considered walking out the back way and testing the resolve of the Wehrmacht. It was apparent to him that someone wanted the British soldiers alive, and his rash experiment had gone some way to prove that. He wondered if they all should group together and make a run for it across the fields to the nearby BEF encampments, and chance that the German reticence to shoot would allow them to escape. He'd counselled such an idea to Sergeant Renyard and his second, the more impulsive corporal, but his plan had metaphorically been shot down in flames. Renyard had injured men to consider – no less the corporal – and thought Ludis' plan suicidal. Well, in his opinion, sitting here surrounded by dozens of armed men was only delaying the inevitable. It was imperative that the shard was delivered to Churchill, and sitting tight until a greater force could arrive to capture and cart them away to some prisoner of war camp was a greater threat to their mission than making a run for it.

The shard was in Renyard's pocket. Ludis considered asking for it back and he would slip away under the cover of darkness and make it to the BEF camp alone. There he'd alert the British to the section's plight and send out a rescue party. Two things stopped him from suggesting his plan: he believed that it had been preordained that Renyard should carry the shard to its heir, and that his plan would be seen as cowardice where Ludis wanted only to abandon the others to their fate. The second notion seriously rankled him, but he understood how scared minds worked. If he mentioned it, he could expect conflict from the very men he had come to think of as his friends. Someone with the quick temper of Corporal Green might even take matters into his own hands and try to shoot Ludis as a deserter. Ludis had no intention of hurting the young man to stop such a lapse in judgement. So he waited, peering out over the flimsy barricade through a window thick with clay dust. Beyond the smudged glass he detected occasional movement as one of the German soldiers shifted to a more comfortable position. There were dozens of them camped out there now, circling the factory.

What were they waiting for?

In fact, what was the entire German army waiting for? The Luftwaffe continued their bombing runs, but the Panzer tanks and infantry had not moved on the BEF all day. It was an unusual battle plan the Germans were following, and Ludis could not come up with a logical answer. Earlier in the day, Sergeant Renyard had suggested that Hitler might have experienced a change of heart – but this was regarding a despotic tyrant who wasn't known for pity. No, something else held back the final push of the German military, and if it wasn't supremely egotistic to think it, Ludis might wonder that *they* were the reason.

The soldier called Whitey was in a poor state of health. A bullet had only creased Corporal Green. It took a chunk of flesh from his side, but the bleeding had been controlled with a field dressing and, other than moving tentatively, the corporal was getting around fine. Blanco Tyler was also wounded in the thigh but his life wasn't threatened. Whitey had been hit square, though, a bullet lodging in his left scapula, having already passed through his chest. His friends had patched him up as best they could, but there was nothing they could do about the internal damage, or the probability that he still bled inside. Without medical treatment he would die. Ludis could tell in the set of Renyard's shoulders that he had considered surrender, in order that the injured soldier might be shown proper care. But the likelihood that the only medical assistance Whitey would receive was a bullet to put him out of his misery held him back.

Whitey had lapsed into a deep, dreamless sleep. His breathing was shallow, a faint whistle that could be heard the length of the factory floor. Occasionally one of the other men muttered or elicited a low curse, but otherwise all were still. Those able-bodied men were at the four corners watching the Germans watching them. Cooper and Watson were at the furthest corners, while Renyard and Ludis were sitting opposite, near to the splintered door. Green and Blanco manned the Bren, and were positioned at the bottom of a flight of stairs directly between Cooper and Watson, a last line of defence if the Germans came in through the front door. Renyard had ordered that all their ammunition be stockpiled, and then he'd dished out equal amounts to the four corner men, so that each had an equal opportunity at fighting for their lives. The bullets for the Bren were not interchangeable with any of the rifles, and they were stacked alongside the gun. Not that there were many left, but enough to slow down anyone coming through the door. The fight – if and when it came – would be short and furious, and Ludis didn't fancy their chances of being the victors.

But he waited, not about to abandon his friends in their moment of plight.

Another two hours passed as slowly as trickling honey, and even Ludis' nerves were beginning to fray. More often than not he found his gaze drifting from the lack of activity outside to the pale faces of those crouching in the darkness within. Each face was drawn with fatigue and tension and he wondered if this was the Germans' new plan for victory: holding off until the allies went mad with frustration or fell asleep through boredom. He looked over at the sergeant and saw that the man had propped his rifle in the corner and was partly standing, trying for a better look through the window.

'What is it?' Ludis whispered. His voice was like a knife slash through the tension and all the others jerked their way. A low mutter arose, soft clinks and the brush of uniform trousers as the men adjusted themselves for whatever was coming. Renyard held up a hand, demanding silence.

'Listen,' he said, still craning for a look without outlining his body in the window. 'There's something going on out there.'

Ludis heard it then; the low grumble of an engine approaching down the same road they had come along earlier.

'Over here,' he said, beckoning Renyard to him.

The sergeant was loath to abandon his post, but he wanted to see what was going on so that he could plan their defence. He scuttled over and went down on one knee next to Ludis.

Through the darkness swept the headlights of a vehicle. They could not see what it was yet, but by the sound of the engine and the rattle of wheels over the rutted surface, Ludis guessed it was a truck of some type. Outside, the Germans surrounding them reacted to the new arrivals, some of them rising up and moving off to meet them.

'Whoever this is, I think it's who the others have been waiting for,' Renyard said.

Ludis grunted in agreement. But it still didn't tell him who the newcomers were, or why they were so important.

Watson, the more hawk-eyed of the section had the best view. 'Sarge, it's more of those Nazis in black. Like the ones back at the barn.'

Ludis shared a glance with Renyard. Suddenly the answer was clear to them both. The Nazi troopers were a crack team whose objective was to capture the fallen angel – most likely their masters had plans to use the devilish thing to their own ends – and it was important to them that Renyard and his men be taken alive. Orders had been sent to watch for them as they fled north, with an instruction that the Nazis be sent for once they had been contained. Perhaps they believed that the British soldiers could lead them to the fiend, or more worryingly, they had witnessed the effects of the shard on the devil and wanted it for themselves.

Ludis gripped the sergeant's wrist. 'We cannot allow the shard to fall into their hands. Armed with both spears, Hitler will be invincible and the rest of the world will fall.'

'I know that. But what else can we do?' He looked to where Rifleman White lay in oblivious sleep. 'We can't fight them all.'

'We can and we must,' Ludis demanded.

'I have injured men here…'

'They are soldiers,' Ludis said gruffly, 'with a duty to fight for what they believe in.'

'I'm aware of that. But they are also men with families who have a right to see their loved ones again.'

'You would have them surrender, and face torture or a firing squad?'

'The Geneva Convention forbids such treatment of prisoners of war,' Renyard began, but immediately realised how stupid he sounded. The arrival of the Nazi troop meant that orders were coming from the highest level of government, and that it was in all likelihood a secret operation. Should they all be captured and given over to those at the top their identities would be struck from the records at the first instance. Even the regular army out there would be sworn to silence – possibly by way of threats should word of this incident ever get out – and no one would ever know of their fate. They were but another section lost following the taking of Sedan, and their graves would go as unmarked as if they had been buried back there in the Ardennes. That didn't matter: Renyard still had a responsibility to the lives of the men under him, and he would not sacrifice them if there were another way out. The problem was, he couldn't see one.

'Sarge,' Corporal Green called. 'Can I have a quiet word?'

Renyard paused, his gaze fixed on that of Ludis. Turmoil danced beneath his features, but in the end he gave a silent nod and then went to join the corporal. Blanco didn't leave the huddle, and though he didn't lift his head, the resignation on his features said that he was in agreement with what the corporal suggested.

As Ludis watched them, he witnessed a lot of head shaking from the sergeant, but it looked like the man was being won over by his younger colleague. He gripped at the shard in his tunic pocket more than once, and by the movement of his lips he was cursing. Both men were whispering harshly, but the acoustics of the old brick building carried their conversation to all ears in the room.

Watson spoke without taking his aim from the activity outside. 'Sorry for interrupting, Sarge, but it looks like we're going to have to do *something* soon. The stormtroopers are preparing their weapons.'

Slinging the silver catchpole on his shoulder, Ludis left his post, moving quickly for where the leaders were still in their huddle. When Ludis was a few steps away, Renyard turned to him and the shivering of his body could be clearly seen. It wasn't fear that shook him per se, but a mixture of emotion, the foremost being regret. Ludis guessed the man was sorry he'd ever fallen into this insane partnership and that it should be Ludis Kristaps who was the man to stay behind.

'Corporal Green has a point,' Ludis said. 'We cannot carry the injured man with us. If we are to succeed in our mission, we have to leave now.'

'I am not in the habit of abandoning my men and am not about to start now.' Renyard dug in his pocket and pulled out the shard, wrapped in its cloth. He thrust it towards Ludis.

'You have to come with me,' Ludis said, refusing the shard.

'That's right, you need someone to speak for you.' Renyard shook his head. 'But it doesn't need to be me. Watson.'

'I'm not leaving, Sarge.' Watson briefly snatched his aim from those advancing on the factory.

'That's not your decision, son,' Renyard said. 'Go with Ludis, make sure he makes it safely to Lieutenant Colonel Miller.'

'Sarge, no disrespect meant, but I'm not leaving. I'm part of this section and I choose to die alongside them.'

'I'm giving you an order, Rifleman Watson. Do as I say.' Renyard beckoned Cooper. 'You, too, Cooper. You're both to assist this man in delivering a very important item…and it's a far nobler duty than sacrificing your lives in this shit hole.'

'Begging your pardon, Sarge, but I'm with Winker. I'm not leaving my friends for anything.'

Renyard smiled, shook his head. 'Any other time your insubordination would hack me off. Go on lads; do what I've asked of you, all right? And don't worry about the rest of us, we'll get through this.'

Watson and Cooper understood that any further argument was pointless. They joined Ludis, who finally reached out and took the shard from Renyard. He secreted it in its place in his satchel, covering it again with the strip taken from Galina's dress.

'You make a poor decision not to come with me,' Ludis told Renyard, 'but it is also the correct one for your injured men. Once we are away from here the Nazis will no longer have a need for them, and it is more likely they will all be spared.'

Renyard looked at the dusty floor, while he gathered the right words. 'I brought the lads here to this place, it's only right that I stay with them. If the Germans don't show them any pity, then I'll make sure they are paid back in spades.' Renyard tapped a bulge in his other breast pocket, and Ludis recalled where the sergeant stowed a couple of grenades they'd scavenged along the way.

Looking to Watson and Cooper, Ludis found faces angry and embittered. But neither man's enmity was aimed at him, but to the situation they had all come to. Both men shared a nod of companionship with him, and then offered brief salutes to their friends that were staying behind. Ludis clapped Renyard on the shoulder, and said, 'There is no need for fighting them. Make noise, tell them you wish to surrender…it should be enough to attract their attention while we slip away.'

'I wish it was that easy,' Renyard said. 'We have to cause a bigger diversion or else they'll realise what we're trying and have their men on full alert.'

The sergeant was right, and as Watson had so recently pointed out they had to do *something* quickly if they were going to have any hope of success. Without preamble, Renyard told Green to swing the Bren towards the windows overlooking the courtyard.

'All right, everyone get ready. We go on three.'

Ludis and his escorts dashed for the furthermost window near to the back of the factory. Ludis pushed open the window and dropped outside. He brought up his rifle.

'One!'

Watson clambered out and quickly went to one knee.

'Two!'

Cooper jumped out and took half-a-dozen paces forwards, and then he dropped to a knee and brought up his Lee-Enfield. Already Ludis and Cooper were sprinting past him.

'Three!'

There was a shout of warning from a German watching the rear of the building, but his voice was lost in the roar of the Bren gun and the cacophony of shattering glass. Before the German could raise the alarm that a trio of the fugitives had broken free of the cordon, a bullet from Watson silenced him.

The roar of conflict rose through the night behind them, but Ludis and his escorts continued to run, passing between the lines of soldiers whose attention was fully on the building.

They kept running as other guns joined the battle, and the voices of men were raised in challenge and counter challenge.

The Bren continued its drum-roll.

Then there was a boom, and Ludis knew that one of the tanks had been called in.

The rumble of falling masonry was punctuated by the single shots of rifles now, and then a different machinegun from the Bren was singing its death song.

A scream.

Shouts.

More gunfire.

The Bren went silent.

More shouts.

Silence.

Then a double detonation, the sound of two grenades dampened by the walls and the growing distance.

Silence once more.

As he pounded through the night, Ludis understood what those final explosions signified. He continued to place one foot in front of the other, every step being one more moment of freedom won for him by

Renyard and the others' selfless act. At that moment he hated the world, hated his God, hated everything: yet he didn't slow, but kept on, because he didn't want those men's lives to have been taken so he could give up now. As he raced towards Dunkirk he could barely see for the tears in his eyes.

Chapter 34

25th May 1940
Dunkirk, France

Lieutenant Colonel Miller wasn't among the many thousands of men spread out along the French coastline, or, if he was, there was no one able to direct Ludis and his companions to him. They searched for the best part of an hour, before finally giving in to the inevitable and approaching a captain, the highest-ranking officer they had come across. The captain, a toff resplendent with walrus moustache, was missing only a monocle and he would have fit in with an army of a previous century. He exuded the blustering air of one who deemed himself above the men in his command, and gave them only as little heed as he could muster, before shooing them away from him with orders that they report to someone who gave a damn to the stories of crazy men. Ludis understood the structure of armies, and the necessity for obeying orders without question, but he couldn't bring himself to be polite to this oaf of a man: Cooper and Watson had to drag him away before they were all arrested for insubordination. They would be no use to anyone locked in a temporary brig and under guard of MPs.

'Let us do the talking,' Watson cautioned as they ushered Ludis between dozens of men camped on the beach. Though it was very early in the morning anyone would think it was mid-day from the amount of activity going on around them. Soldiers couldn't sleep for the hubbub, the least of which was the constant bombing and strafing conducted by the Luftwaffe. The noise was a cacophony of voices, the thud of boots through sand, the clatter of mess tins as starved men prepared emergency rations. Those who weren't eating were seeing to their kit and spread out on the available ground were blankets with rolled anti-gas capes, shaving and washing kits, water sterilizing kits, brushes, dubbing, woollen balaclava, rifle cleaning equipment and other tools of the modern fighting man. While other soldiers were dying further along the beach, the men here looked like they were preparing for an inspection. Ludis thought it was insane, and would have said so, but Watson's caution rang true. With his eastern European accent he might be confused for an enemy spy and torn to pieces by the droves of men gathered here.

'We're wasting our time looking for an officer. We should find a sergeant who'll listen.' Cooper stood taller than most of the men around them, but even he could make out little to differentiate one man from another in this press of men. 'The sooner we catch a sympathetic ear, the sooner we can go back and rescue the others.'

Watson and Ludis shared a glance. Neither man held any optimism that any of those who stayed at the factory had survived the encounter. It wasn't Ludis alone who knew the significance of the two exploding grenades. But they weren't beyond hope, and on the run here had agreed that their priority was to send back a rescue party. All three men had also agreed that they should accompany the rescuers – their way of easing their consciences about leaving the others behind. The task, it seemed, of mounting a rescue party was no mean feat: it seemed that there were far too many stragglers out in the French countryside in need of assistance and their exhortations of the walrus moustached captain had been met with as much disdain as was their need to speak with someone who could help deliver the shard to the Prime Minister.

Watson even considered the option of leaving Ludis here while he returned with Cooper to see what they could do, yet in the back of his mind the young sharpshooter realised that their mission would most likely be suicidal at best. They needed more men and the backup of an armoured division if they'd any chance of defeating the number of Germans back at the factory. Also, it was not lost on them that – should Renyard or any of the others have survived the battle – then already they would have been taken by the Nazis in black and carried off elsewhere for interrogation. Reluctantly he had decided to concentrate on the orders given him by his sergeant, but it seemed that Cooper still had other ideas.

'This is madness,' Ludis snapped as they continued to push through the throng. 'We can see nothing from down here.' He pointed up the sloping beach to where the peaks of buildings were etched in stark silhouette against the war torn sky. 'We should go to the town where command posts will have been set up.'

Watson shook his head emphatically. 'The problem with that thinking is that we'll also be directly in the line of fire. Those tanks aren't gong to hold off forever, and you can bet your arse that the first thing they do is shell the town. My orders were to safely deliver you and your package and I won't be able to do that from under a mound of collapsed rubble.'

Ludis didn't argue. There was logic in the young man's words. Nonetheless, it made him think again about the unusual stalling of the tank battalions. Combining their forces with the Luftwaffe, the German tanks and infantry divisions could move in, tighten the noose and wipe the entire BEF from the beaches. He had to consider that the Germans were thinking exactly that but orders from on high were holding them at bay. He touched the satchel at his belt and wondered if the fathomless power of the shard held more significance to this war than any of them could ever understand. When he'd chosen to employ it against the fallen angel at the barn, had he unwittingly forced a change in the push and flow of this war? It was apparent to him now that those Nazis who'd survived had reported to their master and that Hitler now coveted the shard, as he did the Spear of Destiny. Proof of his theory was in the arrival of men from the same Nazi troop being brought in to corner them at the factory. He thought that should the shard fall into enemy hands then the fate of the thousands of men trapped here would be forfeit. Were there even now spies moving among the British soldiers, seeking them out? Suddenly Ludis found that he was peering at the soldiers around him with suspicion, expecting at any second to catch a furtive glance that would precede an attack, but it seemed that everywhere he looked he saw only men whose spirits were dented but not yet destroyed.

Ahead and to their left a bunker had been erected. Not much of a bunker, being built from stacked sandbags with a dun-coloured canvas awning offering meagre camouflage from the planes in the sky. Watson pointed at it. 'If there's someone in charge, he'll most likely be in there.'

Hundreds of men separated them from the bunker, all tightly packed, as if formed into ranks. The soldiers wore the insignia of various regiments, a hotchpotch of men who were likely stragglers from decimated regiments all brought together in this time of uncertainty. They were standing shoulder-to-shoulder, and extended from the dunes to the Channel, and the only way to get to the bunker from the beach was either through them or to wade in the sea. Cooper had a better idea, and led them through a narrow corridor of reclining men up to the sand dunes and into the deep grasses there. Soldiers were camped in the dunes, small clots of men heating mess tins over small fires shielded from above by cloths so that the light didn't make them a target of the bombers. The smell of cooking brought grumbles from their bellies, but the trio of men continued through the encampments, before turning for where they estimated the bunker to be. The terrain made a pinpointed guess difficult, and when they emerged from the dunes they found they'd overshot the bunker by a dozen yards, and now had to approach it from the opposite side. Soldiers were stationed there, but they barely received a glance from anyone as they pushed towards the bunker. The two riflemen's attention was rapt on the bunker and who of assistance to them might be inside, but from here the interior of the bunker was hidden by the flaps of canvas. Ludis was still conscious that spies might be lurking nearby, and he searched the faces of the many men standing or sitting about the camp. In the past year, he'd honed his instincts to watch for the unusual, the slightest sign that danger presented itself, and but for the one mistake he'd made with the seemingly innocent un-dead child, his senses had been spot on. He trusted that - should he look into the face of a spy - he would recognise the deceit.

As Cooper and Watson pushed on, Ludis' steps faltered. He came to a standstill, his neck twisted to peer back at one face in the crowd. Men milled in the darkness, about tasks of their own, and the face that had caught and held his attention was momentarily lost to him. Ludis shifted, actually moving a burly soldier aside who was blocking his view. The soldier snarled something at him, but Ludis shot him a look that warned of violence and the man muttered and shoved his way off through the crowd. Ludis began searching again. He caught a glimpse of a pale face looking back at him, half concealed beneath a steel helmet identical to hundreds of others in his line of sight and it was the face for which he searched. Ludis glanced round, looking for his companions, but they were already ducking inside the bunker. There was no time for bringing them now, he turned quickly back to where he'd seen the pale man but again other soldiers moving between them obscured his view. Ludis took a step that way, then another. Luckily he was taller than most of those men around him, and he could see over them to where the beach sloped towards the water. Among the hundreds of men arrayed there, the task of spotting one among them should have been impossible, but Ludis' gaze fell on one man moving away between them. Ludis took another step after him, and then stopped. He glanced back at the bunker, but the fact he'd not yet followed his friends inside hadn't been noticed. Logic told him he should go to his friends and alert them, but instinct made him do otherwise. He had accepted the task of carrying the shard, yes, but also he'd set himself his own mission: one where he would challenge the evil things abroad in the land and send them screaming back to hell.

When he'd seen the fallen angel back at the barn, it had morphed into something malformed and less than human, its skin hardened like sun-toughened leather, its eyes flashing like bale fire and pointed teeth bared in feral animosity, yet in the features of the devil he'd been able to picture the face from which it had formed. That same face had so recently spied back at him through the throngs of soldiers and was now hurrying away before he could alert anyone that the devil strode among them. Ludis cast one last look back towards the bunker, then decided: should he run for the others then the devil would make its escape. He began pushing his way through the soldiers, craning to look over the top of them to where a singular figure moved sinuously among them. If he was in any doubt that he'd made a mistake in identifying the fleeing demon, then the faint vibration buzzing against his hip dispelled the notion. As he made progress through the camp the vibration grew stronger, now like an electrical charge passing into his side as he got closer to the fleeing figure. If he was to pull out the shard, Ludis expected that it would be glowing and burning with lust for the demon's life. He had made the mistake of showing the shard the last time, and thought that here and now he would be best served keeping it concealed until the final moment.

The going was difficult for Ludis, yet it was as if the devil slipped easily through the hundreds of men that separated them. Where Ludis had to force his way through, shouts of dismay and anger following him along the beach, the demon seemed to melt and flow among the crowds. More than once Ludis saw the face turned his way, the mouth twisted in a mocking sneer. That angered him, and he began bulling his way forward, now throwing men aside like tenpins, and jumping over others who were seated and not able to get out of his way quickly enough. A ripple of confusion followed him, and many faces were turned his way. He began to gesture and shout, pointing at the fleeing man, but it was as if nobody but him were aware of the devil's presence.

A hundred paces ahead the devil paused. Standing to each side of him was a Tommy in full battle kit. The men continued their conversation, as though a stranger had not interjected himself between them. As Ludis charged towards them all, the two men turned to face him, startled by his yells and the furore that followed him. Ludis screamed a warning to the men, but his shout was deaf to their ears as the devil swung a clawed hand and ripped out first one throat and then the other. Both men collapsed on the sand, causing those nearest to them to turn in surprise and wonder what had downed them. The immediate thought was that bullets from the planes above had hit them and the soldiers began to scatter for cover. That helped open a passage for Ludis, but also gave the devil the room to continue its work. It crouched over each murdered man in turn, pressing a thumb to their foreheads and muttering words that were lost amid the tumult of shouting soldiers. Finished with whatever demented scheme it had concocted, the demon rose up and faced Ludis. It smiled, then turned away from him and began strolling along the beach in no hurry.

There was a reason for its nonchalance.

As Ludis charged forward, his attention was on the receding form of the demon, but all around him voices were lifted in consternation and horror. He snatched his gaze from his quarry to where the pointing hands were all aimed and saw the two slain soldiers stirring. Ludis faltered in his run, thinking to ignore the deviltry and find a way round them, but the press of men made that too difficult. Not only that but faces were now turned on him as if he had something to do with the horror they all bore witness to. The two corpses had clawed their way back to their feet and stood between him and the demon, their mouths hanging open, drooling blood-flecked spittle over their chins. Their faces shone with hunger, and Ludis knew that the risen corpses saw him as the nearest source of fresh meat. On their foreheads similar bruises that had marked those of the un-dead family were livid. Distractedly he thought that his and the fallen angel's paths had crossed long before the events in the barn outside Reims, and that it had visited that lonely farmhouse in the orchard not long before he had. The un-dead family were the creature's vassals, and had been set to await his arrival, just as these two soldiers had now. At the time, Ludis had pitied the family – or the human parts of them that had once existed – but he now saw that he'd been wrong to do so. Nothing of their humanity had existed: their carcasses were but animated clay, driven by an insatiable hunger imbued in them by a devil's mark on their brows. Now, as he charged forward, he understood that to show these soldiers pity was neglectful of the mission he'd set himself.

In a way, they were mindless autonomons, little more than feeding machines, with no memory of their past lives, loves or desires. All they craved now was flesh between their teeth and Ludis eviscerated at their feet. Then they would turn their yearning for further meat on the other men on the beach. Both had forgotten the long-range usefulness of the rifles in their hands, but driven by malicious evil they had not lost all concepts of weapons. A fixed bayonet was something to slash and stab with, a heavy stock something with which to crush a skull. In that moment it was much as if Ludis had also lost all comprehension of the firearms he carried, because, instead of his revolver or rifle, it was the silver catchpole he pulled off his shoulder as he advanced towards them.

Back at the farm the walking dead had been shambling, weak things, slowed by the lack of sustenance they'd found about their home, but these two were newly risen and were as strong and agile as the soldiers they'd recently been. They came at Ludis with startling speed and ferocity and he was hard put to bat aside the first lunge of a bayonet, even as the second snagged at his coat as he swerved to one side. Ludis pivoted the catchpole and rammed one end through the torn throat of one of the walking corpses. The wound hissed and frothed, but it was not enough to immediately stop the revenant in its tracks. Levering up on the pole, Ludis forced the thing down on its back, stamping with all his power between the pole and the rim of its helmet. The soft sand gave, saving the thing a crushing blow to its skull and immediately it grasped at Ludis' boot. It held him as the second swung its rifle like a club. Ludis was not about to be caught out so easily. He ducked low, avoiding the rifle stock, and while his would-be slayer was off balance he ripped loose the catchpole's butt from the throat of the downed one. Swinging it he looped the snare over the second walking corpse's head and pulled on the silver rope with all his might. The throat was already cut deep, but the encircling noose cut deeper, and Ludis continued to strain until the burning silver clove through flesh and ligaments all the way to the spine. The un-dead thing had howled in agony as the noose did its work, but now it had no throat left to make a sound. Ludis gave the noose one final savage yank and the vertebra parted and the head rolled across the sand and came to rest upside down, balanced like a boiled egg in a cup in the bowl of its helmet.

Beneath his heel the second walking corpse strove to fight free. Ludis jammed the butt end of the pole against its chest, holding it to the sand as he stepped off its head. The uniform jacket saved it the agony of silver on its flesh and the thing merely batted the pole aside and came with arachnid-like flicks of its limbs back onto its feet. It had dropped its rifle, and now crouched, ready to leap at Ludis with its fingers flexing. The yielding of the sand had maybe saved it a crushed skull, but his boot heel had mushed its face. In the ruined mess of smashed features its eyes were bottomless pits, darker than the night that surrounded them. It champed jaws now missing various teeth.

'What are you waiting for, damn you? Come ahead, hell spawn,' Ludis taunted, lifting the catchpole like a stave. 'Your tardiness is keeping me from slaying your master.'

The corpse-man leapt and Ludis swerved to one side. He brought the silver pole down and smashed it on the point below the thing's helmet. Such a blow would slay any man, but it was not enough to kill the corpse a second time. It hit the sand in a sprawl, but immediately spun and came back at Ludis, clawing its way along the beach on all fours to attack from below the sweep of his weapon.

Ludis prepared himself, readying to ram the pole all the way through its foul heart.

Then, as he drove forward to meet the thing, there was a swarm of movement, and suddenly many men were between him and the corpse-man. He saw arms lifting and falling, rifles plunging in and out, bayonets piercing the form of the un-dead thing. Soldiers who had been momentarily stunned at the uncanny spectacle had regained their senses and leapt to the fight. Ludis could hear curses and shouts of horror from the men stabbing the corpse repeatedly. Beneath the jumble of men the un-dead creature continued to flail and lash out, but the men's blades were doing the trick and soon it was a shuddering pile of dismembered parts held together by the shredded remnants of a British uniform. When it twitched no more, many of the soldiers turned away, revulsion at their actions painted across their features, while others emptied their stomachs on the sand. Ludis looked down at what remained and saw that whatever life had animated the thing was now long dissipated. He spun round, searching the sands behind him. The press of men coming to see what had happened thwarted any view beyond the first ring of onlookers and Ludis launched towards them, ready to take up the chase.

Hands grasped him, many hands, and he was held back.

He shouted, trying to make his captors understand, but they had just had their first experience of unholy terror, and to them his exhortations only added to the uncanniness of it all.

Before he knew it, Ludis had been forced onto the sand, and many hands held him in place, faces lit by fear and confusion burning all around him. He could barely breathe due to the press of hands at his throat and chest, but that was not what caused the air to catch in his lungs. Men who had been shocked by the presence of walking corpses in their midst had known only one way to respond, and it looked like savagery was still in their minds.

Ludis saw arms rising high, and in those arms were rifles with bayonets fixed.

Chapter 35

25th May 1940
Dunkirk, France

If God should show His hand in Ludis Kristaps' mission He had an unusual way of delivering divine intervention. When he thought about it afterwards, Ludis came to understand that he owed more to coincidence and the circumstance of his location than a thunderbolt from the blue, because what saved him being speared on the bayonets of frightened soldiers was a Luftwaffe fighter plane, flying low along the beach and strafing the gathered men mercilessly.

One second he was surrounded by raised bayonets, voices lifted in command to slay the man who had brought terror among them, and in the next those very same voices were yelling and screaming as red-hot projectiles tore a double swathe along the beach. Men scattered, throwing themselves down, while others were torn to pieces by bullets that could cut through the armoured plates of a tank. The airplane flew on, banking out over the sea to circle and make a second run. The soldiers gathered on this part of the beach were in disarray, some screaming as they writhed in agony from their wounds, others shouting in consternation as they readied their rifles to meet the plane's second attack. Out in the open like this they were as flimsy as paper targets to the plane's guns. Further along the beach an anti-aircraft gun roared as it sent an arching ribbon of fire into the sky, but the tracer rounds fell far short of the plane, and so did the less visible rounds that followed their trajectory. Unabated the airplane came screaming back in, wings dipping from side to side as the pilot lined up on the far horizon to complete his second run. Guns blazed and the sand rose in waves, alongside the bodies of men caught in the hail of death. Everyone that could make a beeline for the dunes did so.

Ludis realised he was suddenly alone.

His captors had abandoned him as they sought concealment from the blazing bullets. Ludis thought to stay where he was, cover his head with his arms and hope for the best, but he could see the sands kicking up, sparkling like phosphorous in the dark and it was a tide that was racing towards him. Frantically, he pulled himself from the floor and – pausing only to snatch up the dropped catchpole - he threw himself towards the nearby sand dunes. The bullets tore up the beach behind him and he sent himself in a flying dive for the nearest reed-covered hummock. Sand pattered down on his back as the plane flew on by, and Ludis sucked in a deep breath for the first time in a minute.

Then the explosions began.

Not only had the German plane strafed the beach with bullets, but it had also loosed its payload of bombs and they were now ripping a series of deep craters in the earth. Ludis experienced compression of his eardrums, and he clamped his palms to his ears to save himself from deafness. Nearby a bomb hit with a dull whump that he felt in the ground beneath him. Sand and body parts were thrown into the air, along with blistering shrapnel that sought the bodies of men trying to find cover in the soft dunes. Ludis felt flame pass over him, and he was glad that he'd shorn his long hair and beard because the sparks of its passing stung his flesh whereas they once would have made a fireball of his head.

The explosions continued along the beach, receding away from him, and Ludis came up to his hands and knees and crawled through the dunes, trying to find somewhere to hide. There was, of course, nowhere in this exposed place that would save him from a direct hit. All he could hope for was that he was one of the lucky ones that the armament missed or he'd end up like the other shattered corpses he clambered over.

Anti-aircraft guns lit up the sky, chasing the streaking Luftwaffe plane. The airplane caught a direct hit, smoke puffing from it, before one wing tore loose and the plane made an ungraceful dive onto the beach. The wreckage exploded on hitting the sands, engulfing many in flame and flying debris, but many voices lifted in a shout of triumph. It was an ill won victory, one German plane against all the lives it had taken, but the shouts were spirited and was what kept the BEF fighting under such overwhelming odds. Ludis gave thanks to God, but in the next instance found he was cursing in an unsanctified manner. The fallen angel was out there still, and he couldn't begin to hope that it had been torn to shreds by any of the bombs or the crashing plane, because there was nothing as powerful as a devil's luck.

He poked his head up from the mound of sand, searching the beach for any sign of the demon, but it was hopeless. The hadn't ended when that one plane had crashed, because other Luftwaffe fighters streaked through the heavens, and most of the men on the beaches were all crouched down, and aiming their rifles skyward. Others were attempting to give aid to their stricken comrades, dragging the wounded across the sands towards the meagre shelter offered by the dunes, all the while yelling for medics, or simply shouting in frustration and anger.

Searching for the demon in the battleground would be a fruitless task now, so Ludis decided he would be best served seeking Watson and Cooper and finding out if they had won passage for them all to the British mainland. He trudged through the dunes, stepping over the fallen, trying not to look into the faces of the dead. Part of him dreaded that the devil might have passed among them and laid his thumb to their foreheads. The last he wanted now was to be engulfed by a wave of walking corpses, because such could be likely when counting the number of dead the demon had at his disposal.

Retracing his run along the sand was a simple enough task – where could he go wrong if he kept the sea to his left? Yet he almost missed the bunker when he came upon it. The bunker had taken a direct hit and all that showed it had once stood there was a carter surrounded by sandbags that had been torn apart, and a canvas that was part buried under a collapsed dune. Here and there he could discern a limb or part of a body sticking from the bloody sand. His discovery came like a clenched fist to his gut, and his first instinct was to rush forward and start digging in the sand, hoping that his two friends were buried but still alive. He ignored the broken limbs nearest to the lip of the crater, because it was apparent that they belonged to corpses, and instead went to where the edge of the dune had butted the back wall of the bunker. There the sand had cascaded down and would have most likely collapsed into the interior of the makeshift workroom – the place he'd last seen Watson and Cooper enter.

He dug like a lizard excavating its prey in the desert, shovelling with his hands, kicking back the drifts with his heels. He found the edge of the tattered canvas, and pulling and heaving on it, displacing yet another cascade of sand, he hauled it up and back, disclosing a shallow depression in the beach. A sightless face stared back at him, the mouth open but choked with earth. He did not recognise the balding man, but that was no source of relief. There could have been upward of a half dozen soldiers in the bunker, so this man was only the first he expected to find buried. Judging by how easily this man had been suffocated he did not give his friends great odds of survival. He pulled on the man's uniform jerkin, dragging him from the sands and placed him on the flattened ground ten yards distant. The man he could now see had stripes on his shoulder, and Ludis growled deep in his chest, recalling another sergeant whose life had been given in Ludis' war. He had to stop thinking that way: he had not caused the bomb to destroy the bunker, and therefore should carry no blame for this man's death. Watson and Cooper's deaths were something different again. If they had not entered the bunker in search of someone to help Ludis in his quest, then the damned bomb would not have killed them. He returned to his digging, and his actions had become more frantic.

On the beach and in the dunes, many others were engaged in similar tasks as they sought to help the injured, or to liberate their dead colleagues from the choking sands. Ludis gave them no mind, rapt on his own work. The Luftwaffe had carried their attack further along the beach and there was a time of respite for now, but the babble of voices, the cries and moans of the injured, the sounds of excavation, rang out from every direction. It was a constant gibberish, as if a wireless had been tuned off-station and all that came through was pulsing white noise that rose and fell in volume. It took Ludis some time to distinguish and recognise one voice among the many. He twisted round from his digging and blinked up at the man standing over him, with one hand resting on Ludis' shoulder.

Rifleman Cooper was panting as if having ran a long way. Perhaps his breathlessness was more to do with the adrenalin racing through his system, or through relief at finding Ludis alive.

'Where in God's name did you get to?' Cooper demanded.

Ludis thought about telling him about the fallen angel, his chase of the fiend and the subsequent battle, but all he said was, 'Where's Watson?'

'He's out there. Looking for you.'

Ludis sank down on his knees. 'Then neither of you was inside…'

'Does it look like it. Here…' Cooper offered his hand and hauled Ludis back to his feet.

'I thought I'd lost you both,' Ludis said.

Cooper surveyed the devastated bunker. 'Maybe I should thank you for running off. If you hadn't we'd have all been inside *that* when the bombs hit. But I'm not going to thank you. Bleedin' hell! We're supposed to be looking after you. You're supposed to stick by us at all times.'

Ludis wasn't used to being scolded like a child. The last person to treat him that way was his wife, Galina, but she'd always done so with a particular look and a wry smile. He understood that the rifleman's words were tinged more with relief than anger, and didn't offer an excuse. Instead he thought to go directly for the truth.

'He's here?'

'Who?' Cooper squinted. 'You're talking about that blasted demon?'

'He was following us, disguised as a British soldier. I saw him and gave chase.'

'Tell me you killed the bloody thing.'

'Unfortunately…no, I did not. But there is one thing that I'm thankful for. The devil ran from me.'

'How's that a good thing?'

'It means that he fears me. Or, more rightly, he fears the weapon I carry.'

Cooper glanced at the silver catchpole, where Ludis had discarded it before digging in the bunker.

Ludis touched his satchel. 'I'm talking about this: the spear tip. I believe now that the shard does have the power to slay the devil. When I had him cornered he resorted to reanimating two murdered men to slow me, in order that he escape.'

As had all the others of the section, Cooper had experienced the supernatural on too many occasions to be stunned by Ludis' revelation of walking dead men. Nevertheless, he grimaced at the notion that others might have witnessed the resurrection. Ludis read the concern on the soldier's face. 'You need not worry that others might report what they seen. There was so much confusion; I doubt anyone would have made sense of what they saw. And, at any rate, I'm not sure any of those nearby survived the Luftwaffe attack. I was lucky to escape: many others didn't.'

'I can't believe I'm happy to hear that fellow soldiers died. I'm not, it's terrible, but it has saved us a lot of explaining.' Cooper hung his head, ashamed at what he was implying.

'You didn't report anything about the devil or the other fiends loose upon the world?'

'No. If we did that, we'd have all been placed in straightjackets and carted off to the nearest field hospital. We thought it best to say that we were escorting an allied soldier who had important information, information for the ears of the Top Brass only.' Cooper cast a wave in the general direction of the sea. 'Tomorrow we begin evacuating, and we secured us all a place on a boat to England. Not that it means much now-' he had taken note of the sergeant laid out on the sand '-seeing as the man who was organising our passage has been killed.'

'The British are evacuating? Everyone? Then that is a good thing.' Ludis forestalled Cooper's grunt of dismay with a lifted palm. 'It means we need not concern ourselves with organising a boat: we can simply board with everyone else. But you do realise what this might also mean?'

'The devil, disguised as a Tommy, can do the very same thing.'

Ludis spied across the sea. Out there across the wind-tossed waves lay the English coastline, such a short hop away, though there was no hint of it through the darkness. He thought again about the journey that had brought them all to this time and place, and how the devil had always been a few steps ahead of them. They had all been on course to arrive here on the eve of the British Expeditionary Force's disembarkation from France. He had heard old tales that evil spirits could not traverse a body of flowing water without the aid of a human emissary. What more would the fallen demon require than some well-meaning officer ordering him aboard a ship alongside all the others? The devil's plan had been to make its way to the British mainland all along, but for what reason?

Whatever that turned out to be, it did not bode well for anyone.

Ludis said, 'We must find Watson quickly. We need all the help we can get to find the damned thing before it can board a boat to England.'

Chapter 36

26th May 1940
English Channel

Operation Dynamo had began in full earnest. Almost a week earlier, Prime Minister Winston Churchill had authorised preparations for a mass evacuation of the British Expeditionary Force and its allies, and Vice-Admiral Bertram Ramsay, understanding that the hard-pressed Royal Navy couldn't possibly supply the number of boats necessary had called on the British public for assistance. At ports all along the English coastline, a ramshackle flotilla of craft had been assembled, people rallying to the call to save their heroic soldiers from being decimated on the beaches. Royal Navy destroyers sailed alongside civilian sailing schooners, cabin cruisers, ferries, yachts and even paddlewheel steamers, with a view to evacuating more than three hundred thousand men. The crossing was treacherous, with the boats having to navigate a maze of German-strewn contact mines and the continuous harassment of *Luftwaffe* fighter planes and Stuka bombings.

The stalled Panzer divisions and heavy artillery battalions had joined the battle once more and the perimeter of the BEF defensive line was shrinking hourly. Dunkirk was ablaze and the port facilities were destroyed, so the boats were forced to risk running aground in the shallow water along the beaches or to tie up alongside hastily constructed breakwaters, formed from rubble and planking, where the soldiers awaited rescue in full view of the German guns. Many men had perished along the beaches, and everyone there knew that there would be many more deaths to come. It was hellish, but nothing like the real hell that would alight should the fallen angel make it to Britain and carry out whatever nefarious plans it had in mind.

Ludis and Cooper had found their companion the day before, and they'd conducted an exhaustive search of the beaches and, once, Watson – despite his earlier argument about doing so - even went into Dunkirk to try to locate the fiend. All their efforts proved futile, and they'd finally collapsed in weary defeat in a jerry-rigged camp alongside thousands of others. Come the dawn they had taken up their search again, but it had been as empty as the day's before had proven. To aid in their search, and to avoid awkward questions, Watson had brought Ludis a serge jacket and trousers so he could blend more easily with all the other men. They risked Ludis being confused for a spy, with the necessity to keep their heads down and board the first available boat. Feign deafness, Watson had cautioned, and try not to speak. Ludis' speech, though his English was now quite good, was still heavily accented and a dead giveaway.

Boats had been landing at the beaches for hours now, but there were thousands queuing for passage out of France, and Ludis and his companions had been forced to join others standing three abreast on one of the jetties pushing out into the Channel. Twice they'd weathered attack from the Luftwaffe, but the spaces made by those that fell were quickly filled with others pushing onto the boardwalks. While they stood among the press of men, all three were alert for any sign that the thing they sought was nearby them, watching them in turn from out of the sea of faces peering towards England and salvation.

It was mid-afternoon by the time they boarded a boat crewed by civilians, on their second shuttle run of the day. Ludis, Watson and Cooper joined another twenty-five soldiers aboard the thirty feet long pleasure cruiser, which showed signs of having already narrowly missed sinking earlier in the day. Bullet holes peppered the hull, but thankfully above the waterline. The space below was full of salvaged equipment, so the men sat or stood where they could on the deck. They cast off, watching the hopeful faces of other men waiting their turn on the breakwaters, all of them wishing that it was them who had boarded and didn't have to endure further bombardment on the beach. The danger was not over for those on board, because already there was gossip among the men that some of the civilian craft had been sank by Luftwaffe attacks out in the Channel. Some – the non-swimmers among them – swore they'd rather die on the beaches than be left to the mercy of the pitiless sea.

'There's a sight I never want to see again,' Watson said with a nod towards the mainland. Dunkirk was ablaze, and even now in the late afternoon the Luftwaffe bombardment was relentless. Oily smoke made the sky as black as pitch, and flame writhed through the buildings from one end of town to the other. In the harbour boats had been sunk, and only the tallest chimneys and stacks protruded from the high tide. From this vantage the numbers of men yet crowded on the beaches was astonishing, but they were less than quarter the number hiding in the dunes or in the lands between the beachhead and the canals. 'Makes me thankful,' Watson went on. 'You ask me, we're the lucky ones for getting away when we did.'

Cooper nodded out to sea. In the distance a Navy destroyer, packed with evacuees, sailed for England. Between them and the destroyer was a small flotilla of civilian boats, some of them nigh on swamped under the weight of desperate men. Wallowing in the water much closer to them was an upturned hull of a boat that hadn't made it. 'Tell the poor saps who were on that boat that they were lucky.'

Ludis found a place alongside the port gunwales, propping himself against the rail and holding onto the silver catchpole like he was an angler seeking to pull in a mermaid. Obviously the evacuees had more on their minds than the weird figure he struck, because nobody commented. Ludis hailed from a fishing village on the shores of the Baltic, and was no stranger to boats, but it had been some time since he'd experienced the pitch and swell of waves beneath his feet. Within minutes of leaving the land he felt nauseous, but he wasn't the only one who tossed their meagre dinner over the bows. Bilious, he sat down and nestled his head in his hands, the catchpole propped behind him. Cooper offered water from a battered canteen, but Ludis declined. The big gunner grinned and put the canteen away.

'Can't say as I blame you. I'm looking forward to a proper mug of tea,' Cooper said. 'First thing I'm going to do when we get home. Nice cup of tea and a bacon sarnie.'

A round of acknowledgement went up from the other soldiers in hearing distance, and conversation struck up about imminent reunions with loved ones, favourite food and special places they'd visit. It should have been an uplifting moment, but too many of them were aware that their voyage home wasn't over yet, or if it ever would be. Soon the chatter stalled.

The soldiers were all of a type, young men who'd witnessed too much in their short lives, and they all sat or stood with similar expressions of dejection on their features. Operation Dynamo, for all that it was starting as a success, was destined to be one of the worst defeats of an army in history, and there wasn't a man among them unconscious of that fact. Only the civilian crew maintained their spirits, and Ludis looked on them as the true heroes of this episode of the war, and thought that they should be rightly remembered as such. However, if the demon's plans came to fruition, he wondered if there'd be any man left alive to recall their heroic endeavours in years to come. He had no doubt now that the devil had set its sights on England, and that it sought to usurp control of the land, from where it would take its war back to the men who had set it loose. That was the folly of tampering with powers beyond mans comprehension, he thought. The Nazis had sought to utilise the supernatural to meet their own ends, but it had backfired on them and now they faced an enemy more potent than the combined British Forces. Recalling again how the devil had resurrected the two murdered soldiers – not to mention the family of farmers – he feared that the devil could defeat all on the British mainland, and then use them as its puppets to send against Germany. He could not begin to imagine the magnitude of horror, or the devastation that could be caused, of an un-dead army marching across the continent. It would be unstoppable. Ludis felt sick once more, but this time it had nothing to do with the continuous movement of the boat. He returned to his previous position, leaning over the rail and watching the rush of water pass beneath the bow of the boat.

He was still there twenty minutes later when there was a stir among the men on the decks. Twisting round he searched their faces, saw that they were all looking in the same direction. Following their gaze, their pointing hands, he saw a black dot appear from the scattered clouds. The dot grew exponentially as it dived like a falcon from the sky. Soon he heard the siren shriek, and heard more than one man yell *Stuka!*

The bomber grew and grew, and it was apparent to all aboard that the pilot targeted their boat. The soldiers fought to bring round their rifles, and a volley of rounds was sent towards the diving plane. The bomber came on, and another salvo was fired, again to no avail. By the time anyone thought to seek cover, the pilot could be seen through the cockpit. At the last second the plane's nose lifted and the bomber made a shrieking curve back into the sky, but not before it released a bomb towards the cruiser. Men yelled in terror, but it was replaced a moment later by shouts of relief as the bomb tumbled over the stern of the boat and struck the waves a hundred yards distant. The bomb detonated, but all that hit anyone on board was a spray of water.

Quarter a mile away a Royal Navy destroyer's guns belched thunder, tracking the Stuka through the heavens, but the elusive plane flew on. Nearby the evacuees on another boat were yelling encouragements to them across the water, having witnessed the near miss. Now that the men aboard this boat realised how lucky they had been they too joined the cheering.

Celebration was a short-lived thing, because the Stuka came back, this time flanked by two Messerschmitts. The fighter planes sent withering fire among the boats crowding the sea, and the Stuka's load struck pay dirt this time. A steamboat was hit and erupted into flame and black smoke. On board all the nearest boats men shouted in anger and dismay, and some of the boats adjusted their course to attempt to pick up anyone lucky enough to have made it into the water before the ship was destroyed.

Overhead the scream of the fighter plane engines filled the heavens, punctuated with short bursts of fire from their guns. Ludis saw another boat hit, men's bodies being thrown skyward by the impact of bullets through their bodies. On his boat the soldiers fired at the speeding planes but it would take a miracle to bring down the fighter planes with rifles alone. Even Watson, who was a superb marksman, could only manage to shoot after the planes raced overhead, and only at their retreating tails. Whether he gained a hit or not, Ludis would never be sure.

A good half-mile distant, and barely visible as it rode the tide, another boat was struck squarely and exploded – its demise marked by a fireball rising into the heavens.

Anti-aircraft guns blazed from the accompanying destroyer, but the planes continued to buzz around it like annoying insects, delivering their stings at will.

There was a stench upon the sea now: burning fuel, cordite, and blood. Even the stiff sea breezes couldn't clear it, but simply swirled the smoke around, shrouding the view of even the closer boats.

Ludis had gripped the catchpole. Little use it was against the attacking airplanes, but the boat was rocking violently and he couldn't afford to lose the weapon. He caught a look from one soldier that said: *What are you going to do? Catch a Stuka by its tail and reel it in by hand?*

Ludis shoved the pole down on the deck and brought out his Webley. The handgun was about as little use as was the catchpole in a fight with the planes, but at least it was a conventional weapon. Chances were that a plane would have to be so close for him to hit it with the revolver that it would already be crashing along the deck. Nonetheless, the presence of the gun in his hand dispelled any awkward questions from the soldier should any of them make it out of there alive.

Ludis was standing thus, his gun aimed ineffectively at the sky when another clamour arose. He swung to where the shouts were aimed and saw another boat looming out of the battle smoke. Whoever was at the helm was blind, or he was dead, because the boat was on a collision course with theirs.

From the cabin there were loud exhortations for their captain to steer clear of the other boat and Ludis felt the deck disappear from beneath his feet, as someone pulled down hard on the wheel. Ludis fell against the railing, his revolver spinning from his hand and into the sea. The second boat, a larger craft with a high prow, loomed over him, filling Ludis' vision and he threw himself backwards to avoid being crushed. The prow struck the point where he'd been standing, and boards and metal rail alike were crushed as if they were eggshell. The smaller boat shuddered and a chorus of cries went up, some of them ending in watery splutters as men were thrown overboard. The larger craft continued to plough alongside them, shoving and butting the cruiser aside, until both boats rode the water adjacent. Ludis had fallen among the feet of others who were all struggling to stay upright and he had to haul on their legs to pull up to his feet. He blinked in incredulity at the place where he'd so recently stood: the entire side of the boat had been crushed inward, the decks shattered and the rail gone. Had he not leapt away when he did he would have been a crimson smear on the prow of the larger boat. Crewmen were leaning over the side, checking the damage, and with relief one of them shouted that the cruiser remained sea worthy, that the damage was all above the waterline. Thankfully, the emergency manoeuvre had saved them from being hit square on and the damage – though an untidy mess – was superficial to the buoyancy of the craft. On the opposite side, arms reached out to help haul aboard those that had spilled into the sea.

The boat that had rammed theirs was still only a few yards away, sitting higher in the water and Ludis looked up to meet the faces of those staring down at them. In convention with all the other crafts on the Channel, the boat should have been packed with evacuees, but he was surprised to find there was no one at the rails. He glanced around him, and could tell that some of his companions had also noted the lack of men clustered on the deck of the ship. Ludis looked again, and this time noticed one figure move stealthily out of the way.

His view of the single man had been for a split second only, but it was all the time he needed. He had imprinted that face indelibly into his brain.

Ludis searched the deck for the catchpole.

Damn all the demons to hell! The catchpole was gone, lost when the larger boat struck and probably back there sinking into the depths of the Channel.

He cursed himself this time, for foolishly putting down the weapon for appearances sake.

Then there was no time for cursing anything, because the captain of the cruiser was making sure a second collision didn't occur. Ludis didn't have time to think. He took a short run up and leapt, his fingers reaching for the starboard rail of the larger boat.

Behind him, he could faintly hear Cooper and Watson yelling in consternation at his idiocy, but there was nothing for it now. If he'd to halt the fallen angel before it achieved landfall, he had to do so now.

All he had to do was hold tight to the rail, then swarm up on board, then beard the demon in its lair.

Except that he missed by a good arm's length and plunged into the brine.

Chapter 37

26ᵗʰ May 1940
English Channel

Ludis held tight to a trailing rope.

His hand had found it as he struck out blindly for the boat that was tantalizingly out of reach, and he had grasped it and clung on for all he was worth. In his mind he recited a prayer that he'd once learned, and since forgotten, but must have retained in some corner of his brain for just such a moment as this.

St Michael the archangel
Defend me in battle.
Be my protection against the wickedness and snares of the devil.
And do, thou, oh prince of the heavenly host,
By the divine power of God.
Cast into hell, Satan and all the evil spirits,
Who wander around the world,
Seeking the ruin of souls.
Amen

Whether St Michael would heed his plea it didn't matter, because the prayer served to embolden him, and his new strength of faith ignited a righteous fire in his gut. He began to haul on the rope, and with each tug the boat grew closer in his vision. Perhaps he could not reel in a Luftwaffe bomber by strength of hand alone, but it seemed he could so with a boat. He laughed at the ridiculousness of the notion, and the mirth helped galvanise him to greater strength. On his hip he could feel the tremor of the shard as it began to vibrate wildly.

Within seconds he found himself in the wash of the boat itself, then he had hauled himself head and shoulders above the spume and he was able to place the soles of his boots against the hull. Hand over hand, step by step, he walked up the side of the boat and finally threw an elbow over the rail. He found he was to the aft of the boat and could see all the way along the deck to where a foredeck and cabin rose up like a castle tower. The cabin was of no concern to him; his gaze fell on the mounds of torn humanity strewn across the deck. They looked like they had taken a direct hit from a bomb, except there was no damage to the boat. There had been no salvation here: soldiers who had survived the terrors of war had discovered far greater horror aboard this boat. Ludis swarmed over the rail and planted his boots on planks awash with blood and viscera.

He had to ignore the dead around him, could not falter from his task for even a second. He walked forward, stepping over bodies ripped limb from limb, their cavities opened like carcasses in a butcher's shop. One distant part of him told him to be thankful that the bodies were in no shape to be reanimated, but that was a spiteful thought that he cast aside.

He could not see the fiend, but proof of its presence was all about him, and he was in no doubt that the sole figure he'd seen on the deck had been the demon. He felt for his weapons. Handgun, rifle, and silver catchpole: all had been lost, but none of those weapons mattered now. He delved in his satchel and pulled out the shard. It was glowing with internal heat, and a tickle of energy ran the length of his arm. He held the triangular blade clenched in his fist, the strip of Galina's dress protecting his palm from the jagged edges.

Then he rocked back on his heels, and throwing back his head, he roared, 'I am here devil. Face me. It is the reckoning you have sought to avoid, but I have found you. Come out…instead of hiding like the cowardly thing you are.'

The sounds of battle faded in Ludis' ears. The shouts of the men on the nearby boat came only as a weak murmur, the shriek of war planes sounded like the insignificant buzzing of gnats, the rat-a-tat of guns merely a spider tapping its legs on its web. All that came clear to him was the bubbling laughter from the foredeck.

Ludis strode forward, hearing the laughter rise in volume.

Corpses hampered his route, but he picked a way through them, ignoring the guns and even the grenades that lay among them. All the while he watched the singular figure that had stepped from the cabin to stand on the foredeck, watching him in turn.

When ten paces were all that separated them, Ludis halted. Seawater dripped from his clothing and pooled at his feet, mingling with the gore on the planks. Ludis settled his feet, bending his knees and lowering his centre of gravity for more stability. He expected the demon's attack to come quickly and with the ferocity of a hurricane: something capable of slaying every man aboard this ship wasn't an enemy to be taken lightly.

The demon took a stride forward, stepping from the shadows of the cabin to be caught in a ray of light punching through the clouds. Ludis saw that it had cast off the disguise of a British soldier, and stood in resplendent nudity on the deck. The face was similar to that it had worn throughout, but its body was sculpted as though by a master artist, both beautiful and an abomination at once. Never had Ludis seen a more perfectly formed specimen of humanity, but by its very nature that also made it inhuman. Hair as white as snow poured down from its skull and hung over each shoulder, otherwise it was hairless, but that was not all: there were no genitalia for it was both male and female, yet neither. The fallen angel opened its arms wide, as though mocking Christ on the cross, but as Ludis watched great pinions unfolded from its back to frame both arms and body alike. Its wings were golden and flared with sparkling iridescence.

Ludis shook his head in denial.

'Deceiver,' he shouted. 'Show your true form.'

The creature cocked its head bird-like, studying him like he was a tasty morsel to be pecked up. Finally its laughter subsided, and it rested one hand across its keeled chest.

I am Abaddon.

The demon's voice rang as clear as a bell, yet Ludis had not seen its lips move. Trickery had allowed the woodsman, Borvo, a similar talent, wherein it seemed like his words were delivered by some psychic connection, whereas it was nothing but a ventriloquist's act. But this was different. He did not doubt that an arch-demon should have the ability to speak directly in a man's brain. His teachings had shown that the devil and his emissaries did so all the time, cajoling and prompting man to acts of sin. He even recognised the name, and it boded ill, for Abaddon was indeed the name of one of the rebel angels cast down by Michael, and buried in the abyss for all time. In some religions, the demon was known by other names, Asmodeus or Apollyon, but more frequently as the "King of Locusts", or more pertinently as "The Destroyer".

I see you know and fear my name.

Ludis conjured up a laugh, but it carried little weight. 'I fear only the Lord God, not a foul thing like you. Now, stop your lies and show me your true face…so I can smite it.'

The hand fell from the demon's breast, to point instead at Ludis. *You place too much faith in that sliver of metal. Do you really expect to vanquish one who has laughed in the face of Yahweh? I do not fear His weapons. Put it down, Ludis Kristaps, and come to me and I promise you a clean death.*

'Put it down, you say?' Ludis brought out the shard, holding it in full sight, and ribbons of light streamed out from it. He saw Abaddon flinch. 'For such a great deceiver of mankind, you are a poor liar. You fear the shard and so you should, because I am going to ram it into your heart.'

You are a pitiful fool, Abaddon said. *I could have destroyed you at any time I chose.*

'Then why didn't you?' Ludis took another step forward, holding the shard out between them.

I have enjoyed the chase. It has given me much pleasure observing the destruction of all those you cared for. For countless millennia I've been trapped in the Abyss. Have you any concept of the boredom that I've endured? Your escapades have helped lighten my return to this realm. Abaddon offered a feral smile. *But that is over now, and I have new delights to occupy my senses. You are of no more value to me.*

'So meet me,' Ludis challenged. 'Let's get this over with.'

I will crush you like an insect.

'Then you'll find I'm an insect with a poisonous sting in its tail.' Ludis launched forward, stepping over one corpse, planting his feet on another and bounding up at the devil. As he did so he made a wide slashing arc of the shard.

Abaddon moved with unnatural agility, springing away to the far side of the boat where it planted its back to the port rail. Ludis almost skidded inside the open door of the cabin, but he thrust out a hand, halting himself against the doorjamb with juddering force. He span quickly, bringing up his weapon to ward off a counter attack. Abaddon still stood at the rail. Its left hand was cupped over its opposite shoulder, and from between its fingers black ichor trickled. Its face came up, a picture of unearthly beauty that transformed in a blink. Its lower jaw opened wide, elongating to encompass sprouting tusks of teeth. Mockingly, Ludis said, 'See, I knew you had another face.'

Abaddon roared, and there was nothing about it that was a psychic connection this time. It was like the keening roar it had emitted back at the barn in Reims, full of hatred and loathing, but also tinged with a demand for slaughter. The body began to twist and deform, and the illusion of golden feathers fell away from its wings, replaced by leathery tatters attached to bony rods like elongated fingers. Even the bat-like wings were an illusion of sorts, a recollection of ancient times before The Fall, and they burst into bilious flames, charred, and then collapsed as ash to the deck. All the while the body continued to shudder and grow, the skin darkening and toughening, and horny protuberances began to sprout along the ridges of its collarbones and spine and the centre of its skull. The legs shifted, stretched, muscles bulging and ligaments elongating, and the heels rose from the deck to form a new joint. The feet splayed, toes now sporting talons that dug into the wood. Abaddon's arms also changed, growing colossal in girth, pulsing with the killing power racing through them.

Ludis had intended goading the beast, and he'd achieved what he'd set out to do, but he must act now before Abaddon fully transformed into its genuine likeness. While it still contorted he had a chance at taking it down. He rushed it, ramming forward with the glowing blade.

Abaddon swatted him almost languidly.

It was as if a tree trunk had slammed him, and Ludis was sent tumbling across the deck feeling agony in every atom of his being. He crashed into the cabin, splintering the wall with his shoulder and almost separating the joint. Tasting blood in his mouth, Ludis struggled up from the deck, surprised to find he hadn't relinquished his hold on the shard.

'Is that all you've got demon?'

Abaddon came like a runaway truck, bolting across the deck with its head lowered. It caught Ludis in the gut with its horned head, and continued on, wrapping him in arms as solid as steel cables. The wall of the cabin was no contest and burst inwards and both of them crashed into the instrument panel. Ludis thought his spine must be shattered, but he was still able to feel the floor beneath his boots. Before the relief that he was not crippled could sink in, Abaddon had caught him by the front of his jacket. It spun him off his feet with a flick of one wrist and hurled him through the opposite wall. Ludis landed on the starboard deck, his jaw hitting so hard he could feel his teeth crack.

Stunned, he could barely crawl over onto his side before Abaddon was over him.

His vision swam, but the wicked claws it raised to rend him apart were stark against the sky and he fixed on them.

The claw began its fall and in Ludis' overwrought mind it seemed to slow as if it moved through treacle.

Inches from his face the claws were snatched aside.

Ludis blinked in wonder, watching sparks light up against the creature's breast. Another flash came from the side of its skull, and the monster turned away. Only briefly was it deterred, because it soon swung back again, and leaned out over Ludis to roar its fury across the waves.

Having no idea of the source of his salvation, Ludis wasn't about to think about it now. He rolled from under the beast and came up on one knee, his right elbow propped on the rail, the shard still tightly held in his fist. Abaddon was screaming hatred at the boat Ludis had escaped Dunkirk on. Ludis glanced that way and saw a severe-faced youth standing in the prow, his rifle jammed to his shoulder as he fired shot after unerring shot into Abaddon's shoulders and face. Watson's bullets did little to harm it, but they were enough to sting the demon's pride. Ludis dreaded to think what Abaddon might do to Watson if it wasn't stopped. The thought galvanised him into action and he powered up, throwing his shoulder into the demon's side and carrying him along the deck towards the mounds of shattered humanity. While he drove the creature forward, Ludis' right arm pistoned in and out, jabbing the shard continuously into Abaddon's stomach and side.

Abaddon dug its clawed feet into the decking.

Ludis felt a hand clamp down on his left arm, and in the next instant he was hauled bodily into the air. The demon shook him like a carpet seller unrolling a rug. The tendons in his elbow and shoulder ripped, and Ludis experienced the searing agony of bones splintering in his forearm.

'I tire of you,' Abaddon said, for the first time given human voice.

He gave Ludis' arm another yank and then the big man was airborne once more.

Ludis crashed to the deck with sickening force.

He looked up, clearer of mind than he ever expected. He thought that he would see the demon wielding his dismembered arm like a truncheon, but the thing's hands were empty. Ludis checked and saw that – though it was severely injured – his arm was still attached. Thanking God for this small mercy, he snatched his gaze to his other hand. Miraculously it was fisted around the shard. Ludis knew that it wasn't through any presence of mind, or strength of will that meant he'd retained a hold of the weapon, but that something else was in command of his hand. Even as he thought it, he began to crawl up again as the shard pulsed brightly, tugging him back to face the demon once more.

'Say your goodbyes to your God,' Abaddon crowed as he stalked forward, 'for you have a new master now.'

Ludis swiped at the thing's face, but Abaddon merely reared away and immediately leaned in again. It laughed as it stamped him down to the deck. Then it flicked him over and held his right hand to the deck with a taloned foot. 'You have given me much entertainment. So much so that I have decided to keep you around. You, Ludis Kristaps, shall be my new vassal. You have seen my work before, but those wretches were dead before I placed my seal upon theirs brows. You, I shall keep alive.' The beast paused to elicit malicious glee at its plan. 'Those revenants were mindless things, but you, Ludis, shall fully retain your mind. Your body shall die and rot around you, and you will be fully conscious and will scream as the gases of decomposition split your skin and the putrefying meat sloughs from your skeleton. When you are but tatters of tendon and yellowed bones, still you will live, and I will delight in splintering each bone in turn and sucking the marrow from them.'

The demon stretched forth one hand, folding in its fingers and extending the fleshy bulb of its thumb. Upon the flesh glowed a sigil that burned like an ember. It began to mutter, and the language it spoke was so ancient that there wasn't a man in history who would have understood it. Abaddon reached for Ludis' forehead.

Ludis wasn't afraid to die.

Not in the normal sense, for he held the Christian belief of an afterlife, where he'd be reunited with Galina and his unborn child, but that was not what the demon promised. His was to be an eternity of living death, from which he'd never ascend to stand at God's side in Heaven. Was there anything he feared more than that? He roared in denial, twisting round his hand and he dug the tip of the shard deep into the meat of Abaddon's foot.

The demon howled in agony and stepped off him, its thumb snatched away.

'I've changed my mind,' Abaddon snapped. 'I think it much more preferable to rend you apart and feed you to the creatures of the sea.'

So there was a grain of goodness in the monster's shrivelled heart, Ludis thought.

That would explain the silver halo that had just flared over its head.

Ludis would have laughed at the absurdity of the thought if the situation weren't so desperate. He clamped his mouth shut, holding in the pain as he fought to right himself, watching in a mix of shock and delight as the halo dropped over the demon's head and settled on its shoulders. Then the halo contracted, cinching tightly round the thick throat. Abaddon was caught in mid-stride, and was jerked forcefully to a halt. Stunned it took a moment to realise what had happened.

Behind the demon Ludis caught sight of another figure, a big man, dripping wet from having swam to the boat. Rifleman Cooper, having discovered where the silver catchpole had slid to along the deck – not into the sea as Ludis had feared – had come to join the battle. Their eyes met for the briefest of moments, and they each shared a look of mutual respect. Then the demon felt the burning touch of the silver and it went into a rage.

The silver catchpole was just that: nothing that could kill or ultimately harm the beast. It had to be used in conjunction with the trident-headed spears that the Nazis had originally carried if there was any hope of holding the monster in its tracks. Now it was simply an inconvenience to Abaddon, and he twisted round, intent on tearing apart its wielder. Cooper was canny enough to stay out of reach of the swiping claws, but it put him off balance and Abaddon easily wrenched the pole from his grasp. It tore the noose from about its neck, regardless of the burning touch on its palms, and then threw the pole aside. It roared, bending at the waist as it prepared to launch itself in rending fury onto the rifleman. Cooper was caught against the rail, and had nowhere to go.

Suddenly the demon buckled at the knees.

Cooper thought it was about to spring, and threw up his arms in a futile attempt to ward it off. But then it spun about and he saw Ludis Kristaps hanging onto the monster's broad back. He had wrapped his legs round Abaddon's waist and locked his ankles together. His left arm, even broken, was snared around the demon's throat while his other hand continuously rose and fell as the big Latvian drove the splinter of metal deep into the flesh of its right shoulder and neck. Where the shard struck, black blood jetted out. Abaddon was screaming, and the note of desire had gone, fully replaced by one of pain.

The demon was in a blind rage, its arms sweeping around and where they struck the gunwales and decking deep gouges marked their passing. It tried to rip Ludis from its back, and made tatters of his jacket, and furrowed deep wounds in the flesh of his face, yet Ludis was remorseless, driven.

The sounds of battle were horrendous, and almost drowned out the shouts of warning from Watson and others on the other boat. Cooper snatched his attention from the fighting to look across to where Watson was at the helm of the second boat. The young man was jumping up and down, pointing in hard jabs towards the sky. Cooper spun to see what he was pointing at and saw the airplane falling from the clouds. While Ludis' battle had raged with the demon, another had been contested above the Channel. Elsewhere evacuees on other boats were cheering the success of the Royal Navy for bringing down the German bomber. Cooper stood open-mouthed, but only for a second or two. He glanced from the spiralling plane, to the deck where Ludis and the demon still strove, then let out a yell of alarm.

He ran forward, jostling to avoid the demon's sweeping claws, and grabbed at Ludis.

'We have to go,' he screamed in the Latvian's ear.

Ludis didn't hear, or he didn't care. He had one thing in his mind and that was to finish the monster once and for all. He continued to stab and slash, the violence of his work sending splashes of his own blood and the black ichor of the devil over Cooper's chest. Cooper ignored the gore, and pulled on Ludis' bad arm with all his strength. At the same time he stared up at the imminent death descending on them all.

Suddenly there was a moment of pause. Whether it was Ludis or the beast that sensed the sudden displacement of air, the shrieking howl of the dying plane, or something else, Cooper didn't know. All that he was aware of was clutching onto Ludis' jacket and both were being propelled across the deck, either by his feet or his companion's, and they both slammed against the rail.

A snapshot image was burned into both men's vision as they saw the demon rear up. One side of its neck was open and black blood spurted from the wound, but didn't seem to hamper the beast as it reared back its head and roared in frustration. It was standing thus as the airplane slammed down on it, smashing through the deck, the hold, and the hull in one terrific collision. Debris exploded outwards, flying shrapnel that tore apart more of the boat. Flames erupted, even as the aft of the boat was forced deep into the water, the prow lifting skyward. Splinters of wood and metal were carried on the flames, as were larger chunks of the aircraft and boat, and comingling with them all were the eviscerated parts of the soldiers and crew who had died at the demon's hands. Also two men were lifted by the blast and their bodies were cast far out from the boat, slapping the waves as they landed, where finally they lay still in the water.

On the second boat, Watson had ducked along with everyone else, but now he was up again, his sharpshooter's gaze flicking from the sinking remains of wreckage to where his companions lay adrift in the sea, surrounded by debris and pockets of burning aviation fuel.

Though he was a lowly private, the young rifleman began yelling orders at the crewmen and more experienced soldiers alike. The boat steered towards the nearest lifeless figure, but there was little hope in the hearts of anyone aboard.

Chapter 38

4th June 1940
London, England

In the pre-dawn hours the final rescue run had delivered the last of the British Expeditionary Force and many of its allies to the British mainland. Thousands of soldiers had to be left behind, those that were too injured to make the voyage, and those that had chosen to remain at their sides. Many of those left behind would face internment in the days to come, for most their imprisonment would last for almost five years. Many wouldn't survive the incarceration. On the beaches of Flanders the dead were too many to count, and people tried to cover the fact of Britain's massive failure in the miracle that more than three hundred and thirty-eight thousand men had been liberated from under the Germans' noses. People spoke of heroism, and trumpeted the success of the evacuation. Townspeople had poured out of their homes with gifts of food and drink for the routed Allied troops, welcoming the famished men home as heroes. It wasn't lost on those politicians or servicemen fighting the Nazi that wars weren't won by evacuations. Dunkirk to them meant one of the greatest defeats in British and French history. Royal Navy destroyers had been sunk, as well as more than three hundred of the civilian vessels drafted in to aid Operation Dynamo. Most of the army's heavy equipment, their trucks and guns and tanks, had been abandoned on the beaches, alongside the thousands of comrades captured or killed.

Heroism wasn't the only thing celebrated. Some people spoke of miracles. A small boatload of infantrymen had arrived at Ramsgate on the first day of the evacuation, and soldiers and crewmen alike boasted of witnessing a great miracle. Some thought the men touched in the head, or drunk or both, and did not believe their claims. When the men were rounded up by military policemen, and shuttled away for debriefing and medical care, those that had heard their account of battling a monster at sea had waved them off with laughter and turned their attention to the wild stories of others arriving fresh from Dunkirk. On their return to service, that couple of dozen soldiers who'd been snatched away by the MPs, never talked about what they had seen out on the Channel, choosing instead to bury their heads in their cups or to totally refuse to relate the story of their evacuation, even when pushed. Of the two dozen, three of them were never seen again: not in the capacity that they'd been carried away, and any that thought about them suspected that at least two of them had perished from their wounds.

Their suspicions were wrong.

Both severely wounded men had survived, though one of them more ably than the other. Rifleman Cooper had lost an arm when the downed bomber crashed onto the boat, his limb pulverised by the flying wreckage. He had also lost the use of one eye and an ear, because his rescuers couldn't fish him from the burning sea before it had done its work on him. Because the gunner had turned at the last moment, throwing himself in the way to shield his companion from the blast – undoubtedly saving his life – the big Latvian had fared better. His face was scarred, cut some thought by flying debris, and he'd suffered a broken arm and numerous superficial wounds, but he had been lucky to have been scooped from the water concussed but otherwise alive. If it could be called as such, there was another strange wound upon the man, and all the military surgeon's attempts to rectify it had failed. It was a talking point among those that had witnessed the surgical procedures, but only until men arrived from the MOD, and then the doctors had nothing further to say on the subject. The man's hand was bandaged, and kept that way for the duration of his stay in the hospital.

Today was the first in which the three men had been reunited.

In a wheelchair, Cooper balanced a bacon sandwich on one knee, while juggling a mug of stewed tea to his lips. He joked that his coordination was off; being right-handed originally he was having the devil's own time getting used to using his left. He made a crass remark best kept in the barracks room and blushed like mad when realising a nurse was in earshot. If he recalled that Ludis had once been a minister, it didn't show and he whispered another joke once the nurse had fled the ward. Then he pointed at Ludis' bandaged hand and said, 'Looks like you might have similar problems when it comes to toileting.'

Ludis was out of bed, sitting in a chair in a corner of the small ward. Next to him on a nightstand was a copy of the Holy Bible, but he hadn't glanced at it since the others had joined him. He didn't need to, recalling all its words implicitly. Eight days with nothing more to do had been well spent in making his peace with the Lord he'd once put aside. The big Latvian looked fresh and alert, his clothing pristine and his hair and beard professionally shaven. If not for the raw scars on his face, no one would have believed the trials he'd endured. He looked like your typical bank manager or stockbroker from the City, according to the nurse who'd inspected him, and ready to meet the prime minister in person. Ludis felt uncomfortable in suit, starched collar and tie, but endured it, the way he did all the other discomforts sent to test him.

James Watson was also suited and booted, as he put it, a right ol' spiv, and looked almost as uncomfortable with the rigmarole as what Ludis was. He wasn't the most social of blokes, he knew, being gawky and not too handsome, but felt even more awkward with his hair Brylcreamed flat and as shiny as his shoes. He didn't know what to do with his hands, seeing as he'd no rifle to hold onto, and continually slipped them from his jacket pockets to his trousers and back again.

'Are you juggling a hot potato there, Winker?' Cooper asked. 'I wish you'd sit down. You're making me nervous now.'

'What's to be nervous about? It's not as if we're about to meet the most important man in England or anything, is it?'

Ludis frowned at his companions, still struggling to comprehend their particular brand of ironic wit. 'You have nothing to fear,' he said. 'He is a nice man.'

Cooper and Watson gawped at him.

'You've already met him? Winston-bleedin'-Churchill? The Prime Minister?' Watson asked.

'He visited my bedside on the day of our arrival here.' Ludis cocked his head at the young man. 'I thought it was through your influence that he came.'

'Not me, mate…I had nothing to do with it.'

Ludis looked over at Cooper, but he had dipped his head over his cup, offering nothing. Ludis doubted that Cooper would have been in a fit state to say anything that day. Tales spread by the boat's crew, or the other soldiers evacuated from the beach with them, must have carried to the ears of the prime minister.

'Did you give him the shard already?' Watson looked miffed that he'd missed the ceremony, despite his unsociable demeanour.

'No.'

'But you told him about it?'

'Of course I did. Britain must be ready for the next attack. It was best that I tell Churchill everything I have learned. We stopped Abaddon, but there are other creatures of the Abyss abroad in the world. And Hitler still has the Spear of Destiny: who knows to what end he'll put it to next?'

'So why didn't you give the shard to the prime minister? I thought that's what our mission was all about. Sergeant Renyard and all the others gave up their lives to ensure we did just that.'

'That was our mission, but it seems that the shard had other ideas.'

Ludis lifted his bandaged hand, and with his left began to unwind the dressing. The going was slow, with the big man working with his broken arm, yet he persevered. Cooper had lost interest in his tea now. He placed both cup and sandwich on the hospital cot and wheeled his chair over next to Watson. He was watching Ludis as keenly as his friend, nodding in fascination. He had been there on the deck as Ludis fought with the demon, had witnessed up close the ferocity with which Ludis plunged the shard in and out of its body, and thought that he must have been causing irreparable damage to his own hand. He also recalled how the shard appeared to glow, as if white-hot. He had assumed that Ludis' hand was both torn and scorched, but now he began to suspect otherwise.

Allowing the bandage to fall away, Ludis peeled back a final gauze pad. He flexed his fist, curling his fingers over the palm, as if testing he had full use of it, then lifted the hand as if offering his friends a blessing. He did not form the sign of the cross, simply opened his hand.

The two soldiers gasped as they stared at his palm.

They were silent for a long time.

Cooper finally asked, 'Doesn't that hurt?'

Ludis turned his palm to himself. He looked at the blued silver triangle of steel fused to his hand. At its edges remnants of Galina's dress were embedded in his palm, the rest cut away by the surgeon's scalpel, but otherwise untouched, unburned. The flesh of his palm had melded with the cloth and with the steel alike, feint veins of silver spreading across his hand. That was strange enough, but there were also reddish veins that extended from his flesh and into the steel. He could not explain how – but for the will of God – but the shard had become part of him, or he had become part of it, a truly remarkable symbiotic welding together of man and steel.

Ludis looked at his friends in turn. 'Without offering him my hand, I could not give the shard to Churchill. Therefore I offered myself into his service. Like I said…there are still creatures of the Abyss loose in the world. He will need someone to kill them while he deals with Hitler.'

'Wait a bloomin' minute!' Cooper looked like he was ready to spring up from his wheelchair, and Watson placed a calming hand on his shoulder. Cooper looked up at his friend, then back at Ludis. 'Are you telling me that you're now taking the prime minister's shilling? That's just bloody charming that is. What about us? Jesus Christ Almighty! I'm a bleeding cripple with no hope of going back to my job…'

Watson clapped his hand on the big gunner's shoulder. 'Cooper, there's a reason why we made you do all the heavy lifting.'

'What?'

'You're too thick-headed to do anything more intricate than hauling that Bren around.'

Ludis laughed at the scandalised look on Cooper's face. 'What our friend Watson is saying is that there's more I have to tell you. If only you'd shut up for a second and listen.'

'You'd best speak into this ear,' Cooper said, cocking his head, 'the other one's gone if you hadn't noticed.'

'Yes,' Ludis went momentarily dour. 'You have lost much, as have we all. It is for that reason that I was able to add…what do you Englishmen call it? – a *clause* to the contract - in that if Churchill accepted my offer of servitude, then he also accepted yours.'

Cooper eyed the stump of his right arm. 'And he agreed?'

'Of course.'

'You'd better wipe the bacon grease off your chin, Cooper,' Watson said, 'or else the prime minister might have second thoughts.'

Cooper returned his stare to Ludis.

'Are you telling me that's why Churchill's on his way over here?'

'Yes. He wants to personally swear us in to his newly formed team of *specialists*. Hitler has his team: you remember the Nazi stormtroopers in black? Well, it seems we are to be the spearhead of a team set to combat them and the monsters they loosed on the world. If you are in agreement, let me welcome you both to Churchill's counterforce.'

Cooper whooped with delight. 'I'd shake your hand if I could!'

'Let me do it for the both of us,' Watson offered. 'A chance at getting revenge for the sarge and our mates…neither of us is going to refuse that.'

He leaned in extending his palm, then jerked to a halt.

'Oh, sorry,' he said.

Ludis smiled, offered his hand in return. 'It doesn't hurt me, and it won't hurt you either. I can't say as much for the monsters we're destined to confront.'

Cooper was still laughing spiritedly. He pointed at Ludis' hand.

'What is it?' Ludis asked.

'You made a joke right? We are to be the *spearhead* of a team?'

'No, I did not joke.' Ludis held his face flat, until it creased and laughter lines edged across his cheeks. 'I was being ironic.'

Epilogue

5th June 1940
English Channel

The sentry almost missed the men that emerged from the sea.

Since the thorough routing of the British Expeditionary Force and its French and Belgian allies, the next step for Germany had to be a move on the British mainland. Hitler would surely covet the island, and due to his successes on the European continent would want to monopolise on those by a quick and devastating invasion of England. In pill boxes and hastily erected shelters, sentries were strung all along the coastline, looking out towards France, but the men were watching for the Luftwaffe to lead the advance, with ships coming in their wake. No one expected for divers to emerge from the cold waters of the English Channel, nor to be so few of them when they did come.

The sentry had been training his binoculars on the horizon, watching for movement, and if not for the sound of the trudge of heavy feet through the shale he wouldn't have looked down at the beach. He allowed the binoculars to droop in his fist as he stared at those men already on the sand, then out to where other heads and shoulders emerged from the foamy tide and came on towards the shore. The sentry thought this had to be some kind of joke, or a test to ensure his attention was fully upon his duties: maybe it was an exercise to gauge just how he would react should a real invasion be imminent. What other explanation was there? These men could not have swum all the way across the Channel, not without scuba tanks or wet suits. Not unless they had come from a submarine sitting just off the coast, he realised.

The sentry reached for the telephone, but paused.

He looked again down at the men shambling up the beach towards him, now numbering more than twenty. Something that struck him was that most of the men wore British battledress uniforms, yet none of them carried their ubiquitous Lee-Enfield rifles, or wore the tin hats synonymous with the Tommy. The sneaky bloody Jerry, he thought, was looking to infiltrate spies into the country. Well, not on his watch. No, Sir.

He reached for the handset, winding the power handle to make a connection with the local HQ, his gaze all the while straying back to those nearing him.

What the heck, he thought. That poor sod has no eyes!

He looked from one face to another and to yet another, and every one that he saw was sightless, the eyes missing or white with cataracts, almost as white as the water-bleached flesh hanging from their bones. If he wasn't mistaken those men weren't German spies. No, oh God, no. They were men drowned in the Channel and compelled to return home by some malignant force. And, though their eyes had been fed upon by aquatic creatures, or had rotted through the processes of decomposition, they still could see, and they were all looking at him. Their mouths were open and drooling. They looked...*hungry*.

The sentry screamed, dropping the phone, and he tried to flee his tiny hut.

A figure barred his way.

He was a man unlike the others.

This one was alive, regardless of the terrible wounds in his neck and chest that were matted with black scabrous tissue. Plus, he was naked as a newborn, built like an athlete, but as sexless as the mannequins in one of those fancy London boutiques. He smiled, showing the sentry one canine tooth that was too long and thick to be normal. Then he raised a hand, and from the fingertips sprouted long curving talons.

The sentry cried out, but his yell was cut short as the clawed hand ripped through his throat.

A moment the figure bent over the dead sentry, extending a thumb to his forehead. When the figure stepped from the hut, the sentry rose up and followed, a livid bruise between his eyes. Along with the twenty or so resurrected corpses, the sentry marched inland.

The invasion of Britain had begun, but not by the enemy everyone feared.

Thanks

Certain people have shown real enthusiasm for the completion of this project and I thank them for their passion and assistance: Lee Hughes, Richard Gnosill, Col Bury, Jim Hilton, Nicola Birrell and Luigi Bonomi.

Acknowledgements

This is a "What if?" story.

It is generally accepted that both Hitler and Himmler were deeply interested in the occult and their search for magical icons has been attested to on a number of occasions. It is true that Hitler claimed the supposed Spear of Destiny on annexing Austria and he held great faith in its legend. Ironically Hitler was to die in his bunker forty-five minutes after General Patton took control of the Spear in the final moments of World War II. Other spears claim to be that belonging Longinus, and there is a Holy Lance of Rome, and the tip was broken off it and lost during the French Revolution, however there is nothing to support that this was either the spear thrust into Christ at his crucifixion, or that it was originally forged by the first metal smith, or that it was cursed. Some people have claimed that at a secret location, a castle at Wewelsburg in Germany, the Nazis did experiment with the Spear of Destiny in an attempt at opening a gate to 'the other side'. This story asks the questions: What if the Nazis succeeded and what would have been the outcome?

I have taken liberties with history for the purposes of the story. It is true that Hitler did halt the advance of his Panzer divisions for a full two days on the outskirts of Dunkirk – a mystery that military scholars still debate to this day – but not to allow his troops to regain any mystical shard or to capture a fallen angel. Nevertheless, I have attempted to keep the details of the war chronologically correct, while injecting the timeline with both Ludis Kristaps' and Sergeant Geoff Renyard's fictional quests, and for that reason relied heavily on un-credited sources discovered on the World Wide Web; Wikipedia in particular. I also consulted the following reference books and relied somewhat on them to inject detail into the story:

Great Battles of World War II edited by Dr Chris Mann (Parragon Books Ltd 2010); *World War II Infantry Tactics – Squad and Platoon* by Dr Stephen Bull (Osprey Publishing Ltd 2004) and *German Special Forces of World War II* by Gordon Williamson (Osprey Publishing Ltd 2009).

Everything else I made up and I had a ball doing so.

About the Author:

Matt Hilton quit his career as a police officer with Cumbria Constabulary to pursue his love of writing tight, cinematic American-style thrillers. He is the author of the Joe Hunter thriller series, including his most recent novel 'No Going Back'. But as you've probably realised Matt loves to write in a second genre, that of horror. Watch out for other horror thrillers coming from Matt Hilton.

Matt is a high-ranking martial artist and has been a detective and private security specialist, all of which lend an authenticity to the action scenes in his books.

Books:

The Joe Hunter thriller series

Dead Men's Dust

Judgement and Wrath

Slash and Burn

Cut and Run

Blood and Ashes

Dead Men's Harvest

No Going Back

Rules of Honour

Six of the Best (Ebook collection of Joe Hunter short stories)

Horror:

Dominion

Darkest Hour

Short stories:

The Skin We're In (Even More Tonto Short Stories)

Apocalypse Noo (Holiday of the Dead) – writing as 'Vallon Jackson'

The Skin We're In (Mammoth Book of Best British Crime 9)

Payback: With Interest (True Brit Grit)

Misconceptions (Uncommon Assassins)

Confetti For Gabrielle (Ebook only)

Satisfaction Guaranteed/Trench Warfare (Action: Pulse Pounding Tales Vol 1)

YA Novels:

Deliver Us From Evil (writing as J.A. Norton)

Find out more about Matt Hilton at www.matthiltonbooks.com

Printed in Great Britain
by Amazon

87773464R00159